"You're evil," she tells me. "You might call yourself kongelig, and you might wear your pretty dress of white, but you're just a dog taking scraps from your masters."

I could have her executed, too, for being a slave who has shown disrespect to her Elskerinde. The guards, watching closely, will wonder why I don't. I'm already weak, wavering on my feet, but I close my eyes, and I sink into her—feel myself in her veins as her face tightens, her arms and legs cramping. She steps forward, then lowers to her knees. The woman struggles, fights against me—leans forward to kiss my feet.

She watches only the ground as I walk past her.

I return to my horse, Friedrich following closely behind, and pause by the brush. Most days, I'm able to pretend I'm not caught in a horror of my own making. Easy to pretend I'm not the monster who deserves the hatred of her people. Friedrich looks away when I heave into the leaves.

BY KACEN CALLENDER

ISLANDS OF BLOOD AND STORM

Queen of the Conquered

This Is Kind of an Epic Love Story

Hurricane Child

QUEEN OF THE CONQUERED

Islands of Blood and Storm: Book One

KACEN CALLENDER

www.orbitbooks.net

Copyright © 2019 by Kheryn Callender
Excerpt from *King of the Rising* copyright © 2019 by Kheryn Callender
Excerpt from *The Court of Broken Knives* copyright © 2017 by Anna Smith Spark

Cover design by Lisa Marie Pompilio
Cover images by Arcangel and Shutterstock
Cover copyright © 2019 by Hachette Book Group, Inc.
Map © 2019 by Charis Loke
Author photograph by Beth Phelan

Orbit
Hachette Book Group
1290 Avenue of the Americas
New York, NY 10104
orbitbooks.net

First Edition: November 2019

Orbit is an imprint of Hachette Book Group.
The Orbit name and logo are trademarks of Little, Brown Book Group Limited.

The publisher is not responsible for websites (or their content) that are not owned by the publisher.

The Hachette Speakers Bureau provides a wide range of authors for speaking events. To find out more, go to www.hachettespeakersbureau.com or call (866) 376-6591.

Library of Congress Cataloging-in-Publication Data

Names: Callender, Kacen, author.
Title: Queen of the conquered / Kacen Callender.
Description: First edition. | New York, NY: Orbit, 2019.
Identifiers: LCCN 2019019777| ISBN 9780316454933 (trade pbk.) |
ISBN 9780316454919 (ebook) | ISBN 9780316454926 (library ebook) |
ISBN 9781549150371 (downloadable audiobook)
Subjects: | GSAFD: Fantasy fiction.
Classification: LCC PS3603.A44624226 Q44 2019 | DDC 813/.6—dc23
LC record available at https://lccn.loc.gov/2019019777

ISBNs: 978-0-316-45493-3 (paperback), 978-0-316-45491-9 (ebook)

Printed in the United States of America

LSC-H

10 9 8 7 6 5 4 3 2 1

For the black and brown bodies that know this pain.

PROLOGUE

My mother kissed my forehead with a smile when I cried, upset that the party would carry on as I was sent away to sleep, and while I lay awake in my bed of lace, huddled beneath my covers and shivering in the cool trade-winds breeze, I heard when the tinkling piano stopped and when the laughter turned to screams. I slipped out of bed and went to my balcony of stone to see the garden below, streaks of yellow light falling from the windows and across the grass where my mother's guests were ushered to the rose mallow by the men with their drawn machetes. I saw my sisters crying, my brother struggling, my mother pleading as they were forced to their knees. A hand covered my eyes, but I heard the moment their tangled screams were swallowed by silence.

Tante carried me away from the balcony, breathless, the front of my dress covered with red that was already turning to rust. My voice had been stolen away, but she still kept her calloused hand over my mouth as we ran down the shadowed hall, into an abandoned chamber, snapping a door shut behind us. Men shouted, their boots echoing on the marbled floor.

"Do exactly as I say," Tante whispered to me, "or the Jannik guards will find you, and it doesn't matter that you're only a child—they'll kill you, just as they killed your brother and sisters."

Tante wouldn't release my mouth until I nodded that I understood. She opened a closet, then fell to her knees to unlock a trapdoor. She told me to climb down the ladder and walk to the end of the tunnel until I reached the groves. There would be a saltwater river. I was to follow the river until I reached a cave. I was to wait, hidden, until a woman came to look for me. We both knew that woman would not be Tante, because Tante would stay behind in the manor, and she would be killed.

She saw the fear shining in my eyes. "Your mother would want you to survive. Do you hear me, Sigourney? Your mother would want you to live."

I ran, salt drying on my cheeks and nose.

Guilt that I hadn't done anything to save them tightening around my neck.

Most days I find that I still can't breathe.

CHAPTER ONE

The invitation is a plain piece of yellowing parchment, folded shut—thin enough that I can see the red of my fingers shining through, as though the paper is a layer of skin in my hands. The paper itself hasn't been perfumed with the scent of crushed flower petals, as most posts from the kongelig tend to be. Only the seal of white wax, with the sunburst insignia of Hans Lollik Helle, marks the letter in any way.

It's an invitation I've been waiting to receive for nearly ten years: a symbol of all I've worked for, and everything still to come. I hold it in my hands, staring at the seal, my heartbeat drumming through my veins. Now that the moment has finally arrived, I can't bring myself to read the words.

Marieke sweeps into my room with a woven basket of fresh sheets. She sees the letter in my hands, noting the tremble in my fingers before I have a chance to steady them.

"What's that?" she asks briskly, even though she knows exactly what it is. She strips the sheets from my bed, and when I don't answer she says, without sparing me another glance, "Aren't you going to open it?"

I place the invitation atop the stand beside my bed.

Marieke watches me as she straightens my new sheets. Marieke has always valued patience, so it's almost amusing when she sucks her teeth as she fluffs my pillows. She thinks I'm falling apart. She can't blame me, she knows—the pressure I've put on myself with this goal of mine would be enough to break anyone. I've whispered to her at night that this plan is the only reason I'm still alive. Marieke believed me when I told her, and she thought it was sad, too, that a child should ever say that they want to die, but Marieke has known many children who've felt life wasn't worth living.

There's been another slave uprising, this time on a sugarcane planation in the fields to the east, so I ride with my twelve personal guardsmen across Lund Helle, through the groves of tangled brush and branches and thorns, weaving beneath the blessed shade of coconut and palm trees, crossing the fields of guinea grass shimmering in the breeze. Lund is the flattest of its sister islands, so the grass stretches on for miles, without any relief from the sun, which seems to reflect against everything here—the white of my dress, the blue of the sea forever shining in the corner of my eye, even the air itself. The heat is a living thing. It burns the corners of my eyes and lips, already cracking from the salt that's carried from the ocean on the wind.

The ocean has always terrified me. It isn't meant for the living. The water, burning my eyes and nose and throat, can so easily fill my lungs; the power of the tide can pull me beneath its waves. Most frightening of all are the spirits. My sister Ellinor would whisper to me that they walk the ocean floor, waiting for their chance at vengeance against the living; that their hands will pull you into the depths, so that your body, like theirs, can turn to salt and sand, and you can join them in waiting for a chance at revenge.

She'd told me this when I was a girl child, so young I could barely walk anywhere on my own without clutching at my eldest sister's skirts. I'd wanted to know if what Ellinor said was true, so I walked into the water—walked until I could no longer feel the sand beneath my feet. I took a deep breath and let myself sink beneath the surface and opened my eyes, stinging in the salt. There were no spirits standing in the sand, waiting for their revenge. All I could see was the coral, the schools of fish flashing silver in the light, the seaweed swaying beneath the waves. I decided Ellinor was a liar and turned to swim back to shore, but the tide was strong that day. I was pulled away from the shore. I would have kicked my legs, just as I'd been taught, but it was like I'd become stationary, unable to move. I swam, swallowing saltwater, unable to cry for help, but I was only pulled farther and farther, until I began to wonder if my sister had been right after all and if the spirits had grasped me by my legs, even if I couldn't see them or feel their hands.

My limbs became weak and numb, and I sank, my lungs burning and my vision fading away. I should've drowned, but when I opened my eyes again, I was back on the sand, salt drying on my skin. No slaves were nearby to claim that they'd jumped into the water and rescued me; my family was still in the gardens, enjoying their tea. It was just me, alone on the shore. The spirits weren't ready to take me yet.

I know that the path we take is dangerous. It leaves us too vulnerable, too much in the open. We're practically inviting an ambush. This would've been a silly thought, once, on an island like Lund Helle. The island only has a few sugarcane plantations, with houses scattered in between, but there've been three slave uprisings in as many months. Before this, the last uprising was nearly twenty years ago, when Bernhand Lund was still alive and Herre of this island. All the masters of the plantation had been killed. Herre Lund ended the uprising swiftly. Every slave on the plantation, whether they claimed innocence or not— whether they were children or not—was executed, their bodies staked and hung from trees so that the other slaves of this island could see. No other islander has attempted an uprising since, not until now.

Friedrich rides beside me. "You didn't have to come," he says again for the second time this morning. "It's a simple group of slaves that have now decided to call themselves rebels."

"I'm capable of deciding where I need to be, Friedrich."

He looks away, scathed. I feel that there's regret in his gut, regret he hopes I won't see, though he knows any emotion he has, any thought of his, belongs to me. If I will it, I can hear his thoughts the way I might think to myself; his emotions become my own. It requires effort, yes—energy, to make my mind become one with another's—but after holding this kraft for so many years, it's a skill that comes with the ease of racing across the fields of Lund Helle, or holding my breath beneath the sea. I know that Friedrich doesn't want to kill his own people. Before these uprisings, Friedrich had never killed before, not once in his entire life. He'd been trained to—had learned how to stab and maim and disembowel straw-filled opponents, as have all fifty of the guards of Lund Helle—but he never expected to see his sword shining red. He was surprised how easy it was to take the life of another man. His sword had pressed against the skin of the slave rebel who had run at Friedrich with a machete, and then his sword sliced through that skin and into pink guts, and it stopped as though hitting a rock—the man's bones, Friedrich later realized—and the man was still alive as Friedrich pulled back his sword, yanking at it with effort. The man looked as surprised as Friedrich felt before he fell to the dirt.

Friedrich killed three more men that day and, when the fighting was done, walked into the brush so that no one could see him or hear him vomit the cold oats and the juices of the sugarcane he'd swiped from the kitchens that morning. He prayed to the gods of the masters, asking for forgiveness, even though the masters don't believe that taking the life of an islander is a sin, and so there would be nothing to forgive.

Friedrich had hoped he would never have to kill another man again. How disappointed he was to hear of another uprising. "The fight won't last long," he tells me. "They never do."

My horse jerks back and forth beneath me. There's a clopping of hooves against the rocks scattered across the dirt, kicking dust into the air, already heavy with heat. My cloak sticks to my skin, and my neck and shoulders ache beneath the blistering sun. It's always hot on this island of mine, but the dry season has lasted a little too long. The crops are failing now, the plantations earning this island less coin every year. Bernhand Lund was put into his grave four years before, and since the title of Elskerinde was passed on to me, there have been nothing but droughts and uprisings. Proof, according to the Fjern of this island, that I shouldn't have the power that I do.

Lund Helle has no cities, no towns, only isolated collections of houses, which form small plantations holding its slaves and are owned by the few Fjern who live here. An abandoned house we pass leans to its side, as though the wind blew a little too hard one night. A rotted body hangs from a lone mahogany tree, bones visible through the rags it still wears, flies like a layer of living skin. It's always difficult to tell in death what color a body had once been in life.

I see the smoke of the plantation's houses before we arrive. It gushes black into the bright blue sky and burns my eyes, even from such a distance. There are brown bodies of islanders in the green field, already swelling in the heat—but there's no way to tell if these men, women, and children fought alongside the slave rebels, or if they were innocents killed in the clash. I see fallen Fjernmen as well, with their pink skin turning purple and blue. The masters of the plantation. I shouldn't be so pleased, seeing their bodies on the ground.

I ride closer to the plantation houses, a circle of wooden shacks and lean-tos ablaze. Some bodies have already begun to attract flies. My horse snorts nervously as I throw a leg over and leap to the hard ground, Friedrich and my eleven other guardsmen following. It's silent—the only sound is the crackling of the fire as it burns each house, splitting wood and stone, making it impossible to get too close as the heat sears the air. I can feel the heat on my skin, my eyes. We stop before a smoldering house that is already crumbling to the ground in embers. A fine layer of sweat and dust and ash covers me.

"Be careful. Some might have kraft," says Malthe, the captain of my guard.

"You think everyone has kraft," Friedrich mutters, smirking at me to share his joke.

Malthe has heard. "What was that?"

Friedrich hesitates. "Nothing, sir."

"Do you think this is funny, Friedrich?"

Embarrassment, then resentment, pulses through Friedrich, but he hides his emotions well. "No, sir."

It'd only been a joke—a joke born in discomfort, I know. It's always uncomfortable, seeing the dead. The sight of corpses reminds people of the first time they witnessed death: for me, the guests of my mother's manor, throats and stomachs cut, painting the flowers with their blood as my mother and sisters and brother were forced to their knees. Friedrich's memory comes to him as well, I can see now: A child, a boy no older than Friedrich had been, hung upside down by his feet as the master of the plantation taught his son archery. Friedrich often thinks about how easily he could have been chosen instead as the living target. That boy haunts his dreams at night, sometimes even now. The child will watch Friedrich with the same empty stare, arrows riddling his body. What had been the difference between them? The boy wants to know.

Malthe orders the guards to search for survivors. I walk down the path of the desolated plantation. Bodies are sprawled across the floors and straw beds of the slaves' quarters. In the distance, the fields of sugarcane are alight. Burning fields, charred houses, slaughtered people. This is my legacy.

Movement in the corner of my eye, a flare of rage—I spin and shout a warning, but too late. A man with a drawn machete has cut a guardsman's neck, so deeply that his head nearly falls. The rebel, machete shining, swings at Friedrich, but I focus on the slave, his rage and fear of death, yes, he wants to live more than anything else, and his mind becomes my mind as he slices his own gut, mouth open in surprise. More islanders burst from behind blackened houses with yells and screams. Machetes and knives drawn, the rebels clash with the swords of my guards, but there aren't many of them, and they have to know that they'll die. I enter another rebel, overtaken for a moment by his hopelessness as I see myself through his eyes, the traitorous island woman in my dress of white, my eyes fluttering as my kraft works through my veins, and he turns on his friends, cutting his fellow rebels down. Each man falls dead to the ground until only the man I've used is left. He slices his own neck. Pain sears, blood flowing, weakness filling him as he falls. For a moment, I feel death—know what it is to die, just as I have felt a thousand times. The sudden jolt of a heart stopping in your chest, the shock as your own body betrays you. This is what my mother and sisters and brother must have felt.

Friedrich uses a handkerchief to wipe clean his sword before dropping the cloth to the dirt. He's now killed his sixth man. He's heard other guards, such as Malthe, say they'll always remember the face of each man they've killed, but the faces of these slave rebels are already starting to blend together for Friedrich: the anger twisting their mouths, the surprise and pain in their eyes. How easily these men could've been Friedrich's friends, family, Friedrich himself. They were driven to desperation, he thinks. He'd had a cruel master once. He knows what it's like to wonder whether it might be better to fight, knowing he'll likely die, if there's a chance he might find a better life.

I walk to the body of my fallen guardsman. I don't even know his name. He was young—probably no older than twenty. His neck is cut, showing the red muscle beneath, the white of bone. Though his body lies on its front, his head is twisted, eyes stuck open. Some would say this was a good way for the boy to die. He stares at the gods and so will know which direction to turn in death. The gods were brought to these islands by the Fjern many eras ago; gods to be worshipped instead of the spirits of our ancestors, as our people had done since the islands themselves rose from the waters. Islanders are no longer allowed to pray to the spirits. If we do, we are hung, and so we learned the way of the Fjern gods. My enslaved people are told that if they worship the gods, they will be granted freedom after death. Most would rather pray to the Fjern gods, hoping for freedom, than fight for their freedom in life. In a way, I admire the dead rebels at my feet.

"His mother and father are on Solberg Helle," Malthe tells me of the dead guard, "working for a Fjern merchant family." *Working*. This is easier than saying his parents are slaves.

My eyes are still on the boy's face and the blood seeping from his neck and into the weeds. "Have his body returned to them." I should simply have his body sent to the sea, I know; it's easier, less work for everyone involved, but I can't help but think that the boy's parents would like to bury him themselves.

Blood has sunk into the dirt. The smells of iron searing under the heat of the sun, of the smoking wood and the charred stone, overwhelm me. My guardsmen sheathe their blades and walk into whichever remaining homes are still untouched by the flames to check for survivors and conspirators, kicking over the fresh bodies that lie at their feet. I watch their work as I walk,

Friedrich beside me. There've been rebellions before, but this has been a particularly devastating uprising; it seems nearly one hundred have died, and the damage to the property and crop won't please the regent of Hans Lollik Helle.

The Fjern of Lund Helle have used the slave rebellions as an excuse to call for me to step down as their Elskerinde. To them, the rebellions prove that I don't have the necessary intelligence to control my own people. I'm an islander, after all, who should be a slave along with my brown-skinned people—not ruling over them and this island. Flower-scented letters are sent to me with open threats: *Elskerinde Sigourney Lund might soon find her own throat cut one night.*

"You don't feel any guilt," Friedrich says as he bends over to check the pockets of one of the fallen rebels. There's no question in his voice, just as there isn't any question for the guilt he feels. Friedrich worked hard for his position in my guard—he wasn't handed his title—but this doesn't take away from the comforts he knows he has over the other slaves of Lund Helle and all his people in these islands. He lives in the barracks, which have beds, not the overcrowded slaves' quarters, where his people sleep on dirt floors. He receives a meal of oats and banana in the morning and goat stew at night. He's even allowed to drink guavaberry rum, when he isn't escorting me across the islands. He isn't beaten, except while in training with the other guards as they practice their skirmishes; he isn't whipped for his mistakes. The scars he bears are fine, thin lines in comparison to the thick scars that cover the backs of the slaves who work the fields. It isn't easy for him, knowing his people suffer while he lives in comfort—knowing it was simple luck that allowed him to be sold into training for the guard. He could just as easily be trapped in the fields, whipped and scarred; just as easily have been hung upside down by his feet while his master's son practiced archery.

Friedrich stands from the body, mouthing a quick prayer to the gods. The gods don't bring him peace. He knows that these are the gods of the Fjern, and that these gods only care for people whose skin is paler than his own. Still, he prays to them. This, like most of our people, is all he knows.

"Do you think I should feel guilt?" I ask.

He glances at me, my mouth, my neck. "It's not my place to tell you how to feel."

"That is true," I say, and though he'd suggested the fact himself, shame still flourishes in his chest. "But I still want to know what you think."

Friedrich doesn't answer, not at first, and so I sink my consciousness into his, feel the pulse of his veins in my own. A jungle of voices echo in my mind: He wonders if I'm using my kraft on him and hopes that I don't; he fears, as he always does, that I might decide I don't want or need him anymore—fears that, though I would have no reason to, I might take control of his body in the same way I've taken control of so many others and force him to stab his knife into his own stomach. He thinks that the stomach is always the slowest, most painful way to die. Death should always be quick and clean. Ever since the first man he killed, Friedrich is careful to give merciful deaths to the slave rebels he fights.

And still, even with his fear of me, I can feel the emotion in him rising as though it's my own: desire—for me, for my body, for my freedom, for my power. He thinks of me at night, dreams that he's inside of me again even now. He doesn't think the words, not consciously, but whenever he's in my bed, he's able to imagine for a moment that he's not my slave. I'm not surprised. I know what Friedrich has convinced himself he feels: that he believes he, a knight in a Fjern fairy tale, has fallen in love with his mistress, his Elskerinde.

Friedrich glances at me again and swallows thickly, knowing

that I'm in his head. He pauses beside another body, this time a pale-skinned Fjern—a woman, her face twisted in fear, her stomach cut open and spilling onto the ground. "I don't think you should feel guilt." He lies to himself, even he's aware of this. "These men were rebels, murderers. They would've been executed eventually, even if they hadn't died today."

"Is that really what you think?"

It's a cruel question. I know he's too afraid to tell me the truth. The truth is traitorous, the words of rebels, punishable by beheading. But his feelings are clear: None of these men can be blamed for wanting, and fighting for, their freedom.

"They were driven to rebel and murder because they preferred to die rather than live as slaves to the Fjern," I say. "I'm an islander. These are my people. I haven't done enough to help them. At least, this is what those who hate me will say."

Friedrich looks at me with pity. He thinks he knows me: his poor, misunderstood mistress.

He checks this woman's pockets as well, then murmurs a prayer for her. Remarkable, watching a slave pray over the body of a slaver and to the very gods that oppress him. But I can't judge Friedrich too harshly. These are my gods, too. I was never taught how to pray to my ancestors. Any thought of our ancestors, the spirits, was supposed to have died generations ago. I wait until Friedrich is finished, and we walk quietly for some time.

Friedrich says, "Only people who envy your power will hate you. The poor hate the rich. The slaves hate the kongelig. It's only natural, isn't it?"

I want to ask Friedrich if his envy of my freedom, my power, means he actually hates me as well, but the corners of his lips twitch into a smile, and he remembers an image, hoping that memory will become my own—a memory of only a few nights before, sneaking into my chambers, into my bed, beneath my sheets. I should be disgusted with myself. Ashamed. The boy is technically my property. Property, like the goats fenced in and awaiting slaughter. That is what the laws of these islands decree: Friedrich, and all other islanders, are not human. The color of their skin, the blood in their veins, make them undeserving of life. And so they must give their lives for the Fjern. There's nothing beautiful in this, I know. In the same way there was nothing beautiful in the fact that my mother technically belonged to my father, before she was given her freedom; in the same way there was nothing beautiful in the fact that my father's ancestors belonged to the Fjern, who took these islands. If I cared for Friedrich, I would give him his freedom, along with all the slaves of Lund Helle. I wouldn't take Friedrich into my bed, pretending my company is something he wants, something he chooses, when he has no choice in a life he doesn't own.

I refused him, at first. This is what I remind myself in consolation. I refused him and told him that he's a child for thinking he wants me. But though I own my life, it's not a good life I live, and Friedrich is a distraction I desperately need. He's young and foolish in his ambition, cocky in his thoughts of surpassing his peers to follow Malthe and become captain of the Lund guard— but still handsome, with his dark skin and sculpted muscles and his smile, a smile that isn't easy to find on these islands, and certainly not this island of mine. And even I can't ignore that my body has its own needs, its own desires.

I tell Friedrich I'd like to make a trip to Jannik Helle, and I can sense his impatience. It'll be my second trip this month alone. Still, he nods his understanding as he kneels beside the body of one of the slave rebels, machete still clenched in his hand where he fell. Checking the rebel's pockets, Friedrich pauses with a frown and withdraws his hand, staring into his palm.

"What is it?" I ask him, though I see a flicker of his vision.

He offers his hand to me. He holds a rusted red coin. I pick it up and turn it over. The coin has the crest of a crude zinnia flower, the symbol belonging to the Ludjivik family.

Friedrich stands, brushing off his knees. "Do you think they were behind this?"

"I wouldn't put it past them," I say. "An ill-fated attempt at supporting and supplying a slave rebellion against me."

"Unless they meant to lose. What if this was meant as a distraction, or they hope to make you feel secure before attacking again?" *They will take this island from you.*

I toss the coin into the dirt. "It isn't incriminating to find a coin. Maybe one of the slaves recently traveled to Ludjivik Helle and took it."

Friedrich doesn't look convinced. I don't need to enter his mind to know his thoughts: There are those in the islands of Hans Lollik who want to see me dead, and if I'm not careful, eventually one will succeed.

Friedrich and I start the walk to our horses. The rest of my guardsmen will stay, searching for clues and valuables under Malthe's watch, before starting the back-bending work of burying each of the slaves' bodies at sea. The dead masters of the plantation will be returned to the Fjern for a ceremonial burial so that they will easily find the gods.

Before we get far, a guardsman hurries down the rocky path.

"Elskerinde Lund," he says, breathless. He catches my eye, and when I look to his thoughts, a wave of his fear crashes into me, dread sinking into my bones. Fear that I'll learn of all his secrets, of the extra goat stew he's been stealing at night, and maybe even of the little boy he watched drown so many years ago—

"Spit it out," Friedrich says.

The man hesitates. "We found survivors." He doesn't look at me as he continues to speak. "One of them has kraft."

We follow the guard back up the path to the burning plantation houses with my nine other guardsmen, waiting in a circle
and turning to watch my arrival. A line of the survivors stands
in the center of the circle, all slaves. A man, middle-aged and
frail—thinner than most, it's clear that he holds a sickness in his
lungs, perhaps caught from the last storm season, something he
never managed to shake. A woman, her skin a maze of wrinkles,
toothless so that her lips sink in like a skull. She watches me. She
isn't afraid. She's already so close to death. What could I possibly
do to make her afraid? There's another woman as well, breathing heavily as she grips the hand of the girl beside her. The girl is
young, perhaps no older than thirteen. She and her mother have
the same eyes, the same mouths.

Though he'd been so willing to joke about kraft before, Friedrich takes the matter seriously now. "Do you think the one with
kraft caused the uprising?" he asks me, eyes on the islanders.

That would depend on the power, and the strength, of the
kraft itself. My chest burns. "Which one?" I ask Malthe.

He marches to the villagers and pushes the girl forward, forcing her to let go of her mother. The girl winces, struggling not
to cry, shoulders shaking with the effort. My heart drops. She
reminds me too much of my sister Inga, crying as she was forced
to her knees.

My mouth is dry, words scratching my throat. "How do you
know she has kraft?"

"She tried to use her power on us—confused us for a moment,
made us forget who we were, what we were doing here, then
tried to run with the others. When we captured them and
threatened to kill them all if no one spoke the truth, she stepped
forward."

The man in the line of slaves speaks. "She's just a girl. She was
afraid, thought you were rebels. They were killing all of us, not
just the masters—"

Malthe jams the hilt of his sword into the man's nose. The slave falls with a shout of pain, blood streaming between his fingers as he clutches his face. If he thought he was safe, facing his own people with not a single Fjern in sight, he was mistaken.

"You'll speak when we ask you a question," Malthe says to all of them. "Is that clear?"

No one moves or makes a sound. The woman with her skin of wrinkles watches me.

"Were you fighting with the rebels?" I ask the girl.

She glances up, terrified, before looking at the ground again. She's willing to tell us anything and everything if it means she'll live. Even if she doesn't own her life, she still wants it. "No— I wasn't, I promise you. They weren't of this plantation. No one recognized them. They came here and attacked us. Killed everyone. They weren't from Lund Helle, they were speaking of returning to their ships."

Friedrich gives me a pointed look. I ignore him, glancing Malthe's way, and he nods. The ships will be found and searched.

I ask, "Where were the rebels from?"

The girl doesn't know the answer. She's frightened I won't be pleased. "I—I think maybe Niklasson Helle." She's lying. There's no reason for her to think the rebels came from Niklasson Helle.

I pause. I can feel their fear. Fear that they'll all be killed for failing to protect their masters. Fear that I'll decide they're lying, and that they were all a part of the rebellion. Fear from all— except for the older woman. She stares at me, blue film over her eyes. She's seen more hatred, more evil, than I ever have— probably more than I ever will. The Fjern, who gave me the power I hold, stalking through the plantations in the dead of night when she was a child. Raping her mother and her sister and herself, slicing open the bottoms of her feet and burning the palms of her hands and making her work the fields, threatening death if she stopped for even a breath, hanging her father for daring to meet his master's eye, beating and whipping and tying up a little boy child and leaving him outside in the sun to be eaten away by the salt air, and all because he wouldn't stop crying for his mother after she was sold away. Islanders, tying rocks around their ankles and walking into the sea to escape the hell of Hans Lollik.

To the slaves before me—to all the islanders—I'm the traitor to her own people. My skin might be brown, and my blood might belong to these islands, but I'm no better than the Fjern. My heart thumps harder. I close my eyes. Try to push their thoughts aside—their hatred for me, their fear of me—but I realize that the feelings are my own.

When I open my eyes, the man is still bleeding. The elderly woman still watches me. The girl's mother clutches her hands together so tightly they shake. The girl tries so hard not to cry.

I have no more questions—no way of delaying what I know has to come. Malthe stares at me expectantly. I'd hoped he'd let this pass. No one need know we found a slave girl with kraft in the fields of Lund Helle.

When I speak, my voice doesn't sound like it belongs to me. "The law of Hans Lollik is clear."

The girl's mother begins a low wail. This woman will inevitably feel a guilt I'm familiar with—guilt, that she didn't do enough to save the person she loved. But the guilt will only simmer beneath the rage, the hatred, for me—the one who ordered her daughter's death.

I don't even know the girl's name. "You stand accused of holding kraft, a power that belongs only to your sovereigns of Hans Lollik, gifted as a divine right by the gods that watch over us."

The woman tries to step in front of her daughter, but the guardsmen pull her and the others aside. The girl shakes her

head. Her face crumples as she heaves sobs, tears dripping from
the end of her nose. I can't save her. The Fjern made it clear
when they claimed these islands over hundreds of years before:
Only they, with their pale skin, are allowed to have kraft; any
slave accused of having the power must be found and killed, no
matter the innocence, no matter the age. The fact that the Fjern
can't own kraft is one that they despise. My people, descendants
of the first islanders before the Fjern ever came, believe the abilities to have come from our ancestors. We whispered that those
with kraft were blessed by the spirits. The Fjern disagreed. They
don't believe in the spirits of our ancestors; they declare that
their gods pass the kraft on as divine gifts to only the worthy,
and to the Fjern, my people are not worthy. I was born with my
freedom, and so I'm allowed to keep my life, even with kraft
simmering in my veins. This girl wasn't born with her freedom,
and so she'll die. She'll become a martyr. The hero in every
story but my own.

I recite the words memorized, heavy on my tongue. "Anyone who isn't of kongelig descent and dares possess kraft, which
belongs only to their benevolent rulers as a divine right, must
die by execution."

The woman screams now, fighting against the guards that
hold her. I nod at Malthe, and he moves forward dispassionately,
pressing down on one of the girl's shoulders so that she'll fall to
her knees. I look away when he swings his sword.

Silence, but for the crackling of the fires. The girl's mother
has fainted. My hands are shaking. I wipe them on the white of
my dress as I turn away, but before I can take another step, the
older woman comes forward. She spits at my feet. The metallic
smell of blood burning in the heat sickens my stomach, and I feel
faint. I don't have the energy or the will to read this woman's
thoughts—to feel her hatred. But she wants me to know.

"You're evil," she tells me. "You might call yourself kongelig, and you might wear your pretty dress of white, but you're just a dog taking scraps from your masters."

I could have her executed, too, for being a slave who has shown disrespect to her Elskerinde. The guards, watching closely, will wonder why I don't. I'm already weak, wavering on my feet, but I close my eyes, and I sink into her—feel myself in her veins as her face tightens, her arms and legs cramping. She steps forward, then lowers to her knees. The woman struggles, fights against me—leans forward to kiss my feet.

She watches only the ground as I walk past her.

I return to my horse, Friedrich following closely behind, and pause by the brush. Most days, I'm able to pretend I'm not caught in a horror of my own making. Easy to pretend I'm not the monster who deserves the hatred of her people. Friedrich looks away when I heave into the leaves.

CHAPTER TWO

Herregård Dronnigen is a manor I'd visited many times before as a child. It was where my paternal cousin Bernhand lived with his wife of the family Lund, nestled right on the edge of Lund Helle, its back fortified by the wall of stone, dirt pathways leading to the sea. I'd enjoyed the sticky mango tarts and the flowers of the gardens and the shallows of the beach, where I would pick up sea urchins with their spiny needles and starfish, feeling their tentacles tickle the palms of my hands. As a child, I never questioned why so many people with brown skin, brown like my own, worked the fields of the plantations; why my nursing maid, and all the cooks and servers and guardsmen, were islanders. I only wondered why the Fjern with their pale skin wouldn't smile my way as they would with the other little girls in their dresses of lace, why they refused to speak to my mother if ever we passed one another in the streets of other islands of Hans Lollik.

My mother wouldn't take me or my sisters or brother away from Rose Helle often. I think she wanted to protect us from the hatred she knew we would face—the same hatred she bore every day from the Fjern—but she couldn't keep us trapped on our little island, in the paradise she had built for us. Inga was left behind in the manor of Rose Helle while my mother brought me, Ellinor, and our older brother, Claus, to Solberg Helle. She had business, I don't know what. She held my hand on one side and Ellinor's hand on the other, while Claus walked behind. We had no guards. This I remember. I don't know why—perhaps my mother wanted to show everyone that she wasn't afraid of the Fjern. Whatever her reason, it was foolish. She brought us to the main town of Solberg Helle, streets cobblestoned and air salted by the docks. There was a market, dozens of stalls selling stewed mango with cinnamon and stalks of sugarcane. Even I, who would normally stare only at the sweets, was distracted by the gazes that followed us; the Fjern, who stared at my mother with her dark skin, wearing her finery, and at her brown-skinned children, also dressed in lace and pearls. She went into a house, spoke briefly with a Fjernman and exchanged our island's rose-mallow coin for papers, I don't know the contents, and I suppose it doesn't matter—and just as quickly as we'd gone inside, we were out again. But this time, the Fjern who had stood behind their stalls now had words for my mother. They asked why she walked with no master. A Fjernman stood in front of her and demanded to know which family she belonged to. Another suggested he might take me, Ellinor, and Claus away from her, to be sold on the docks of Niklasson Helle. More Fjernmen came, surrounding us. They followed her. They shouted at her. They spat at her feet. Claus grew pale, Ellinor cried, and fear was heavy in my gut. I hadn't been afraid often as a child—I didn't know I'd had anything to fear—but I was afraid that day. And through it all, my mother only walked forward, her chin raised, as though she were taking a stroll with us down the shoreline, with nothing before us but the sea.

My mother was usually kind and gentle, but once we returned to the ship that would bring us to Rose Helle, she slapped Ellinor for crying. She told us never to let the Fjern see our fear again.

"This is what they want to see," she told us. "Don't ever give them what they want."

Dronnigen shines, stones painted white faded by the everlasting sun. I jump from my horse, rocks crunching beneath my sandals, and hand the reins to Friedrich before I step into the hall. Paintings of the deceased Lund and Rose families line the walls, portraits that Bernhand Lund had installed out of respect before his own death. There's my father, dead shortly after my birth—I was too young to have any memories of him now—along with my mother and two sisters and one brother. My mother was beautiful, with black hair curling atop her head, skin as dark as the purples of the night sky, brown eyes lined by lashes so thick it's as though she wore kohl, and a proud, wide nose sitting above an even wider mouth. I remember that she had scars lining her arms and back, and one thick scar from her ear and across her neck, but the scars aren't in her portrait. I look more like her painting every day.

She was born of slavery, given freedom and married to my father when she was fifteen. When I ask, my personal servant Marieke tells me that my mother and father never had a loving relationship. He liked to keep my mother by his side to show off her beauty like a trophy, but nothing more. He would take my mother into his bed as often as he could, hoping for an heir worthy of the Rose title and inheritance. Claus had always been a weak child, and Koen Rose wanted a son who didn't seem like he would die from a single storm-season sickness. He was unlucky in this. I try to imagine my mother standing beside my father, slapped and beaten if she ever misspoke; the years she must have waited, patiently watching and observing and learning everything she could, so that the moment my father died, she could inherit and control the title of the Rose. Sometimes

I wonder if my mother had a hand in Koen Rose's death, but there's no way to know something like this now.

Even before my father's death, my mother had been so dearly loved. She only ever spoke to islanders with respect and kindness, even though she had been handed the power to consider them beneath her. She would walk the plantations of Lund Helle with baskets of mango, sugar apple, squash, and banana bread, handing out the food to anyone who worked the fields. Marieke told me, once, that my mother had heard of a slave's whipping at the hand of my cousin Bernhand Lund and went to the shack where the islander lay. She rubbed aloe on the man's back with her own two hands. It's difficult to know if any islander would've done the same if in her position. I'm in her position now, and this is something I've never done myself. Perhaps this is why the islanders loved my mother yet have such hatred for me. Before she was murdered and after my father had been beneath the sea for many years, she'd promised freedom to each and every slave of her household and of Lund Helle following Bernhand Lund's death. It's a promise I can still feel burning in the slaves' hearts. The chance to escape these islands without the fear of being hunted down and killed.

But my mother is dead, and this is a promise I can't keep. I need the slaves around me. My mother had the respect of the regent, the power of the Rose and Lund families; I have nothing. Nothing, but the coin of the Lund inheritance, which will only get me so far. To release my slaves would be to release the last of the power I have, and if I'm going to succeed in my plans, I'll need them. Disgust radiates from the slaves of Herregård Dronnigen whenever I cross their paths. Most of the slaves I'd known as a child died in the Massacre of Rose Helle, but the slaves of Dronnigen still remember me from the visits I would make when I was young. It must be only out of respect for my mother's memory that none creep into my room at night to cut my neck. I make it a habit to avoid my slaves whenever I can, to keep a barrier between me and their thoughts. I hold enough self-hatred. I don't need to expend the energy to use my kraft and read their minds, confirming the thoughts I already have for myself.

The shade of the hall is a relief from the sun, but not from the heat, which is so thick it's something I must move through, something I must breathe. The heat swarms my skin, filling my veins, and I can see the girl standing before me, crying; hear her mother's screams. The screams grow louder when I close my eyes.

Friedrich's voice startles me. "Are you well?" he asks, walking into the hall behind me. I can't be sure if he asks out of genuine concern or if he asks because I'm his Elskerinde. I don't think he knows the answer himself. When I turn to face him, his eyes scan my own, perhaps searching for a humanity I'm not sure I have.

I need a distraction. Friedrich is a good distraction. I ask him to my chambers, and though he doesn't speak on it, I can feel his hesitation. His fear. But he doesn't argue. He can't argue, I remind myself. My self-hatred rises, but I push it down again, allowing myself to pretend for a moment that I'm not Elskerinde Lund, and that Friedrich is not my slave, and that we are two islanders who have escaped Hans Lollik, living in the north, in freedom and in love. It's the only lie that allows me peace whenever the boy shares my bed.

Friedrich follows me up the winding stairs, closes the door behind him, and allows me to kiss him without complaint, lets me press myself against his body, wrapping my arms around the back of his neck.

"Elskerinde Lund," he says, "perhaps this isn't the right time..."

I raise a brow and let my hands fall over his shoulders, the buttons of his shirt. "But you're always so eager to please me, Friedrich."

He steps away from me now, a flicker of hurt crossing his face, pinching through my chest. He wants me to respect him, to think of him as someone who is strong, intelligent, could easily become captain of my guard. He spends much of his time trying to make others laugh. He goes to the kitchens, flirting with the cooks and tasting their guavaberry tart. He drinks rum with the guards by the stables, telling stories of how he'd get himself in trouble with the head of his guard when he was a child, running away from his beatings. He wants to make others laugh, but he doesn't like it when others laugh at him. This is the worst thing that I could do.

My hands smooth over his chest and down his arms, lined with thin white scars. Friedrich honestly believes he's in love with me—the knight forever ready to protect his princess—but this isn't love. It's no more possible for Friedrich to love me than it is for me to love any of the Fjern, just as it wasn't possible for my mother to love my father, her master. It's simply a fairy tale that Friedrich has told himself—another lie to help make this life of his bearable. He was born to an enslaved family on Årud Helle. He only has a vague memory of his mother hanging a white sheet, ballooning in the breeze. He was sold to another Fjern family, at first to be an errand boy and then to be trained as a guardsman when Friedrich began to show talent with a wooden sword. I bought him myself, to join my guard under Malthe, five years before; bid on him from the docks of Niklasson Helle. His life, apparently, is worth six silver coins with the guinea-grass insignia of Lund Helle imprinted on the front.

I lean forward to kiss Friedrich's clenched jaw, the corner of his lip. His lips loosen against mine. He lets me guide him to my bed and helps me pull my white dress over my head. Friedrich is young and clumsy, but he makes up for it all with his enthusiasm.

He won't stop until I find my pleasure. When we're finished, we lie in my sheets, sticky with sweat. I stare at the invitation, still waiting atop my stand. Friedrich notices, and curiosity hovers over him. Friedrich can be annoying after he's shared my bed, and I want him to leave, but I'm afraid of being alone now, too.

Friedrich lies on his stomach, propped up by his elbows. "Have you ever considered escaping the islands of Hans Lollik?"

He speaks to me as one slave might speak to another. *Escape.* I don't have to escape, hidden away on a ship, praying to the Fjern gods that I'm not captured and hung by my neck. I'm free to leave anytime I please. "And go where?" I ask.

He shrugs. "Anywhere. Another island, another empire." He dreams of seeing the lands to the north, where the pale-skinned Fjern of Koninkrijk and dozens of other empire nations have days and nights so cold that ice like frozen sand falls from the sky.

"Why would I?"

"You could do anything you wanted. You could become another person."

His eyes are earnest, and because he's risen through my guard so quickly, I sometimes forget that he's young—eighteen, two years younger than me. This only reminds me that I'm young as well. "Do you think I should?" I ask him.

"I think you should be happy."

"Do I seem so unhappy now?"

He hesitates, and in my impatience I push my way into his thoughts. His memory takes me to the afternoon sun, the screams of a woman, and what I'd looked away from but what Friedrich forced himself to watch: the white flash of the sword, the blinding red, the girl's body crumpling into the dirt, her head with her eyes clenched shut rolling in the grass.

I sit up, dizzy in the heat. "You should leave."

He kisses my bare shoulder, still watching me.

I ask him, "Do you really think you're in love with me?"

His brows pull together. "Why do you say that?"

"Because I see it in your thoughts. You believe you're in love with me, but your love for me is a child's, before he even knows what love is. You tell yourself you love me, to stop yourself from hating me instead."

"You always do this," he tells me, voice low.

"And what is that?"

"Push me away. Try to hurt me. Why? So that you won't feel weak? Because you might start to love me, too?"

"I don't love you, Friedrich."

He stands up, abandoning the sheets, and bends over to pick up his shirt and tug it on over his head. "I'm sorry. You're right. Why would you love a slave?"

I'm silent as he buttons his shirt and pulls on his pants. "Even if you think you love me," I say, "you shouldn't waste it on me. Fall in love with a sweet island girl instead. One who'll smile every time she sees you."

He shakes his head. "What do you mean, I shouldn't waste my love on you?"

I can feel his heart, thumping with anger, begin to soften—can feel the pity in him as he walks back to my bed and sits on the edge. "I'm not wasting my love on you."

He truly believes he loves me, but this love isn't real. It's imagined, a story he tells himself, and while he sees me as the princess in the fairy tales we heard as children, I'm nothing more than the wicked queen. I'm not deserving of this false love, even as I take it and use it to comfort myself. I'm only deserving of his hatred. This I can sense also—embers of his hatred for me, burning beneath his skin. If he admitted his hatred of me, he might not be able to stand the sight of me, the woman he's meant to protect. He might take the sword meant for killing rebels and cut my neck instead.

I tell Friedrich that Marieke will come by any moment, and

I can feel his frustration, but he nods his understanding and kisses me again before leaving my chambers, boots in his hands. I sit in my bed, knees curled to my chest. My room is usually a welcomed sanctuary—a slight reprieve from the island and its responsibilities, though not from my own thoughts, my own ambitions. That's never something I'll be able to escape, maybe not even when I'm dead and in my grave of the sea. But today, I look again to the table beside my bed and the awaiting letter I haven't had the courage to open or read. I already know what it'll say—have waited for its arrival for nearly half my life.

The marbled floor of my chamber shines yellow in the bright sunlight that spills from the open balcony windows, lace curtains leaving intricate patterns on the walls. It's a clear day, and I can see three of the other dozens of islands under the rule of Hans Lollik in the distance: Solberg Helle is farthest, green hills faded in the distance; Niklasson Helle is a jagged rock that reaches for the sky. Rose Helle is closest. I can see the browning of the trees, the bald spots where fires spread so many years before. My mother's island had been beautiful, once. It was the smallest of the islands of Hans Lollik, with no plantations and only a scattering of houses. I would run through the groves with Ellinor and hold Inga's hand as she took me to the shores. Claus had been the quietest of us, the shyest. He would spend his days in the library, reading his books on the histories of Hans Lollik Helle and the northern empires. Ellinor had only been interested in the fairy tales. She would beg Inga and our mother to read them to her, no matter the time of morning or night. But I would come to Claus. He was fourteen. He had the lightest skin of us all and curly brown hair that showed the blood of the Fjern ancestor who lived so many eras before. Claus was lighter-skinned than even the Fjern who worked long days under the hot sun. The Fjern didn't like Claus and the color of his skin. It was too strong a reminder of how close the islanders and the Fjern truly were, despite the Fjern's claims to higher intelligence, and their divine purpose in oppressing the dark-skinned islanders. It was their justification: The Koninkrijk Empire claimed that the Fjern must spread their rule over the lesser savages of this world.

Claus didn't lie to himself. He knew that the color of his skin wouldn't make the Fjern accept him, knew that the Fjern would hate him more than any of us. Our father had taken Claus with him on all of his meetings across the islands. He showed Claus and his son's lighter skin with pride. Claus had hated our father. He told me this, plainly, when I asked my older brother to tell me about the man who had given us our name and our freedom. He said that our father lovingly kissed the feet of the Fjern, who would kick him in the mouth. Koen Rose didn't want to be seen as a threat. He was happy to be treated like a dog if it meant he could continue his family's legacy in the sugarcane business.

My father, though an islander, wasn't a kind master. He would have the slaves beaten, just like any of the other Fjern, and though he wouldn't torture the slaves as some might, Claus knew it was because he saw each slave as an investment and a profit. It didn't matter that their skin was as dark as his own. My father had no feeling for them and did whatever he could in the eyes of the kongelig to distance himself from them—to make it clear that, though he looked like an islander, he'd still had an ancestor of the Fjern generations before. He had tried to marry into any of the Fjern families, but none would have him, so he decided on my mother, the most beautiful islander he had seen, even with her scars.

Claus didn't want to inherit the sugarcane business or the island of Rose Helle if it meant he had to pretend to hold love for the Fjern. Claus would tell me the histories he learned, since I was still too young to read about the north myself. There are seven nations to the north, three more to the east, and two to the west; only our islands cross the sea. Claus explained to me that the Fjern came from their empire of Koninkrijk, which was the farthest north and by far the coldest of them all. The northern empire is oppressive, with little mercy for those who disobey the laws of the land, which they believe come as direct orders from the gods above. Claus had laughed when I asked if the Fjern envied the heat of our islands—if this is why they took the land from us.

My bedroom door opens without a knock, and Marieke strides in as she always does, a pan of water in her hands. "The girls are gossiping about how your guard was seen walking barefoot down this hall," she says. "You need to be more careful. You don't want these rumors spreading to your betrothed, do you?"

"Good day to you, too, Marieke."

She sucks her teeth when she sees my clothes strewn across the floor, white dress stained yellow and brown from the island, ash from the fires. "It's not too hard to pick up and fold your own clothes, is it?"

She walks into the adjoining room, and I hear her pour water into the tub. I stand, naked, and walk across the marble to join her.

"Why do you feel the need to mess with that boy?" she asks me.

I hesitate. I'd needed a distraction from the memory of the girl, a memory that returns to me now. Marieke is the only person I can trust with the truth, but there are some truths even she won't want to hear. Instead, I change the topic, telling her to prepare new clothes for a visit to Jannik Helle in the morning.

"You're visiting Elskerinde Jannik again?" she says. She believes I've accomplished enough with the woman.

"It's not really your place to question, is it?" I ask. I sink into the white clawfoot tub and withhold a contented sigh.

"I'll question whatever the hell I want. This isn't only your life you're playing with, Sigourney, and I have no plans to follow you to the gallows."

"Good. Maybe then I'll have a break from your nagging."

Marieke begins to scrub at my arms, my shoulders, my back.

I ask, my eyes still closed, "Why do you stay if you hate me so?" Marieke is the first and only slave of the Rose household whose freedom I have granted—and yet, over the years, she's remained.

She doesn't pause in her scrubbing. "You already know that I have nowhere else to go."

I can't help but smile. This is why I love Marieke—her honesty, perhaps knowing there's no point in trying to keep the truth from me, is refreshing. She stands and pours more water into my tub, and I open my eyes now and look at the wrinkles of her brown skin, the thick curls escaping her bun. She'd been the woman who found me waiting by the bay so many years ago, the night that my family had been massacred and Tante whispered that my mother would've wanted me to live. I'd climbed down the ladder, falling the last few feet and twisting my ankle so that it swelled and throbbed. I limped through the brush, thorns catching my dress and hair and skin, tripping over roots and rocks. Every now and then, I would hear a crunch, and I would stop, trying hard not to cry, fearing the guards had found me; and when no one came with their machete, I would keep moving—following the salted river as Tante had told me to, straight to the bay. I found the cave and sat motionless, knees to my chest. The entire night had passed and the sun was starting to rise, and Marieke found me there, covered in dirt and scratches and salt from my tears. A safeguard, I realized as I got older—a slave of the Rose family who had never come within the manor walls, and who knew to come to the cave if anything ever happened.

Marieke brought me to Lund Helle. I didn't yet have my kraft, but it was plain to see that my cousin Bernhand Lund was shocked to see me alive. He'd watched the fires of Rose Helle in the early morning and had heard word of the massacre. He'd been told my entire family, myself included, had been killed. Marieke asked for shelter, but Bernhand Lund didn't think this wise. In retrospect, it's possible that he didn't want to be tangled up with my family's deaths, didn't want my assassins to come back for me and decide to take his life as well. I'd been numb in those days, and have little memory of the conversations between my cousin and Marieke, but I imagine now how terrified Marieke must have been; scared that my cousin might simply decide to make both of us his slaves and take the coin of Rose Helle for himself. It would've been easy. My mother was no longer alive to stop him, and I was supposed to be dead.

But he did not. To this day, I honestly can't see why he didn't. It wasn't out of love. My Lund cousins didn't love us, and were often embarrassed to depend on my family for the sugarcane business, and if Bernhand Lund was afraid of my assassins, he could've offered me to the kongelig in exchange for his life. Perhaps he'd already considered the fact that he had no heir, and as shaming as it would be for him, he would need me to continue the Lund legacy. Maybe he simply decided to do what was right. Whatever his reason, my cousin sent me away for my protection. He gave Marieke coin so that I could travel the northern empires, from villas to cottages to cities. We became the guests of Bernhand Lund's acquaintances, spending months in the grandest of manors; we would travel to a city and spend just as much time in an inn that smelled of ale. We lied about my roots to anyone who asked, and allowed the rumors to spread. The bastard child of Bernhand Lund's and a forgotten slave, perhaps, or an orphan of the northern empires that Bernhand saw in the streets and took pity on. I became known as Sigourney Lund.

The northern mass of land is carved up into its own separate empires. Koninkrijk—home of the Fjern—is the farthest north, and the smallest of the other empire nations. Perhaps it's because of this that the Fjern have spread themselves across the world, starting wars and claiming more land for Koninkrijk on behalf of their gods. The Fjern give those lands to regents so that coin and trade can be sent back north. The regents rule without mercy, slaughtering anyone who attempts rebellion. The islands of Hans Lollik are far from being the only lands that have suffered under the hand of the Fjern.

My islands are well known in the north for their beauty. Some strangers Marieke and I met even knew of my mother, the woman who had been a slave but rose among the kongelig. It was possible that some were spies, sent from my family's killers to murder me. Marieke insisted that if I was to truly hide, I should change my birth name as well, but even as a child, I refused. It was the name my mother had given me, the name she had whispered as she kissed my forehead at night.

I've met some who have wondered—thought on how there was once a little girl named Sigourney Rose, who might've been the same age as me if she hadn't been killed nearly ten years before, found dead in a pretty little dress beside the rest of her family, but no one has stepped forward with such a claim. No one has attempted to kill me for being a daughter of the Rose.

I spent seven years traveling the north with Marieke. I was thirteen when I decided I would sacrifice my freedom to return to the islands and take the power from the kongelig. I studied each of the kongelig: the Niklasson, Nørup, Solberg, Årud, Larsen, and Jannik families. My plan required the inheritance of the title of Elskerinde. Bernhand Lund didn't have any plans to retire his title, and I held no love for him, as he held no love for me. I asked Marieke to slip a drop of poison from oleander flowers purchased from the Solberg markets into my cousin's tea, and over the months he became ill. He left me everything in his will when he died. I could sense at his deathbed that he was grateful to have a name to write down on his paper, embarrassed that he'd lived such a long life but hadn't grown to love anyone but himself, ashamed that he had no choice but to ensure his legacy continue by placing his wealth and land into my hands. Now only Marieke knows with any certainty my true identity.

Marieke's rough fingers make their way into my hair. "And I don't hate you," she says. "You already know that."

There's an unexpected warming in my chest. I'm tempted to slip into her mind to see if she really means what she says, but Marieke is the one person whose privacy I've always respected. Besides, she has a way of knowing when I'm reading her thoughts, and she always has harsh words for what she calls "evil's trickery." Any other kongelig would have her killed for slandering what they consider the divine gifts.

"If only more people were like you, Marieke," I tell her.

She sucks her teeth again. "What's this? The grand Sigourney Rose, worried about what people think?"

I don't answer. She's silent, waiting for me to speak my worries. "Someone with kraft was found at the uprising today."

Marieke pauses for a brief moment before her hands continue to make their way through my hair. "Someone is always found with kraft."

I try not to think of the others—dozens—who had been brought to me over the years since becoming Elskerinde Lund after my cousin Bernhand's passing. I had to announce their rightful deaths and listen to their screams and cries, their pleas for mercy. They would've been honored, once. Before the Fjern came and declared these powers belonged to only them, an islander with such a gift would be considered blessed by our ancestors. They would devote their lives to using their abilities to help others. Now an islander with such an ability only becomes ash.

"It was a girl this time—young, couldn't have been any older than thirteen."

Marieke's fingers are stiff. Disgust emanates from her. I was right. Marieke wouldn't have wanted to hear about the death of a child. The death of a child by my own hand, no matter if I have a choice in declaring her execution or not.

Still, she tries to comfort me. "It was your responsibility as Elskerinde."

"Yes, it's my responsibility to kill my own people. How many will have to die because of me, while I kiss the feet of the Fjern who enslaved our people and killed my family?"

"What do you propose you do?" she asks. "You knew what was in store the day you decided to return to Lund Helle. This shouldn't come as any surprise," she tells me.

I raise my hands and stare at my wet palms as if I can see the blood that stains them. The next words I can't speak aloud, so I risk slipping into Marieke's mind, implanting a thought of my own: *It isn't easy to be so heartless.*

"You've never cared before," she says, her voice lowering. "Why start now? There's no harm in keeping your goals in sight." Marieke tips another pan of water slowly over my head, water cascading over my face. She likes to nag, but I know Marieke holds the same wishes as I do. Her family had been inside my mother's manor that night, too.

"Focus only on yourself and your ambitions," she says, "and soon you'll find that you care not what a single person thinks. Not even your gods."

CHAPTER THREE

My guardsmen and I race across the fields of Lund Helle, cutting through valleys where goats graze on guinea grass and houses dot the horizon. We travel to a bay and its crescent alcove of white sand. A private ship is anchored at sea, the clear blue water reflecting the cloudless sky. Friedrich rows me out on a smaller boat, and we climb a ladder to the top deck, floorboards swollen with salt beneath my feet. The islands of Hans Lollik are grouped nearly in a circle while the royal island of Hans Lollik Helle rests in the center. It can take only hours to reach any of the neighboring islands, but to venture farther out to the other end of the circle, the journey can take days. Ludjivik Helle is one of the islands farthest away from all the rest. Malthe told me no ships that the executed slave girl had mentioned were found. It's difficult to believe the Ludjivik family could truly have been behind the uprising.

Jannik Helle is only half a day away. Rose Helle is at our backs as we pass Niklasson Helle, then Solberg Helle, until finally the faded green of Jannik Helle is in the distance. Lund Helle is known for its farmland, its plantations and crops; Jannik Helle is known for its gambling dens, brothels, and rum. Jannik Helle had once thrived, providing the Fjern with entertainment, but when we arrive at the docks, it's empty of sailors; the few anchored trade ships appear to be abandoned. Malthe leads me to an awaiting carriage, its arrival prepared in advance. Though Malthe is the captain, Friedrich is my bodyguard, trained to be at my side at all times; he follows me into the carriage, while my remaining guardsmen wait behind. It would be an affront if I brought them all to Elskerinde Jannik's manor.

We ride for some time, out of the town of uneven streets that become dirt roads, the carriage clattering into the rocky coun-tryside of Jannik Helle, until finally we arrive. Yellow elders of the Jannik insignia bloom on the path leading to the Jannik manor, Herregård Mønsted. The house is a pale blue, two stories tall, with a balcony that wraps around each floor, windows dark with their gauzy curtains. We step from the carriage and walk through the garden, blossoming with its fruit and flowers, bees and hummingbirds flitting through the air, flies surrounding the overripe mango and guava that hang from their branches and fall to the ground to rot.

Friedrich knocks on the door and announces us to the answer-ing slave, who allows us into the manor. It's not so different from my own. Dead family members, sitting in their portraits, line the opening hall here as well, and the wooden floors gleam in the dim light that manages to shine through the cracks in the curtains—yet there's a smell here that's sunken into the walls. The smell of decaying skin, yellowing teeth, of fruit rotting in the heat.

The slave is a woman with graying hair. She has one hand, warped with white scars. When I send myself into her mind, it's only to know whether Elskerinde Jannik is awake and well enough to take visitors; instead, I'm overwhelmed with a mem-ory that sits with this slave woman in the forefront of her mind, always lingering: She was a baby, barely able to stand on her own two feet, not yet sold to another island or Fjern family, when her mother—young, not any older than me—spilled hot tea on Elskerinde Freja Jannik's hand. The woman's pale skin blistered and stung. And so she had the young girl's child—the woman who stands before me—taken to the kitchens, her hands forced into a pot of scalding-hot water. One hand had to be cut from the bone. The other is barely usable. The young mother was sold away, and the child remained here, serving Freja Jannik by sweeping and opening the door and carrying shaking trays of tea. She wonders about her mother sometimes, blames her for the loss of her hands. She doesn't think to blame Freja Jannik.

The woman won't meet my eye. She's heard that I executed a little girl for having kraft, and she's afraid I'll somehow believe she has kraft as well. She believes that I'm evil, unworthy of the power I hold. Most of my people hold hatred for me, hatred that feels like water from the sea filling my lungs. I leave her mind so that I won't have to see these thoughts.

"Herre Aksel Jannik is away," she says.

"I'm not here for Herre Aksel Jannik."

The woman stares at the ground beneath her feet. "The Elskerinde isn't well enough for visitors."

"The Elskerinde will never be well again," I say, "which is why I must see her while I still can."

She steps to the side and allows me into the shaded heat of the house. The smell of rot gets stronger as the slave leads us down the marbled halls. The windows are closed, the gauzy curtains attempting to block the sunlight. We turn corners and climb a flight of stairs until we stop outside the grandest door of all, the heavy mahogany wood even darker in the hall's dim light.

The slave bows and leaves, and Friedrich waits in the hall beside me. "Would you like me to come inside with you?" he asks, even though I always have the same answer for him. It's curiosity that makes Friedrich want to see the dying Elskerinde Jannik.

"No," I say, ignoring the pinch of disappointment from him. "Wait outside. I'll only be a moment."

He opens the door and, after I step in, clicks it shut behind me.

The room is cluttered. The Elskerinde Jannik had been a collector when she was young, and bells of every possible color and shape sit atop their shelves, and painted dolls with pale skin and red lips brought from the Elskerinde's homeland of Koninkrijk line the wall in their own private glass cases. The dolls are precious antiques. They aren't made quite the same way anymore, and they're worth thousands of coin in the northern empires— coin that could've helped to settle the debt of the Jannik family, if only the Elskerinde had not refused to part ways with the dolls. They bring memories to her, memories that are forever slipping away, however much she grasps at their edges.

She has memories of holding her mother's hand as they walked the cobblestoned streets of Koninkrijk, clumps of ice falling from the pale-blue sky. They bought dolls with lace dresses that looked like her own. Freja was only six years old when her mother and father came to these islands to begin a new life. Freja didn't understand why they'd had to leave Koninkrijk, but as she grew older, memories were like the pieces of a puzzle, snapping into place: the wealth their family had acquired so quickly; her father's disappearance for what felt like years, but could only have been weeks, before he returned one night. He hurriedly whispered to Freja that they had to leave, and she could only choose her favorite possessions. Her mother helped her pack the dresses and the dolls, still in their cases. They left that very night for a ship that waited in the harbor, and the Jannik family escaped into exile to live in these islands. Freja Jannik had cried every night once they arrived. She missed her home in Koninkrijk, the manor she'd been raised in with its gardens, the cobblestoned streets. Even as she grew and became a woman, she always longed to return to the country she'd been born to, but she never could, for risk that she would have to pay for her father's crimes.

Paintings cover the torn, yellowed wallpaper—portraits of the different landscapes of Koninkrijk, with the crowded towns and white mountains and endless forests. There are paintings, too, of Freja Jannik when she was younger, holding her baby boy in her lap. The largest painting is of her late husband, Herre Engel Jannik, which rests directly above her bed, watching her every move, even in death. He'd been a large man with a thick neck, brown hair that was stark against his pale skin, a heavy brow.

Elskerinde Freja Jannik lies beneath him. She's still, and for a moment I think she has passed—but I can feel the life thrumming through her veins, and her chest moves, her eyes blinking as she turns her head toward me. Her pale skin looks yellow in places. The tips of her fingers are blue, as if she'd dipped them into icy water. Even when dying, she's still had her slave put rouge blush onto her cheeks and painted her lips red, all with her one hand, so that Freja looks like one of the many dolls atop her shelves.

"Elskerinde Lund," she says, her voice still as melodic and strong as if she were a young woman of twenty years. "It's always so nice to see you."

I work my kraft and sink into her thoughts, as I came here to do. The Elskerinde lies. I can feel it in her bones. The woman despises me. She's disgusted, greeting a woman with skin as dark as mine, when I should be working the fields. Elskerinde Jannik has only known slaves since she came to these islands of Hàns Lollik. There are people with brown and black skin in the nations to the north, but the town they lived in within Koninkrijk was far from these empires; it was only when she got on the ship that would bring her to these islands that she saw people with skin as dark as mine for the first time. It was easy to believe the lies she was told: that people with dark skin are

closer to animals than she, that the gods have marked our skin to
show that we are evil and must be shown the ways of the good
through obedience to the Fjern. She thinks of this now as she
watches me entering her room, as though I'm her equal. I'm not
obedient. I watch her in defiance with my dark skin.

I sit at the chair aside her bed. A thin layer of dust covers the
arms and cushion.

"How are you?" I ask, taking her hand, the disgust in the
Elskerinde seeping into my skin. She wants to pull away, but
she doesn't want to risk offending me. She knows that she
needs me. Her hand is cold, damp, but I force myself to grip her
fingers, blue veins running like rivers over her wrist.

"The same," she says. "I just won't die, will I?" A shadow of
fear passes over her.

"I hope you'll stay with us as long as you can."

Her thinned white hair sticks to her cheek. Her own people
have forgotten her and left her to die alone in this room. Not so
long ago, Freja Jannik was practically the queen of these islands.
Before Jannik Helle fell to its debt, the Jannik name had been
the wealthiest in all of Hans Lollik. After Freja and her parents
fled to Hans Lollik, they started a life on this island. They'd
lived in town near the docks, where Freja had to wake to the
smell of fish blood and guts every morning, when she'd been
used to the fresh scent of pine and ice. The heat scalded and
burned her pink skin, and the salt cracked her lips. Her mother
passed only a year after they arrived. The woman had become ill
during the storm season and died only days later. Freja became
isolated, quiet. She could see how the other young Fjern ladies
of her school laughed at her, but Freja had an ambition of her
own. All of the girls clamored for the attention of Engel Jannik. He'd been like a prince to them, the handsome son of the
owner of this island. There were garden parties, balls, and only

the wealthiest and most respectable families of Hans Lollik were invited to attend.

Freja was neither of those things, but she'd been clever. She left her isolation. She showed only a joyous smile and complimented everyone around her, with never a nasty thing to say. She befriended the girls with her pretty smiles and easy charm, happy to make herself subservient to them, until finally she received invitations to follow along to these grand parties; and there, from afar, she could see Engel Jannik watching her. She feigned innocence, making sure the sunlight shined through the yellow in her hair. And when the handsome Jannik son invited her to the gardens, away from the crowds, Freja allowed him to slip a hand into her skirts so that he might know what he could have were he to marry her. She whispered sweetly in his ear that afternoon, and soon Freja found herself invited again and again to Engel Jannik's manor and to his gardens; found that she no longer needed her friends, who were now her enemies writhing in jealousy.

Engel Jannik proposed a month later. His parents retired from their positions, and so Engel and Freja inherited the titles of Herre and Elskerinde Jannik. The two threw the grandest parties in all of Hans Lollik. The music, the drink, the glamour—it was like magic, these parties. Guests would come one night and leave days later, swirling with memories of drunken laughter, as though they'd been bewitched by someone with kraft. Even the regent of the islands had come once, leaving his island of Hans Lollik Helle, an honor that to this day has still not been shared with any of the other kongelig. This manor had once been filled with guests, music, laughter, the clink of glasses filled with sugarcane wine. Now no one visits Elskerinde Jannik but me, a descendant of islanders, a person who ought to be a slave—and how pathetic it is, she thinks, that she's even begun to look forward to seeing me so that she won't die alone.

When I begin, I close my eyes. The Elskerinde is no longer a dying woman but a girl child, sitting on her father's lap, laughing at a joke she doesn't understand but desperately wants to, her mother glowing in a dress of white; and the little girl stands on the sand of Jannik Helle, clutching her father's hand, watching her mother's body float away on a boat that's been set afire. I clutch the Elskerinde's hand as I peel the memory away, filling the images with darkness.

I open my eyes again, and Freja Jannik stares at the canopy of her bed. "Even my own mother won't visit," she says, slipping her hand from mine and clutching the sheets at her waist. My own hands shake as I rest them in my lap. It's exhausting work, reading the thoughts and emotions of those around me, as though stretching my spirit between two bodies; it's even more tiring to manipulate Freja Jannik's mind as I do, taking away her memories.

"Do you miss your mother?" I ask, thinking on how much I miss my own. It might be a childish thought, but it's one that comes to me every day. I miss my mother, and the years that I never got to have with her. Marieke was always there for me—supportive, able to offer her advice. But it was my mother that I needed: a woman who understood what it means to be an islander in Hans Lollik with her wealth and the respect as a member of the kongelig, never swaying under their hatred for her.

Freja Jannik has stopped listening. She's lost in a memory again: her belly swollen and cramping, bruised from the fist that had hit her. Praying that the child is nothing like its father. She'd always known who Engel was, from the first moment she followed him into the gardens so many years before, when Engel Jannik had slipped a hand into her skirts and gripped her wrist with the other so tightly that she'd had to hide the bruise for days afterward. It was no surprise when he hit her in anger. It was a price Freja had thought she'd been willing to pay.

This memory I strip away, too—not to ease her suffering but because it seems that the more memories I take, the faster she dies; and so I search, careful not to take so many that my visits would be suspicious and that Freja Jannik won't look to be anything other than a woman dying of old age. I've come to Freja Jannik for the past two years now. At first it was only to speak with her—to see how I might become her ally. When it became clear that she would never be an ally by choice, I had to think of ways to convince her otherwise. I try to push away the guilt. I must remember who Elskerinde Freja Jannik is, and everything that she's done.

As I look through the caverns of her mind, I see flashes of her life: Engel Jannik, broad-shouldered and young, standing to greet her—she'd thought he was so handsome then, and he'd been so in love with her, so attentive, even if he had never been very kind; men and women in outfits of white, their glasses of sugarcane wine gleaming; walks through the groves, as she watches my enslaved people; a little brown boy running past, the Elskerinde's burning hatred for him.

And then there's her son. He's a squirming pink thing in her memory, wailing with a toothless mouth, pail of red water splashing onto the floor, pain unbearable—there had been complications and the boy had nearly strangled himself with the cord around his neck—but happiness, too, happiness that both she and the child survived.

I slip a thought into her mind: *My son is the perfect match for Elskerinde Sigourney Lund.*

"My son is the perfect match for you," she says, eyes shining.

He may not love her—I hope he never will—but the Lund name is our only savior.

The Elskerinde smiles, smoothing her hand against the sheet, unwilling to share her true thoughts: The Jannik family is in ruin. Engel adopted an ugly habit of cards and rum, and the endless parties proved too expensive for the Jannik family. Failed businesses attracted the more sordid crowds of the Hans Lollik islands. Freja Jannik became pregnant three times, and three times the child died in her womb. Her husband had never been kind, but he became angrier at the smallest of offenses: not speaking loudly enough, walking too slowly, not wearing Engel's favorite dress—suddenly, all were crimes deserving of his fist.

And, though Engel Jannik had no kraft to his name, Freja could see in his eyes that he blamed her not only for the deaths of their children but for the weak ability of their son as well. Freja Jannik has no control over the power of her son; it was only ill luck that Aksel was gifted with such a weak kraft by the gods—a weak kraft that has wrecked their chances before Konge Valdemar. Her family is lucky they've even remained members of the kongelig. There've been some who have called for the Jannik house to step down. The Ludjivik family has been most vocal, but there have even been members of kongelig families, Freja knows, who have whispered among themselves. "Pathetic," the Jannik family has been called. It's only out of pity, embarrassment, that they've been invited to Hans Lollik Helle over the years, invited to the garden parties and balls.

Freja Jannik hates me. She hates the darkness of my skin, the thickness of my eyelashes and hair, the wideness of my nose and lips. She hates that I was born of these islands, and she hates most of all that I am her family's last hope. But she at least knows my blood is strong and that coin has never been an issue for the Lund family.

There's a twist of unease that thrums through Freja and into me—her eyes widen, and she inhales a sharp breath. I can feel kraft steeping inside the Elskerinde, a tingle over the skin.

"Are you all right?" I ask, leaning closer. It's perverse, the genuine concern I have for her, this connection I feel with Elskerinde

Jannik after visiting for years, even as I aid in her death. I hold no love for the Elskerinde, but I do have understanding—knowing her story, feeling the pain she's felt, keeping her thoughts as though they are my own.

The fear in her eyes subsides. "The whispers. They happen more now. They tell me I'll die by the hands of someone I trust, but they won't tell me who it is."

I force a smile. "I can't imagine who would want to betray you, Elskerinde Jannik."

She laughs, but her laugh turns into coughs—her body, her bed, it seems even her entire room shakes with each one, until she takes another deep, wheezing breath. "I can think of a few," she says. A memory appears in Elskerinde Jannik's mind, images flashing through my own. A memory of my mother, standing before all the kongelig, dressed in white.

I wait for the storm ripping through my veins to subside. "May I ask you a question, Elskerinde Jannik?"

"Of course, Elskerinde Lund."

I grasp my hands together. "What do you know of the Rose family?"

Her expression is still. I've seen these memories, too, when I sink into her mind—memories of sitting on sofas, sipping sugarcane wine, wishing she hadn't been in the room when her husband discussed the plans with the other kongelig, agreeing on exactly how they would send in Jannik guards to slaughter every single man, woman, and child who happened to be in my family's manor. How they'd clinked glasses, silently signing away the lives of people I knew, people I loved. My sisters, my brother, my mother.

The kongelig hated my mother and the Rose family. They couldn't understand why the regent of these islands would seem to hold my mother, an islander, in such grand esteem, or why he would invite her to Hans Lollik Helle for the storm season.

Some feared that the king even planned to pass Mirjam Rose the title of the crown, and power over all of Hans Lollik; and so, the kongelig planned for her death.

The ghost of my mother haunts Freja Jannik at night. My mother never speaks. She simply comes to watch Freja. She watches with no judgment or hate—only a reminder of the sins Freja has committed before the gods. My mother has come to visit Freja Jannik so often that the Elskerinde has even started to question if, after all, the islanders had been right to believe that the spirits of the dead will always seek their revenge. The Elskerinde's thoughts have whispered their regrets to me. Regrets that Freja hadn't taken Engel's hand and insisted that they find another way to convince Konge Valdemar of their own value. That killing the Rose family, and slaughtering everyone in the manor, was not worth their ambition.

Elskerinde Jannik has many regrets, yes. But her regrets won't bring back my family. Her regrets mean nothing to me.

She finally speaks. "Why would you ask that?" she asks. "I'd rather not speak about such a tragedy."

It's what any member of the remaining six kongelig families of Hans Lollik say when asked. It's what they agreed upon: to never speak on the atrocity they've committed, in the hopes that the gods will forget their sins. The kongelig don't believe they've sinned in killing my family; they don't consider islanders to be human, and so there's no sin in taking our lives. But there'd been other Fjern that night: cousins of the Skov, longtime allies of the Lund family's plantation business, and the Koch family, a poorer family of the Fjern but still Fjern regardless, perhaps excited for an invitation when normally ignored by the kongelig. Their families had been slaughtered as well.

I watch Freja Jannik in her bed, dying—and suddenly, even her death isn't enough. "What happened to the Rose family, Elskerinde Jannik?"

"They were killed," she says, and her frown deepens as she's unsure why she's speaking, why she's answering me, why she's unable to stop. "Murdered by guards."

"Whose guards?"

She hesitates, then says her own family's name.

She trembles, and tears threaten to fall from her eyes as she begins to breathe her apologies, but I give an unspoken order of silence, and she quiets in her bed. "Why did you have them killed?"

Freja shakes her head, but the words fall from her mouth. "Konge Valdemar had invited Mirjam Rose to join Hans Lollik Helle for the storm season, to join the kongelig. By the gods, I couldn't fathom why he would invite a former slave, but the king had been ill, weak of mind. I feared he would consider passing his title to her family in his confused state."

"And so you brought the idea to your husband?"

"It was my suggestion first, yes, but I only meant for Mirjam and the boy child, Claus, to die. The boys are so much more likely to become heir, and I thought the girls could be spared. I suggested killing both separately. Mirjam Rose, by poisoning so that it would seem she'd died naturally of an illness, and Claus Rose, by sending a guard to break his neck as he rode his horse, as he was known to do each morning on the shore, so that it'd seem he'd fallen. But Engel—he didn't want to take the risk. He didn't want anyone from the Rose family to survive. And so he waited until the annual ball thrown by Mirjam Rose in her late husband's honor, and had our guards kill everyone. Every single—"

She gasps, and I think for a moment that her heart really has stopped, but no—it keeps beating, and she closes her eyes. "They didn't all need to die. The Koch family. The Skov family. So many people. My husband's guards had to set fire to the manor to burn the bodies, because there were too many to bury at sea."

I've already seen Freja Jannik's memories where she tried to spare me and my sisters. I know she would think her hope to save us from herself would mean she deserves my pity, my mercy. My hand, shaking, reaches for Freja Jannik's cheek—slides to her neck, where my fingers tighten a grip around the woman's throat. Her eyes widen, her mouth opens as she tries to suck in the air she can't breathe, and I watch, my entire arm trembling with the effort. Her eyes become glazed, her mouth slackens.

Yes, she thinks. *This is exactly how the gods described it.*

I release her.

She chokes on air.

I can hear Marieke's voice. *Patience, child.*

CHAPTER FOUR

I strip the woman of her latest memories and leave Elskerinde Jannik's chamber to race down the hall, down the stairs, a surprised Friedrich following me, his thoughts and questions interrupting my own—*Is she crying? What happened?*—but he says nothing as we rush toward the doors.

I turn a sharp corner and nearly run into the man I'm least expecting: Aksel Jannik.

He's tall—taller than his father had been, with broader shoulders. His pale hair, the same color as his mother's, is combed away from his face. His white shirt is buttoned to the neck, despite the heat in this airless hall, and his riding breeches and boots are spotless. He's alone. Aksel never has guardsmen with him—a foolish move on his part, an oversight based on his own arrogance. He hates the idea of being followed everywhere by a slave, having to share the same space with someone who has skin as dark as mine. He doesn't think he needs to depend on a slave to save his life if he's ever attacked. He thinks he's above death. I can't wait to prove him wrong.

Aksel doesn't seem as surprised to see me. He's probably been here all along. I'm weak, feeling faint after working through Freja Jannik's thoughts, and Aksel has become rather good at hiding his mind from me over the past year. It was only in the beginning that I could feel how much he despised me.

"Elskerinde Lund," he says in greeting.

"Aksel," I say, forcing a smile.

His eyes, the dark brown of his father's, flit to Friedrich, still standing beside me. "Leave us," he says.

Friedrich doesn't move. "Elskerinde Lund?" he questions. I can hear in his voice that he takes particular pleasure in ignoring Aksel's command.

"Prepare the carriage," I tell him. "I'll only be a moment."

Friedrich's footsteps fade, and Aksel and I are left alone in the hall.

Aksel isn't so different from Friedrich: One emotion I can still sense is his envy. Aksel Jannik's kraft allows him to sense when another has an ability in their veins, and to know what that power is, the level of that person's strength. Whenever he meets me, my kraft flows into him, and he knows that I'm strong and that he's weak.

He eyes me. "I'm surprised you're here again."

"I enjoy visiting your mother."

"But so often?"

"You don't resent my visits, do you?"

Of course he does.

His arms are stiff. "She needs her rest."

"I'd like to think I bring her peace."

"You don't know what brings my mother peace," he says, and I can feel the rage simmering beneath his calm facade. I'm not sure even I understand the depths of his hatred for me, the islander he's being forced to marry. He doesn't trust me, and with reason. It was only when I began to call on Elskerinde Jannik two years before that she started to insist that I marry her son. Even Aksel, as dim as he can be, is suspicious. That his mother had even agreed to accept me as a guest had been worrying to him; then for her, a year after meeting me, to tell him that she wanted us to unite in name, he knew that his mother had fallen victim to my manipulation. He doesn't know for sure if it was my kraft—has no proof I've used my abilities on his mother—but he suspects I might have. Still, he doesn't complain. He loves another member of the kongelig, a Fjern woman I've only ever met in his thoughts, but her coin and her blood is nothing in comparison to the Lund family's wealth and the power of my kraft. Marrying her might as well mean forfeiting any chance he has to receive the blessing of Konge Valdemar.

"I heard there was another slave uprising on Lund Helle." He says this without a smile, though I can hear it in his voice.

I flinch, remembering the slaves—the girl, crying on her knees. I don't bother asking how he knows such a thing, or searching for the answer in his thoughts; word travels fast in these islands, and gossip flows stronger than blood. "And they failed."

"If you aren't careful, the Jannik family might inherit your enemies."

"The Lund family is strong enough that it doesn't matter which enemies you inherit. You should be grateful."

His thoughts stab through me—thoughts he throws at me, wanting me to hear: *I will never be grateful to marry you. I'll wake up every morning, knowing that I've sacrificed my life, my happiness, for the sake of my family—but never think I'll be grateful to marry you.*

He turns his back to me, marching down the corridor, dismissing me without another word.

I leave the front hall of Herregård Mønsted and return to the carriage where Friedrich waits. I feel his curiosity, but Friedrich doesn't ask about my feelings toward Aksel and if we really hate each other as much as we seem to.

We journey back to Lund Helle. By the time the ship anchors in its bay once more and we're outfitted atop our horses, the sun peeks over the ocean's horizon, sky a transparent pink, the air fresh with the relief of a salted morning breeze. My twelve personal guardsmen ride behind me in a line, as always, and Friedrich's horse clops alongside mine as we cut through valleys. These are my brief moments of peace: closing my eyes, feeling the heat of the island on my cheeks. I pretend to have a different life. One where my family is not dead, and I'm still in the home where I spent my first years on Rose Helle, running through my mother's maze of hedges and stealing mango tarts from the kitchen; Inga singing her clear, high voice through the halls.

I remember the stories my mother whispered to me and Ellinor as we sat upon her lap in the gardens. Stories about our people, and these islands that had once been our own. All of the sea belonged to us—all of the sand, the dirt, the fruit, the trees. The powers that flowed through the veins of the blessed were celebrated and nurtured—gifts from our ancestors and the spirits that surround us. These islands had a name, a language, a history, before the Fjern ever arrived. A name, a language, a history—now lost. Even as a child, I mourned for what the islands had once been, longed to know the name my people had once called these lands.

The Fjern came over hundreds of years before. They raided our villages, taking our homes and slaughtering our people. The lands we had once called home were renamed the islands of Hans Lollik, and the Fjern replaced our language with their own. Anyone who dared speak the mother tongue had their own cut from their mouth. I sometimes feel a disgust for myself, that I speak the language of the Fjern and hold a name with their roots. What would my name have been had the Fjern never come to these islands? The hollow in my chest wishes to know.

The Fjern claimed these islands as Koninkrijk territory and granted a regent to rule. The regent has his advisers, known as the kongelig, who are born of the wealthiest and most powerful families of these islands. It's no coincidence that every member of the kongelig has kraft, allowing them to rise above the other Fjern who have left Koninkrijk to come to Hans Lollik. The Fjern claim only the kongelig and their descendants may hold kraft, but never once have I seen them execute one of their own, while my people with kraft are routinely rooted out, hung, beheaded, drowned. There'd once been hundreds of thousands of my people across these islands. Now half of that number remains—and of those who survive, I'm the only one who has my freedom, beyond Marieke, whose freedom I have given.

But the Fjern have always been pragmatic. Islanders were promised to be released from slavery if they managed to pay for their life. My ancestor Wilhelm Rose did just that. He'd been a slave on a plantation of Niklasson Helle and was to work the fields for his master from dawn until dusk; after dark, he returned to his own garden behind the slaves' quarters and grew lemongrass, which he then sold on the dock's markets before the sun could rise.

The Fjern who bought his lemongrass didn't question if the coin would go to Wilhelm's master or stay in his own pocket; they assumed he'd been sent on an errand, as so many other slaves in the market were. If they'd known Wilhelm sold the lemongrass for his own profit, they never would've bought his lemongrass; but his loyal customers had to admit that there was something special about his grass, the strength of its taste, the brightness of its flavor. His grass seemed to cure any ailment, to cheer any mood, and it became popular enough that he earned more coin than even some of the Fjern selling their grass and herbs. Wilhelm worked like this and saved his coin for ten years, I was told. He buried the coin he saved in the very garden where he worked into the night, without his master's knowledge.

Claus told me that another slave saw Wilhelm burying his coin and attempted to dig up and steal the treasure for himself.

Wilhelm caught the man and struck him in the head with a stone, killing him, then dragged his body to the rocky shore to make it seem he'd fallen and hit his head as he attempted to escape the island. Claus had told all of this to me, though I can't see how my brother would've known something like this. Claus, like my sister Ellinor, had a habit of telling stories for the sake of entertainment, regardless of whether they were true or not. Still, the ending must be the same, whether our ancestor was a murderer or not: Once he had enough coin saved, he approached his master with the price of his life.

At first, the master reneged on the promise of Wilhelm's freedom and simply took the bag of coin for himself. But when my mother told me the tale, she said that the master's wife had a softer heart—rare for the Fjern. She convinced the man to release Wilhelm, and he was allowed to leave the plantation with only his name and the clothes on his back. My mother tells me that the plantation had been covered with rose-mallow flowers, so Wilhelm, as he left with his freedom, decided to give himself the family name of Rose. He had nowhere to go and no coin to depend on for survival. Wilhelm knew he could easily be captured by any Fjern, who would sell him or accuse him of escaping and have him killed, but he also had no way of making it to the north, where he had heard others with brown skin lived with their freedom.

Wilhelm took a risk. It was the only choice he had. He approached Fjern families on the streets of Niklasson Helle, claiming he had a knowledge of working the fields that no other islander would share because of their anger at being enslaved—a knowledge that no Fjern held, as they didn't know these islands as he did. Wilhelm boldly promised he could help their business grow if they allowed him to become a partner in their crop. At first the Fjernmen found him amusing, this islander who had bought his own freedom and thought he could become their equal. Their amusement quickly dwindled. Within days, laughter turned to shouts and threats. He was spat at, until one day, a Fjernman knocked him across the face, and the man and his friends kicked Wilhelm as he lay curled up on the ground. If he'd fought back, he'd undoubtedly have been hung for striking a Fjern.

It was Wilhelm's luck that Patrick Lund happened to walk by at that moment. Patrick was no better than any of the other Fjern of these islands: He thought himself above islanders as well, but he pitied Wilhelm the way he would if he saw a gang of boys kicking a dog. He insisted Wilhelm be left alone. Patrick Lund, my mother told me, was a soft-spoken gentleman, but commanding all the same. The Fjernmen left Wilhelm on the streets, and Patrick offered him safe passage from Niklasson Helle. When asked why he'd been attacked, Wilhelm explained that he wished to become a partner in a Fjern family's crop business. Patrick Lund was intrigued. The family's tobacco plantation had been failing for some time and was near ruin. Wilhelm was invited to Lund Helle to teach any tricks he might have in exchange for coin. Wilhelm, it turned out, could see the issue clearly: The soil was not right for tobacco. He suggested the Lund try their hand at sugarcane instead. Patrick Lund did this, and the sugarcane thrived within months.

The Lund family had been on the precipice of ruin, and Patrick still needed Wilhelm's knowledge of the crop. He agreed to allow Wilhelm to become a partner. Wilhelm lived on the plantation, in a house he built himself, and he married a slave girl. They had a child, and by the end of his life, the Lund sugarcane business had become so profitable that Wilhelm had acquired more wealth than some of the poorest Fjern families.

His family line continued, and the Lund and Rose sugarcane business survived the attacks of anyone who felt a man of my people didn't deserve such wealth. Eventually the Rose married into the Lund family. This was Ellinor's favorite story to tell: a son of the Rose, who fell in love with a daughter of the Lund.

Ellinor found the story romantic, and would add elaborate tales of how they had to secretly meet in the gardens to keep the love they had for one another hidden. I was too young to understand the stiffness in my mother's gaze whenever Ellinor would tell this story of hers, but I do understand now: Our people have no love for the Fjern, and the Fjern have no love for us. This must've been a painful business proposal.

Still, it was the best political move for both families. No Fjern would agree to marry the Lund after they joined in business with a family of islanders. The Rose had been their only allies. The families joined together were fortified all the more, and eras later, ten generations of free Rose sons, with their black skin and thick hair, had maneuvered the politics and coin of the islands so deftly that my grandfather managed to claim an island of his own. It was a small island, useless for plantations, but it was his. He was the first and only native of these islands to do so, passing Rose Helle on to my father.

Even after my father's passing, my mother held the family's strength, and the Rose name continued to grow. She seemed to possess all knowledge of the workings of the islands: she managed the sugarcane business alongside the Lund and the politics of the kongelig so swiftly that some still whisper that she had been blessed with kraft, though no one ever directly accused her of it. When the family line of the kongelig Holm family ended with no heir, the regent of Hans Lollik invited my mother to stay on the royal island for the storm season, officially making ours the seventh family of the kongelig.

But the regent is aging now, and Konge Valdemar has no successor. Ten years ago he announced he would choose one at the end of this era from any of the viable kongelig families. The era concludes with the end of the coming storm season, in two months' time.

And so I will have two months to convince Konge Valdemar to choose me.

Two months to destroy the remaining kongelig families.

Wind rushes across the fields of Lund Helle before it dies down again. The winds bring dark, mountainous clouds that block the sun, threatening rain and thunder, but the clouds don't stop over Lund Helle, and the sky is blue and bright again within moments, the sun scalding my hands as I grip my horse's reins. The rain showers steam far out at sea in the distance.

"By the gods," Friedrich says, "sometimes I forget how beautiful this island is. It's enough to make me want to settle a small piece of land and build a house of my own."

This is a joke of his, knowing that he'll never be able to do such a thing without his freedom. The hatred in Friedrich for me simmers, but he pushes it aside. There's no point in allowing himself to hate me, no point in giving in to his rage. He'd have nowhere to place that anger, unless he wanted to attempt to take my life, forfeiting his own. I wonder if, in a way, I've forced Friedrich to think that he loves me. I didn't place the thought in his mind, as I've placed thoughts in Elskerinde Jannik's—but if Friedrich isn't able to hate me, perhaps the only other choice is for him to believe he loves me instead.

I try to ignore the desire for a peaceful life that bubbles inside me. It'd be easy. No one knows I escaped the slaughter in my family's manor. A little slave girl's body was found in one of my dresses, so my family's murderers think I was killed along with everyone else who was there that night. It'd be easy to let my cousin Herre Bernhand Lund's legacy pay for a cottage house in the countryside, perhaps with a view of the ocean and some goats of my own. I could marry a gentle farmer, or maybe even Friedrich, and have children—daughters and a son—whom

I'd name after my sisters and brother. It would be easy. Easy to ignore the invitation to Hans Lollik Helle.

We cross the fields before turning to the shadow of a grove, mahogany trees' leaves shining green, bristling in the breeze. A bird calls and another answers. These groves remind me of the ones on Rose Helle that I would dash through with Ellinor, our nurse racing after us. Ellinor had whispered to beware the woman in white: She was one of the many vengeful spirits, my sister had said, who looks like a beautiful woman with pale skin and yellow hair, until she smiles her mouthful of needlelike teeth.

Friedrich stops his horse beside me, a frown of confusion marring his face. He grips his reins tightly as his horse steps back nervously. I look ahead to see a tree fallen across the road. A single tree, so thin it could be chopped in two with the right machete and the right muscles, roots pulled from the dirt and tangled in the air like branches. There must have been a windstorm that pushed the tree over, yet Friedrich's uncertainty spreads.

"What's wrong?" I ask him. His answer comes to me as he speaks.

"Could be a setup for an ambush. We should turn around."

I try not to laugh. "It's more likely just a fallen tree, Friedrich. It's in their nature to fall."

He turns to me to speak, mouth open, but before he makes a sound, an arrow flies and lands in his throat. Red splatters across my face. Air is sucked from the grove.

The horse stands on his rear legs. Friedrich's body leans, and thumps to the ground. Malthe shouts as my guardsmen leap from their horses. I follow, stumbling to the dirt, Friedrich unmoving beside my feet, blood and muscle blossoming where the arrow protrudes from his neck, his eyes wide with surprise—islanders have emerged from the trees, the brush, machetes drawn. There aren't many—only four, no, five—but these aren't slaves now calling themselves rebels. These men are trained. They clash with my guards, swiping left and right, dodging expertly, stabbing swords into my soldiers' chests and necks. Six of my own fall to the ground, and only six more stand. This is a fight we could lose. A fight that we are losing.

I pierce one mind, and I can feel the man fighting me as if he'd been warned about my kraft—but then he turns and stabs his machete into the stomach of one of his comrades, then another, before he cuts his own neck—

One man aims his bow at me, and an arrow whisks by, nearly piercing my cheek. I haven't recovered before the man races toward me, knife drawn—I try to sink into him next, but my kraft ricochets. I barely manage to jump back, to escape the knife aimed for my neck, my feet tangling in my dress as I fall to the dirt. The assassin moves to follow, to stab my chest—I grab his hand, pushing back as he grips the handle, the tip piercing my skin above my heart. I kick out with a scream, push him off with all my force, and he rolls from me and jumps to his feet. My soldiers have gained control of the battle, three of the assassins falling, red gushing from their throats, their chests, their stomachs; it's now four of my guards against the one remaining assassin. He sees the situation, his dead friends, and begins to run.

Malthe follows—grabs the man's arm and yanks him to the ground, twisting the knife from him. My guards are on the assassin, pulling him to his feet as he struggles against them. The dead surround us. Friedrich is one of them. Blood on his lips, his neck mangled, eyes empty. Pain wells and burns my throat, but I swallow my tears. I learned early that it doesn't help to let anyone see me cry.

Malthe knocks a fist into the assassin's mouth, and he stops fighting against the hands that hold him. He spits blood into the dirt. The man has a young face, even if his expression is grim, mouth set in a firm line. Now that he's lost, he stands calm under the force of my guards, eyes on me, waiting for me to give the order that would take his life, but he doesn't seem afraid. There's even a shadow of a smile on his lips. As though he thinks this is funny, that he's killed Friedrich and my men and attempted to kill me.

I move toward him, bending over to pick up a fallen machete as I walk, leather handle rough in my palm, blade gleaming with sunlight and blood. I press the edge of the machete to the man's neck.

"Who are you? What's your name?"

He doesn't answer me. I try to force myself into him again, but it's as if I'm walking into a glass wall, bouncing back with surprise—agitation, as I press a hand against the glass wall and try to push. The man winces, but only for a second. His face returns to the same expressionless mask.

"Who sent you?" I ask. "The Ludjivik?"

I'm so used to asking a question and finding my answer, but this time there's only silence. People have tried to hide their thoughts from me, and many have succeeded—a jungle of confused thought to hide the secret they don't want me to know, or a quiet and meditative mind—but to be blocked out completely . . . This is different. This is new.

The assassin only stands, chin raised, peering at me as the corners of his lips twitch into a smile. He taunts me as though he knows of my kraft and knows, too, that I can't see into him like I can see into anyone else of my choosing. I study him. His dark brown eyes are the same color as his hair, curling and sticking to his face in the heat. His skin is a golden brown, bright even in the shaded grove. Though his dead friends were all islanders, it's difficult to tell if this man is a descendant of the men and women who invaded these islands, or if he has the blood of an islander as well. The longer I look at him, the more questions appear, and the more my frustration builds.

"Elskerinde Lund," Malthe says, his face steeled though his eyes are wet. It'd been his responsibility to protect these guards, and though Friedrich had been a pain in his side, I could tell that Malthe also cared for the boy. "What should we do with this man?" he asks me.

I should kill him. Slice open his neck as he and his friends sliced open the necks of the men on the ground. An execution, for attacking and attempting to kill me, is the only action anyone would expect. I open my mouth, ready to give the order... But there are still too many unanswered questions. Not only about why he has tried to kill me but about why my kraft doesn't work on him as well. I can't kill him—not yet. My hand holding the machete trembles before I drop the blade to the ground.

"Take him to Herregård Dronnigen. I'll question him there."

The guards hesitate. Shock, anger pulse across their faces. I'm sparing the life of a man who has killed their fellow guards, their friends—who has tried to kill them. If I read their thoughts, I might feel a confirmation of what I've feared has been there all along: their hatred of me, their judgment. Malthe remains steady.

"Elskerinde Lund," he begins, his tone grave—but he doesn't push when I hold up my hand to silence him. There's even, for a moment, the barest flicker of relief across his face, and he lowers his head, perhaps glad that he won't have to argue for another islander's death.

One of my guardsmen gets onto his horse to race ahead to the manor, to be sure it's safe for my arrival. Two of my other guards bind the assassin, throw him over the back of a horse, and start their journey to the manor as well. Malthe tells me that we must leave immediately. The groves might still be unsafe. Other assailants could be hiding in wait. I know that he's right, but still I have a hard time leaving. I force myself to keep my gaze on Friedrich. His body is empty. I can still feel the remnants of his being inside of him, dust settling, but this is no longer Friedrich. There's no energy that vibrates through him, no humor, no gladness that he's alive even if he doesn't own his life.

I ask Malthe to give Friedrich a proper burial at sea, and he promises that he will.

Herregård Dronningen appears on its hill, faded white as though a ghost of itself. The guard who had raced ahead has already arrived, waiting on the path to acknowledge that the manor holds no threat. Marieke and other slaves await my return on the front steps. Malthe helps me from my horse, my hands and knees weak. Marieke is by my side immediately, taking my gloves as I yank them from my trembling fingers.

"Is it true?" she says beneath her breath. "Is Friedrich dead?"

I nod, sweeping past her.

"Spirits remain," Marieke murmurs, following closely behind. Marieke often murmurs her prayers to the ancestors, even knowing that if the wrong ears hear her, she could be hung. It doesn't normally annoy me, her prayers to the spirits, but it annoys me now—the idea, that spirits remain and protect us. Friedrich has been killed. He isn't here. He doesn't remain.

I throw open the doors to my chambers and turn to the stand beside my bed, but the letter is gone. "Where is it?"

Marieke squints at me in confusion as though I've lost my mind. Maybe I have. "Where is what?"

"The letter from Hans Lollik Helle. The invitation."

Marieke hesitates, closing the doors behind her. "You've just had an attempt on your life," she says, "and though you won't likely admit it, you're grieving the loss of your guard. It's all right for you to take a breath."

I shake my head, and as I look to the ground, I see the splotches of brown—Friedrich's dried blood along the collar, the front of my dress. My stomach churns. I try to yank it off, struggling

with the collar and the sleeves, until Marieke moves to help me
and I'm able to step out of the dress, leaving it a crumpled mess
on the ground. Even if the stains are removed, I won't be able to
wear the dress again.

"I nearly died today," I tell Marieke.

She nods, but she doesn't understand, and it's difficult for
me to form the words, to describe what happened—Friedrich's
death, and the man who tried to kill me. Two guards are riding
back with the assassin now, expected to arrive by evening.

I stand naked and catch a glimpse of myself in a mirror. The
cut on my chest, right above my heart, has already started to
scab. The dirt and grease smeared across my face, my tangled
hair, the panic in the shine of my eyes, the pain knitted in my
brow. I look close to tears. I harden my expression.

I watch myself as I speak. "Give me the invitation."

There's no doubt in my mind now: I'd grown too comfortable with myself, my position, my plans—I was too confident,
and now reality has come to confront me. A group of islanders,
so well trained, couldn't simply have found their way to Lund
Helle and attempted to kill me. These were guardsmen. Someone sent assassins for me, and the only people in these islands
able to afford such a group of assassins are the kongelig.

Marieke folds her arms for a moment before walking to my
bookshelf and pulling the invitation from a stack of papers. I
snatch it from her fingers, palms sweating as I tear the seal and
unfold the paper to read the script with shaking hands. As the
betrothed of Herre Aksel Jannik, the honor of my presence
is requested on the royal island for the coming storm season.
Should I accept, I must arrive within one week's time. The paper
is signed by the regent, Konge Valdemar, himself.

I'd envisioned reading these words for so many years now. If I
accept, there's little chance that I'll survive the storm season. It's
become a tradition of sorts to see which member of the kongelig

family will be found dead, drowned on the beach or strangled in their bed, poisoned at a dinner party, or in the middle of the woods with their neck cut. To be invited to Hans Lollik Helle is an honor that's bestowed upon few Fjern, and for them to be gathered during the storm season is the perfect time to settle old grudges—to kill whoever stands in the way of their goals. As the only islander, I know I'll be targeted all the more. Even when I was young, I knew there was little chance I would survive the storm season on Hans Lollik Helle, but it had become my only goal: to receive an invitation from the king himself. To convince him of my worth, and to be named the next regent of the islands of Hans Lollik, so that I would have the power to destroy the people who killed my family.

I tell Marieke to begin preparations for Hans Lollik Helle. We leave tomorrow.

CHAPTER FIVE

Herregård Dronnigen isn't the same without Friedrich. I've lost guardsmen before, but with Friedrich there always seemed to be a smile upon everyone's faces—the kitchen staff's as he chatted with the cooks, picking at desserts; the stable boys' as he told stories about his days in training over rum. And mine, whenever he accompanied me to the nearby villages. When he laughed against my ear under my sheets, speaking of escaping the islands of Hans Lollik. I didn't love Friedrich, not as he believed he loved me—but he didn't deserve to die. Not because of me.

The manor is silent. No chatter in the kitchens, no laughter in the halls. Guards are positioned at the entryway and on the porch. I can feel their anger. My guards have never held love for me, but the anger they now have boils. I've allowed the man who attempted to take my life—the man who killed Friedrich and most of my personal guardsmen—to live, when he should have been hung from his neck. There's a reason I don't read the thoughts of my people. The Fjern—yes, I know that they hate me, and always will—but the hatred from my own people is what cuts me open. It's the hatred in their eyes that lets me know I'm truly alone.

There aren't any dungeons in Herregård Dronnigen, so the

assassin has been locked away in an abandoned wing. I haven't wanted to face him, knowing he was responsible for Friedrich's death. I'm not sure I can trust myself not to have him killed the moment I see his face. But now, with only hours before I must leave for Hans Lollik Helle, I have little choice. I plod through the halls barefoot. Dust has gathered and floats, shining through the yellow light that streams from the closed windows. The air of the hall is heavy, the curtains unmoving. Heat rises through my skin, and sweat pricks my brow. This had been the wing my sisters and brother and I shared with our mother when we came to visit our cousins as children.

I didn't have my kraft yet, so there's no way for me to be sure, but as a child I thought it was easy to see the discomfort of our cousins. The Lund knew it was our ancestor, Wilhelm Rose, they had to thank for their wealth, but even this didn't stop them from placing us in these quarters that had once belonged to slaves. This didn't stop Bernhand and his wife, before her death, from repeatedly failing to invite us to their sitting room for tea or to the dining room for supper. More often than not, my mother would come here with us, and we would stay only a few days as she conducted her business, observing the crop and meeting with Bernhand Lund, until finally we'd return to Rose Helle. While my mother was locked away in the office with Bernhand, Ellinor and I would run laughing through the halls, hiding from our nurse and Inga. We explored the manor, searching for hidden and unlocked rooms, rummaging through drawers for buried treasure. The wallpaper, like an old memory, has faded. Dust covers the porcelain vases, which once held bunches of flowers of every color and scent, but only sit empty now.

I walk to the main chamber, hand hesitating on the golden handles of the large mahogany doors. Ellinor and I would run to these doors, burst them open, and jump onto the bed where our mother slept. She would open her eyes, a smile already on her face, as she'd wrap her arms around us and tickle both of our bellies until we could no longer breathe.

The sound of laughter dies away. I push open the door and step into the room. The lace curtains are still the same, the canopy bed and the vanity table and the balcony that gives a glance at the blue sea. The only difference is the man standing in the center of the room, watching me, as if he'd been waiting there in exactly that same spot for the past night and day. I snap the doors shut behind me.

I can't read his mind. I can't control his body. My kraft has allowed me to do both for years now, since the days I spent traveling the north with Marieke. First, the ability was an uncontrolled burst of power: The thoughts and emotions of others came to me as though they were my own, and I would crumble under the weight of other minds. Slowly, the power faded into what it is now: my conscious effort in deciding to read the thoughts and emotions of those around me. The ability to sink so deeply into those thoughts that I could become that person, even for a moment, developed over time as well. Every person, each mind, each body, has belonged to me for half of my life now. No one has ever been able to resist me and my kraft—not until the man who stands before me.

I walk across the room, eyes still on him. His ghost of a smile is gone now. It might have something to do with the bruise that blossoms across his cheek, the cut on his lip. He wears the same loose-fitting shirt and pants as when he fired the arrow that killed Friedrich, and when he tried to take my life. There are rusted bloodstains on his clothes, splattered across his shirt. His hands, his nails, are dried with red as well.

I try again—try to press into him—but the wall remains. This wall—it's almost something I can feel, an ache growing in my own mind whenever I attempt to force my way into his thoughts.

"What's your name?" I ask.

He blinks, but doesn't look away.

"Did the Ludjivik family send you? Was it one of the kongelig?" Any of the kongelig could've learned that Konge Valdemar sent me an invitation to join him on Hans Lollik Helle for the storm season and hoped to see me killed before I could arrive. This wouldn't surprise me. The kongelig are ruthless. Just as I plan to destroy them, they undoubtedly plan to destroy me.

The assassin speaks, his voice broken and hoarse. "If you're going to kill me, then please—kill me. But don't force me to listen to the same questions over and over again, spirits remain."

I can't help but smile. He has a bit of a bite. "You're bold, to praise the spirits in front of a kongelig."

He finally looks away, his face showing a twitch of annoyance—an annoyance I share, since I can't feel the emotion for myself.

"You killed my personal guard, you know," I tell him.

"Was he your favorite?"

"He was," I say with enough force that he looks at me again. "He was childish, but he was passionate about life. He didn't deserve to die, not by your hand."

He clenches his jaw. "Then have me executed as punishment."

"Why're you so eager to die? Were you sent to kill me, not expecting to survive yourself?" I gesture at the balcony, the curtains, the bedsheets. "You could've taken care of this yourself, if you were determined to. Maybe you're only asking for your execution because you know it's your duty to die, but you don't want to—not really. You want to live. Which makes me think that you were sent on a mission to kill me, not expecting to survive, by force. Forced to kill, forced to die—who would do such a thing to you? You couldn't have any real loyalty for such a person."

"Not any more loyalty than I have for someone who would lock me in a room and threaten to have me killed."

"I can see we're going nowhere."

There's a flicker of fear in his eyes at the suggestion that I'll follow through and have him executed for killing Friedrich and my other guardsmen. A part of me does want to see him swing for taking my Friedrich's life, for acting like Friedrich had meant nothing. But I know that I need this boy alive. I need answers from him still.

The journey to Hans Lollik Helle begins within hours. I leave last-minute preparations in the charge of Marieke and take my horse for a ride with Malthe, racing over the green fields of guinea grass, the hills that allow me to see Lund Helle for what could be my last time: its white-sand shore, the cloudless sky, the yellow sun reflecting on the ocean of clear water that turns turquoise, then blue, the nearby islands resting in the distance.

I ride my horse to the top of a hill, and directly across sits Rose Helle—and down in a valley, appearing as though it is nothing more than the scattered pieces of a broken toy, rests the ruins of the manor where I'd lived my first few years. Even from here, I can see the gardens—now overgrown, filled with weeds and wild flowers. The garden where my family was killed. The balcony where I stood, listening to their screams.

I tell Malthe that I'd like to visit the fallen manor, and he doesn't argue. We ride to the bay and take a small boat across the still sea. Malthe's hair is gray, but his height and strong muscles are intimidating, even to me. His skin is dark, face peppered with unshaved white hair. He has a quiet mind, which can be frustrating when I search for his thoughts. I wonder how he feels about me keeping Friedrich's murderer in my home rather than killing him and returning his body to the sea.

Malthe jumps from his seat to pull the boat onto the sandy shore of Rose Helle. I hold my sandals in my hand as I step into the water, dress ballooning around my legs, becoming sheer as

I wade, feet sinking into the wet sand. Water foams around my ankles as I stand before the ruins of my childhood home. My mother's house is the same as I last saw it. The entrance I have memories of, chasing after a laughing Ellinor as we returned from the groves or the shore. Windows are shattered and glass is scattered on the ground. The door splinters from its hinges. Black dirt covers the hallway floor, and porcelain bells are smashed across the marble. The only thing not touched is my mother's rug, glowing gold and hanging on the wall because my mother didn't want to get it dirty. She'd told me that the rug had been the only thing her own mother had kept as a slave. She took the rug from the slaves' quarters where her mother kept the rug on Lund Helle, before the woman caught the storm sickness and died, returned to the sea. I used to catch my mother touching the rug sometimes, tracing the edges of patterns as though she were touching her dead mother's hand.

I move through the sections of the house that still stand. The air feels sucked in, as if the walls were holding their breath. In the kitchen, red sunlight used to bounce off copper pots and pans. It was a room stuffed full of heat and grease from boiled banana and goat-meat stew, with big flies zooming around everyone's heads as Ellinor laughed too loud. Now it's full of blue shadow, with pots and pans covering the floor, and stains of red on the walls showing where the Jannik guards cut everyone down.

I step into what had once been the sitting room. Stone walls, blackened with ash, crumble into rocks. I walk into the sunlight. The garden sprouts flowers of red and pink and orange, and grass covers the ground where my family screamed for mercy. Jannik sent the guards, but each family was involved in the planning. Each family had a hand in their deaths. Now I'll have a hand in theirs. Once Konge Valdemar chooses my husband as the next regent, I'll cut his neck and take the throne for the Rose. The guards of Hans Lollik Helle will be at my disposal, and the Fjern of these islands under my rule. I'll be slow in my plans—enjoy pitting the kongelig against one another, tearing each family apart until none are left standing. I'll have the power to kill them all. It's what I promised my mother I would do when I returned to these islands. It's what I promise her now.

Malthe stands behind me in the water, hand still on the boat, and when I turn, I see his eyes fastened on mine. He thinks no thoughts, but I can feel the emotion vibrating through him. His suspicion. His distrust.

He says nothing. I walk back to the boat, and we continue on.

Malthe and I make the initial crossing to Hans Lollik Helle. Marieke and my prisoner will follow after with my belongings. Lund Helle will be without its Elskerinde for the storm season, a tradition of the kongelig that has been met with ire by the people of Hans Lollik for generations. We set sail from the bay of Lund Helle, through the churning waters of the sea, rougher as the winds grow stronger, past the dozens of islands the Fjern have claimed. We sail for a full two days, until finally the royal island is on the horizon, glimmering as though a jewel in the rising sun, sitting in the center of the islands under its rule.

Hans Lollik Helle is its own private island, guards lining the beaches as though it's a fortress that must keep the enemies of the poor and sick out, a place for the noble families to celebrate themselves while their own people starve and succumb to disease around them. I suppose I can't complain. I play the part of a kongelig well.

The ship anchors, and before long a boat paddles out to bring me ashore. The salty breeze cools my neck, my cheeks, in the early morning before the sun rises and all the island falls to its mercy. My guardsmen will stay on the ship and return to Lund Helle—bringing them onto the royal island would only be seen as an invasion, an insult—but Malthe will escort me as my personal guard until I'm able to appoint a new one and he can return to his usual duties. The heads of the guards of the kongelig make up the guardsmen of the island, keeping watch on the shores and relaying any information of threats to their masters. Malthe climbs down the rope ladder first and onto the awaiting boat and helps me down the last few steps.

An older slave, a man with a white beard and brown skin, begins to row. He knows better than to look at me or to speak as he paddles, the boat rising and falling with every wave. As the man rows, the water is clear enough for me to see the shine of the rising sun reflect against the white sand on the seafloor, the silver flashes of fish as they weave between the coral, green seaweed swaying back and forth with every wave. The island has jutting rocks and sheer cliffs, leafy groves beyond the shorelines, and a single, sloping hill. At the very top of the hill is Herregård Constantjin, shining white. This is the main house. Its smaller houses, the homes of the kongelig families for the storm season, are placed about the island. I can see one now, standing on the cliffs on the far side of the island; the others must be hidden among the trees, or perhaps on the opposite shores.

We come closer, and the mangrove trees with their spiraling roots weave through the water and line the east side of the island's shore, blocking view of the main manor. We enter the mangroves, water still and smooth, branches reaching out to snag my hair and the collar of my dress. I use my hand to block the salty leaves from brushing my face until we reach land.

I step out of the boat, my feet sinking into the warm, clear water, sand settling like dust beneath the waves. In the time it has taken to paddle across the sea, the sun has risen higher, bright light reflecting on the white of the sand and forcing me to raise a hand to shield my eyes. I slip off my sandals, clutching them to my side, toes sinking into the dry grains that are as soft as powder, still only warm so early in the morning, though I know they will be as hot as embers by the time afternoon comes. The breeze pushes against us as we walk, the front of my dress clinging to me while the back whips in the wind. We reach the grass and the entrance to the groves, tall coconut trees with their bladed leaves shimmering in the light. A slave, a woman with scars wrapped around her hands, greets us before leading the way down the dirt path, which becomes cooler, firmer, as it cuts through a shaded grove of coconut and palm trees, which then become neat rows of banana and guava and mango trees. It seems the worked groves wrap around the base of the hill that holds Herregård Constantjin on its pedestal. Men, their skin as brown as mine, are careful not to look at me as they collect green bananas. A Fjernman sits atop his horse as they work, whip firmly in his hand. His head turns to watch me pass. He'd heard that I, an islander, would be joining the kongelig for the storm season, but he had hoped it'd been the joke of his friends as they shared guavaberry rum. He wonders now what has become of these islands.

The islands of Hans Lollik had been the pinnacle of the territories of Koninkrijk in his youth—islands of unimaginable beauty and unending opportunity. Everyone in the streets of his small waterside town had been desperate to smuggle themselves onto a ship that was headed for the islands of Hans Lollik. And now? Most of the islands are in ruin, and even the islands of the kongelig families aren't what they once were. And here I am—an islander, who should be a slave, wearing a dress of white. These islands have fallen, he thinks. He grips his whip. I can feel how he wants to lash my back. Remind me that I was born of these islands, and that there isn't much that keeps me on the other side of the fields.

I've kept the slaves of my household, knowing that they'd been promised their freedom, but never have I forced my people to endure what so many others on these islands do. I see the horrors marked across the bodies of my people. Their limbs, missing. Eyes and noses and lips and tongues, gone. The scars write the past across their skin. It's a past that I've never experienced. The scars are what tie my people together—but since my skin is unmarked, perhaps this means they aren't my people after all. I would never whip a slave of my household, or punish them for attempting to escape, if any ever tried. I tell myself that in this, at least, I'm not like the Fjern, who take such pleasure in torturing the people of these islands. I try to ignore the fear that this is only a lie I tell myself so that I can fall asleep at night.

The path climbs toward the cliffs on the southern end of the island. The Jannik house awaits at the top of the path. The house isn't impressive. It's two stories and has a porch of white trim, with creaking wooden shingles and panels that threaten to blow from the foundation in the morning breeze. The slave bows and leaves us, and I look over what will be my home for the next coming weeks—possibly the last home I'll ever know.

Malthe forces open the front door and steps aside, allowing me to walk into the front hall. The windows have been closed for some time, judging by the heat that seems to emanate from the walls, the wooden floors. The stained and torn wallpaper is a pattern of birds that clashes with the seats of the small entryway greeting room. The floorboards are covered with dust, mud, blades of grass, piles of wood and stone, and burnt pots piled in a corner.

Malthe releases a heavy sigh. "Marieke will have her work cut out for her."

I ignore him and continue walking, floorboards threatening splinters with every step. I find a sitting room through glass doors, one of them cracked. A shadowed hall with candleholders buried in melted wax brings me to a dining room, overwrought chandelier hanging from the ceiling over a table covered in white cloth with no chairs. The adjoining door takes me to the kitchen. There's an iron stove, ceiling stained with soot, ashes smeared across the floor. A wooden door leads outside. I clutch my sandals as my feet crunch the brittle grass and rocks as I walk into a dead garden.

The garden behind the house ends with the edge of the cliffs of Hans Lollik Helle. The field of grass crumbles into stones that fall sharply to the sea. I walk toward the edge, water churning into the rocks below. For a moment, I think there's a woman standing on the rocks—yellow hair, pale skin, one of the many ghosts of Hans Lollik—but when I blink, she's disappeared.

A hand claps on my shoulder and I spin around, heart racing, but it's only Malthe.

"You don't want to get too close," he says, but for a flash I feel how easy it would be for him to push me over the edge. The thought ends, and I can't be sure if it was me or him who'd imagined it.

"At least we'll only need to worry about assassins making their way in through the front door," I say, glancing back down at the rocks again.

Inside of the Jannik house, I walk up the creaking wooden stairs. There're two bedrooms. Malthe will stay in a separate house of barracks with the guards, and Marieke will stay in the island's slaves' quarters, so thankfully I won't have to share my bed with Aksel more than necessary. I don't know where Aksel is, or if he plans to come to the manor before our wedding.

I sit on the bed, as hard as the ground itself, and take in a deep, shuddering breath. A whisper within suggests it isn't too late. I can still leave—can still escape these islands; can live, as my mother had wanted for me.

But I know those were only the fantasies born of weakness—of fear. Hans Lollik Helle is the only place I can be now.

CHAPTER SIX

I tell Malthe I'd like to explore the island, to prove to anyone who might be watching that I'm not afraid, but I don't argue when he insists he stay by my side. The truth is that fear builds inside of me with every breath. Hans Lollik Helle has long since been known for the murders that mar each storm season, and one of the kongelig has already tried to take my life. I have no way of knowing how long I'll have until another tries again. I might be killed before I'm even able to meet Konge Valdemar, let alone convince him that I should inherit the title of regent.

The royal island is small in comparison to the others under Hans Lollik rule, but still large enough that it can accommodate the dozens of houses of the Herregård Constantjin estate and their gardens, along with the groves that seem to feed the island's guests. Malthe and I walk down sloping hills and through the groves and over rocky dirt. Above us stands the main house of Herregård Constantjin. It rests on the highest point of the island, a house of white stone that seems almost to be a part of the island itself as it dips and curves with the rock at its base, green vines and moss crawling up the walls. This is where the regent himself lives. Konge Valdemar has been king for nearly fifty years now—one of the longest reigns of any regent of Hans Lollik

Helle. But the era is coming to an end now: a chance for any of the kongelig to rule over these islands.

I stop in a grove empty of slaves and pick three golden mangoes. I carry the fruit in the skirts of my dress, yellow juices and sticky sap leaking onto the white fabric—Marieke will be incensed, I can already feel it—and we take a path cutting through the rows of guava trees, deeper into the groves, until the coconut trees end and the groves come to a clearing. There I see a house belonging to another of the kongelig. It's large—certainly larger than the Jannik house—and is made of stone, painted a faint white. We linger for a moment, mosquitoes biting my legs.

"Shall we call on the master?" Malthe questions.

I hesitate. I'm curious to see another of the kongelig—to see the men and women whom I have for so long only known through the thoughts and memories of Elskerinde Jannik, her son, and my cousin Bernhand Lund. I never met any of the kongelig when I was a child growing up on Rose Helle. My mother would take me and my sisters and brother to the other islands at times, though she could have easily left us in the comfort of our home. I believe she wanted us to learn a specific lesson that couldn't be taught in our manor's library poring over books. I suspect she wanted us to witness for ourselves the hatred in the eyes of the Fjern, their cold dismissal whenever we crossed their paths. We did learn the hatred of the Fjern, but still, the six other kongelig families were never included in these lessons. I'm sure my mother would've wanted us to meet the kongelig, but I never saw them on our travels. We weren't worthy to be invited to their garden parties, and they never visited my mother or attended the balls she invited them to in turn. Before I met Elskerinde Jannik, the members of the kongelig families had always been an amorphous shadow in my imagination. I know each of their names, the kraft that runs in their

veins, the strengths and weaknesses of each family—have studied them relentlessly since the moment I decided to return to
these islands as a child. It's almost like reading about characters
in books for years, and knowing that any moment now, those
characters will walk from the page.

I hesitate in front of the house of the kongelig. I want to meet,
in person, those responsible for the murder of my family. And
the perverse curiosity I have—I can't ignore that, either, this
desire to look upon a member of the families that have been so
upheld in these islands for generations, the people I have studied
religiously as the Fjern study their own gods, even as I can feel
fear and hatred pulsing in my veins.

"No need," I tell Malthe—but curiosity gets the better of
me as I begin to slip closer to the house, mangoes still bundled
together in my skirts.

I walk into the gardens with the flourishing rose mallow surrounding me, breath unsteady. I don't see any slaves walking the
path. The manor's windows are black. The house might as well be
abandoned. It might be, in fact. Not all of the houses on the royal
island are occupied, though the houses that are have been passed
down from one generation to the next in each kongelig family. My
mother never made it onto Hans Lollik Helle. If she had, the regent
would've offered her one of the houses that now remain empty.

Just as I've decided to return to Malthe, I feel someone's gaze.
I spin around to see a Fjern woman. She's young, as young as
me, with unblemished skin, pale under the sunlight, and yellow
hair tied tightly in a bun. She's what the Fjern would consider a
princess: what they declare is beautiful, intelligent, what a person should look like in order to rule the islands of Hans Lollik. She'll have an easier time convincing Konge Valdemar of
her worth in inheriting the title of regent of these islands, while
I will not. She doesn't even want the regency. I can see this,
too—see how unambitious she is, especially in the face of the

kongelig that surround her. She's the head of the Larsen family, only because it's her duty; she comes here to Hans Lollik Helle every storm season, only because it's her responsibility. I've had to work for my position, while she does nothing, wants none of this, and still she's respected more than me. I hate her for it, but I have my other reasons for hating her, too: I've seen her before, in Aksel's thoughts and daydreams.

"I'm sorry," she says, her voice a wisp that immediately makes me want to strangle her. Her eyes widen in fear. "I didn't mean to startle you."

She knows who I am, knows of my kraft. She looks to the ground, breathing too quickly. She tries to hide her thoughts, but it's easy to sink into her mind—she's too open, too vulnerable. I can feel fear, and unmistakable sadness. She's afraid that I'll know the truth of her relationship with my betrothed. Not only might I learn her thoughts but I might decide to have my vengeance on her as well: take control of her body, force her to walk into the sea until saltwater fills her lungs.

"You're Beata Larsen," I say, "isn't that right?"

She seems surprised that I've spoken to her. "Yes, I am. And you're Elskerinde Lund. No, sorry—Elskerinde Jannik."

"I'm not married to the Jannik name yet." I eye her—the pretty white dress of the kongelig, her trembling fingers. "You shouldn't apologize to me," I say. "I'm the one wandering your gardens without permission."

"These aren't really my gardens," she tells me. "They belonged to my parents."

Now dead, I know, killed by bandits in their own home many years before, when Beata was just a child. In the sitting room of the Jannik manor, the Herre and Elskerinde Larsen hadn't been vocal in their agreement to kill my family, but they weren't vocal in their disagreement, either, so I celebrate their deaths as much as I do the deaths of any of the kongelig.

The Larsen family had been one of the most beloved of the kongelig. The islands across Hans Lollik suffered a drought, and the plantations began to fail; the people—islanders and Fjern alike—began to starve. Besides the Jannik name, the Larsen family had always been the poorest of the kongelig. Even so, they did what they could for their people: They collected coin, fruit, and bread, and handed out what they could to the starving villagers. This hadn't been enough to save the island. The few plantations that belonged to other Fjern families failed as well, and the island was abandoned, save for the small villages that remained. It was from one of these villages that a mob sought to punish their island's rulers. The gifts and the Elskerinde's kind smiles were forgotten. Bandits arrived at the manor one night and slaughtered everyone inside, slaves included—everyone, except for little Beata Larsen. She'd been smart enough to hide and to not make a sound, even when she'd wanted to cry. The bandits had searched for her until the sun began to rise, but the smoke from the fires set to the Larsen plantation had alerted other islands, and the kongelig sent their guards. The bandits had to escape or risk the gallows. Beata was found by her rescuers, still too afraid to make a sound. She didn't speak for the next two years.

Beata lived under the patronage of the Solberg family, who took her in—perhaps not out of kindness but in an effort to minimize her as a future threat; to convince her, from a young age, that becoming regent of these islands wasn't something that she could handle, or that she would want. Beata is still hesitant to speak, to make herself heard, her voice never louder than a whisper. We have similar histories, Beata Larsen and I, but our lives still managed to be so different.

"You've inherited the Larsen title and property," I tell her. "The gardens are yours."

She's embarrassed now, I can feel, because she knows she lacks the confidence a woman of her age and standing should have, regardless of the tragedies she's endured. Everyone has endured a tragedy. She isn't special in this. She can't meet my eye, red coloring her cheeks. But there's another reason she doesn't look at me. She's so terrified that I'll be able to sense the love she has for my betrothed. She shakes at just the thought that I might see a memory of hers, of Aksel taking her into his arms and whispering into her ear that she belongs to him and he to her. If only he had his freedom from me, he'd murmured, he would marry her and together the two of them would leave the islands of Hans Lollik—

"You're too soft," I say.

Her gaze snaps to my own, breath catching in her throat. By the gods, she's so frightened of me. Maybe she should be.

"Let me give you some advice, Elskerinde Larsen," I tell her. "Aksel doesn't deserve you."

She's surprised. Not that I've sensed her feelings as she feared I would but that I would say such a thing. *You're wrong. I'm the one who doesn't deserve him.*

No anger. No judgment in Beata Larsen. Her innocence enrages me.

"I can see what you feel for him—can tell that your heart is genuine—but I need you to stay away from Aksel, because while I could care less about who he brings into his bed, I won't allow him to risk the Jannik name."

I don't bother waiting for a reply. I leave the gardens, her shock and her fear following me. I'm ashamed to revel in the power I feel after frightening Beata Larsen, this woman the Fjern consider worthier than me. The Fjern are cruel. Perhaps that's proof enough that their blood runs through my veins.

As Malthe and I return to the Jannik house, walking up the sloping dirt path, one of the island's guards approaches from the groves, waving us down. The man sweats in the island's heat, and he's breathless.

"There's news," he tells Malthe—he won't speak to me directly. Malthe is impatient, perhaps just as tired as I am. "What is it?" The guard hesitates. "I'm not sure this ought to be heard by a lady's ears."

Malthe's impatience becomes my own. I almost sink into the stranger's mind, just to hear the truth for myself, but it's only as I stagger on my feet, so close to my new bed in the Jannik house, that I realize how exhausted I am. Days of travel and confronting the Larsen heir has tired my mind, and I don't want to spend the energy knowing this man's thoughts, not when I know I'll only be met with the hatred I always find in my people. The Fjerns' hatred, I know and expect; my own people's hatred is the one that strips me open and tells me that I'm undeserving of the life I live, unworthy of love and acceptance. I don't bother to read the minds of the slaves around me.

Malthe's tone is curt. "Elskerinde Lund isn't delicate. You can tell us what you came to say."

The man hesitates, even with the express permission given, but finally he speaks, voice low. "There's been a death on the island. Dame Ane Solberg, cousin of Jytte Solberg, was found dead just an hour ago."

"Dead?" Malthe repeats, surprised, though I don't know why he would be; this is Hans Lollik Helle, after all.

"She was found in her bed. It seems she'd passed in her sleep."

"The woman was old, ailing," Malthe tells us like he's arguing a point, perhaps making the suggestion that her death isn't suspicious. The guard nods, as though he agrees with this, but he won't meet Malthe's eye. There are any number of poisons to ensure that when a person falls asleep, they won't wake again. It's never just a coincidence when someone dies on Hans Lollik Helle.

Malthe offers to stay with me until Marieke arrives. I can't pretend that I don't feel unnerved by the news of a death so soon in the storm season. I know what I've risked agreeing to come here; with so many enemies together in one space, murder is inevitable. It's become a tradition, here on Hans Lollik Helle; a game of sorts, to kill without being caught, and to survive the storm season yourself. It's a game where I know I'll become a target. The kongelig hate me for being an islander where they feel I don't belong, just as they hated my mother. They killed my mother for daring to go beyond what they considered her station, and for daring to earn the respect of the regent.

I'm afraid on this island. I would be a fool not to be afraid for my life. Still, I'm also exhausted, and eager to be alone, and so Malthe leaves for the island's barracks. After I rest in my bed for a few hours, I wander the Jannik house's garden of brush and weeds, bending over to snag thorny leaves and pull them from the dirt, back and shoulders aching in the heat. The afternoon passes as I explore the house itself—discover a hidden library with dust-covered volumes, and a particularly nasty surprise as a fruit bat screeches and flaps around the room desperately, until I'm able to unstick the window and it escapes into the sunlight.

Evening comes, and Marieke still hasn't arrived. There isn't any food besides the mangoes I'd earlier picked, but I've gone days without eating before, on our journeys across northern empires. The empire of Rescela, along the coast; the Aldies, fields that grow into mountains that seem to be pillars of the sky itself. The towns of the islands of Hans Lollik were so much smaller than the cities of the northern empires. The cities had piss-covered streets of stone, mazes of crumbling houses, and people everywhere I turned, people packing the roads and the windows of uneven houses and doors. The people were my favorite part about the north. There were so many different sorts, from all around the world, even the western empires, that I'd never witnessed before with my own eyes; people who wore wooden beads and scarves around their hair, people with markings drawn across their skin, people who had their eyelids and lips sewn shut. The languages, the scent of the different foods and their spices, the music and beat of drums that would follow my ears—and the colors of skin, from the pales of white moonlight to the darkest of black night. Hans Lollik isn't the only land that holds slaves. There are empires to the west, and some of the empires in the north as well, who sell humans as one might sell cattle. But the empires I journeyed through with Marieke, using my cousin Bernhand Lund's coin, were nations where each and every single person was free.

It was the first time I saw people who looked like me and who also had their freedom. They walked with their heads in the air, their gazes not stuck to the ground; their skin was smooth, untarnished by a whip's scars. They smiled and laughed with ease. There were even a few I saw who I could sense had come from Hans Lollik, slaves who had managed to escape, stowed away on ships. I shared in their awe at these people who looked so much like us and yet were so different—and only because they'd had the luck to be born somewhere other than our islands. I'd escaped Hans Lollik as well, I realized—escaped the Fjern who would have me killed. It wasn't an easy decision returning to the islands, knowing that anyone who looked my way would only ever see a slave.

I had always been so enamored with the north and its people, but the north didn't always return this love. Marieke and I had just returned from one of the short visits to Lund Helle. Bernhand hadn't been a particularly gracious host when we came to visit. He rarely joined me for dinner, and when he did welcome me into his sitting room for tea one afternoon, he commented on the color of my skin and how it seemed to be getting darker. "Perhaps not as much sun," he'd suggested.

I was thirteen, and I'd had my kraft for a full three years already, but I hadn't yet mastered the power. If I tried to read another person's thoughts, I would become lost in their mind and emotions, unable to distinguish them from my own. We sat for tea, and I decided to try to read my cousin's thoughts so that I could know what I should say to please him. I could feel his disgust. He wanted to pretend he was benevolent, that he loved his family, but he was embarrassed to call me his cousin. Bernhand Lund had always held a smile for me, but now that I had my kraft, for the first time I could see his hatred. I was curious. Curious to know of other hidden thoughts. I became lost in his mind, so lost that for the barest of moments I looked out from his eyes and saw myself sitting opposite him, this child who should never have survived the massacre that took her family's lives.

It was the first time I realized the extent of my kraft. Marieke knew of my power to feel the emotions and thoughts of others around me, but not to the point that I could nearly become another person. I could already feel how much she hated my kraft, and I knew I couldn't go to her for guidance on this. We left Lund Helle on a ship that returned us to a northern coastal city. Normally Marieke and I would travel various cities and towns and stay at the local inns as I explored and learned of other cultures, continuing my studies in any library we found, but this time Bernhand decided he would finance my education with a tutor, and pay an acquaintance to allow me to stay in their townhouse as a guest. To keep me out of the sun as much as possible, I suppose.

It was a townhouse in a row of others in the center of the wealthier section of the city, with brick walls and vines that wrapped around the windows. Upon arriving, I learned that my cousin's acquaintance didn't live in this house, but rather that the house was filled with his guests: other girls from across the empires, either the bastards of the wealthy who wanted their daughters hidden away from polite society or the exiled who had nowhere else to go. There were even a few who'd been taken from the streets in mercy. In all, there were ten of us. Marieke took residence with the other servants of the household, and for a time, I had what I considered a home that wasn't Hans Lollik.

Marieke made it clear to me that my kraft was to remain hidden. No one could know of it. In this city we'd traveled to, anyone with kraft was hunted, as my people often were in Hans Lollik; but instead of being killed, they were made to devote their lives to the divine gods of the north. They were placed in churches and temples and forced to take oaths that they wouldn't marry or have children and would devote their lives to the divinity in gratitude for the gifts that had been bestowed upon them. It was a different sort of slavery, and the fact that I wasn't from this city wouldn't save me.

I don't have particularly fond memories of this time. I was used to my independence: traveling with Marieke at my side, deciding what I would learn and study each day, eating and drinking whatever I craved. Now I was at the mercy of a nurse who was stricter than Marieke. She had her ideas of what it meant to be a proper lady of the north, and though she was used to seeing people with brown skin like my own, she had her own ideas of what it meant for me to come from the southern islands. She didn't like the way I pronounced my words. If I said anything that had the lilting tone of the way my mother had spoken to me, the nurse would hit my knuckles with a stick. If she ever caught me sipping the lemongrass tea I would often buy from the markets, rather than the proper mint that was more common in the north, she would spill the scalding tea on my hands. If I ever talked back, or gave a look that let her know exactly what I thought of her, she would have me raise my skirts before the entire class and beat the backs of my legs.

She wasn't the only person who didn't treat me well in that year. Though I was the only girl from Hans Lollik, I wasn't the only girl with dark skin. There was another, named Andela, who had skin as dark as mine and had a following of girls whose skin was all colors, some pale and some brown, all from different empires in the north. I looked to her, and I saw the commonality between us: To me, her dark skin meant that she understood the world and its hatred of people who look as we do.

Her people hadn't been enslaved in Hans Lollik, but she had to have understood the pain of others looking down on her, the isolation of feeling that hatred surround her. She would be my friend, I'd decided. I'd never had any friends; besides my sisters and brother, I hadn't even known anyone my own age before, as Marieke and I had been solitary in our travels.

Andela was beautiful, with a loud voice that seemed to command the attention of everyone in a room. She demanded respect with the raise of her chin. I was enamored. The first few days following my arrival, I only watched from afar—watched the way the other girls flocked to her. Watched the way she could have any of them do her bidding—bring her gifts, cups of tea, her favorite books—with the smallest of smiles. We would do our quiet, ladylike activities in the sitting room each day at noon for an hour. I would glance from the pages of the book I read to see Andela whispering to her friends with that same smile.

My kraft had developed enough for me to know her thoughts and her memories at my will. Her past hadn't been easy: She'd been born with her freedom in another nation to a wealthy merchant family, but her family's wealth quickly crumbled under new taxation laws that secured the coin of particular families in power. Andela's mother had died in childbirth, and her father became sick; unable to afford medication, the man had little choice but to sell their home and their belongings, until finally they ended in the slums of the city. Our benefactor, whoever he was, had taken mercy on Andela, and she was brought to this house three years before. Her father had since passed away, what little left he owned sent to the benefactor to help pay for Andela's schooling, food, and clothes. Andela didn't speak of her worries to her friends; she didn't say how she was unsure what was to become of her after her education at this home was complete. She would have no money, no prospects, nowhere to go. She hoped the benefactor would allow her to stay as the new nurse, but she wouldn't admit to this aloud; there was nothing beautiful or glamorous in this.

I worked up the courage to greet her one night as we took our supper at the table. I sat across from her and said good evening. This grabbed the attention of the other girls. So far, I'd been quiet—to them, I could feel, I was mysterious and strange. I never spoke, only watched the others and always had a blank expression upon my face, as though I could already tell what they each thought and felt. I was intriguing to a few, but to Andela and her friends, I was mostly boring.

Andela looked at me with a quirk of her eyebrow. "Good evening," she said in return.

I can't remember what we chatted about—books, perhaps. I'd taken Claus's love of books when I was young, sinking into worlds and persons who were not my own. Andela, I could tell, was still bored by me and my presence. She wished I hadn't spoken to her. She didn't consider me important enough in the ranking of the girls of this school. I was determined to change her mind.

The following day we were taken from the house for our morning stroll. We would line up as pairs and walk the cobblestoned streets as fog hung heavy in the air. I'd been traveling the north for some time already, but I had not and could never become used to the constant chill, or to the white steam of breath that left my lips. I shivered as I walked beside another girl whose name I couldn't remember, directly behind Andela.

She spoke of rose mallow. I inserted myself into her conversation, letting Andela know that this is the flower that had inspired my last name.

"Really?" she asked with a touch of curiosity. "I've never seen a rose-mallow flower before."

"When we return, I can paint one for you."

She was grateful, and when I fulfilled this promise, she gave me a smile. I was then allowed to sit with her friends at the din-

her table, and allowed to continue to walk behind her as we took our daily strolls. The other girls—four of her friends, now five with me—seemed interested in the fact that I was from Hans Lollik. They asked why I wasn't a slave in these islands.

I didn't notice it at first, the favors Andela requested of me: to bring her a glass of water or mint tea, to hold an umbrella over her as icy rain began to fall on our morning walk. I did, however, begin to notice the way she delighted in humiliating me. I sat with her and the others in the gardens as the sun was setting.

"You're beautiful in this light," I told her, meaning for it to be a compliment.

She scoffed. "Do you suggest I'm not beautiful in other lights?"

"Of course not," I said. The others laughed, and it was a silly thing, but I was filled with hot shame. The following day, I accidentally brushed against Andela, and she spun to me and yelled to never touch her again. I could feel the disgust building in her. I could feel her thoughts plainly: She thought me beneath her, for having come from these islands. She thought me a savage. Beneath those thoughts, there was a vibration of jealousy—jealousy because Andela feared that I was more beautiful than she. She was used to being the only one in this house with her dark skin and her convincing smile.

What angers me about those days wasn't Andela's hatred for me, the betrayal I felt simmering beneath my skin; what angers me most is that I continued to sit at her feet, that I attempted to convince her that I was worthy of her respect and love. Months went on like this, me fetching her things and doing her errands and taking her harsh comments, the laughter of the girls around me, the shame boiling inside me.

Finally, one morning, we all walked the cobblestoned streets. The seasons had changed and it was a hot day, sun bright, the market filled with clattering stalls and horse-pulled carriages making their deliveries. There were slaves, marked by the chains around their hands and legs. This particular nation held no slaves, but they allowed merchants to pass through with their property, as long as the slaves weren't sold on these docks. The slaves also had dark skin, like mine, and like Andela's—and yet, she laughed.

"Sigourney," she said to me, "is this not your people? Isn't that where you belong—in your chains?"

The other girls laughed with her, and the flare of anger in me was unexpected. It was the building of rage and humiliation, yes, and also of Andela's dismissal of my people and their pain; but also there was her dismissal of me. Her suggestion that I was only worthy of such a life because of the color of my skin and the islands I'd once called home. I did it without thinking: I sank into her, as I might to feel her emotions, but sank so deeply that I could feel myself within her body, another soul possessing her skin, and I could see through her eyes—could feel, for a moment, the pain as I forced her to step in front of an oncoming horse pulling a carriage to make its deliveries.

Andela lived, though she had multiple broken bones. She was unconscious, taken away from the house where we lived. When I admitted to Marieke what had happened, she told me that we had to leave at once. We couldn't allow anyone to know what I'd done; we couldn't allow ourselves to wait for Andela to wake up and declare that I had used my kraft to attempt to kill her. But it was the first time I truly understood the extent of my power.

The trade winds make the islands cooler at night, and they become much stronger at the start of the storm season, whistling through the wooden cracks in the house. Even with the windows closed, the curtains shift as if on a breeze. I shiver, placing cut wood and branches in the fireplace and sparking a flint until the fire comes to life, filling the room with light and warmth. I take the white sheet covering the dining room table, wrapping myself in a seat before the fireplace, biting into the mango's skin so that its juice leaks down my arm.

I think on my mother. How she must've felt when she was first invited to the royal island. My mother must've been afraid. She must've been scared every day of her life, with her four children and dead husband, knowing that the kongelig hated her, suspecting that they might attempt to kill her. She never showed her fear to me or to my sisters or brother. She would have a smile as she tickled me and Ellinor and read us our fairy tales, plaited Inga's hair while they sang their songs together in the sitting room by the unused fireplace, while she fed Claus chicken broth and lemongrass tea, smoothing down his hair and whispering her encouragements whenever my brother fell ill, as he often did. She had loved us so much.

So why, then, did my mother accept Konge Valdemar's invitation? There's a bitterness in me, an anger at my mother. She must've known what the kongelig would do if she did accept. She knew she was entering into a dangerous game, and that she would be risking all of our lives. Instead of accepting Konge Valdemar's invitation, my mother could've moved us all to the north; she could've done this the day my father died, in fact, taking all the coin of the sugarcane business and starting over in a place where we wouldn't be hated for the color of our skin—in a place where our freedom wouldn't be questioned.

But I knew, too, that my mother would never have made such a choice. My mother would've wanted to do everything she could to inherit the title of regent from Konge Valdemar. She hadn't been born with her freedom. She knew what it was to live in these islands she called home, these islands she loved, these islands of our ancestors, and have her happiness taken by the Fjern. She was the true heroine: sacrificing her life, and even the lives of her children, for the chance to free her people.

The wind becomes stronger, the fire flickering. Rain begins to lash against the windows, and I can hear water dripping. I stand, sheets wrapped tightly around me, and see water pooling at the entrance, leaking in through the door. I open the door and step into the night, chilled rain stinging my eyes and cheeks, wind pressing against my ears, my thin dress and sheets sticking to my skin. I can see now that there's a hole in the wooden paneling above the door—nothing can be done about that now, I'll have to wait for the help of Marieke and for the other slaves to arrive.

Something moves in the corner of my eye. I spin to look, my heart quickening. I expect to see someone come at me with a knife. Even in the night with nothing but the moon, the lashing wind and rain, I recognize her—this woman who had earlier stood on the rocks. Her yellow hair glints in the moonlight.

A roll of thunder, and the woman is gone—disappeared, like she'd never stood before me, like she'd only been a part of the rain, sent away on the wind.

I return inside, closing the door behind me, and stand there for some time, staring at the torn wallpaper, willing my heart to slow, for the fear to stop pumping through my chest. I pour a pail of water into the steaming fireplace and, in the dark, make my way to my room, where I lie on the hard bed, listening to the lashing storm. I've heard stories of the ghosts of Hans Lollik. Marieke would speak of them as warnings, and Ellinor would whisper about them under our bedsheets with her wide eyes—but I'd never witnessed one myself. I'm surprised. I expected that when I saw a spirit of these islands, it would be one with skin as black as night, coming to me with vengeance in its eyes.

CHAPTER SEVEN

Marieke arrives at the front doors in a flurry before the next morning's end. A comforting warmth spreads through me as I watch her arrival from my porch. I haven't seen Marieke in days now, and I'm used to her steady thoughts, her fierce reminders of why I need to continue to pursue my goals. And though I won't readily admit it, I've been afraid to stay in this house alone.

The house comes to life. It's almost easy to forget about the woman who appeared in my gardens, like forgetting the details of a nightmare after waking—though I do have a harder time forgetting Dame Ane Solberg. It's possible, yes, that she really is only an older woman who passed in her sleep, but it isn't likely. The Solberg family has enemies among the Fjern; families like the Årud hold a jealousy for Jytte Solberg's success, and it's possible that one of these families hoped to strike at a weaker member of the Solberg family, perhaps force Jytte into a state of grief, or intimidate Elskerinde Solberg into leaving the island. Ane Solberg's death only serves as a reminder that the kongelig are ruthless. If they're willing to kill one of their own so early in the storm season, how long until another attempts to kill me again?

I can hear Marieke shouting orders, smell the spices from the kitchens, hear the chatter of the slaves who followed from

Lund Helle. It's a chatter that silences itself the moment I come within hearing; the slaves' eyes downcast, they murmur proper greetings and fill the air with songs so that I won't know their thoughts if I attempt to see their minds, though I never do. I'm used to the silence and to these songs. It's as much my shadow as is the hatred that follows me.

When Marieke has a moment, she comes to my room with steaming lemongrass tea. It's always too hot to drink tea on these islands, but the scent is still calming. We sit together, speaking of her journey. She allows me to distract myself. To give myself a reprieve in thinking about the fact that after so many years of planning, I'm finally here, on Hans Lollik Helle—and that the storm will soon begin. We share stories. She tells me of a memory that I was too young to hold myself: Before my mother gave Marieke the order to leave our manor, she'd worked alongside Tante, nurse to me and my sisters and brother. Inga, Marieke tells me, had been made of light. Inga would wake in the mornings and pray on her gratitude to the gods. She didn't mind that the gods belonged to the Fjern and that our people had been forced to forget the spirits of our ancestors. These were the gods she had been taught, so she prayed to them with her thanks every morning and every night. She would take baskets of bread and fruit, along with bowls of water, to the slaves who worked the groves and the fields, just as our mother had done; and though the Fjern held no love of her, Inga would bring her basket of bread and fruit into the poor villages of Lund Helle as well.

Ellinor had been made of light as well, but she was more mischievous. Ellinor hadn't been born with kraft, Marieke tells me, but with a trickster spirit; she says this with a laugh, but even still I can feel the exhaustion in her from the memories alone. It seems that girl never learned to walk; she simply stood one day and ran, and she never stopped running. She'd run from her baths, suds and water splashing all over the marble floors; she'd run from her dress fittings and out into the mud, so that she would become as dirty as the goats; she'd run right into the sea like she was a wild thing, an untamed spirit brought back from the land of the dead. The girl didn't like to listen, Marieke tells me, but she still had a light inside her, so that while chasing her, even Marieke couldn't help but smile.

I was born after Ellinor. I'd been born screaming, so angry to be pushed from my mother and into this world. The rage never left me, Marieke tells me. I liked to listen to Inga's songs as she braided my hair, and loved to laugh with Ellinor as we ran from our nurses, but I had an anger in me that neither of my sisters held.

"I suppose I got that anger from my father," I say, relying on the memories I have of my mother, always gentle, always smiling.

"No," Marieke tells me, voice hard. "Your father was a fool. He was afraid of the world, afraid of upsetting the Fjern, always so eager to please them however he could so that he wouldn't lose the power he'd managed to scrape together. No," she says again, "you got your anger from your mother." She sees my surprise. "She hid her fury well. She knew it was dangerous to not be seen smiling, dangerous if the kongelig were to see her unhappiness. But your mother had a horrible anger, as though a vengeful spirit entered her body and never left. Sometimes I wonder if, when she was killed, that spirit left her body and entered you."

Shouts interrupt us. The yelling gets louder, and slaves who'd been bustling about hurry beneath my balcony, across the lawn of weeds.

I jump to my feet, peering over the edge of my balcony's railing. My gaze follows the slaves into the searing light. I squint my eyes to see Malthe below, and the man who is my prisoner.

The two face each other. Somehow, the assassin has slipped free from his bindings. He holds a knife, pointed straight at Malthe, who holds his own blade steady.

"Spirits, boy, don't be foolish," Marieke murmurs beside me.

Attempting to kill Malthe will only mean the end of his own life, the man has to know; I realize, with a flinch, that this could very well be what he wants. They circle each other for only a moment before the man lashes forward, aiming for Malthe's chest—the guard dodges, kneeing him in the gut. The prisoner falls to his knees but swipes out a foot; Malthe falls back, and the assassin has an opening, but he hesitates. Malthe kicks, and the prisoner is on the ground as well, Malthe holding the blade against the man's neck.

Malthe looks up, right at me, as though he knew I was watching from the balcony all along. The assassin struggles, until finally Malthe yanks his arms behind his back and holds him to the ground.

Marieke stands beside me, hand to her mouth. "Are you sure it was wise to bring him onto this island?" She asks this automatically, mechanically—she's too used to nagging me.

The man is dragged to his feet. Malthe stands, chest heaving, sweat shining across his skin. He addresses me now. "Elskerinde Lund," he shouts, calling to me; heads turn, and the assassin's gaze flicks to meet my own. "This man is too dangerous to keep."

I know what Malthe implies. If I were a true kongelig, I'd have Malthe execute him now, just to show what happens to anyone who attacks my guardsmen. The man is silent. A clearing in the center of a tangled wood. The still waters of a mangrove surrounded by a churning tide. Blood trickles from his nose, his mouth. He should be executed, beheaded, whipped to within an inch of his life, at the very least, for attacking the head of my guard—for killing Friedrich, and attempting to kill me.

My voice carries on the breeze. "Bring him inside for questioning."

I turn my back, walking into my chamber and its heat. Marieke is beside me.

"Why do you keep him here?" she asks, voice low. "He's too dangerous. He could break free again, kill everyone in the house—kill you, as he'd initially intended to do."

"I don't need to explain myself to you, Marieke."

She's offended by this. Marieke raised me for more than half my life, and now here I am, thinking I'm beyond heeding her advice. She's the one who held me on the nights I woke screaming, memories of my family's deaths overtaking me; she's the one who wiped my cheeks when I cried, telling her that the voices of others were driving me to madness. I shouldn't dismiss her, not so easily. I apologize, and Marieke presses her lips together, looking away in annoyance, but my apology is accepted. I can feel her regret as she leaves my room.

I close my eyes. I need to know who the boy is, and which of the kongelig used him to have me killed—but this power he holds over me, his ability to block my kraft. The curiosity for him fills me.

Malthe tells me that he has brought the prisoner to the library. There wasn't anywhere else to hold him. The walls are lined with shelves, the smell of mold and dust hanging in the air. The spines bloat in the heat. The books remind me of hiding away in the libraries of my mother's manor with Ellinor, begging Inga to read us fairy tales, picking up the books ourselves and attempting to sound out the words, filling in the sentences we couldn't decipher with our own imaginations.

A shadow moves, and I see the prisoner standing beside a far shelf, book in his hand. Islanders aren't allowed to read.

Punishment has often meant the loss of an eye. I wonder again about his lineage: His skin is a light brown that reminds me of Claus, but if he is an islander, he shouldn't be able to read. The bruise on his cheek is yellow, and the cut on his lip is scabbed. His nose swells, blood dried on his skin. He's washed since he attempted to kill me in the groves, by the looks of his hands. The silence that surrounds him remains. He looks up at me from the pages of the book, his dark eyes hardened. I can only assume that the hardened emotion in him is rage. Hatred. Disgust. His lips twitch into a smile, even with such an angry gaze. A challenge, perhaps? Yes, I think so—he means to let me know that he's fully aware of what my kraft is, and that he's the only person who can resist it.

"I didn't take you for a poet," I tell him, seeing the cover of the book he holds.

He shuts the book and returns it to its shelf. "I'm not."

"Has Malthe been treating you well?" I ask.

"He threatens immense pain and death," he says.

He's laughing at me. That, he allows me to sense.

It's infuriating, not knowing what the man feels and thinks. Infuriating knowing that I can't take control of his body. I should be afraid of him. I should be terrified that he could try to kill me again, and I wouldn't be able stop him; and I am, but I also feel curiosity. I have questions for him, yes, many questions about which of the kongelig sent him to kill me—but more than anything else, I want to know why my kraft stops with him.

"Do you hate me for bringing you to Hans Lollik Helle and keeping you against your will?" I ask.

"I'm grateful," he says, leaning against a table, arms crossed, blinking as curls fall into his eyes. "I'd probably be dead if you hadn't taken me prisoner."

I can't tell if he's being genuine.

"Though you could still have me killed whenever you wish."
He watches me carefully, trying to see the answer on my face,
but I'm expressionless.

"I don't hate you," he goes on. "I feel sorry for you."

I know that he's baiting me. I take the bait anyway. "Why do
you feel sorry for me?"

"Your own people hate you. You've betrayed them. Abandoned them, for coin and comfort, while they're enslaved and
raped and tortured and murdered around you. No one has any
love for you, even if you pretend they do. Even if you force them
to. You have no true allies or friends. Those closest to you want
you dead."

"Are you trying to anger me so that I'll have you killed?"

"You're an island woman who fancies herself a royal. The
kongelig laugh at you. They see you as a goat in a dress. Amusing,
kept alive for entertainment, until you become too inconvenient."

"I won't have you executed, if that's what you want."

"You asked me a question, and I feel compelled to answer it
as honestly as I can." He smiles, a sliver of white flashing in the
dim light. Laughing at me again, always laughing at me.

"Who ordered you to kill me?"

He doesn't respond.

"You can't have any true loyalty to them," I say. "You
would've tried to kill me again by now if you did."

"I still might," he says, smile beginning to fade.

"I think you have no loyalty to whoever sent you to kill me. I
also think you've given a false impression of your identity."

He raises a brow at this.

"You have the blood of an islander," I tell him, "but you also
have the blood of the Fjern. I can see it in the color of your skin,
your hair. You're a slave of whichever kongelig sent you to kill
me. Kongelig that you're also related to, perhaps?"

He watches me, waiting as though bored, but I can see the twitch of uncertainty in the corners of his mouth.

"Which family do you belong to? Which of your cousins want me dead? Nørup, Solberg, Niklasson? Your family has sent you on a mission to sacrifice yourself, and I, by default, want to destroy anyone who wants me dead. I would say that we're allies."

"We're not allies."

I step closer to him, lowering my voice. "Which family?" He doesn't move, only watches me. "Tell me," I say. "Was it Jannik?"

He clenches his jaw and glances at the shelves of books.

I let out a laugh of surprise. "Elskerinde Jannik?"

"That woman doesn't even know where she is," he says.

"Then it was Aksel."

There's a flash of pity in his eyes, which I turn away from. Emotions come to me, slowly. Embarrassment first. The slave might have a point. Everyone really might be laughing at me. While I'd considered myself a master in this game of the kongelig, I've been nothing but a piece on a board game myself. Anger comes next. Rage, twisting through me, growing into a fury that makes my fingers tremble and makes my stomach lurch. Aksel Jannik has become much better at hiding his thoughts from me.

I'm quiet for too long, and the slave is watching me carefully now. I ask him, "Why would Aksel Jannik want me dead?"

"That's something you should ask Aksel Jannik."

I can barely look at him now. A thought strikes through me: how much better I might feel, if I'm able to see this killer hanging from his neck. It's because of him that Friedrich is dead, and it would feel nice, I think, to kill him and have his head delivered to Aksel.

"You have your answers," he says. Hesitation in his eyes—

maybe a glint of fear, fear that I'll have him executed now that I know who tried to have me killed. Maybe he can sense the rage in me, see the way I look at him.

But curiosity still burns inside of me. I don't yet know why I can't work my kraft on him. "Not all of them."

I may not be able to feel his emotions for myself, but the more I watch him, the clearer they become, in the flicker of his gaze, the shifting of muscles beneath his skin. He tries to hide his relief. He pretends to be brave, pretends to be a willing martyr, but he doesn't want to die. I wonder if I'd be able to do the same. If I hadn't been born to the Rose name, and had been taken from my mother's hands; if I'd been forced into the fields because of the dark of my skin; if a pale-skinned master had ripped at my clothes and forced his way into me, between my legs, and then tore out a child from me, taking the screaming baby away—would I tie rocks around my ankles and walk into the sea, like so many of our people have done before?

He doesn't say anything else when I leave him in the library, locking the door behind me.

CHAPTER EIGHT

In the days that pass, golden mornings followed by sunsets that light the sky afire, I hope that I'll begin to feel settled, but I do not. The habits are familiar: waking in a bed with sheets that are sticky with sweat; allowing Marieke to scrub my shoulders and back in my warm bath and stepping into the white dress she has laid out for me; wandering the gardens of the Jannik house where slaves work, replanting mango and guava and sugar-apple trees and yanking out the dried weeds; sitting on the porch with lemongrass tea, closing my eyes in the trade-winds breeze. The days begin to mirror my life on Lund Helle—but here, every shadow that passes in the corner of my eye makes my pulse race beneath my skin. Every creaking floorboard has me whirling around to see a startled slave carrying a handful of sheets or a basket of fruits. Closing my eyes, I feel the loose skin of Freja Jannik's neck beneath my fingertips, the tip of the blade piercing the skin above my heart. I can never feel settled or at ease on this royal island of Hans Lollik. Especially not when I should be preparing myself to meet Konge Valdemar—to convince him that I am worthy of the title of regent.

It's on the third day that one of the new slaves, a young girl that I've heard Marieke call Agatha, comes to my chamber with news, twisting her hands with nerves: My betrothed, Aksel

Jannik, has arrived. I thank Agatha and leave her in my chambers. I walk down the stairs and a hall with sunlight pouring in through windows before I pass the open glass doors. Marieke stands at attention against the nearest wall while Aksel sits on a sofa on the opposite side of the room. His boots have tracked dirt onto the rug. Aksel doesn't stand when I walk in, but I give the customary curtsy, straining to keep my expression serene so that he won't see the fury twisting through my veins. He's tried to have me killed, and yet he sits here as he does, daring to look me in the eye without any shame. It's because of him that Friedrich is dead.

"Herre Jannik," I say when I rise. "I'm glad you've arrived safely."

There's a roiling of emotions, of thoughts, that knock into me at once—complete confusion, a jumbled mess—but Aksel's face remains impassive. He's trying to hide something from me. Trying to hide the fact that he sent assassins to take my life. Another layer of anger is added, and bitterness for my own ignorance: Had I not gotten my answer from the slave locked within my library, Aksel might've succeeded in keeping his secret from me.

I move to sit across from him. "How was your journey?" I ask.

Aksel waves his hand impatiently in response.

"Will you be staying long?"

He looks at me as though it's a ridiculous question, and I suppose it is. "This house you've occupied, Elskerinde Lund, is my own, and you're only here on Hans Lollik Helle because we're engaged to be married."

My rage reminds me of when I faced a laughing Andela, and the anger that would come to me at night when I couldn't sleep, thinking about my family that had been taken from me. I could kill Aksel, I know. I could sink myself into him and force him to stop breathing, pressure building in his lungs and throat. I could have him walk to the kitchens and pick up a knife to cut open his own neck. I could have him walk off the cliffs of Hans Lollik Helle.

But I need him. I need his name if I'm to fulfill any of my plans on this island.

"I haven't forgotten, Herre Jannik. I'm glad to be welcomed here."

He's silent, struggling, a swell of emotion and thoughts. Finally, he says, "My mother is dead."

It takes me a moment to understand the words. There's a spark of satisfaction, but darkness also churns through me. Though Elskerinde Jannik's death had been a part of this plan of mine, I still feel a twist at the knowledge that she's dead in part because of me.

"I'm sorry to hear that, Aksel," I tell him, and surprise myself when I mean what I say. I know how it is to lose a mother.

"I'm not," he says, his eyes fastened to the ground. "She was suffering. Now she's at peace."

I don't speak. The silence curdles as remorse grows in me. Elskerinde Jannik would've died eventually, but she may have had a few more years of life if I hadn't made her a piece in my game against the kongelig. I try to remember that she's a part of the reason my own family is dead, try to grasp that rage and hold it close to my chest.

I don't realize Aksel still has more to say and is struggling to speak until I look up and see him watching me, jaw clenched.

"I heard word just the other day," he finally says, "of an attempt on your life."

I sit unmoving for a moment, before I ask Marieke for lemongrass tea. She nods her head and leaves the sitting room, closing the glass doors behind her.

He continues. "I had a visitor to Jannik Helle who'd come from a town your guardsmen had passed through, with news that the guard named Friedrich is dead. Is that true?"

Aksel mentions this now only because he knows hearing Friedrich's name will hurt me—and it does, a stab to the chest. I flinch, but I don't blink, don't look away from Aksel.

"Poor Friedrich," he says, though he doesn't feel sad for the boy at all. Anger rips through me. "He had a lot of potential. I'd considered adding him to the Jannik guard, once we were married."

I fold my hands together in my lap. "Let's not pretend, Aksel," I say. "You tried to have me killed."

The churning of emotions, of thoughts, stops within him.

I watch Aksel, his surprise and confusion. "I knew you hated me, but I didn't quite realize how much. I underestimated you."

Silence flows for some time before he manages to speak. "So you survived, and decided to come to Hans Lollik Helle anyway?"

"I must be here if we're to be chosen by Konge Valdemar."

He struggles to meet my eye now as thoughts storm through his head. "How did you know?"

"A prisoner," I tell him, but that's all I will say.

Aksel sits still for some time, his darkening emotions clouding the air. There's only a jumble of thoughts and emotions, tangled together, and it's impossible to latch on to any single thread. The doors reopen, and Marieke steps inside, placing a silver tray of steaming porcelain cups on the center table. The tea will stay untouched—it's just a formality, and besides, it's too hot to drink on a day like this.

"You may leave, Marieke," I tell her, and I feel her irritation prick me, for acting like she's a mere slave who can be easily dismissed. Still, she bows her head before she walks out of the sitting room, shutting the doors behind her again.

"I don't like that one's attitude," Aksel says, his eyes having followed her to the door, as though I hadn't just told him that I know he tried to have me killed. "She should be replaced."

"Marieke will stay wherever I am," I say with enough finality that he doesn't argue. "Why?" I ask. "That's the one thing I can't figure out."

He takes an impatient breath—a sudden shift in tactic, attempting to pretend he holds the power in our dynamic. I realize with a spike to my heart that he does. He's a pale-skinned Fjernman on the royal island of Hans Lollik. He will always have more power than me.

"Take a moment to think." He wants to pretend he's indifferent, but I can feel the discomfort ripple through him.

"I've considered one possibility: It would be easy for you to blame my death on an assassin sent from the Ludjivik," I tell him. "Easy enough to spark a war now, and destroy the family while the Jannik guard remains in a stronger position." When he doesn't answer—only watches me, unblinking—I ask, "Is the Jannik name really so weak that you feel the need to eliminate the Ludjivik now, before they become a threat?"

"Perhaps the idea of being tied to you for the rest of my life is reason enough to want you dead."

"I'm not afraid of you, Aksel," I tell him. "You want to have me killed, but you can't see that the Jannik family is nothing without the Lund name."

He stills. His jaw tightens, and he watches me, eyes cold, thoughts swarming—until he clears a path through his mind, a path that leads me to what he wants me to see: a memory of the gossip, the gossip that holds its own value in these islands, whispers that had reached Aksel's ears—the mention that there had once been a little girl named Sigourney Rose who might've been my age had she not been found dead in a pretty little dress beside the rest of her family.

"The Lund name," he repeats.

Aksel doesn't know the truth, not for sure, but he suspects. He's suspected for some time now.

"Ask me," I tell him.

He doesn't ask.

"Ask me if it's true."

"I don't need you to tell me if it's true."

"And so because I'm not Sigourney Lund," I say, "but Sigourney Rose, you want me dead? What does my name matter, when any name is better than the Jannik?"

There's a splinter of surprise in his chest, yes—curiosity, even, as he knows with certainty now that he looks upon someone who had been thought dead for the past twelve years. But engulfing that surprise is a fury that swells inside him. It infuriates Aksel that I'd try to sweep away this lie and pretend it isn't worth discussion. My bloodline, and my attempt to trick him into an alliance with the Rose, is unforgivable. Bad enough that Aksel is being tied in marriage to an islander with skin as dark as mine—but to be deceived into a marriage with an enemy of the kongelig not only makes a joke of Aksel Jannik but makes him a target of the kongelig as well. They could think that he truly is an ally of the family that his father had ordered killed, and that he means to help the Rose rise to power once again.

"You believe the Rose name is stronger than the Jannik?" he says. "The Rose is dead."

"I'm alive, and I'm stronger than you."

"You give yourself too much credit."

"No, your ego is too bruised to see the truth," I say. "You need me when faced by Konge Valdemar. It's doesn't matter if I'm Sigourney Lund or Sigourney Rose. You're a fool if you don't see that."

"You're a fool if you think I could ever allow myself to marry you."

"Why? Because you don't love me? Are you really so childish, Aksel?"

"It isn't childish to love and be loved. I doubt you've ever felt love. I doubt you ever will."

I push away the wave of hurt—the memory of Friedrich telling me that I deserved his love. It's impossible to continue the
lie without Friedrich here to uphold his end. Aksel is right; I
can't be loved, not by any of my people, not when I allow them
to remain slaves. A Fjern would never in their eyes lower themselves to love someone like me, and I could never hold love for a
Fjern. I want to be the beloved heroine to my people, but I want
the power and respect of the kongelig as well. I know that both
are impossible.

Aksel is silent now, biting his lip. I'm exhausted from confronting Aksel and from reading his mind, but still I sink into
him one last time. He has a tangle of thoughts, emotions, and
memories, but one becomes clear: an image of the woman he's
loved all along, her yellow hair and pale skin and blue eyes. It's
almost enough to make me laugh. Not the politics of the Jannik
and Ludjivik families, not my false identity, not even the fact
that my skin is as dark as night; it's this, something so simple and
plain.

"So your desire for that woman did play a role after all," I say.
"I underestimated your love for her and overestimated your love
for the Jannik name."

He doesn't speak. Even now he's lost in his memories of
Beata; the storm season, years ago now, when he finally found
the courage to tell her that he loved her and that he wanted to
marry her. They'd whispered their dreams to each other. Beata's
patrons, kongelig of the island, wouldn't have approved of her
choice in Aksel, she knew; and Aksel also knew that his mother
would've hoped for him to choose a daughter of the kongelig
who had more coin and a more powerful kraft that would
impress Konge Valdemar. They'd kept their promises to one
another a secret, and every storm season when they were able to
fall into each other's arms once again, they would make plans to
escape the island and travel to the north, be married, and start

their life anew. Aksel thinks, too, about how one year ago, after he agreed to his mother's wishes, he had to tell Beata Larsen that he couldn't be her husband and she couldn't be his wife. She had cried, yes, but even then she had been so full of understanding and love. Aksel's heart aches at the memory, salt beginning to prick the backs of his eyes. It was only out of respect for his mother's wishes that he told Beata he could not marry her; it's out of respect for his mother's wishes that he remains here on Hans Lollik Helle.

"Understand that I'm showing you a mercy," I tell him. "I could have you killed and declare to all we'd been married in secret, taking the Jannik name. I don't need you to impress Konge Valdemar. It's a mercy that I'm allowing you to live."

He blinks too quickly, too many times.

"But betray me again," I tell him, "and I'll cut your neck. Do you hear me, Aksel?"

He watches me, fury building in him.

"Say it. Tell me that you understand."

I feel a wave of the depth of his hatred, splashing onto my feet, rising to my knees. "I understand, Elskerinde Lund."

"Good." I stand, clenching my hands so that he won't see them tremble, and walk out of the sitting room doors.

Marieke waits for me in the hall. She follows closely behind. "I've heard gossip that passed from a slave of the groves," she whispers to me, "that the prisoner you keep in your library is familiar. He's spent many storm seasons here on Hans Lollik Helle."

I wait for her to speak again, but when she hesitates, my respect for her privacy is overwhelmed by my impatience. In the same moment, I realize this is what she'd wanted—she's known for some time now but has had a difficult time telling me. But she can't keep this secret to herself any longer, not when Aksel Jannik has returned to Hans Lollik Helle, and when my prisoner, named Løren Jannik, is the half brother of the man I'm meant to marry.

Now that Freja Jannik is dead, the family needs a new Elskerinde to inherit the title, and so Aksel declares the wedding that will unite me to the Jannik name will be within three days' time. This is an emotionless business proposal, after all; there isn't any need to wait the weeks it would take to plan and execute a ceremony of the sort of caliber the Fjern are used to witnessing.

I've never been excited for my wedding. Even as a child, I only saw this ritual as something that was meant for the pale-skinned girls with their yellow hair. The ceremonies I heard of, much like the fairy tales I listened to, weren't meant for someone like me. Ellinor wanted a grand wedding, she whispered to me at night, one where her dress was made of white rose-mallow flowers and her husband was a handsome Fjernman. She knew the wedding ceremonies weren't meant for her, either, with her brown skin and brown eyes and brown hair, but Ellinor had a hope in her that was different from my own. She wished to be welcomed by the Fjern. Maybe because her skin and hair and eyes were lighter than mine, closer to those of the Fjern ancestor we'd had generations ago, she felt this spark of potential that allowed her to dream of the smiles of Fjern who might one day greet us in the streets of other islands, rather than the still faces and cold eyes we'd only ever known.

My skin has always been dark, even darker after spending days in the sunlight on the shore, playing in the clear seawater. There was no hope for me to be treated with love by the Fjern, I knew from a young age, and so I never bothered to dream of being in one of their fairy tales, never expected or hoped for their smiles. Still, a resentment began to rise. Resentment, that even after being born with my freedom, I would never be considered their equal. Marieke wonders if a spirit left my mother's body and entered my own, but this anger has always been inside my bones.

I'm not excited to marry Aksel, but this is a necessary step in my plans, as necessary as moving here to the royal island for the storm season, as necessary as having my betrothed killed. And so I'll marry him. All the kongelig of Hans Lollik Helle will be in attendance. My heart begins to thunder at the thought. I shouldn't be so afraid to meet the men and women responsible for my family's deaths, and yet unease flows through my veins.

Marieke selects a simple, modest dress of white, and wraps my hair in white cloth as well. The sun has faded away by the time Aksel and I leave the little house on the cliffs, Malthe following us closely behind. I try to ignore Aksel, but the knowledge that he tried to have me killed pricks me every time I look at him. The sky is a deep purple with streaks of fire coloring the clouds red and orange, the chorus of the night birds and frogs filling the air. The cooling trade-winds breeze presses my dress of white against my body, tickling my skin. A path leads directly from the house and through the groves, to the manor of Konge Valdemar. Walls and towers dip and curve as they follow the slope and rise of the hill itself. Green climbs up the white stone of the tower walls, as if the island is attempting to swallow the manor whole.

Herregård Constantjin seems to glow even in the setting sun; the windows are warm yellows, and as we walk up the path toward the entrance, torches flicker with the wings of gnats and moths, lighting the enclosed garden that surrounds the court-yard of cobblestone and carved benches and a sparkling fountain, tables of fruits and meats and wines, and where each kongelig family and their members of court await. The kongelig of Hans Lollik and their family and friends—nearly twenty in all— have come to bear witness. I know each and every one of their names; I've studied their portraits, their kraft, their legacies. It's disorienting to see them all before me, not simply as figures in paintings, or facts about each written on paper.

The elite stand in celebration of themselves, in their glittering gowns of white and sparkling jewels, drinking the sugarcane wine that has cost the blood of my people and our lands. There's a tinkling of dishes, a burst of laughter, a trail of music floating through the night. Slaves with skin as dark as mine stand along the walls, eyes fixed ahead.

As Aksel and I walk into the courtyard, Malthe trailing behind, I can feel the turn of heads, the widening of eyes. It's like they've seen a ghost. I'm the exact image of my mother—the spirit of the woman they killed, returned for her revenge. The kongelig who had their hands in her death implicate themselves. They're pale, sweating, as they turn away with sips of wine. Other kongelig lean into one another with smiles. The rumor that I'm the survived daughter of Mirjam Rose has spread faster than brushfire, and seeing me now is all the proof they need. Chatter ends, laughter stops. It's been years now since I've unwillingly been overwhelmed by the thoughts of others. My kraft once overpowered me daily when I first discovered the ability in my veins, but as I grew used to my ability I learned to control it, to choose when I would read the thoughts of others. It's only in moments of stress and fear that my kraft takes control of me again, just as it takes control now.

The stream of thoughts begins. The questions, the exclamations, the shock and curiosity and hatred—it bowls into me. The hatred, most of all—this hatred is as thick as smoke, bitter on my tongue, burning my eyes and clogging my throat. Hatred for me, for thinking myself their equal; hatred for the way I walk with my chin raised, eyes not fastened to the ground; hatred for the darkness of my skin, gleaming in the yellow lights. It becomes a living thing, this hatred, come to strangle me, and for a moment I begin to think that they're right. That I don't deserve to stand here among them. That I should be nothing more than ash and bone, dirt beneath their feet. Their hatred becomes my own.

Malthe puts a hand on my shoulder, steadying me. He speaks, but I can't hear his words, because the thoughts—they're too loud, echoing against one another, drowning out all other sound. I struggle to recollect Marieke's training. Though she has no kraft in her blood, she does hold the ability to calm my mind. To help me remember myself when the thoughts of others attempt to overpower my own. *Breathe*, she would say, hand on my back after facing a particularly busy street in our travels. *You are your own person. Focus on your own thoughts, your own mind. The thoughts of others—they matter not.*

"Are you all right?" Malthe asks me, his voice low.

The kongelig before me still watch, whispering to themselves, craning their necks to get a look at me, but their thoughts have become a low hum, until they're silenced altogether. I take a breath, nodding to Malthe, biting back the curse that almost leaves my tongue. This is the kongelig's first impression of me, and now they've all witnessed me walking into the courtyard, looking as though I'm about to faint. They'll see my weakness as opportunity.

The ceremony begins. I stand in my dress of white, Aksel beside me. He doesn't bother to hide his thoughts now when I sink into his mind. He wishes I'd been killed in the groves, as the Jannik guards and his half brother had been ordered to do. He wishes he'd never agreed to his dying mother's wishes—that he'd proposed to Beata Larsen instead, and that they'd escaped these islands for the north years before. I can feel the heartbreak in him now. The fear of trapping himself into a life he doesn't want, and for what? For the approval of parents he no longer has? For the admiration and esteem of royals he cares nothing for? Aksel Jannik doesn't want this. It's only his sense of duty that binds him to these islands.

There's the exchange of vows, and the official pronounces us wed. Aksel and I press our lips together for the first time, and what I wish could be the last. He tastes like lemongrass and sweat. We step through the crowd, hand in hand, toward the front of the courtyard so that the celebrations may begin. In the courtyard, candles flicker around the fountain, music tinkling beneath the pale blue of the night, white stars shining. I stand beside Aksel as the guests come forth to greet us, wishing us well in our marriage. Lothar Niklasson, Patrika and Olsen Årud. Faces I recognize from Freja Jannik's memories, from the portraits I studied. The Fjern before me once stood in a room as they discussed my family's coming death. It was a bloody affair, but necessary; none argued with the proposal of Herre and Elskerinde Jannik. The kongelig can't meet my eye now. They'll kill me the first chance they're given—finish what hadn't been completed so many years before. They'll ensure that I don't survive the storm season. The courtyard fills with laughter and music, chatter as pairs begin to dance, sweeping across the stone. It doesn't seem that the death of Dame Ane Solberg rests heavily on anyone's mind. Death is too common an occurrence here.

There's a clatter, a shatter, the stiffening of bodies. A slave girl with trembling hands has dropped a tray of sugarcane wine. The glass glitters prettily on the cobblestone. She doesn't move, doesn't breathe, as though she hopes that if she stays still enough, no one will notice her, no one will have seen. A woman with white hair twisted into a bun, cousin and guest of Niklasson, marches to the girl across the courtyard and slaps her. The girl's head twists and she falls, hand flying to her cheek, tears already in her eyes as she begins to murmur her apologies. She bows her head, begins to pick up the pieces of the glass with shaking fingers, saying again and again that she's sorry. The Niklasson woman isn't listening. She's humiliated—all gathered know the girl belongs to her; they'll whisper and sneer that she doesn't

properly train her slaves as she should. The woman snaps her
fingers at a guard who stands against the wall. He comes forward
hesitantly. I can see the dilemma in him: He has no whip.

Lothar Niklasson steps toward the woman, hand on her
shoulder, as he whispers to her, "Another time. The girl can be
punished another time." His cousin snatches the slave girl by
her hair while all the other kongelig watch. Entertainment, I
realize, bile burning in my throat. I'm not any better, for I'm
also watching. The woman pushes the girl back down, into the
glass, splinters puncturing her hands, her arms and legs. Blood
mixes with the spilled wine. The girl cries as the kongelig snaps
again at the guard, gesturing at him to take the slave away. Even
as she leaves, limping with shards of glass stuck in her skin, it's
clear to all that her punishment isn't over, far from it. The slaves
still lining the wall haven't moved, haven't blinked, have barely
breathed.

There's uncomfortable laughter all around. The music never
stopped, so the dancing continues, along with the chatter and
gentle smiles. It's hard to ignore the eyes that flit to me. That
scene has only served as a reminder to the kongelig. I, too,
should be a slave, stripped of my beautiful gown and whipped
for all to see.

There's a thunderous laugh. Konge Valdemar himself has
stepped into his courtyard. At seventy-nine, Konge Valdemar is
an old man with a head without hair and a wiry beard of white,
wrinkles lining his face and spots on his hands; but the muscle
of his youth remains on his frame, and with a height that towers
over everyone in his courtyard, he's undoubtedly an intimidating man. He looks like he could live for another fifty years—but
still, he declared that a family of his choosing would take the
crown once he turned eighty at the end of the storm season,
ending the Valdemar era of rule and beginning another with a
new regent. Konge Valdemar has a notable kraft: an ability to

speak with and see spirits of the deceased. The dead would come to him and share their messages with him, ask him to speak to loved ones on their behalf. The Fjern have always claimed that the spirits of these islands do not exist, and so the regent's power was feared, and Konge Valdemar would not share his kraft with others. Yet when the spirits wouldn't leave the king alone, he sought help from the divine gods and prayed for the spirits to leave him be. Konge Valdemar became a religious man because of his kraft, devout, and merciless when it comes to the punishment of those who have sinned. When the king lost his wife and child, he didn't remarry. Without any children of his own, and with no noticeable kraft in his relatives, Konge Valdemar will choose a new family to pass Herregård Constantjin to and the ruling powers and responsibilities of the islands of Hans Lollik that come with it.

If I can become close to him, Konge Valdemar might begin to trust me enough to invite me to his daily affairs—afternoon gatherings in the gardens, or trips out to sea to watch the passing of the whales, as I hear he's so fond of—giving me a chance to slip into his thoughts, as I did with Elskerinde Jannik. He's too strong of heart and mind to sway easily. Elskerinde Jannik was dying, making it simple to plant thoughts of my own. The regent will know of my power and it will be more difficult to trick him. But it couldn't hurt to send notions to the king—thoughts of how the other kongelig families are weak and Jannik is strong.

A gaggle of courtiers and royal families surround Konge Valdemar, speaking over one another, seeking attention—as if the affairs of a courtyard wedding ceremony will affect his final decision. Konge Valdemar sips wine, eyes sweeping over his lavish party, the men and women who would throw themselves to the ground to kiss his feet if asked—and his gaze finds my own.

His eyes stick as he smiles. And I smile back, but my mouth trembles—because while he looks at me, I realize I can't hear any thought or feel any emotion. There's nothing at all. This isn't like Malthe, with his naturally quiet mind; or Aksel, attempting to hide his thoughts. This isn't even like the man who tried to take my life, with a block preventing me from knowing what he thinks and feels. With Konge Valdemar, there's nothing at all. As if there's no soul to feel, no mind to hear—as if I'm looking at a dead man. Nothing more than an animated corpse. And the silence of Konge Valdemar—it sweeps over the party, until his nothingness fills me like a swirling tide.

The night grows long, and my feet grow weary. Questions sear me, and I can't stop staring at Valdemar, who doesn't look at me again for the rest of the night. The party ends, edges of pink light glowing on the horizon. Aksel and I return to our darkened house on the cliffs. I know we'll have to spend our first night as husband and wife. I'm more than tempted to suggest to him that we tell all we performed the act of marriage as required, but I know, too, that Malthe will be listening for the truth from outside the house walls, as is his duty. Neither of us speaks as we walk up the stairs to his chambers. He pauses at the doors.

"We don't have to do this." He sounds sober now—I suppose the idea of sharing his bed with me is a sobering reality.

"To legitimize the marriage, we do."

"No one besides us will know whether the marriage is legitimate or not."

"I won't have you use the lack of consummation as an excuse to force me out of Hans Lollik."

He watches me for a long moment before he pushes open the doors. I follow him into his chambers, darkened in the night, the room itself spare, with only a bed and a chair, balcony doors open so that the cool night breeze drifts through the room. This won't be the first time for either of us. Aksel hasn't lain with the one woman he's always wanted to, but he's spent many nights in the brothels of Jannik Helle, enjoying the treatment he receives as Herre Jannik, regarded like a king. I feel a pinch of pain at the memory of Friedrich, but even before him there were other guards of Lund Helle whom I welcomed into my bed. I never saw much point in attempting to hold on to my purity for the Fjern, when the Fjern would never consider purity a possibility for someone like me.

We don't need to draw this out longer than necessary. I begin to undress, and Aksel follows suit as we look at each other in silence. My dress slips to the ground, crumpling in a pile. I'm not ashamed of my body and don't feel the need to hide it. He steps out of his breeches, pulls off his shirt, and folds both, leaving them on the chair.

I step toward his bed, sitting on the edge, and wait for him. He pauses, as though considering whether he'll tell me no once and for all, though I can feel desire quickening his pulse— shocking, overwhelming, he didn't want to think of me this way. He should be disgusted by me. He'd been taught that my skin, the thickness of my hair and wideness of my nose and lips, are ugly—inhuman, belonging to the savages of these islands. But he can't continue the lie he tells himself. I see myself as he sees me: I'm beautiful, dark skin luminescent even in the night. But still, even with the attraction he begins to feel, he can't ignore that I'm not the woman he loves. He closes his eyes and tries to imagine that it's actually Beata he's about to lie with for the first time, and he leans toward me, but I put a hand to his chest.

"I won't be substituted for her."

Frustration ripples through him, but he nods his agreement as he leans toward me again, letting me wrap my legs around his waist. He hides his face in my shoulder now as he pushes into me, but I can feel the pleasure that grips him. It seeps into me, and I can't be sure if the pleasure I feel is his or my own. He moves, but this isn't something for either of us to savor and enjoy for hours until the sun is high in the sky. It's over quickly. Aksel collapses to the bed beside me, content, but satisfaction sours into disgust once again.

I stand, using his sheets to wipe between my legs before discarding them on the floor, picking up my dress and slipping into it. The wine has made Aksel dizzy. The night's been long, and he's spent in this heat. He falls asleep on the bed, breathing easily. He's a fool for trusting me as he does. I've just married him before all of the kongelig of Hans Lollik Helle. I now have his name, the only thing I'd needed from him—no one can dispute this. I don't need Aksel to face the kongelig, not when I'm now Elskerinde Jannik. It'd be easy to kill him now. Stop the air in his throat and, once he's died, wrap a sheet around his neck so that it seems he decided he would rather be dead than be married to an islander. The kongelig wouldn't argue this possibility. I planned to kill Aksel once Konge Valdemar had chosen the Jannik name to follow as regent, but why couldn't I simply kill him now?

It's cowardice that stops me. I worry that the kongelig will know the truth too easily, worry that the slaves might hear Aksel wake and struggle to breathe and tell the Fjern the truth of his murder. I'm afraid that even though I have the name I need from him, I might still need Aksel's body as well—the fact that he's a man, along with his pale skin—to convince the kongelig of my worth.

I watch Aksel as he breathes, eyes roaming beneath his lids, lashes fluttering against his cheek. I don't often slip into another person's mind when they sleep—it can often be unsettling, to see their dreamscape, to fall victim to their nightmares—but I slip into Aksel's mind now. I see Hans Lollik Helle from his mind's eye: Herregård Constantjin, fused with the Jannik Helle manor. The former Elskerinde Jannik, walking the halls in her white dress, dirt staining her feet and hands, roots tangled in her hair, as though she crawled from her grave. She stops walking and turns her head to look at me.

I ask her, *Did Aksel know what you and his father did to my family?*

And Aksel's memory rushes forth: a child, hearing the adults speak on topics they don't think he'll understand—and he doesn't, not yet. But years later, when he remembers the way they spoke of sending the guards to Rose Helle, when he thinks on the night the news arrived that everyone within Mirjam Rose's manor had been slaughtered, he realizes what his mother and father had done. He knows, too, that this is the reality of Hans Lollik.

I leave him in his room, door shutting heavily behind me— and for a moment, in the shadowed halls, I see Freja Jannik standing by an open window, skin even paler in death, hair glowing white in the night. But I blink my eye, and the hall is as empty as it was before.

CHAPTER NINE

The sky, normally so blue, turns gray—and by the end of the morning, the trade-winds breeze turns to a wind that lashes rain upon the islands, blackened storm clouds rolling over the hills and waves crashing into the cliffs of Hans Lollik Helle. The roar of the wind vibrates through me, and I worry that the house will be blown from the cliffs and into the sea. The roof rattles as though it means to be taken. I sit alone beside my closed balcony door, watching the storm as it continues for a full day and into the night, candles flickering until they're blown out as the wind rushes through the cracks in the house's walls. It's not until the following afternoon that the winds finally slow, and the storm has passed.

Marieke receives a letter that informs me of the damages to the groves on the Lund plantation of Herregård Dronnigen— scores of mango and banana trees pushed over by the wind, saltwater from the mangroves leaking into the sugarcane soil. I ask her to keep watch over the slaves as they plant new trees to replace the old, and she sets off that day. I ask Malthe to collect information on both Lund and Jannik island's damages, which he leaves to do as well.

Aksel left at some point in the early morning following our wedding. Days later, and I still don't know where he is—if he stays with Beata Larsen or one of the other kongelig, if he's left the royal island for Jannik Helle, or if he'd gone to roam the groves with his guavaberry rum and was killed in the storm. With Aksel having disappeared altogether, and without anything to do but wait for Konge Valdemar to call on me and the rest of the kongelig, I find myself alone in my chambers with nothing but my spiraling thoughts. The expressions of the kongelig, their smiles and widened eyes, pale faces turning away as they sip their wine; the fear that lives and breathes inside me, the continuous waiting for any of the kongelig to take my life. The emptiness of the king and his thunderous laugh, his cold eyes that laugh at me. The gleaming white of Freja Jannik's hair, the maggots that crawl across her rotting skin. The hardness in Løren Jannik's eyes. That image comes to me time and again. I busy myself with the duties of the Elskerinde, fussing over decoration and curtains and rugs, more out of a need for distraction than genuine care.

I leave the house in the early evening, sky a deep red, stir-crazy from seeing the same walls and their paper, the same furniture, the same views of the sea. I step into the heavy heat of the island and walk along the path that cuts through the groves, where slaves are busy replacing the fallen trees. The path takes me to the shoreline. I give the slaves a wide berth, just as I do whenever I'm able, shame crawling through me. My heels sink into the soft dirt still damp from the rains. Part of the beach has been washed away by the high tides of the storm, and brown seaweed straggles across the gray sand. I take off my sandals, toes sinking into the grains, and bend over to pick up the pink shells as I see them. I'd once heard a song when I was a child, sung by Inga as she plaited my hair, a song about a girl who spends a lifetime picking up the prettiest pink shells on the beach—hundreds of thousands of shells—and on the day she is to leave this world, an old woman with death in her soul, she releases all of the shells back into the sea so that another little girl may walk along and find them on the beach.

When I come to the edge of the bay, the jagged rocks sticking from the sea beneath the cliffs, I see him. Løren stands on the rocks that crumble into the water, staring out at the ocean, as though he's replaced my ghost. The sea is still rough from the passed storm, and waves rush around him, threatening to pull him beneath. Perhaps this is why he stands there, waiting.

I call to him, and he looks at me, startled. Shells clink in my hand as I watch him hesitate, then walk over the rocks. They're jagged, sharp, the sides wet with algae that has to make them too slippery to walk on, yet he moves effortlessly, as though he were raised by the rocks themselves, until he jumps from the last one and into the shallows, walking across the sand toward me. As he comes closer, I feel the same block, an invisible wall raised around him, and I think again how senseless it is, how reckless, that I'd willingly stand before the one person I have no defense against.

He stops before me, silent, his dark eyes staring. He wears the same loose-fitting shirt and pants as the slaves of Hans Lollik Helle, but he doesn't bow. I can see that a new bruise blossoms across his cheek. It's clear from his empty expression that he's waiting for me to speak, and so I do.

"Why're you outside of the library?" I ask him. "Who let you free?"

"Aksel Jannik," he tells me.

"Your brother, you mean?"

If he's surprised I know the truth about him, he doesn't show it.

"Why is my kraft blocked by you?" I ask him, and it strikes me how comical this could be, that my concern for my kraft overpowers concern for my life.

He only stands, chin raised, peering at me. His dark-brown eyes are the same color as his hair, curling and sticking to his face in the heat. His skin is a golden brown, brighter here under the setting sun. I can see now that they have the same brow, the brothers—but one, born in freedom, is higher than the other in its arrogance.

"You're a slave of the Jannik household," I tell him, "and as your Elskerinde, you should answer me when I've asked you a question."

The hatred he holds for me is clear. He stares at me evenly, still not speaking. He reminds me of the woman I'd encountered in the fields of Lund Helle as I ordered the girl executed—watching me, wanting me to know that she isn't afraid.

I eye him, feeling my heart speed with anger, frustration growing inside me. "There's plenty of work to be done after the storm," I tell him. "You shouldn't be standing here idly staring at the sea."

Finally, he looks away—but only back to the water that swells, rising onto the sand. What have I done for this man—for any of the slaves of Hans Lollik—to hate me the way they do? Shouldn't they be glad to see one of their own free and among the kongelig, to gain the power to potentially release us all from the Fjern? I've sacrificed myself for this—my freedom, my peace, perhaps even my life—and rather than meeting me with thanks and love, I'm met with such hatred.

"Return to your work," I tell him, frustration leaking into my voice.

He looks back to me again, and his mouth twitches into the familiar smile he's given me before—one that somehow manages to fill me with shame. There's a split in the wall between us, a crack—and suddenly a memory comes to me unbidden: Løren was a boy, brown hair stuck to his face as he ran out of the pale-blue manor. He tripped and fell, scraping the skin from his elbows and knees, but he barely felt the sting. He tried to scramble to his feet, but Herre Engel Jannik appeared on the steps.

Løren was barely off the ground before Engel Jannik strode to him with three long steps. He reached down and grabbed the boy by his hair, ripping him from the ground and to his feet.

The slaves working the nearby grove wouldn't look at Løren, who clutched at Herre Engel Jannik's hand. Løren hated the slaves who wouldn't look. He hated that they ignored his pain, and for what? Their own fear? The slaves could have easily left that grove. Left the grove with their machetes and descended upon Engel Jannik, tearing him apart, chopping off his limbs and head until the man was nothing but a torso of pale skin and ribs. But they did nothing. They left Løren to be beaten by their master.

Engel Jannik's fist swung, and Løren went flying, mouth filled with blood. Engel Jannik's foot caught the boy in the stomach hard enough that he gasped, bile burning his throat. He looked up to see Aksel Jannik standing on the house's porch, watching with wide eyes.

Løren hadn't stolen the tart. It had been taken from the kitchen, and he'd been hiding in the library all day, reading books he wasn't supposed to read. There'd been an older slave, a woman who had known and loved Løren's mother. She'd taught the boy the written words of the Fjern, and though he was so young, Løren took to reading so easily that he began to pick up the largest of volumes he could find. Løren enjoyed reading. He could escape into the lands of the Fjern, could escape into the bodies of people who weren't his own, and learn—for one blessed moment—what it might have felt like to be free.

The woman who had taught Løren to read had passed away years ago, and Løren paid respect to her every time he dared to open a book, even though he knew he might lose an eye. If anything, reading in the library should have been the reason

Løren was punished, but instead he was accused of stealing a tart from the kitchens. The kitchen staff promised it wasn't any worry at all—they would simply bake a new one in time for dinner, it would take no more than an hour—but Aksel had blamed Løren. This wasn't something Herre Engel Jannik could simply overlook. And so, Engel took a whip and beat the boy on his back and legs until he bled.

Løren had been beaten many times before, for offenses even greater than this—for spitting at the feet of a visiting Fjern who commented that Løren had a little too much defiance in his eyes, and once for hitting Aksel after Aksel had hit him—but for whatever reason, this stolen tart had sent Engel Jannik into a frenzy. He beat Løren without stopping. Løren was afraid he would die.

But Engel Jannik did stop. The boy was left bleeding in the dirt. Herre Jannik reminded him to know his place. Løren wasn't a kongelig, no matter his blood.

Usually, when I choose to slip in and out of the thoughts and minds of those around me, it can feel like slipping in and out of my own daydreams, memories coming and going as they please. But when Løren's memory is finished, I feel the jarring sensation of being snapped back to reality, as though he had suddenly pushed me from his body. Løren stands before me, a man. The wall is between us once more. He speaks. "Is that all, Elskerinde Jannik?"

He's mocking me. He knows that he's managed to block my kraft, and that he knows, too, how much my inability to control him enrages me. He shares with me this piece of his past—not for pity, but to show that he has no reason to fear me. He has survived Engel Jannik, and there's no one on this royal island who is worse than the person his father had been. Certainly not me.

"Yes," I say, "that's all."

He doesn't wait for me to finish speaking. He dismisses himself, turning his back to me and leaving me to stand alone by the sea.

As the sun begins to fall, I lie down on my bed, still in my dress, my hair curling out of the bun atop my head, allowing my thoughts to race freely: thoughts on the slave and his hatred of me, the kongelig, and the regent. The silence that swarms Konge Valdemar, like witnessing an animated corpse. The king's kraft allows him to see and speak to the dead. Is it possible that his kraft has evolved somehow? Allowed his ghost to remain, perhaps without even realizing that he's already gone? Sun burns against my cheeks and eyelids, and gnats stick to the sweat on the back of my neck. I'm lying in the grass. I think vaguely on how strange this is, given that I'd been in my bed only a moment ago. Green blades crunch and fold beneath me, marking my white dress, as does the wet dirt sinking beneath my fingers. I look up, blinking at the sun, which is shining yellow through the green leaves that sway in the breeze, the branches of the mahogany tree that stands in the center of the garden. I used to sit here in the shade with Ellinor, picking at the grass with a book in her lap. Inga's voice reaches my ears as she sings—high and clear, like the sound of a bell tinkling in the early morning.

Ellinor isn't here. I don't see Inga, either. And I have to remind myself that they're dead—but then what am I doing here, in the old gardens of the Rose manor? The gardens look as they did before: flowers of all colors bursting in the sunlight, hummingbirds and bees flitting from one petal to the next, pruned hedges of the maze inviting me. I walk across the grass, warm rocks digging into the undersides of my bare feet, and slip into the shadows of the maze. The hedges were taller when I was younger—now they only reach the top of my head, but I walk as I did when I was a child, turning left and right and then right again, toward the center, where I knew my mother would be waiting sitting on a bench with a smile on her face...

I jolt. I'm standing on solid ground, but I feel as though it's falling out from under me, something sharp scratching my foot all the way to my knee, biting the backs of my legs—I blink, and the scene has changed. Rocks dig into my back, my elbows and shoulders, blood rising from cuts across my skin. I'm on the cliffs behind the Jannik house. I've slipped, clinging to the ledge, but a few feet more, and I would've fallen off completely—over the rocks that crumble and fall sharply into the sea, which foams and crashes beneath me.

I scramble back up the ledge, rocks slipping down to the ocean, until I'm on the grass again, running to the back door of the house. Air wheezes from my throat. My blood is heavy in my legs, my hands cold and shaking. I'd been in my room one moment, in the gardens of the Rose manor the next, walking through the maze—and then I was behind my new home on the Herregård Constantjin estate, inches away from my death.

I look around me, peering through the brush of the gardens, searching for a presence with murder on its mind, for the feeling of someone with kraft pulsing through their veins—but I feel nothing, see no one.

Sleep doesn't come to me for days. When I do sleep, my eyes too heavy to keep open, I hear tangled whispers, see flashes of the blue sky from beneath rippling waves, listen to a soft melody, feel blood dripping onto my hands. I wake, skin cold in the trade-winds breeze, sheets wet with sweat, my bones too heavy to lift. My mother begs, Ellinor smiles over her shoulder at me as laughter echoes through the halls, a woman with yellow hair and blue eyes stares at me through the mangrove trees. A hand pats my head, soft cloth wipes sweat from my neck. Marieke forces me to sit up, to drink the lemongrass tea and sip the chicken-bone broth. She tells me I'm lucky that I'm alive. She found me like this, fever on my skin and in my eyes.

"Was it poison?" I ask her.

"No," she tells me, dipping the cloth into a bucket and wringing it out, bringing it back to my shoulders, my neck, my cheeks. "Just a storm-season sickness and a good amount of stress."

I've almost managed to kill myself before anyone else on the island could. This is funny, so I laugh. Marieke smiles down at me. There's a sound she hasn't heard in a while. There'd been a time, once, when she thought I would never laugh again. Sailing with me to the north, she thought that my spirit had been taken over by grief. It was a year before she could coax a smile from my face. Even longer before I outright laughed. It was a sound that had shocked both her and myself. I remember the very moment: While we were traveling in the north, a Fjern who didn't like the dark of our skin told us we wouldn't be able to stay at her inn because we couldn't afford such a thing. At that exact moment, a northern acquaintance of Bernhand Lund happened to be passing through the city. He called upon us, shocked that we would ever think to stay in such an inn when we should be inside a manor. The woman, learning of the coin we had to spend, tried to convince us to stay, but it was too late as we left with this acquaintance. Marieke and I had looked to each other and laughed.

"You aren't in my head again, are you?" she asks me, and I tell her that I'm sorry; the kraft tends to overpower me whenever I'm weak. She tells me to rest. I close my eyes again, and I let sleep take me, knowing that at least Marieke is here to watch if I try to get to my feet and walk over the cliffs. In my sleep, I find Løren standing on the shore again, roots winding around his feet, trapping him to this island of Hans Lollik Helle, refusing to let him escape into the sea.

When I ask Løren, his eyes answer me. His mother was already

dead when he was cut from her stomach. A knife was put to his
wailing throat, but his own eyes were too much like his father's,
brown and steady. He should've died. The slave should've died
a thousand times. When he spat at a kongelig's feet and when he
dared to hit his brother across the face and when he tried to run,
only to be caught the next morning, and most of all when his
gift had been found. The Fjern believe that this gift isn't meant
for slaves. They say it's a divine right, an offering from the gods
above. Kraft is a rare trait, seen only in those who are revered,
generations of people who have ruled empires and led armies;
the gifts aren't meant for savages. Any islander who dares to have
a divine gift is a trickster who has managed to steal the power
that isn't rightfully theirs.

This slave had such a power, and finally he was meant to be
hung from his neck.

I wake up, tongue stuck to the back of my throat, breeze rustling
the curtains of my bed's canopy, streaks of yellow sunlight falling across the walls. My limbs are heavy with disuse, my joints
creaking as I pull off the sheets and get to my feet. It's hard to
know how much time has passed. Memories of my dreams feel
as real as memories of waking: a young brown-skinned boy
running across the rocky shoreline, the bottoms of his pink
feet bleeding; blue eyes fastened on me through the trees of
the groves; listening to an old song as I walk through the green
maze; opening my eyes to find myself on the edge of a cliff, only
a few feet away from my death.

Marieke wants to know why I'm out of bed when I pass her
outside my room. The slaves won't look at me as I walk by, slipping through the halls. The door to the library is shut, the key
still in the lock. I twist it with a click, scraping the door open.
He'd been free just days before, standing on the rocky shore, but
it's hard to tell now if that had only been another dream. The

man named Løren had been asleep, I can tell, and I woke him with all my noise; he's on his feet now, standing up from his corner on the floor where someone took pity on him by bringing him a blanket and a pillow, a cup of water, and leftover chicken broth. The skin around his eyes is dark and heavy, the corners of his mouth lined as they tug down, making him look much older than his twenty-two years.

It's obvious, I realize—this power he has in his blood, his kraft to hinder the ability of anyone else around him. It isn't easy for him. It's something he must put his energy into, watching me the way he does, careful not to leave open a crack, careful not to let me slip inside him and take control. This is a great fear of his: Though he might not own his life, he can at least control his body and mind. This is something he prides himself on. Not everyone who is a slave controls their own mind.

His breath catches in his throat when I tell him that he will be my new personal guard to replace Malthe, effective immediately, and stride away, leaving the library door open behind me.

CHAPTER TEN

The ghost of Konge Valdemar sends a letter of invitation to join him and the other kongelig for the evening. I leave for Herregård Constantjin with Aksel. It's the first time I'm seeing my husband in over two weeks. He'd left his Jannik house after our wedding night and hadn't returned since. I know he wouldn't tell me the truth if asked, so I sink into his mind and see now the days and nights he'd spent: drinking with his friend Erik Nørup, and once Herre Nørup could drink no more, drinking alone in the shadows of the groves, lingering outside of Beata Larsen's house, refusing to leave even after she begged him to, her finally coming to him and allowing him to kiss her, to whisper his love for her. She took mercy on Aksel, brought him into her house and bathed him, washed his clothes. He cried to her, admitting what he had done with me on our wedding night, though he wouldn't admit to the shame he felt for his desire. He apologized for his betrayal; but for Beata, there was nothing to forgive. He kissed her again, and Aksel and Beata made love for the first time, although they risked ruining Beata's reputation and the Jannik name. It was the greatest pleasure Aksel had ever known.

He doesn't hide this memory from me now. He wants me to see, in fact. His eyes are rimmed red with rum. Slaves might have seen Aksel leaving Beata's house in the early-morning light, and gossip might spread across the island quickly, but he doesn't care. He isn't desperate for the king's favor—not like I am. Anger ripples through me, but I won't spend energy on what can't be undone. I can only hope that the regent won't hear word of Aksel's betrayal and that this sham of a marriage won't fall apart at its seams. Even if the king is nothing more than a ghost—a corpse, dangling on invisible strings—this is the game we must still play.

Aksel has questions about his brother, and why Løren stalks behind us as my new guard, but he doesn't ask them. He assumes that the slave is my new pet, just as Friedrich had been, and also thinks that I use his brother's presence to flaunt the fact that Løren failed to kill me. If Løren has his own assumptions about his new position, he doesn't let me know them.

Cutting through the courtyard, we walk up the stone steps and through the heavy doors that allow us into the entrance hall. Løren waits outside with the other guards lined up in the court-yard, and Aksel and I continue on. Aksel is used to these meet-ings; he's been attending in his mother's place for the past storm seasons. He's used to the notion that, at any moment, any one of the other kongelig might decide that he would be more useful to them dead, and has relied on the weakness of the Jannik name to spare him his life. He's witnessed the other kongelig die around him, watched the cousins suddenly fall ill or their bodies washed ashore. He rarely worries for his life, but Aksel has always been a fool. With his marriage to me, there's more reason now for the kongelig to decide the Jannik name is more of a nuisance than a joke, and to target him and me both.

As we enter the main house's walls, Aksel doesn't blink at the luxury that surrounds us—but for a moment, my breath is taken away. These are the riches the Fjern hoard to themselves, created on the backs of my people while the islanders suffer. The floors are made of white marble, and intricate wallpaper that seems to glitter with gold covers the walls. We're led by a slave down another hall that holds grand paintings, larger than even myself, with portraits of the past regents of Hans Lollik. I can hardly meet the slave girl's eye, so much shame fills me. I'm angry at the Fjern, but I've enjoyed riches and wealth and freedom just as much as they have.

The girl is familiar, one of the island's, I realize. She's been introduced to me before, helping Marieke around the Jannik house, though I forget her name now. She keeps her gaze obediently on the marble floor as she takes us through what could nearly be a museum, statues and busts on display. Another turn, and we reach the open doors of the meeting room.

This is a room of mahogany, velvet, and gilded gold; plush seats surround the wooden table. We aren't the first to arrive. My heart feels heavy in my chest as I see the kongelig. It will take energy, but I need to use my kraft on each of the kongelig at every opportunity. This creates its own danger. The exhaustion might make it difficult to think as clearly as I normally would, but this is worth the risk. I need to know if any of the kongelig plan to see me dead—if one had meant me to walk to my death over the cliffs, or if it really had only been a dream.

Beata Larsen takes her seat as the head of the Larsen family, not meeting my gaze, and Erik Nørup sits alongside his twin sister, Alida. The Nørup family, symbolized by the lily, is known as one of the more powerful among the kongelig in terms of wealth and ability to provide and trade multiple crops, though the family isn't as competitive when it comes to their guard. They have only one hundred men, last I heard, though I suppose I can't be too judgmental, when the Lund guard only has fifty, and the Jannik only thirty.

I can feel Erik's curiosity as he glances at me and nods his greeting, but Alida stares only at the table, deeply lost in thought, completely aware that more guests have arrived but not caring in the slightest. The Fjern believe that Alida Nørup might make a better head of the Nørup family than her brother, who drinks and frolics through the lands, if it weren't for the fact that she's a woman; even so, her desperation to be anywhere but the meeting room is easy to see. She doesn't want the crown, nor does her brother. The Nørup twins are not a threat.

Jytte Solberg also sits in waiting. The Solberg, with their oleander crest, are even more powerful than the Nørup clan. They've been by far the most successful in building a military presence, with over three hundred guards that actively train as though preparing for a possible invasion. The Solberg family has an inherited wealth, which they've been careful with for generations, unlike the Jannik. The Solberg family would be a clear frontrunner to be next in line for the crown were it not for their mistake in having a woman as their heir. Jytte Solberg seems to take her family's mistake gravely. She's a grim, silent woman, her pale eyes sweeping across the room before landing on me. She's nearing thirty years and is small in stature, and her skin, her hair, her eyes remind me of sand. Disgust rolls from her in waves when her eyes meet my own, but it's not the disgust I'm so used to seeing in the pale-skinned Fjern around me. She doesn't see me as her equal, this is true; but Jytte Solberg's hatred of me is seeded somewhere else. She simply does not trust me. I'm lucky, I suppose, that Ane Solberg had been poisoned before I arrived, found dead when I'd been on Hans Lollik for barely an hour; otherwise, Jytte Solberg might have accused me of the woman's death, whether she thought I was innocent or not. It's almost a relief, this hatred, for it to not be rooted in the color of my skin and the thickness of my hair and the wideness of my nose and lips.

I remember Jytte Solberg's kraft with a rush the longer she

holds my gaze with her own, and my heart begins to race with panic: her control is over fear. She continues to watch me, a challenge, and the longer I keep her stare, the faster my heart pumps in my chest, palms becoming cold with sweat, as my thoughts fill with death and the fact that I won't succeed on Hans Lollik Helle, will not survive—

I blink and look away with a shuddering breath, and Jytte smiles.

"I believe this is the first we've had a chance to speak, Elskerinde Jannik," she says.

I nod my head to her. "A pleasure."

"I'm sure." She glances at Aksel, who has turned his attentions to Beata. "Congratulations on your wedding."

She's taunting me, and she wants me to know. Aksel and I sit at the far end of the table, Aksel still gazing openly at Beata, while Beata refuses to meet his eye. Beata regrets allowing Aksel into her house and into her bed, regrets giving her virginity to a man who isn't her husband, a man who is married to someone else. If news of this spreads, she will lose all of the respect of the kongelig, the legacy her parents and her grandparents had built for generations. Beata Larsen would be forced to leave the islands of Hans Lollik in shame.

We aren't yet properly situated when Patrika and Olsen Årud storm into the room, a wave of haughtiness sickening the air. They take their seats, looking smugly at each of us without formal greeting. The Årud family with the crest of the crab claw flower; it's only their grandiose self-esteem that makes them any sort of threat. Though wealthy from the multiple businesses their family holds, their crop has always failed, and they have an army of only seventy guards, yet they manage to act as though they are better than any of the other Fjern, and because of their arrogance, somehow they have convinced others to believe the same. I don't find them a threat to the crown, but I think the two would be happy to kill whoever they feel is in their path.

Patrika and Olsen are two of the few remaining kongelig who belonged to my mother's generation. They would've looked her in the eye, smiled, and exchanged pleasantries over wine, knowing that she and her children were about to die. They would do the same to me now—may have even already begun to plot how I'll find myself dead in just a few days' time. I think of the cliffs and how I nearly fell from the edge. It could've been the storm sickness, yes—a dream brought on by fever that nearly walked me to my death—or it could have just as easily been any one of the kongelig, using a secret kraft to guide me.

Though the Årud say nothing to me, I can see a crack in their mask of conceit, feel their discomfort: I look like the ghost of my mother, taking a seat at the table that she'd previously been denied.

"Why is Lothar always the last to arrive?" Patrika says with annoyance, readjusting her skirts in her seat.

I've heard of Patrika Årud's powers to cause excruciating pain with just a glance. Patrika had been beautiful once, I can tell: Her hair, a curling red, swoops over her shoulder, while her painted lips are full; but in her aging years, her cheeks have become gaunt, and powdered makeup cracks in its attempt to hide the lines around her eyes, her mouth. Olsen, from what I've heard, has never been particularly pleasing to the eye: his bulging eyes, his thick neck and fingers, his thin mouth, and hairless, weak chin. Instead he covers himself with jewels—rubies, emeralds—to show his wealth.

Olsen snaps his fingers at a waiting slave girl to pour him wine, and when she's finished, he picks up the glass with thick fingers and swallows. Olsen holds no kraft in his veins. It's only his wealth that has afforded him a seat on Hans Lollik Helle. He watches me, eyeing my face, my chest, as he slowly sips his wine. *A pretty little thing*, he thinks. *Too bad she has the skin of a slave.*

"I've heard rumors of your kraft, Elskerinde Jannik," he says. "A powerful ability to enter minds—even take control as you wish." His eyes glitter like his jewels. "Is this true?"

I have no reason to hide my power. "I think you must already know the answer, Herre Årud."

I can feel the eyes of the others on me. He smiles. "A curious ability. Couldn't it be said that you might've forced your way onto Hans Lollik Helle?"

"I think the same can be said of anyone with kraft," I answer. "Perhaps Elskerinde Årud has threatened the king to perform her kraft on him if she were not to receive an invitation to join the kongelig."

"Is that an accusation?" she asks.

Olsen sips his wine, eyes fastened on me, in an attempt to unsettle me—part of his game, I know, because he holds no kraft himself.

"Perhaps it'd be best if you stopped watching me," I say to him.

"I can watch whomever I wish," he says.

I enter him—see myself sitting only a few seats away, disgusting that an islander with skin as black as mine should sit at the table as I do—and his neck twists with a gasp, eyes turning to stare instead at the front of the room.

"What're you doing?" Aksel hisses.

Olsen wheezes as I let him go, and he leans forward over the table, as though he might be sick. He keeps his eyes on the table, and only furtively glances up at me, enraged—he wants to have me whipped, tied to a tree by my wrists and beaten—but I can also feel his prick of fear. Patrika looks to be on the verge of laughter as she sips her sugarcane wine. She holds no love for her husband.

The door opens, and Lothar Niklasson strides into the room. Herre Niklasson is easily the oldest of the heads of the families, with graying hair and a lined face. The Niklasson family is symbolized by the orchid. Besides the regent, the family is by far the most powerful of the kongelig, in wealth, crop, business, and with an army of four hundred guards. Everyone knows that they are the family most likely to inherit the crown. Lothar Niklasson is also the one who holds the greatest threat on the royal island: a kraft that forces others to speak the truth to any question asked. If he grows suspicious of me, and knows exactly the right question to ask, I'll have no choice but to tell him everything about my plans here on Hans Lollik Helle—to win the favor of the king, only to have my husband killed and claim the throne for the Rose; to use my power to destroy each of the kongelig who sit before me, one by one, until they're all in their graves of the sea.

Lothar takes a seat, silently nodding his greetings, and from the stillness in the room, I know that the others fear him as much as I do—a man who potentially has access to each of our secrets and all of our plans. Yet I remind myself that I, too, know a secret of his: He, along with Patrika and Olsen Årud, murdered my family.

I look to each member of the kongelig, silently remembering the ranking I had conceived with Marieke: First choice for the crown would undoubtedly be Niklasson; second, likely a tie between Solberg and Nørup, for the simple fact alone that Erik Nørup is a man, and Jytte Solberg is not. The Årud family would follow, embarrassingly directly ahead of me and Aksel. The Jannik would be considered only in front of the Larsen family. Before the next two months pass, I'll have to ensure that this ranking changes.

We all sit silently, waiting. A moment passes, and Konge Valdemar walks through the heavy doors and into the room. We stand with a scraping of our chairs as he faces us. Ice runs through my veins, seeing the regent standing so close by: There is no life in this man. It's like watching a doll, or a scarecrow, suddenly move and turn with a smile. I'd come here to Hans Lollik Helle believing that I would have to focus on charming the regent… but now it's clear that my goal has shifted: Something is wrong with the king. He could be a ghost, yes, an animated corpse; but another possibility strikes me: The regent could be a product of kraft. He could be an image, a puppet, its strings pulled by one of the kongelig in this very room.

Konge Valdemar doesn't greet any of us as he moves to the head of the table. He waits as the slave girl pours him a glass of wine, then nods his thanks as she returns to her station. He looks to us all, still standing, then says gruffly, "You may be seated."

We sit down once again.

Konge Valdemar takes a healthy sip of wine, then waves his hand at me, a smile suddenly upon his face, eyes bright—though I still can't sense any happiness, any emotion, any life from the man. I suppress a shiver. "We have a new addition."

The heads of each family look to me.

"Elskerinde Sigourney Jannik," he says. "Welcome."

"Thank you, my king."

There's a moment's breath of quiet, before Patrika Årud turns to me, clearly unable to control herself, even in front of Konge Valdemar.

"Elskerinde Jannik," Patrika says, eyes fastened on me. "I'd heard a rumor that, while Bertrand Lund had been your patron, you are actually a member of the late Rose family. Looking at you now," she says, but it's her thoughts that finish for her: *She looks so much like Mirjam Rose that this must be true.*

All of the kongelig and Konge Valdemar watch me silently. Aksel's brow is furrowed; I've already taken too long to speak.

"Yes," I say, "it's true. I am the daughter of Mirjam Rose."

Silence fills the room. This is the first I've acknowledged my bloodline publicly. Beside me, I sense Aksel's anger, and at the root of that anger, his embarrassment.

"My condolences on your family's deaths," Elskerinde Årud says, her heart speeding, a surprising amount of fear sinking into me, though she controls her expression well. "May I ask how you survived such a tragedy? I'd thought all in the manor that terrible night had been killed."

"With the help of a slave," I say, "who sacrificed her life for mine."

Lothar Niklasson's gaze is narrow. "And why did you keep your name a secret all this time, until you are now conveniently on the royal island of Hans Lollik?"

I can feel tendrils of his kraft reach for me, and I know that no false words can now leave my tongue. Yet there's a truth I can easily speak without revealing all my plans: "I kept no secret," I tell him. "I would never denounce my mother's name."

"But you can't be here as a member of the Rose," Patrika says now, irritation leaking into her voice, her condolences a thing of the past. "Mirjam Rose may have been invited to Hans Lollik Helle before her death, but you were not."

"I'm not here as a member of the Rose," I say. "I'm here as Elskerinde of the Jannik name, wife of Herre Aksel Jannik."

Aksel is silent in his seat. His embarrassment, his anger, his hatred for me radiates heat.

"Do you see how your wife used you, boy?" Olsen Årud says.

Patrika turns to the king himself. "Surely we cannot allow this. Such devious plans, such a snake among us. At the very least, she must be exiled from Hans Lollik Helle at once," the woman announces, looking to me once again, "if not executed for her crime of falsehood."

Yes, Patrika certainly does want the title of regent for her own family name. More than a few of the kongelig shift in their seats,

Jytte Solberg repressing a laugh. Even she finds Patrika ridiculous, her desperation amusing.

The regent speaks. "And what crimes of falsehood would that be, Elskerinde Årud?"

"The falsehood of her lineage."

"Sigourney Jannik didn't lie about her lineage," the king says, "and to imply that I have been deceived by Elskerinde Jannik only suggests that you believe me a fool."

Patrika Årud's face freezes. She leans forward in her seat, shaking her head. "No, my king, I would never—"

"I knew of Sigourney Jannik's lineage," Konge Valdemar interrupts, chin raised, eyes fastened on me. His words, for a moment, distract me from the cold emptiness within him. He smiles. "I'm most careful about whom I invite onto this island of mine. Sigourney Jannik, formerly Sigourney Lund, had been under the patronage of Bernhand Lund for over ten years until his death—but there were no records of you, Elskerinde Jannik, before those years. It was easy enough to see that your appearance coincided with the deaths of Mirjam Rose and her children—obvious that you are actually Sigourney Rose. This did play a role in my invitation to you," he says. "Though I knew most would be disgusted by your presence here, I see your value. You remind me of your mother. She knew so much about these islands, these people—would know how to placate them before me. She could stop these ridiculous rebellions and unite her people under us so that we could continue our rule without expending so much of our resources. She would've been useful here. Perhaps you can be useful, too."

And so this is why the regent invited my mother to Hans Lollik Helle—why he considered passing her the crown. He wanted to use her as a symbol, use her to stop the rebellions; he couldn't have realized the sort of woman my mother was, and that she would've taken her power and led a rebellion against the Fjern herself. There's no way to know if the real regent would've thought the same of me had he not been the ghost that stands before me, or the puppet, strings pulled by one of the kongelig in this very room. If Valdemar is being controlled by one of the kongelig, which one would it be? I try to glance at them all, looking for obvious signs, but there are none.

There're few thoughts from the kongelig following Konge Valdemar's words—only a swelling of emotion from each at the table. Frustration, disgust, yes—confusion as well, confusion that Konge Valdemar, of Fjern descent, would suggest that he might turn his title over to someone like me, who should rightfully only be a slave.

The old fool has lost his mind, Patrika thinks to herself, and I know that more than a few at the table agree. But I'm sure his words aren't brought on by insanity. I feel the depths of uncertainty. This could be the king—echoes of him, a man who doesn't yet realize that he's dead—but why would a ghost play such a game on his advisers? It's more likely that the king is only a false image, a product of kraft. Whoever holds the king puppet's strings has made the choice to pretend that Konge Valdemar stands behind me, and it's clear that by the regent's words alone, the target on my back has grown.

Konge Valdemar says that there's much to discuss, and so we silence ourselves, heads bowing and jaws clenching. Patrika throws a nasty glance my way, as though she's thinking of using her kraft on me here and now. The hatred she held for my mother—an islander who dared to see herself as a kongelig—has been transferred to me.

"Since the slave rebellion of Lund Helle, there have been more outbreaks on the sister island of Nørup. Elskerinde Jannik, you helped quell the latest uprising of Lund Helle, did you not?"

I suppress the memory of the girl pleading for her life. "Yes," I say, voice steady under the heated gazes of those around the table—but beneath the anger, I feel the growing curiosity from the twins. Erik and Alida both see me now as a good source of entertainment in these otherwise dull gatherings. "It was a minor slave rebellion, nothing more."

"So it would seem," Konge Valdemar says. "Except there is reason to believe that the slaves had been sent by the family Ludjivik."

Patrika sucks her teeth in disgust. "When will they cease this mockery of a rebellion?" She doesn't appreciate the attention I've taken in this rare chance to impress the king, and so will speak whenever she sees a chance.

The regent slides a cold gaze to her. "It's nothing to laugh at, Elskerinde Årud—this 'mockery of a rebellion' has now altogether cost several hundred lives, and damages to farmland and crop."

Beata's voice emerges, a whisper that's barely heard. "There isn't—I mean to say, there couldn't be any truth to their claims, could there?"

"That the Ludjivik family should be chosen for regent?" Patrika says, openly laughing now.

"They take the claim seriously enough," Lothar Niklasson says now. "As one of the first Fjern settlers, they believe it's their divine right to be granted status as kongelig and hold a place at this table." Konge Valdemar leans forward, seeming to listen carefully. I'd heard that Lothar Niklasson is a close adviser to the king, and has been since the two were young boys on these islands—another reason Lothar Niklasson is the king's clear choice to inherit Hans Lollik Helle.

Lothar continues. "The Ludjivik family won't easily stop their attacks, not until we put down a firm hand."

Konge Valdemar looks to me. "We did have the chance, but

with the destruction of property and loss of life, the Ludjivik see the Lund Helle rebellion as a success."

I can see gladness in faces around me; smugness, that I have clearly hurt the Jannik name, and my own chances of taking Hans Lollik Helle. Aksel sits beside me, meeting my gaze with the echo of a smile. *Do you hear that, Sigourney?* he asks. *You have cost us Hans Lollik, and Konge Valdemar. How could he ever give the crown to you now?*

But I see an opportunity: Though this is only a puppet king, I still need to play this game and impress Konge Valdemar. "My lord, please," I say, "allow me to confront the Ludjivik family myself. I will act as a messenger of Hans Lollik Helle and negotiate the end of the uprising."

Surprise raises brows around the table. Konge Valdemar eyes me for only a moment. "And what will you offer them?"

"Their lives," I say, simply. "They must know that when they attack one family of Hans Lollik, they threaten all of Hans Lollik. We've seven armies to their one. We will crush the Ludjivik name if they don't end their claim to the throne."

Konge Valdemar leans back in his seat, watching me with approval, though there's no way to know what he actually thinks, what he really feels.

"With your permission," I say, "I will leave for Ludjivik Helle at once and face Herre Gustav Ludjivik."

"We've threatened Herre Ludjivik before. What makes you think you will succeed? No," he continues before I can speak, "perhaps it's best that you go to Herre Gustav Ludjivik, as you suggest, and once you arrive, fulfill what has been previously threatened. You will execute him yourself."

Those around the table hold their tongues, but I feel the stunned silence. There's a spark of gladness from Aksel beside me, as he thinks that he will finally be rid of me—for if I leave for Ludjivik lands and murder Herre Gustav Ludjivik in his own home, this will be an act of war. The Ludjivik guards would never allow me to leave alive. Konge Valdemar waits for my response, a smile playing on his papery lips, and I know that whoever holds control over him must have realized I know the truth: that the regent isn't alive, doesn't have emotion and thought and soul as he should. They mean to be rid of both me and Herre Ludjivik. I sense confusion in the other kongelig; Konge Valdemar suggests that I might take the throne one moment, then sends me to my death the next. Jytte thinks this is a test, perhaps, to see if I deserve the crown; Patrika believes it's another symptom of his madness. I don't know the goal of whoever holds the puppet king's strings, but it's clear they enjoy this game they play.

Before I can speak, Lothar Niklasson interrupts. "Are you sure that's wise, my lord?" he asks, and I know that it's only Lothar Niklasson who can openly question the king. "Executing Herre Gustav Ludjivik will only draw ire from his cousins, who will continue the uprising in full force. Nothing more than a costly pain, to be sure, but they will inevitably find a way to attack again."

Konge Valdemar turns an icy gaze to Lothar, who shifts in discomfort—Konge Valdemar has been different since the start of the storm season; he hasn't taken Lothar's advice as readily, has turned to him in anger more and more—

The regent speaks. "Yet we cannot allow these actions to go unpunished. They'll continue to attack whether Herre Gustav Ludjivik lives or not. We must send a message—not only to the Ludjivik, but to all the islands."

Lothar bows his head in understanding.

There's silence, and everyone at the table waits for me to speak. "My lord," I say, "I would be honored to execute Herre Gustav Ludjivik and fulfill my duty."

CHAPTER ELEVEN

My husband should be with me when I confront Gustav Ludjivik, but the coward is nowhere to be found the next morning. I can't completely blame him, I suppose; I'm not sure how I'll manage to execute Herre Ludjivik and leave the island alive, when I'm sure his guards will be waiting to take their revenge. The Ludjivik aren't particularly powerful; last I heard, Gustav has ten personal guards in training at his manor. I know that I should plan for another battle, at the very least. Marieke has a carriage prepared; Malthe arranges my usual personal guardsmen of twelve as well as an additional twenty of the Lund guards to follow as we take a two-day boat ride to Ludjivik Helle, far from all the other islands of Hans Lollik. We arrive and ride into roads that cut through lands I haven't seen before. The island is rocky, barren, with no farmland and no trade. There are no villages, no plantations, no crops—only the rare crumbling house, enslaved islanders stopping in their duties of chopping wood and washing to watch us pass, children running alongside the carriage for as long as their legs permit. That the Ludjivik have managed to stretch their reach across the islands with their rebellions humbles me. I've underestimated them, just as Friedrich warned me not to nearly a month before.

My new guardsman Løren takes Friedrich's place across from me in my carriage. He pretends to ignore me, staring out at the passing island, but I can feel his intense focus on me, this constant wall he must carry between us. It's exhausting for him, keeping this barrier of his. I can see it in the furrowing of his brow, the heaviness of his breath. He won't look at me—won't even glance at me—and I wonder if it's easier for him to keep me outside his thoughts if he pretends he doesn't sit across from me. I don't pretend. I watch his every move openly, watch the curl of his brown hair and the blinking of his dark eyes. His eyes are so much like Aksel's—so much like his father's, Engel Jannik's, staring down at me from the painting above Freja Jannik's bedframe. Is his portrait still there, or did they bury it at sea with his wife? I suddenly want to know.

Løren tries hard not to let his mind wander from me. If he loses focus, I'll have access to all of his thoughts, and I'd even be able to control him. This is the worst thing I could do to him. But his eyes glaze, and finally after a few hours of silence, I feel a question slip from him.

I begin to speak, the first words I've said to him all day, and I describe to him the maze my mother kept on Rose Helle, its green leaves and thorny branches that would prick my skin if I ever got too close. "My sister Ellinor and I would play in that maze until the sun went down. I dreamed of the maze," I tell him. "I dreamed I was back between its walls, lost, searching for my mother, who always waited in the center for me. And when I woke up and opened my eyes, I had nearly walked over the edge of the cliff of Hans Lollik Helle."

Surprise now—Løren can't hide that from me, though he tries. He glances at me, only for a second, before he goes back to staring at the passing Ludjivik Helle. He's never been on this island before. He's been on others, yes, when he'd been sent on errands and when he lived on Jannik Helle and when he attempted to escape to the north, but he's never come to this island before. He's had no reason to.

"I wondered for a while if it was the sickness that nearly killed me, or the stress of being on the royal island. But nothing is an accident on Hans Lollik Helle, is it? You hold the power to stop the kraft of others," I say. "The kongelig want me dead. You can protect me from them."

Why would I? This he wants me to hear.

There's such hatred in his tone and in his eyes as he stares at the passing rocks and browning grass. He would rather see me dead. I ask him why. "Why would you want me dead? You say I've betrayed my people, but I've sacrificed myself for these islands." He lets out a laugh of disbelief, but I continue. "I could have taken my freedom and left, but I'm here. I could have gone to the northern empires with my cousin Bernhand Lund's coin and built a new life for myself, one where I wouldn't be seen as a slave everywhere I go, but I returned."

"Returned to your manor of comfort while your people bleed around you."

"I'll be able to change that if I live long enough to take power from the kongelig. If you help me live."

He's refused to look at me all the while, but he looks at me now. "Convenient that your sacrifice will end with you on top of a throne." His eyes are narrowed, but the holes in his wall grow wider, and I can see his incredulity, his pity for me. "Do you really believe the Fjern would ever let an islander become their regent? They would rather burn the throne to the ground than let you sit on it."

"Then I'll sit on its ashes."

He laughs, but there's anger in his eyes. "Those ashes will hold the skin and bones of our people. These islands can burn, and

the Fjern can leave, but the islanders—our flesh, our blood—
will have nowhere else to go."

"We can rebuild the islands."

"With you as regent," he says. The anger is gone now, and the
stiff emptiness isn't filled with judgment, only fact.

"Would that be so wrong?" I ask him. "Am I really so hated
that I couldn't free my people and be considered their queen?"
My mother would've been welcomed with open arms. She
would free our people, return the islands to what they'd once
been, the stories she'd told me as I sat on her lap in the center of
the maze. Our people don't see me with the same hope. Perhaps
they see the selfishness, the greed, better than even I can see it. I
want the love of my people as well as the power of the Fjern. It's
difficult to admit, but I know that I can't have both.

"You would only replace the kongelig," Løren tells me, "but
nothing would really change."

"It would be a victory for our people, to see an islander rule."

A muscle in his jaw jumps and he turns his head back to the
window and the countryside. "You want to see," he tells me. He
doesn't give me any time to respond before the wall between us
crumbles.

I'm in a different place, a path cutting through the groves and
the salted waves foaming onto shore, the mango and plantain
picked in bushels, Herregård Mønsted with its pale-blue paint
glowing beneath the yellow sun. The boy named Løren slept
on the dirt floor of the house meant for slaves, alongside the
ten other boys who were being trained as guards. He heard
their whispers in the night—how easy it would be, to take the
machetes they were given and cut the masters' necks—and he
saw, too, how they stared at him, knowing that his brow looked
so much like that of the master and the master's son. They hated
him for it. Løren was beaten and whipped and bled by the mas-

ters more than any of the other boys, but he had the blood of a Fjernman in his veins. Don't tell him your secrets, they said, or he'll betray you.

There was something else in his veins, too—he knew this ever since the afternoon he served the Elskerinde Jannik one afternoon, pouring her lemongrass tea, and accidentally spilled a scalding drop on her hand. She stood and slapped him across his face hard enough that his lip bled. The sting was with him for days, but all he could think of was how he could hear the whispers that afflicted the Elskerinde. He heard them as though the thoughts were his own. Thoughts of how she'd never be able to forgive herself or her husband for the mistakes they'd made. Whispers that she'd die alone, with no one to love her, not even herself. Her son would come to hold nothing but bitterness for his mother, that he would feel tied to these islands by his mother's wishes. He would wish his own mother dead, and Elskerinde Jannik would attempt to fix this bitterness by doting on her son, but nothing would change. Løren could also feel, just as easily, how he could reach out with his being and silence the whispers in her head, like a hand covering her ears. Løren knew this was kraft, and that if anyone learned of his kraft, he would be killed.

Aksel knew. His kraft emerged within days after Løren realized his own, for Aksel could look to anyone and see the power in them. Kraft wasn't always guaranteed, even if one or both parents had kraft, and so a large celebration was thrown, and the other kongelig of the islands were invited so that Aksel's kraft could be known. Aksel had discovered his kraft when he passed through the plantation days before. He looked to an older man, nearly one hundred years old with his dark skin lined with wrinkles, who sat and shelled peas and peeled potatoes for the kitchen every day, from morning until night. Aksel said that this man had the kraft to see others' dreams as they slept at night, so the man was hung by his neck that same day. Aksel looked

to one of the boys who'd whispered about cutting the masters' necks while everyone else slept, one of the same boys who
looked at Løren with hatred for having the master's blood. This
boy had beaten Aksel in training, as he'd been ordered to do
by Engel Jannik, roaring at Aksel to not let himself be bested
by a slave. Aksel hadn't been pleased that he'd lost and that his
father had hit him in the face and called him a disgrace. Aksel
came to the plantation shed and said that the boy had the kraft
to weaken his opponents. The boy had no such kraft, Løren
knew, but this didn't matter. The child was hung from his neck
beside the old man, who'd already been dead a full day. The
slaves were all forced to gather and watch and were told they
couldn't leave, even after the boy's body stopped twitching,
even as it swung like a wind chime in the breeze. Their bodies still hung as the Fjern arrived to join in the garden party's
celebrations.

And Aksel watched Løren. He smiled at his half brother,
knowing the other's secret. Løren lay awake at night, waiting
for the hands that would drag him to the hanging tree, but they
never came.

Løren trained every morning for hours, preparing to become
a member of the Jannik guard; and after training, he would work
on the plantation, pulling weeds in the lines of crops or running errands for the Elskerinde, who always had such a burning
hatred for him. One afternoon, Løren was sent to pick fruit for
the kitchens, when he found Aksel already waiting for him in
the groves. Aksel held a machete. Løren was afraid his brother
had finally found the courage to kill him, but even still, Aksel
wouldn't swing the blade. Løren asked him why he wouldn't—
asked him why Aksel hadn't yet told their father of his brother's
kraft.

Aksel had intended to kill Løren himself, but Løren could see
the uncertainty in his brother's eyes. Aksel dropped the machete.

"I'll have you killed one day," Aksel had said, and Løren could feel the truth in his brother's promise. "But not yet."

Løren doesn't speak. I struggle to catch my breath, my mind still reeling from the memories, the thoughts, the flood of emotion. After nearly a decade of seeing into the minds of others, I've learned that most live just above the surface, gliding from day to day. But this mind knows what life is worth. Løren is so fully aware of his own impending death that his spirit radiates, honoring his life with every ounce of being. He feels like a bolt of lightning striking and searing the earth.

I want to know more. The wall isn't back up yet. I sink into him once again, and memories rush through me: Løren, crying at night after a beating, running through the groves as Aksel hunts him; Løren, sure that this time his brother would hang him from a tree and watch as he fought to breathe—

"You want to be the heroine of your story," he tells me. "You don't want to be the villain to your people. You want to convince me of your worth. If you convince me of your worth, then perhaps you're worthy of the love of our people, too."

Embarrassment runs through my veins, growing stronger as I realize he can sense this emotion in me. The shame clogs my throat, making it difficult to swallow, impossible to speak. I hadn't realized that Løren could see into me, just as I could see into him when he brought his wall down. His kraft allows a path between us. His ability to see my thoughts is weak, more an aftereffect of my own. He can sense only the strongest emotions in me. He can't control me, though he's tried. When I came to visit him in the library, he held the wall between us, but for just a moment he tried to reach into me, to control my body as I'm able to control others. He couldn't do it. He would've had me cut my own stomach open if he could. He would've had me kill myself, and he would've run.

He wants to run, even now, and escape the islands of Hans Lollik. But his brother would happily use the excuse to have Løren captured and finally killed, as he should've been so many times before. Løren had been sent to his death when he was ordered to kill me in the groves of Lund Helle. I wasn't supposed to have survived and taken him prisoner. But he's grateful, that much he can admit to himself, no matter how much he hates me. And he does hate me. He looks at me and sees fire, tastes blood, smells the rot of his people's bodies. I saved his life, but he wants to escape me as much as he wants to escape his brother. He's my guard, but I can see that Løren will kill me if he has the chance.

There's no block between us. I wonder if he's using kraft on me now—looking into my thoughts, feeling my fears and my hopes, just as I see his own. I now know what everyone around me feels: the uncertainty, the fear that my body isn't my own. But there's another emotion also, one I don't completely understand. I hope that Løren will look into me and know me completely, more than anyone else ever has—that he won't feel pity for me, or a false love for me, but an understanding. I want him to understand me. To realize that I'm not the villain everyone says I am. To comfort me, and tell me there's no need to hate myself as much as I do.

Løren watches me with his steady eyes. "The kongelig will never let you become regent," he tells me. "Konge Valdemar will never choose you or the Jannik name to succeed him."

The wall is between us again, hard as the rocks that stand against the crashing sea.

CHAPTER TWELVE

After stopping at an inn for the night, there's only a day's more journey over particularly rocky hillsides of browning grass, as though the rains haven't fallen on this side of the island in quite some time. There are villages here, houses cramped together on roads of dirt and stone jostling me and Løren back and forth, while Malthe clops alongside the carriage. My other eleven personal guardsmen flank the carriage, while the remaining twenty Lund guards follow behind in close procession. Fjern villagers and their few slaves pause, watching us pass, distrust in their eyes.

The Ludjivik estate emerges over the crest of a hill. There are no guards awaiting an attack, prepared for battle. The groves surrounding the stone manor are failing, that much is easy to see, and the house itself seems to be crumbling before my very eyes. I try to remember what I learned of the Ludjivik as a child. The daughter who died at a young age, the wife who took her own life in grief. Though he has cousins scattered across all the islands of Hans Lollik, Gustav Ludjivik lives here alone. The pity in me for the man grows, yet this is the man I was sent here to kill.

The carriage stops outside the doors, and a slave hurries to greet us with downcast eyes. She invites me into the manor, but puts a hand up to Malthe.

"I'm sorry," she says. "No guardsmen are allowed inside."

Malthe must think the slave is joking, because he only continues on toward the doors, but she steps in his way. "It's an order from Herre Gustav Ludjivik himself."

"It's okay, Malthe," I say. "I can defend myself if I need to." This is what I say, even though I'm not sure it's the truth—but I'm also sure that if we argue for the guards to join me, the bloodshed will begin here and now, before I've had a chance to kill Herre Gustav Ludjivik, as I'd been ordered to do. If there are guards waiting within, I'll have a chance to run back to my own guardsmen, who will easily overpower the Ludjivik.

The floors here are made of wood, not marble; they've lost their shine after generations of scuffing by shoes and heels, and some of the floorboards seem to be accumulating mold. The wallpaper is rotting with stains—water, leaked from the ceiling. There are no paintings, no rugs, no grand furniture. The Ludjivik family is barely hanging on by a thread.

I follow the slave to the sitting room, where Herre Gustav Ludjivik already waits. His scouts must've warned their Herre of our oncoming arrival days before. Gustav Ludjivik seems to be falling apart just as much as his own estate: his pale skin, so white and translucent that I see the veins beneath, as well as the tremble in his legs as he struggles to stand, suggest that a disease has entered his bones. A quick scan of his jittered mind confirms my thoughts. He survived a storm-season sickness years before, but his lungs haven't cooperated as they should, and every night the man wakes coughing and wheezing, skin slicked with sweat.

He presses his lips together. "Please, sit down." He gestures to the couches, fabric thin after years of wear.

It's perverse, being welcomed into the house of the man I'm meant to kill, but still I move to sit. I clench my hands together. I shouldn't waste time. I should complete what I came here to do.

I take a look around the sitting room and the old furniture

that once must've had value, though they're now out of fash-
ion. I think of how lonely it must be in this manor—how easy
it could be to convince yourself that you're more than you're
worth and that you deserve to rule all of Hans Lollik. Gustav
Ludjivik is sick, in both mind and body—but that doesn't mean
he deserves to die, or that I should be the one to kill him.

The man's mind is open in its weakness. I can see flashes of
memory. He was born in these islands. He thinks of them as home
as much as I do. He's never even seen the empire to the north. His
father had whispered to him when he was a child: Their family
has always lived in ruin, yes, but they are kings. They deserve the
crown. They've been blessed by the gods with their divine gifts.
They have skin paler than all the other Fjern, even after generations of being under this sun on these islands. They deserve to
have their family name rule as regent.

The pale-skinned Fjern often believe they deserve so much.
And why shouldn't they? They're told they own the world from
the moment they're born, brought wailing into this world and
put into their smiling mother's arms rather than taken away and
sold to the highest bidder. If I'd been told as a child that I deserve
to own all I see, maybe I would believe it, too. But it's because I
haven't been told this, and they have, that I'll succeed over them;
this I know, because while they sit and wait to be handed this
world, I'll work and I'll fight for my position. I'll succeed, while
they wait for me to fail.

Gustav Ludjivik knows that he'll never be named regent. He's
sent nearly all of the slaves and guardsmen of his manor to the
other islands and told them to fight for their freedom. He has no
use for the slaves of a dying estate. He knows they won't return.
He knows he won't succeed in his rebellion. He knows, too, that
I've come to kill him.

I speak, still delaying the inevitable. "How long have you
been sick, Herre Ludjivik?"

"Does it matter?"

"I suppose you haven't had visitors in some time. You don't want anyone to know you're sick. You wouldn't want to be seen as weak."

"Why're you here, Elskerinde Sigourney Jannik?" he asks, and he doesn't mean his estate. He knows why I've come to him. He means to know why I'm here, in these islands. "Do you feel you're a royal of Hans Lollik now?"

Gustav Ludjivik is like so many of the other kongelig. Watching in amused wonder as I make my way up the ranks of the islands of Hans Lollik. Astonishment that the king doesn't seem to realize that my skin is as dark as a slave's as he invited me into his meeting room, as though he considers me one of the kongelig—as though he really might consider handing me the crown. *Entertainment.* Yes, that's the word Løren had used: I'm entertainment to these kongelig, who haven't yet bothered to kill me because they keep waiting for someone else to do it first rather than waste their own energy and resources.

This is Gustav Ludjivik's last regret: that he'll be killed by me, a slave. The king should've sent my husband to take the man's life. My husband, or even any of the pale-skinned women of Hans Lollik Helle. But to send me is to make a mockery of his death.

He'd been ready to die. Had been willing to take the blade with honor, fearless; but now this insult angers him. "I remember your mother well," he tells me. "She also thought she was a royal of Hans Lollik Helle."

The mention of my mother jolts me. He sees this and smiles. "She was beautiful, your mother," he tells me, "for a slave. She was never insulting. Forever polite, knowing that if anything she said was taken as an insult, she'd be hung by her neck. Always pleasant, so pleasant. And still, she was murdered in her own home, along with the rest of your family. How does that feel, Sigourney Rose? Knowing that even after trying so hard to bend to the will of the kongelig, they killed her?"

He's angry that I'm the one who's been sent to take his life. He thinks he'll die with dignity if he reminds me of my place. He's imagined his death many times now: swift, a blade across the neck, or maybe even his head removed completely. These are the fastest and easiest ways to die, the killings of a merciful executioner. There're so many awful ways to die on these islands. Herre Ludjivik has witnessed them all, and even ordered a few of those deaths himself: burned at the stake; tied by the wrists and left to have the seawater, breeze, and birds pick away at your skin until you're nothing but bones. Being hung from the neck could be merciful if the neck snaps, but it would likely end with you kicking desperately, choking on your own tongue. Drowning: That's what Herre Ludjivik fears most of all. He fears having rocks tied to his ankles sinking him into the depths of the sea, lungs burning as he swallows water. Out of the many ways to die, I have to agree. I fear drowning most of all.

"You, a slave, believe you'll be chosen as regent by marrying that fool of a boy, Aksel Jannik, but the Jannik name carries no weight in these lands, or on Hans Lollik Helle. It holds no respect or power. There isn't a chance Konge Valdemar will choose your name to follow his own."

I humor Herre Ludjivik. "And so you'll have your family replace the Jannik on Hans Lollik Helle?" I ask. "Why would Konge Valdemar choose you?"

"I have my successors—equally worthy."

"In no one's eyes but your own," I tell him. "The rebellions across Lund and Nørup Helle—"

"I thought they might get your attention."

"You've declared war not only on the Jannik and Nørup names, but on all of Hans Lollik."

I've now started the path I must complete. Gustav Ludjivik

clenches his jaw. "Do you believe in dying for what you believe in, Elskerinde Jannik?"

The question surprises me. "I do."

"And so you believe in killing for what you believe in, too."

He says this as fact, not a question. It's not one I'd be proud to admit the answer to aloud, but I know the truth as well as I know air, as well as I know the sea. This, ultimately, is what makes me a kongelig.

Gustav Ludjivik watches me from his seat, waiting for me to begin, and so I enter his mind. There's overwhelming hopelessness in him. It's the sort of hopelessness that's dangerous as it seeps into my own skin and makes me wonder if there's any point to continuing as I do. There's his hatred for me, his disgust—and a warmth flourishing in him as he thinks that if the stories of the gods are true, there's a chance he might see his wife and daughter again soon. I force his lungs to constrict, his airways to close. He begins to choke. This is how it would feel, he thinks, to drown—gasping for air, his chest on fire, his head tightening with pressure. I watch him, hands going to his own throat, grasping—his heart stopping in his chest.

There're no guards waiting to take their revenge. He sent all the fighting slaves to other islands and to their deaths. I return to Malthe and the carriage, Løren still waiting inside, and we leave the estate to arrive at the same inn previously used by nightfall. I try not to think of the monster I am, for when I do, the sickness rises. I might pretend that I had no choice but to take Herre Gustav Ludjivik's life, but I did—yes, of course I did. I could've disobeyed the king, could've left the islands of Hans Lollik and found myself the life of peace that still comes to me in my dreams.

Løren plans to sleep in the slaves' quarters of the inn with the other guards, but I ask him to follow me to my room. The room is cramped, dark, and filled with heat, even as a breeze flows through the small window. The room makes me feel nostalgic. It reminds me of my days traveling the northern empires with Marieke at my side. The cities were so large, made of stone and wood, piss and filth slicking the streets. No one cared about the color of my skin there. They would try to take advantage of us, yes—we didn't know the languages that slipped off tongues, didn't know the customs, and had too much money. It was days after my tenth birthday, when I began to bleed between my legs, that I heard their whispered thoughts and felt their deceit.

My sisters and brother, older than me, didn't have kraft, and neither did my father. My mother had never sat me down and warned me of the possibility. I'd heard rumors that she might've had kraft, but she never denied or affirmed this to any of us. And so, though she'd once warned me of the blood that might come between my legs, cramps splitting through my stomach and my sides, she didn't tell me that I might begin to feel a power in my veins. I thought I was going mad. I could hear the whispers of sellers who sneered at us with bright, pleasant smiles. The cost of bread was half of the coin they were asking from us; the cost of the room where we stayed was only two coins, when they had asked for ten. I was afraid to tell Marieke. Afraid that she would say I'd fallen sick, and would no longer travel with me.

It was only one night as we sat by the fire at an inn when I heard Marieke think on the daughter she'd lost and the man she'd loved. They'd been my mother's slaves, living inside the manor but free to visit Marieke every morning and night. Marieke had waited, wondering why her family didn't come, a potato and pumpkin stew prepared and going cold. Early the next morning, she saw the smoke and the ruins of the manor.

Marieke ran. She ran down to the bay, along the path of the saltwater river, feet sinking into the wet dirt and mangrove branches scratching her. She wouldn't stop running until she found the cave.

I told Marieke that night at the inn that I hadn't known she'd had a daughter, and she looked at me with surprise. She hadn't said a word. She asked me how I'd learned this. I tried to lie. I said Marieke had spoken aloud without her realizing it, but Marieke was hard to fool. Even as she demanded the truth, I could hear the thoughts in her mind, again and again: *The child has kraft. Spirits remain, the child has kraft.*

Marieke had been afraid, yes, this she couldn't keep from me either. Kraft had once been considered a gift of the spirits by islanders, blessings to be nurtured and beloved, but our beliefs were burned away when the Fjern came. With the Fjern and their law to kill any slave with kraft came the fear that islanders who had the power in their veins were cursed. Marieke was afraid of me and of my power. I thought that Marieke would abandon me, or send me back to Lund Helle. But she'd made an oath to my mother, and she stayed by my side. I quickly learned to stay out of Marieke's head, and she in turn taught me to calm myself when I couldn't control my kraft.

I tell all of this to Løren while he sits on the single chair by the window. The wall between us remains, but I can plainly see on his face that he wonders why he should care about such stories.

Friedrich had loved listening to me speak about my journeys in the north. He'd wanted to see those cities for himself, and thought he one day would, once he finally received his freedom from me. He'd say these things and think these things as he kissed me, pulling my dress over my head.

When I peel my dress from my skin, Løren doesn't react. It's only when I walk toward him that he stands. I raise a hand to his cheek, and it's easy to pretend that he's Friedrich for a moment— but he snatches my hand, yanking it away from him, disgust lining his mouth. Shock vibrates through me. No slave has ever dared to touch me like that.

He meets my eye with an expressionless gaze. He waits for me to try again, and I know that if I do, he'll only react the same way. He isn't Friedrich, and he doesn't pretend to want me. I can't use him to pretend I'm accepted by our people. I can't force him to have any love for me. He wants that to be clear, the wall between us gone.

"I'm your mistress," I tell him. "The wife of your owner. Elskerinde Jannik."

He knows this. I'm not the first Elskerinde who has come to him, expecting him to watch as they pulled their dresses from their bodies, ordering him to touch them as though he loved them, even when he'd been only a child. He's been used by multiple women over his years of growing up in these islands, beaten whenever he refused, threatened to be hung and drowned. He isn't unique in this. So many of my people have been used by the Fjern, forced into their beds. Sickness churns through him at the memory of being forced to pleasure women he hated. He'd always known that he was a slave—had understood that he didn't own his life—but the first moment Elskerinde Freja Jannik passed him along to one of her dear friends, he learned for the first time that he didn't own his body, either. He'd thought wrongly that at least his skin was his own, his flesh and bones, but even this belonged to the Fjern as much as they owned their furniture, their crops, the islands themselves.

Løren only feels a coldness at the thought of sharing another's bed. He's never been with another woman of his own accord and has experienced little desire in his life. There was a time when being called to the beds of these women, the cruelty of his father and brother, and his long days training to be a guard, beaten again and again in the hot sun, brought him to the rocks that grow from the sea. He stood there, waiting to find the courage to dive into the waves, hoping that the tide would do the work for him—but the courage never came. And so he returned to the life that was not his.

The fury he has at the thought of sharing my bed sinks into me. It sickens me that I could attempt to do the same to him as so many other women of Hans Lollik Helle have—that I could attempt to take away his choice, make him nothing but a body that I own, that exists for no other reason than to pleasure me. That I could pretend, for even one moment, that he isn't a human with his own thoughts, his own emotions, his own choices. Hot shame runs through me. I pick up my dress, pulling it back on quickly, smoothing down its wrinkles.

Løren had wanted to die, he allowed me to see—but it was because of his desire for death that he knows the worth of his life now. His life isn't defined by the Fjern. His life holds the strength of the generations of spirits who came before him. All the islanders who line up behind him like an army, giving him the power to continue the fight that they could not. These ancestors aren't behind me. They've abandoned me—we both know this. I can feel just as easily, too, that Løren will kill me if I try to touch him again. He'll kill me, even knowing that it'd mean the end of his life as well.

CHAPTER THIRTEEN

Hans Lollik Helle is a surprisingly welcome sight after days of traveling with Løren. Any hope I have for an alliance with him, of convincing him to protect me if any of the kongelig try to take my life, is now gone. In fact, I'm sure there's an even higher chance now that he will kill me himself. I know that I should have him removed as my personal guard; lock him in the library again, or have him executed for attempting to assassinate me so many weeks before, and for putting an arrow through Friedrich's neck. But still I can't help but keep Løren close to me, as though I think there's a chance that I can convince him that I'm worthy of his respect. That I might finally prove to him that I'm a kongelig, yes, but I'm also an islander, and that I deserve the love of my people.

I escape from the boat the moment it's close enough to shore, wetting the ends of my dress and hurrying over the hot sand and dirt back to the airless hall of the Jannik house on the cliffs. I walk across the creaking floors feeling as though I've become the ghost of the former Elskerinde Jannik—wandering the halls, forever lost, seeking revenge for my betrayal. I return to my chambers and to Marieke's solace, ridding myself of my clothes and sinking into a tub of lukewarm water, allowing her to scrub my arms, my back, my hair. I don't tell her about Løren. The shame curls through me, wrapping itself around my throat.

Marieke lays a fresh dress on my bed and holds up a towel for me as I step out of the tub before she returns to her duties. She's quiet with me today, when she would normally nag her reminders to stay focused on my goals, my purpose for being here on Hans Lollik Helle. She won't even meet my eye. I told her once that I respect her too much to invade her mind, so I don't slip into her to see what might be wrong. I worry that Løren told the other slaves what I'd done as soon as we arrived, and so Marieke can't stand the sight of me now: me, this woman who is supposed to be an islander, who is supposed to love her people and yet treats them no better than the Fjern treat their slaves.

Another member of a kongelig family, this time a Nørup, has been found dead. It was an older man, Herre Jens Nørup, and he was known for his love of drink. This is why, they say, his body has been found beneath the cliffs on the rocky shore, his neck snapped, but it's been known for some time that Herre Jens Nørup openly complained of the king's favoritism toward the Niklasson family; he suggested, time and again, that Lothar Niklasson might find himself dead by the storm season's end, and that his nephew, Erik Nørup, would become the new favorite of the king.

There's another glittering party in the courtyard of Herregård Constantjin. All of the kongelig are expected to attend. I don't know if the puppet king will be there, watching us. I don't want to attend the party, but it could be a chance to observe all the kongelig, to see who among them might control the puppet king's strings. I leave for the courtyard party with Aksel, who's disappointed I'm still alive. He doesn't bother to hide his thoughts from me: the daydreams he'd had of a messenger coming with news of the death of his wife, being able to declare that the grief was too much to bear and leaving Hans Lollik Helle, before traveling to the north with Beata Larsen. They would go to the Fjern empire of Koninkrijk. Neither had been, and Aksel longed to see the birthplace of his people. He would be free there; free from these responsibilities he doesn't want, free from the savages and the islands, which, he fears, are turning him into a savage as well. Løren follows behind us without speaking.

The courtyard has its lights, the sun setting prettily on the horizon, sinking beneath the blue water and painting the sky with its pink and red hues. The frogs make their noise, the night birds sing, and fruit bats swoop in and out of the sky, their black wings fluttering shadows in the corners of my eyes. Gentle music plays. A low hum of chatter greets us. Løren moves to stand with the other slaves who line a wall, and Erik Nørup dances with a younger cousin of the Larsen family. The puppet of Konge Valdemar isn't here, but Lothar Niklasson greets us the moment we step into the courtyard.

"What news?" he asks.

I tell him that Herre Gustav Ludjivik is dead, executed by my hand as commanded, and Lothar knows that I speak the truth, and so doesn't ask for any proof. He had no other business with me; he leaves, ready to discuss another important matter with a Solberg cousin who waits near the gardens. Beata Larsen stands beside a low stone wall, looking at the sunset; her back is to us, but I can feel how intensely aware she is of me and Aksel, and how much Aksel wishes he could take her into his arms. I can see the love that had begun between them years before, when both were brought onto the island for the storm season. Beata Larsen had always been a sniveling little thing. He was four years older than the girl, and she followed him and Erik Nørup everywhere they went. Finally, one day he got tired of her, and asked her to play a game. He and Erik led her into the woods and told her to close her eyes and count as high as she could. The young Beata Larsen did as she was told, and Aksel and Erik escaped the groves, laughing all the while. The two were free of Beata, and so ran along the beach's shore and drank guavaberry rum they'd swiped from the kitchens. They returned to their homes for their dinner when the sun began to set. It was only when a messenger came with news that the Larsen child had gone missing that Aksel's blood ran cold.

He was a coward, even then, so he said nothing of the game he and Erik had earlier played; but the moment his parents had gone to bed, Aksel snuck from his room and returned to the groves in the dead of night. He could hardly see a thing. The moon's silver shine was all he could rely on as he stepped through the trees, roots snagging his feet. He called Beata Larsen's name. He called and called and called again, but there was no reply. He was afraid the girl had fallen off a cliff to her death.

Just as he was about to give up, his voice hoarse and his feet sore, he saw a glimmer of pale skin in the moonlight: Beata sat against a tree, knees huddled to her chest, waiting to be found. Aksel ran to her and snatched her arm, dragging her to her feet. He demanded to know why she hadn't said anything when she heard him calling her name, and Beata's only response was that she hadn't wanted to lose the game.

Aksel stopped ignoring Beata after that. He thought of himself as her knight, her rescuer; he doted on her, bringing her flowers and chocolates. He began to look forward to seeing her with every year that passed, began to look forward to spending his days on Hans Lollik Helle. Theirs is what the Fjern would consider a fairy tale romance. I look to the slaves lining the walls, and I realize I've never heard such a story of love between two islanders. It makes me believe that love wasn't made for us. Along with the freedom of my people, the Fjern have taken joy and love as well, declared this a thing that belongs to them alone. Løren watches me, though his eyes are supposed to be fastened to the dirt beneath his feet. He watches me, and he wants me to know that he hates me—hates me for forcing him to come here again, among the kongelig, even knowing the pain they've caused him.

I leave the estate to walk through the breeze, winds blowing the clouds, their shadows moving over the blue of the darkening sea. I walk across the white sand, burning the bottoms of my feet until I stand in the cold waves, the ends of my white dress becoming dark and heavy with salted water. I stand there looking over the ocean until the sun sets completely and the white stars begin to dot the sky. The music of Herregård Constantjin reaches me even here, along with the faint laughter. I can sense the presence that appears behind me, so I'm not frightened when Beata Larsen calls my name.

"Elskerinde Jannik," she says again. She looks startled when I turn around. I turn back to face the sea. "I—I apologize, I didn't mean to frighten you."

"You didn't," I tell her.

She's afraid to speak, scared to tell me her thoughts. She wishes I would simply look into her and know them. She speaks to my back, frustrated that I won't turn to face her. "I've come to tell you that I'm leaving Hans Lollik."

At this I turn around. She looks to the sand. "I've found that I can't stay here. Not any longer."

There's a rush of emotion that isn't easy to untangle, but still I find the string—unweave it, to make sense of the feeling that she can no longer stand to be on this island while the love of her life is married to someone else. It's the greatest tragedy she's ever endured, but she hopes that once she leaves Hans Lollik, she can learn to love another as deeply as she does Aksel Jannik. She can marry, have a family. These politics, this crown—she wants none of it.

"From what Aksel tells me, I know that you're ambitious," she says. She forces a smile, even as it trembles with emotion she tries and fails to hold. "You won't stop until Konge Valdemar chooses the Jannik name to inherit the title of regent. I wish you success," she says, and it enrages me, that even after hurting her—even after taking the love of her life—she genuinely means this. "But I also wish you happiness. What is life if you can't find joy?"

"The throne will bring me joy," I say.

"Will it?" she asks. She steps to me, and there's no measure to my distrust—I look at her hands, expecting a hidden knife, but instead she reaches her palms toward me. "May I, Elskerinde Jannik?"

I want to take her by the shoulders (or better yet, the neck) and shake her—tell her to fight for Aksel if she loves him so much. Tell her to accept Aksel's pleas—escape Hans Lollik with him so that they may become a Fjern fairy tale for the pale-skinned children of these islands. But the Jannik name would become nothing if Aksel were to leave. I'm lucky that he's stayed, grappling with his sense of duty to his family name and his mother's memory, even if he doesn't want the throne himself. If Aksel left, I would become the greatest laughingstock in all of Hans Lollik: a slave attempting to become a queen, abandoned by her husband for another woman. I still need him. So I say nothing, and I take Beata Larsen's waiting hands.

The joy that spreads through me begins at the fingertips— warm, stretching through my hands, over my skin, tingling with comfort. I feel as I do in my bath, listening to Marieke's reassuring words; sitting in the sunlight, heat upon my cheeks; the peace I feel rolling through the hills of Lund Helle, seeing the green fields outstretched before me. I feel as I did when I was a child wrapped in my mother's arms, listening to Inga's songs, Ellinor's laughter, Claus's stories. Safety. Love. Yes, that's the secret to Beata Larsen, I realize—she's filled with so much love. Beata Larsen believes me beneath her, in the way that a human might think the goat is beneath them, incapable of true thought and feeling. But still, she tells herself that she loves me, in the

way that a child might begin to love and care for that goat, playing games with each other, until finally the goat is slaughtered.
She sees the pain of my people, and she wonders if it can be right
for the Fjern to treat us the way they do. She prays for all of our
souls, islanders and Fjern together, and hopes that the gods may
forgive the sins of her people. But still, this is all that she will do.

I open my eyes, and Beata is watching me. She tells me she'll
leave for Larsen Helle in the morning, and that by month's end,
she will travel to the north. This will be the last time either I or
Aksel will see or hear from her. She curtsies with respect, and
walks the path from the beach, leaving me in the sand, the waves
crashing around my ankles, foaming onto the shore.

I dream when I sleep. The maze of the Rose manor twists, flowing green in the moonlight, stark against the black sky and its
smear of silver stars; the maze begins to close in on me, roots
attempting to trip me, wrapping around my ankles, branches
reaching as I turn left, then right, then right again—and in the
center of the maze stands not my mother but Freja Jannik. She
waits in her white dress, and when she opens her mouth, she
screams, but no sound fills my ears. I struggle against the roots
that tighten around my ankles, the branches that tear at my hair,
and I reach out for Freja Jannik's neck—wrap my hands around
her cold skin. She begins to rot in death. Her skin peels away
at the corners of her lips, and maggots crawl from her nose, her
eyes. The maze swallows me.

I jump from my bed, sweating, afraid that I'm still tangled in
the brush of the maze—but instead I find myself in my room,
tangled in my sheets. Dawn begins to peek over the hills with
rays of pink streaking through the dark-purple sky. There's a
shout in the morning's quiet.

I hurry to my wardrobe, pull on a thin dress, and race out of
my room, down the stairs and to the entryway. Aksel turns the

corner sharply, knocking into me, but doesn't stop to apologize or to acknowledge me. In his flurry of emotion, he hasn't even seen me—there's no thought, only pain. He disappears down the hall, toward the gardens. I slow down. The slave girl named Agatha speaks to Malthe in the entrance. My eyes automatically search for Marieke, but she isn't there.

"What is it?" I say. My heart hammers at the thought that Marieke is hurt, or worse—but Malthe steps forward, and I force myself into his mind. A messenger came to the barracks in the dead of night, leading Malthe down the dirt path that cuts through the groves, alongside each of the heads of the kongelig guards. He's returned now. He has already told Aksel. Even though I can see the image he's witnessed with his own eyes, it's difficult to believe.

"News from the hilltop," he says. Marieke's girl has already heard—a series of her thoughts come to me, but I push them aside, waiting for Malthe to speak the words. "Elskerinde Beata Larsen," he says. "She's been found dead, my lady."

"Drowned?"

Malthe is unsurprised, nonjudgmental, that I've seen his thoughts. "Yes," he confirms.

I see the image again: Beata Larsen, skin already turning blue, resting upon the shore. The very beach where we'd stood only hours ago. Lifeless, eyes open and staring at the gods, yellow hair tangled with sand and seaweed and shells. She's the first of the kongelig in direct line for the crown to die this storm season. Perhaps a dream was placed in Beata Larsen's mind and she imagined walking from her bed and into the arms of Aksel Jannik, only to wake and find herself at the bottom of the ocean floor.

Aksel. By the gods, I hate him as much as I hate any of the Fjern—more, since I'm tied to him and depend on his name—but I can't help but think of the pain he must be in now, having learned of the death of his beloved. I feel ill. How easily could that have been me, drowned and dead on the shore?

I walk farther down the hall, away from Agatha and the gathering crowd of slaves. Malthe knows to follow.

"Do you have any idea who might've killed her?" I ask, voice lowered.

"The other heads of guards felt—assumed—that she'd—"

"Killed herself?" She'd told me she was leaving in the morning—but she never said how she would be leaving Hans Lollik Helle. Still, though it's possible that she killed herself, I know from the peace she felt yesterday—the joy, the excitement at being alive, the possibility of finding a new love—that Beata Larsen wouldn't have willingly died.

"Forgive me, my lady," he says, "but it's well known that she'd been the mistress of Aksel Jannik. Most felt she'd succumbed to heartbreak."

"An assumption like that only pulls suspicion away from a possible murder," I tell him.

"Elskerinde Larsen had no enemies."

Except, he thinks, *you.*

I nearly laugh, but the amusement dies in my throat. All on Hans Lollik know that Aksel Jannik loves only Beata Larsen. All know that I'm the only person on this island who has any true reason to dislike Beata as much as I truthfully do. None of the kongelig viewed the girl as a threat. She had no ambitions for the crown. She'd only stayed on this island out of a feeling of responsibility to the Larsen name, and since she'd planned on renouncing any claim to the crown, the kongelig had even less reason to kill the girl.

"You don't think I did it, do you?" I ask Malthe.

He pauses. It's the first time he's considered being dishonest with me. "I have my suspicions," he adds after a moment, "but I don't think you'd be careless or foolish enough to murder Beata

Larsen. However," he adds, "my beliefs aren't shared by all, I will admit to that. You'll need to be careful, Elskerinde Jannik. It's clear that someone means to have you blamed for Elskerinde Larsen's death."

Malthe marches out of the hall, leaving me to the tide of thoughts. Death on Hans Lollik Helle isn't surprising or new, but Beata's murder has left me shaken. Even more frightening is that I know I had a dream last night. A dream where I was, once again, in a maze that led me away from my home—perhaps away from my bed, down the halls, to wrap my hands around Beata Larsen's neck.

CHAPTER FOURTEEN

The air of Hans Lollik Helle has shifted. The wind grows stronger, and waves crash onto the shore. I stand among the kongelig, their pale skin turning red in the heat, slaves lined up behind us. Beata Larsen's body is placed on a boat and pushed into the sea. The waves carry her away quickly, the fire that was sparked growing fiercely in the breeze, consuming the white flowers that covered her hair and her dress and the boat itself until it's nothing more than a red flame careening into the distance. The flame, this ceremony, is one that's meant for the bodies of the Fjern. They stay atop the sea, eyes turned to their gods, while my people, with their dark skin, are forced to walk the ocean floor. And when I die, where will I be?

The kongelig around me cry to themselves, wiping their eyes and patting their cheeks. I can feel that for most of them, it's an act—it would be insensitive not to cry at a moment like this. Aksel can barely breathe. He struggles not to let grief overtake him. But he can't stand next to me without letting his hatred leak from his skin. He's also heard the rumors. The rumors that I'm the one who killed Elskerinde Larsen in a jealous rage. He believes them. He wants to wrap his hands around my neck—to shout at Løren, who stands behind us, to cut his machete into my stomach. Aksel's hands twitch with the effort to stay still at his sides.

Many had seen me leave the gardens the night before, Beata following me. There must've been an argument, a fight. I must've asked Beata to meet with me on the shore that very night, or followed her without her noticing, and wrapped my hands around her neck and pushed her into the waves, hoping she would be drawn out into the ocean. The ocean betrayed me, they say, by bringing her body back to shore. Some even whisper that though Elskerinde Larsen had returned to the gardens the night before, is it not possible that my kraft, which I shouldn't rightfully have, could've tricked them all? Perhaps I made them see a vision of Beata Larsen walking into the gardens, when the girl was already dead.

We're meant to stand in remembrance of her, and some of the kongelig do. Beata was beloved. They believe that she never had a wicked bone in her body. Even from a young age, most agreed that had it not been for her family's lack of coin, she would've made a most benevolent queen. Her parents had been kind-hearted, and all of the Fjern gathered have empathy for her, since she had been orphaned as a child and was forced to become an adult long before she ever came of age. They have always shown Beata Larsen kindness. Maybe this is why she had so much love in her, while rage has always filled my veins. Though I had the same fate as the girl, I was never shown the same kindness.

As soon as the ceremony is complete, Aksel leaves. He walks across the shore, in the opposite direction from the Jannik house, disappearing into the groves. I don't know where he's going, and I suppose I don't much care. I'm grateful that he isn't returning to the house, where I'll have to feel his constant hatred for me. I should leave as well, but I linger. I want to show the kongelig that I'm not afraid of them and their rumors, even though I am. The kongelig stay where they are as well, watching me. I want to show them that I'm innocent, looking each of them in the eye, even as doubt vibrates through me. It's easy, when surrounded by people who question you, to begin questioning yourself. And the nightmare—the maze, the roots, Freja Jannik's open mouth twisting in her silent scream, my fingers reaching for her throat…

The kongelig believe I did it. They believe I strangled the poor girl out of envy, out of fear that she would be chosen by both Aksel Jannik and Konge Valdemar. And even if the kongelig hadn't believed this, they would've proclaimed it anyway. They want me dead. They eye me, all of them, images of my death coming to me with every pulse. My body will hang from a tree like a spoiled fruit, and once my body swings in the breeze, they won't put me on a boat, or even let the waves carry me away. They'll let me rot there, under the sun and in the salt air.

Jytte Solberg is the first to speak, under the gaze of all the kongelig. Her voice doesn't shake when she asks me, "Why did you do it, Elskerinde Jannik?"

I tell her I did not. The kongelig murmur to one another. None believe me. Jytte narrows her eyes. Beata Larsen had always been a good girl. Jytte, ten years her senior, had looked over her like a little sister. The Solberg family had adopted Beata into their home once her parents were killed, and though Jytte didn't grow up with Beata in their home—the girl had lived with cousins on a nearby plantation—the two had spent many days together, sipping lemongrass tea on the Solberg manor porch, enjoying the breeze in their white lace dresses.

As the last surviving heir of the Larsens, Beata had become Elskerinde as a child, and came to Hans Lollik Helle for the storm season. The girl had no family and, sitting at the table of kongelig, she was afraid. Jytte had taken her under her wing, told her whom she could trust and whom she should be wary of; how to sit with a straight back and how to meet the eye of the other Fjern. For though she had always been a timid and kind-hearted thing, the other kongelig would likely pick her apart if she showed any sort of weakness. Jytte believes I killed Beata

Larsen, but she blames herself as well. She should've told Beata to run: leave the islands, giving up her family's position within the kongelig, and save herself. Not many survive this island of Hans Lollik Helle.

I think to myself that I'll stand here as the kongelig do, proving to them that I won't be scared away, that I deserve to be here on the shore in mourning as much as they. Jytte Solberg is the first to turn away from me, and then finally all the rest leave as well.

The wait isn't long. I sit on my balcony with Marieke, feeling the question in her pulse whether I want to or not: Did I kill that girl? I want to tell Marieke that I did not, with all my certainty, but I think again of the dream that had taken me into the depths of my mother's maze, where I'd wrapped my hands around Freja Jannik's throat.

"You're distracted by the kongelig's games," Marieke tells me. She's never hesitated to chide me. "You've forgotten why you came here to Hans Lollik Helle."

"I haven't forgotten. The game is changing. The rules are different. I can't simply convince the king that I'm worthy to become regent. Konge Valdemar isn't real. It's like he's an illusion, or a corpse returned to life. One of the kongelig controls him. If I can discover who it is—figure out what's happened to the king—then maybe I'd have a chance of taking the crown."

I tell her that I'm sure it's the same kongelig who attempted to walk me over the cliffs of Hans Lollik Helle, and who means to blame me for Beata's death—the same kongelig who has killed Beata Larsen, and perhaps even Dame Ane Solberg and Herre Jens Nørup as well. "Jytte Solberg wants to see me burn more than any of the other kongelig, besides Aksel, but I can't see how she could have the power to conjure a false image of the king. Her kraft controls pain. And it couldn't be Aksel— he's weak, barely has the ability to sense another's power."

"All of these questions," Marieke says, "and no closer to your answers."

"I'm trying, Marieke," I tell her, and regret the words the moment they leave my mouth. I sound too much like a child, crying to Marieke about the hardships of my life. We'd been in the north, traveling across the empires, when one night she told me to stop my whining—she was tired of listening to me complain. *Yes, you have hardships,* she'd told me. *Now, what will you do about them?*

"You're trying," she repeats, "but you're not trying hard enough. This is a game the kongelig play, and you're losing. Have you forgotten yourself, Sigourney?"

"No," I tell her.

"Have you forgotten your mother? Your sisters, your brother?"

I can feel the frustration building. "Of course I haven't."

"Then continue to fight," she tells me. "Fight until you win."

We sit in silence. Marieke takes my hands. If the kongelig come to kill me, there isn't anything she can do now but pray that the spirits will welcome me. She prays that my mother will be one of those spirits, waiting for me with a smile, arms wrapping around me; my sisters and brother, who would look exactly as I'd seen them last—not ushered into the gardens with their tears and screams—I don't want to think on that—but rather the way they looked as we were getting ready for the party earlier that night: Inga in her pretty dress of lace and Ellinor with ribbons in her hair, Claus with his buttoned shirt and smile. They'd look exactly as they had that night, and the islands would be the paradise they'd once been before the Fjern ever came: the land free of plantations; the people walking back out of the sea with their freedom; houses and villages hidden in the groves, lush with mango and guava and bananas. I would walk the shore with my mother, her hand in mine.

Before the sun reaches its height in the sky, they come for me. A messenger and the kongelig's guards arrive in a line, ready to escort me. We walk the path, dirt burning the bottoms of my feet through the soles of my sandals. The slaves working the groves don't look my way as I'm led to my death. Malthe and Løren follow, and I'm surrounded as I'm brought to the courtyards of Herregård Constantjin. I have no friends here. I know that no one will save me. If I'm declared guilty, Malthe's first loyalty is to the crown always, as is that of all of the guards on this island. Løren will happily see me dead. None of the kongelig will speak in my defense. They'll lie to see me killed; they'll lie, and they'll say that I deserved it.

We gather in the courtyard. White flowers are strung around the walls, petals beneath our feet. The feeling that grasps me now is breathlessness, a calloused hand over my mouth, a whisper in my ear—my mother would've wanted me to live. But here I am now, before the kongelig, with their pale, unsmiling faces.

And there's the husk of the king. Konge Valdemar sits in a grand chair at the end of the courtyard, thorns and flowers on either side of him. The crowd of kongelig part, and there's a passage I must walk alone. My legs tremble, my hands shaking. I hold them together as I walk, all of the eyes of the kongelig on me, and the king himself, with his empty gaze, the corners of his lips upturned into the slightest smile. I stop before him and bow until I'm kneeling. The courtyard's stone scrapes my knees through the thin material of my white dress. My eyes should be kept to the ground, this I know, but I let them rise to meet the king's gaze.

The man is a corpse without a soul. His chest moves as though he breathes, and his eyes blink as though he sees, but he's nothing but skin and flesh and bones. The kongelig are fools. This is the true threat to them—this and whoever controls the king now, perhaps even standing here among us in this very courtyard— and they don't realize it. They only bow in their ignorance, hoping for scraps, a chance to rule. And yet here I am, kneeling before the puppet king, waiting for him to sentence me to death. Perhaps I'm the greatest fool of all. I'd come here to Hans Lollik

Helle thinking that I would have to play one particular game—but the rules of that game have completely shifted. I need to know who among the kongelig controls the king. If I can discover who holds the puppet's strings, then I can discover the true murderer of Beata Larsen. I can take their power—fight until I earn the title of regent.

The ruling begins. Konge Valdemar speaks, his voice echoing through the courtyard, even filled with all the kongelig of the island and their families and friends. "Elskerinde Sigourney Jannik," he says, "you've been accused of murdering the Elskerinde Beata Larsen."

My voice is thick, my throat raw. "Who accuses me?"

Aksel steps forward. My eyes meet his, and I can see it plainly, how much he wants to see me dead. He's never wanted anything more. Even his desire for Beata pales in comparison to his need to see my body hanging from a tree.

"My king," I say, "though it's humiliating for me to admit as his wife, we all know that he loved Beata Larsen. My husband is sick with grief, desperate for someone to blame."

"I blame the one who killed Elskerinde Beata Larsen," Aksel says, his eyes back to the regent. "My wife is a hateful woman. She told me she would kill me. Cut my throat in my sleep."

"Is this true?" Konge Valdemar asks.

Aksel continues. "She wishes me dead—all of us. She hates the kongelig, blames us for the deaths of her family. Whoever killed her mother and her siblings should have killed Sigourney Rose that day as well. She never should've stepped foot on Hans Lollik Helle."

"Whoever killed my mother and my siblings?" I repeat. "Was it not your family's guards, Aksel, who killed them, and tried to kill me as well?"

I get to my feet, though the king has not yet given me permission to rise, and turn to face the rest of the kongelig. "Was it not each family who agreed? You all know what you've done.

You all know that you're guilty. Yet you accuse me, ready to sentence me to my death, knowing that I'm innocent."

The kongelig are silent, their hatred burning. The king makes an expression, as though he isn't pleased, though I feel no emotion from him. Still, he says nothing of it as he tilts his head and calls forth anyone else who would like to speak. Jytte Solberg steps forward.

"Sigourney Rose connived her way onto this island," she says. "She's a snake. I hear it was only once she began meeting with the Elskerinde Jannik that the woman made it known that Sigourney Rose was to marry her son. It was no coincidence, and we all know of this woman's kraft. Kraft to read minds, kraft to control. Who is to say that she didn't force the late Elskerinde Jannik to speak these words?"

"I did not," I say, my voice rising. "I made my wishes known to Elskerinde Jannik, hoping for a union, and she agreed."

Elskerinde Solberg ignores that I've spoken. "Sigourney Rose should be nothing but a slave. Slaves are executed for having kraft, not rewarded with positions of power. She doesn't deserve to stand as a member of the kongelig."

"And so because I'm an islander, you'll have me killed?" I ask. "I'm not on trial for the color of my skin. You can lie to yourselves, but I refuse. I will speak the truth. I've done nothing wrong."

Jytte Solberg returns to her place in the crowd with the kongelig.

There's silence but for the blowing of a breeze. The king asks if anyone will step forward on my behalf. All eyes are on me. The slaves, waiting against the wall, stare at the ground—all except for Løren, who watches with a darkened gaze.

"My king," I say, "I ask for Lothar Niklasson to speak."

Lothar steps forward, brow heavy. "I have no words to speak on Sigourney Jannik's behalf, your grace."

"I ask to be questioned by Herre Niklasson. No lie can leave my tongue if he asks me a question. Ask me if I killed Elskerinde Beata Larsen."

The king taps the armrest of the chair he sits in. "You're requesting an interrogation by Herre Niklasson. Do you understand that we won't only ask about the murder you're accused of but also about your tactics in finding yourself on my island?"

I nod my understanding. The crowd parts once again, and Lothar stands beside the king, hands grasped behind his back. I'm sweating in the heat, trying not to show the tremble in my hands, my legs.

Lothar Niklasson speaks. "Elskerinde Sigourney Jannik," he says, "also known as Sigourney Rose: What do you know of Elskerinde Beata Larsen's death?"

I can feel his kraft like vines wrapping around my neck, slithering into my open mouth and down my throat, pulling the truth from me. "I'd had a nightmare where I killed Elskerinde Freja with my bare hands," I say, "and when I woke up, I learned that Beata Larsen had been strangled and drowned."

"And did you do it?" Lothar asks. "Was it you?"

I shake my head, the truth freeing itself from my lips. "No, it wasn't me."

My voice rises through the courtyard. Murmurs follow. The expression on Aksel's face is a twist of rage.

"She's lying," he says. "She's lying, I know she is—she's found a way around Lothar Niklasson's kraft."

"Are you accusing me of weakened blood?" Lothar asks.

Aksel's face flushes and his gaze drops. "No, Herre Niklasson."

Lothar nods his head at the king. "She tells the truth. She did not kill Beata Larsen."

Whispers string through the crowd again, and I can feel the surprise, the frustration, the questions. I stay firm on my feet, raising my head. At least if they kill me now, they won't be able to tell themselves the lie that I deserve it—that I'm being

punished for taking away Beata Larsen's life. If they kill me,
they'll know it's unjustified, and that I've died only because they
hate me.

Jytte Solberg reminds Lothar that there are still more questions to be asked, and so he proceeds.

"How did you find your way onto this island?"

I tell him that Elskerinde Jannik and I agreed that I would
make a good match for Aksel Jannik; because I was betrothed
to be married, the king sent me a letter of invite to join the
kongelig for the storm season. Jytte says that the question isn't
narrow enough, so Lothar tries again.

"Did you take advantage of the late Elskerinde Jannik in any
way?" he asks. "The woman was aging, sickly. Did you force her
to agree to let you marry her son?"

"No," I say, relieved that this is enough of a truth. "I didn't
force her to agree." But I can feel slivers of truth rising. As
though sensing there's more to be said, Lothar continues.

"How did she come to agree to let you marry her son?" he asks.

I'm quiet. When I try to open my mouth, the words that I
hoped wouldn't come linger, swelling in my throat, heavy on
my tongue. The kongelig are waiting; the king leans forward.
Aksel's eyes are red as he watches me, his chest heaving, fists
tight. He's suspected, but he's never known for sure—and now,
finally, he'll know the truth of his mother.

I tell Lothar, "I used my kraft on Elskerinde Jannik."

Aksel demands justice, but Lothar raises a hand to silence
him. "How did you use your kraft?"

"I gave her my thoughts. Thoughts suggesting I'd make a
good match for her son. Her mind was frail; she mistook these
thoughts to be her own. I took away her memories," I add,
Lothar's kraft forcing all of the truth from my mouth, "when I
knew that this would only make her more ill."

"Did you kill Elskerinde Jannik?"

"I did not," I say. "She was already dying, and she passed of natural causes in her old age; but taking her memories helped this process."

"Why did you do this?"

"I wanted her to die more quickly, so that I could wed Aksel Jannik as soon as possible, and so that I could come to Hans Lollik Helle to be considered by Konge Valdemar as the next regent."

Laughter follows this, but there's little mirth in the crowd. There's cruelty in the gazes of the kongelig, a readiness to see me punished. Punished not only for my actions but for thinking myself their equal. The kongelig want to remind me of my place. Aksel, however, doesn't just want to see me whipped and beaten. He's shaking with rage. He wants to kill me himself. I fooled him, this he already knew—suspected that I might've used my kraft to convince the late Elskerinde Jannik that I should marry her son— but Aksel didn't know the role I'd played in his mother's death.

Konge Valdemar raises his hands, and the laughter and whispers are silenced. We all wait to hear what the king's ruling will be. The king is controlled by one of the kongelig, of that I'm sure—one of the kongelig who means to kill each of us until it's too late to stop them, who means to take control of Hans Lollik Helle and all of its islands in a way that will seem innocent, blameless, so that there will be no retaliation or rebellion. And if Konge Valdemar is controlled by a kongelig, that surely means there's no chance the kongelig will let me leave this island alive.

The king speaks. "Not guilty of Elskerinde Beata Larsen's murder," he says, "or of the death of Elskerinde Jannik, but guilty of scheming and conspiring your way onto this island of mine." He leans forward with a smile. "What do you think your punishment should be, Elskerinde Jannik?"

I raise my head, holding my breath. "I believe my punishment should reflect my crime, and not the kongelig's hatred of me."

Konge Valdemar smiles. When he declares that I won't be

killed, whispers stream from the kongelig gathered. Aksel doesn't wait for the rest of the sentencing; he turns on his heel and leaves, walking out of the courtyard, his blistering rage following him.

"You'll instead stay here on Hans Lollik Helle," Konge Valdemar says, "continuing your role as Elskerinde Jannik—attending my meetings, giving your updates on the islands under your rule, Lund Helle and Jannik Helle. But know that I'll never give you what you wanted," he tells me. "You worked so hard to get onto this island, in the hopes that I would hand you the crown; I will never name you or your husband regent. You will never be chosen as my successor."

The king stands, and the judgment is complete. He leaves, Lothar Niklasson following closely behind. The other kongelig are slower to leave. They watch me, waiting to see what I'll do next. It's only when I turn to walk through the courtyard, my palms still shaking, that Jytte Solberg approaches, standing in front of me so that I can't take another step.

"The king has declared that you're to remain on Hans Lollik Helle," she tells me, "perhaps knowing that's a death sentence in itself. You won't survive the storm season."

I push past her before she can say another word and continue on the path to the Jannik house, Løren following closely behind. He doesn't speak, but the wall that remains between us wavers. I feel pity in him. Pity for me. Not for the king's ruling—he couldn't care less about that—but having witnessed me, surrounded by the Fjern who have so much hatred for me, taking their judgment with my raised chin. Løren knows how it feels to be surrounded by those who have no love for him—but I don't want or need his pity. I know now that I've been a fool, like all the kongelig, to kiss the feet of a puppet, when all along I should have been searching for the one who holds the strings.

CHAPTER FIFTEEN

Aksel doesn't return to the Jannik house, and I have no plans to leave. I'm no longer in line for the throne, but I take Jytte Solberg's threat seriously. The kongelig's hatred of me has only grown, and they don't believe that I should be on this island, nor that I should even be alive, after everything I've admitted to in Lothar's questioning. It's clear to me that the second I leave the Jannik house, my life will be at risk. Any one of the kongelig could be lying in wait, ready to kill me and make it seem like an accident—push me from the cliff, or hang me from a tree and forge a note in my hand to make it seem like I'd taken my own life. I'm too afraid to leave the house. Marieke tells me this means the kongelig have won.

"Isn't it all right to be afraid?" I ask her. "My mother must've been terrified for her life, before the kongelig killed her."

"She was," Marieke admits. "And yet she continued. She wasn't fighting only for herself. She was fighting for the islands. She couldn't afford to hide away in her home. She couldn't afford to be afraid of death. Her life didn't belong to her. It belonged to our people. They needed her."

Maybe that's why I'm so afraid now. I don't live for our people the way my mother did. I only live for myself. I live for my own goals, my own ambitions—my own need for vengeance.

To make the kongelig pay for taking my family away. To relish taking their power.

Marieke runs her fingers through my tight curls, strands yanking at my scalp. She used to do this with her own daughter, she allows me to feel. Her little girl had been a wild thing. She'd play in the sea from morning until night. Marieke was sure that the girl had been nothing but one of the spirits of these islands, trapped in the body of a child. Marieke, the girl, and the girl's father lived together in a little house that swayed in the breeze, on the cliffs of Rose Helle, looking down at the manor and the sea. Every morning before the sun would rise, the girl and her father would walk hand in hand down the hillside to work on the plantations for their mistress, Elskerinde Rose, and every night they would return.

The girl would tell her mother stories of what she had done that day—picked mango, pulled weeds. Her father would kiss Marieke good night before he went to sleep. Marieke was grateful, because some nights she could pretend that this is what it might feel like to be free. And she knew, too, that she should have love for the Elskerinde Rose. Mirjam Rose was not like the Fjern. She would not sell Marieke's little girl or the girl's father, and Mirjam Rose would not beat any of them out of spite. Yet sometimes, on the darkest of nights while she lay awake, Marieke couldn't forget that even though her life was not as painful as the lives of so many in these islands, she still wasn't free. And in those moments, she had a spark of hatred for the Elskerinde Rose. She hated the woman, for even though Mirjam Rose had her own scars, and even though Mirjam Rose knew the pain of her people, the Elskerinde still hadn't let them go.

Marieke plaits my hair, and I ask her if she loved her daughter's father. "I've never heard of one slave loving another," I tell her.

"I did love him," she tells me, "though I shouldn't have. Even with your mother, as kind as she was, I knew that there could be no joy for us. He disagreed. He believed finding our joy was the only way our people could survive. Even in the face of pain, the hardships we endured, we had to remember our joy, our laughter, the love we had for one another.

"For a while, I believed he'd proven me wrong. He wouldn't leave me alone when we were young, that boy," she tells me. "Every single morning, he would walk across the plantation before we were to begin our work and he would bring me the most beautiful shell he'd been able to find on the beach the night before. He did this for years. Eventually I had several bowls and jars filled with nothing but the most beautiful shells. Until, finally, I decided to meet him on the beach while he was looking for another, and, well—I won't tell you the rest." She smiles. "But he was wrong in the end. He died, and my little girl died, and you're here on this island with their killers, too afraid to bring them to justice."

I walk the gardens of the Jannik house, the newly planted mango and guava and sugar apple trees' leaves bristling under the sun, the rose mallow and bougainvillea blooming red. I sit on a stone bench, looking out at the blue of the sea, the islands of Hans Lollik shining green in the distance. I think about the kongelig, and who among them could possibly control the king; who has tried to kill me, and has succeeded in killing Beata Larsen, and perhaps Ane Solberg and Jens Nørup as well.

None hold the kraft to control illusions, dreams, or hallucinations—unless their very kraft over illusion has tricked us all. Unless one of the kongelig pretends to have a different kraft, when they actually have the ability to control the reality that surrounds us. I run through the list of kongelig and each of their motivations: Lothar Niklasson with his cold, calculating eyes. The Nørup twins, who have seemingly no need for the crown, though perhaps this is as much a hoax as the king. Patrika and Olsen Årud, who—though foolish and arrogant—might enjoy this cruel game they play. Perhaps Olsen has had a power all along, only pretending that he has no kraft in his blood.

Ironically, I don't think Jytte would be behind the king or these murders, though her ambitions seem to rival only mine. If she had such a power, she'd do as the culprit does now: wait silently for their moment to strike, hidden in the shadows. Jytte does neither of these things, and she mourns the death of Beata Larsen, though I suppose this could be a part of her game as well. I'm certain that Aksel wouldn't have killed his beloved Beata Larsen.

I'd always known Lothar Niklasson to be the greatest threat, but maybe I'd been too quick to dismiss Patrika and Olsen Årud for their foolishness, and too quick to believe that neither of the Nørup twins have any true desire for the crown.

Løren, who's to be at my side at all times whenever I'm not in the house, stands in the shade on the porch. It's a possibility also, I suppose, that anyone on this island might hold the kraft to control this false illusion of the king—even an islander like Løren. He could be pretending to have an ability that blocks my own, hiding his true kraft. He meets my gaze unblinkingly. He thinks I'm brave to be here, when he could so easily push me from the cliffs and into the ocean below.

"But how would you escape?" I ask him. "Malthe wouldn't let you get very far."

"How do you know that?" he says. "Malthe might congratulate me and escort me to the boats himself." When I don't respond, he tells me that he would make his way to the mangroves in the bright of day and hide there until nightfall, which he learned in his younger years was better than running for the mangroves at night, when the masters and guards would expect a slave to run. Once most of the night had passed, and the sky was beginning to show the morning sun's light, he would swim. There would be sharks, and he would be tired, but he'd swim for as long as he could, as though his life depended on it, because it did. He would try to make it to Larsen Helle; it was the closest island, though also the most dangerous, as there were few mangroves to hide in and it has open, rocky shores. He would rest for a few hours before he'd swim again, next for Årud Helle.

"It'd be impossible to swim that long, and for that far, with only such a short break in between. Why wouldn't you try to find a boat?"

"The Fjern look for slaves on boats without masters," he tells me. "I wouldn't last an hour. At least in the sea, if someone sees me, I can try to swim beneath the waves until I've lost them."

"You wouldn't last long," I say again. "You'd drown."

He already knows this, he lets me sense—he's already tried to escape from these islands. The first time he'd attempted to escape from Jannik Helle was when he was eleven years old— had run late at night, while everyone was asleep, and ran until he reached the shore. He'd hidden a raft there, one he'd built over long months, and pushed it across the sand until it was atop the waves. He climbed onto the raft, pushed out with his paddle, and made it past the coral reef and the tide—but the raft began to sink under the rougher water, and before long he was in the sea, sinking in the current, pulled beneath and knocking his head on coral—

He should've died then. So many times the boy should've been killed. But a guard had seen him trying to escape. He pulled Løren from the sea, and the child was hung from a tree by his wrists. Engel Jannik whipped any slave who attempted to run away, whipped them until it was up to fate whether they would survive; but today, he handed the whip to Aksel, and would not let the boy stop beating his brother until Løren's eyes closed and he stopped breathing. He was taken from the tree, and again, Løren should've died—but he always lived, always survived.

Løren didn't stop trying to run away. When he came to Hans Lollik Helle, he tried again two times. In the first attempt he was caught in the mangroves, but in the second, he'd swum from night until morning, swum until he thought it might be better to let himself drown. His feet finally reached sand and rock, and he lay on the bay like a body washed ashore. He was found like that, so exhausted he couldn't move, let alone run. The guards dragged him to his feet. This is what broke him. Not the whipping or the beating he received afterward, not being starved for a week and having the bottoms of his feet cut open. It was finally finding his freedom—for even a moment, lying on the rocks of another shore and knowing he had escaped—but being unable to find the willpower to get to his feet.

"Will you try again?" I ask him.

"Yes," he says, "but not until I know I can escape."

This is bold of him to say, he knows; it isn't something he should so easily admit to his mistress. Not something he should say, implying that he means to kill me and whoever else might stand in his way. But he isn't afraid to speak this truth. He isn't afraid to look away from my gaze, even now. Løren is fearless. He has no reason to be afraid. His life isn't his own, and so he feels he's already dead. Not all islanders of Hans Lollik feel this way, but Løren lets me see that he was dead the moment he was pushed from his mother's hips. His father might as well have run the blade through the infant's neck. What could a dead man have to fear, when he might be fighting for a chance to live?

When I ask Løren if he'll come with me to Herregård Constantjin, he doesn't ask why—he doesn't care to know the reason, and only vaguely suspects it might be another garden party or council meeting. It's his duty to follow me, regardless the reason, so that's what he does—silently, out of the gardens and down the path. Night is falling, and the noise of the island's birds and frogs grows the closer we get to the white manor. I can sense Løren's confusion growing as well. There're no lights in the courtyard, no other kongelig wandering the path with their slaves to arrive at the council meeting. We're alone here.

Though his ability to read my thoughts is weak, Løren must've reached into my mind, because he asks, "Are you sure you want to be caught wandering the manor without permission after you've just been accused of murder?"

I laugh, not because this is funny but because it feels odd to hear Løren speak to me as though we're acquaintances—friends, even. This is usually something Marieke would say, and in exactly that tone of voice, too. "Probably not," I admit.

He asks me what I'm looking for.

"Something. Anything." A clue to this mystery of Konge Valdemar and who might be controlling him. I want to wander the manor with Løren, too—to look at his face and attempt to read his mind, to see if he might let the truth slip. To see if he's the one who's been killing the kongelig.

The courtyard is empty except for the shadows, the sun already disappeared behind the sea, the white-silver light of the moon illuminating the pockmarked cobblestones. Without the glittering lights and sugarcane wine, the gentle music and chattering kongelig, the courtyard looks desolate. The walls of the manor itself seem to be crumbling.

"We shouldn't be here," Løren tells me.

He follows as I walk to the grand entrance doors, but they're barred. I step into the gardens, thorns of overgrown flowers catching the bottom of my dress, weeds crunching beneath my feet. I look into a blackened window, but a gauzy curtain blocks my sight. I ask Løren for a rock, but he doesn't hand me one—only stares at me blankly, like he's become a ghost, or like he's thinking of killing me here and now, where there wouldn't be anyone to witness my murder; I can't tell which, and he's put the wall between us back up again. I bend over to pick up a rock myself and throw it at the window. Glass shatters. I wince, hesitating to hear the voices of confused slaves or guards running to the commotion, but there's nothing.

I rip a strip of cloth from the bottom of my dress, wrapping it around my hands, and climb up. Løren refuses to help, even as I struggle to put one leg over, trying to avoid the gnarled teeth of glass. An edge pierces my thigh, and sharp pain follows the drops of red that stain my dress and dribble down my skin. I pull my other leg up and manage to jump down into the manor itself.

The hall I've landed inside is abandoned. There're no lights, and the wallpaper is torn and yellowed, old water ballooning beneath. The rugs smell of mold and have dirt scattered across them. I wait for Løren, who takes his time climbing the wall and pulling himself up through the window as well, landing silently beside me. He doesn't say anything as we make our way to the end of the hall. I look around the corner, but this hall is also abandoned. I feel a whisper on my neck even though no other windows are open for a breeze.

The next hall, and the next—empty, dark. One takes me to the kitchen. Pots and pans, scattered across the floor. Ash and dust layers the tables, the iron stove. I think that this is a wing the king, or whoever controls him, has had no use for, and that there's another kitchen where the slaves prepare their meals. But the halls take me to the grand entryway. Paintings have been torn down from the walls. The staircase, which had been made of marble, once gleaming in the sunlight, now crumbles. The room that had held the exquisite art is empty; the few busts that remain are cracked and on the floor. The meeting room has its table, its chairs, but the wood is swollen and covered in dust. The mahogany rots. I walk faster until I'm running—I race up the stairs, and there's more of the same. Chambers with overturned furniture and torn curtains and sheets, rooms that look like they'd been set aflame. No slaves. No king. I don't think a soul has lived in this manor for more than a decade.

The pressure in me, as though I've been sinking into the depths of the ocean, builds. I have to leave. I have to get out of the manor. The walls of the maze close, thorns wrapping around me. Løren takes my arm. He guides me through the abandoned halls, to a door to the servants' quarters and out into the night. I sink to the weeds, overheated even in the trade-winds breeze. Sweat makes my dress stick to my skin, my hair itching my neck.

It's all been a lie. Not only the king but even the house— perhaps this entire island.

Løren stands over me. I believe in his innocence now. He would've continued the lie if he could have. It has to be one of the kongelig. They must need to be inside the manor itself, the meeting room and the courtyard, to use their kraft and keep up their illusions. Whoever holds the power of the king has been in attendance for each gathering, each meeting. The kongelig must've had a laugh having us sit in filth while we thought we were surrounded by riches. More frightening than anything else, though, is the power this kongelig must have, to fool so many of us.

Løren helps me walk to the shoreline so that I can clean my stinging cut with saltwater. I take the cloth from my hands to wrap it around my thigh. The water is black in the night, swirl- ing around my feet and pulling back out to sea again, a rhyth- mic pulse that's usually so soothing but now feels like a threat. Løren's wall remains in its place. He shows no emotion at hav- ing seen the ruins of Herregård Constantjin. I remember he has nothing to compare what he's seen to; as a slave and my guard, he never would've been let inside those walls. He's always been forced to wait outside, lined up in the courtyard with the others.

I tell him that the king is dead. "He must be," I say, "for someone to be able to use this image of him as they do, to take over the Herregård Constantjin, take control of the kongelig. What could they want? They already have the crown, with their false image of the king. What could be their goal?"

Løren doesn't care; he listens, but only because he has no choice. He doesn't answer my questions or my thoughts with any of his own. Anger sparks inside me.

"You pretend this doesn't affect you."

"How does this affect me?" he asks.

"Whoever controls the false king will take control of Hans Lollik Helle."

"And when they do, how will my life change? It'll be the same as it was before. There might be fewer kongelig alive, once the fighting is done, but that's not something to mourn."

"You might very well be killed in the fighting, too."

"Then not much will have changed still," he tells me. "Don't misunderstand me. I want my life. But I want my life on my terms."

"That's all the more reason for you to worry," I tell him. "I should be at the helm of Hans Lollik Helle. If I were in power, I would free you. I would free all of our people."

"Would you?" he asks me.

The question angers me, so I don't respond, not at first—I only watch him, wait for him to crumble under my gaze and look away, but he does not. "Yes, of course I would."

"I heard that you were supposed to have freed the slaves who work under you long before now," he tells me, "but you have not."

"I need them still," I say. "I need all of you if I'm to be on Hans Lollik Helle, to be considered equal to the kongelig."

"So you use your people to make yourself seem above them in the eyes of the Fjern."

"I'll free them once I have the power to do so. I'll free all of us."

There's anger in his eyes, even as he laughs at me. "You're lying to yourself, Elskerinde Jannik. Tell me, how do you envision these islands under your rule?"

I think of the land, lush and green with fruit, my people walking free. This is what my mother would've wanted. But even as the image crosses my mind, questions fill me: How will our islands continue to compete in the world's economy if there are no slaves to work the land? We will make ourselves vulnerable for another attack if I release all the guards of the islands as well. The Fjern would send their armies to quell my rebellion, and we would be massacred. It's easy to say that I would be the heroine in this tale, just as my mother was, but fear of the truth swells.

I don't respond, so Løren tells me, "I'll believe you mean to free your people when you decide to free me."

When I'm finished bandaging my leg, he walks me back to the Jannik house and tells me good night as he's expected to. I pass by Aksel's chambers, but I don't feel him inside. Aksel's been gone from the house since Konge Valdemar's ruling. I'm grateful. It's better to have him away than haunting the halls, his rage and depression souring the air and sinking into my skin. I pause outside his door, and a shadow catches my eye. A scream lodges itself in my throat. Aksel's face is blue as he swings, sheets wrapped around his throat, body hanging from the top of the bed's canopy. I shout for help, but none of the slaves are in the house—they're in the slaves' quarters, Malthe sleeping with the other guards—

A shadow moves behind me, and I spin. Nothing's there. By the time I turn back around, Aksel's body is gone.

CHAPTER SIXTEEN

Aksel's eyes are red, and his skin is paler than it normally is; he staggers, talks loudly enough that his voice echoes, and laughs after every sentence he speaks. But still, he's alive. I can't look away from him. He'd been dead, neck swollen where the sheets had cut into his skin, eyes stuck wide open, feet above the ground. The man had been dead. The questions burn through me. It could be the work of kraft—the kongelig with their power over illusion. It could be my stress playing tricks on my eyes. It could be this island itself, filled with all of its ghosts.

When I first saw Aksel in the sitting room that morning, he wouldn't speak to me, but he wanted me to know that he wasn't afraid of me, and that he wouldn't be pushed out of his own home. If we had to share the same space, even believing I'd taken the life of his beloved, then so be it. I couldn't look away from him, even as he ignored me. The body I'd seen the night before was burned into my memory.

Traveling the streets of the northern cities, I'd told Marieke my fear that I was mad. I could've easily convinced myself that the thoughts of others that filled my head were the by-product of my kraft. What if these weren't actually the thoughts of strangers at all, but voices I'd conjured? My madness wasn't difficult to imagine. I'd had thoughts of taking my own life for years, especially after the deaths of my mother and sisters and brother. I had no interest in being alive when they were all dead. I was young, but I started to wonder if there was any real point to life, when in the end, I was going to be met with the same fate as everyone, no matter the color of their skin, no matter if they had their freedom or not: We were all going to be met with death. I wanted to die. I'd never attempted to take my own life, but I told Marieke as much.

In the end, it was a nightmare that turned me. I'd been plagued by nightmares every time I closed my eyes: the echoing screams and the grass shining red and the stomping of boots in the hallway, the men's voices searching for me even so many miles away. But this particular night as I ran through the twisting halls, dodging the bodies of the dead that covered the floor, I heard Tante's voice. She reminded me: My mother would've wanted me to live.

Aksel has invited the kongelig to our gardens. Hardly anyone has come. There are only seven: Erik Nørup, always happy for an excuse to drink. I take the opportunity to watch him closely and to invade his mind—to search for any possibility that he and his sister might have performed the killings and created our false king—but I only find thoughts of boredom and memories of wine and the women who've shared his bed. Patrika and Olsen Årud are also here, too snooping to decline. I decide I'll keep a closer watch on them both throughout the afternoon. A few cousins of the kongelig have also come out of nosiness and curiosity; I don't know which families they belong to, and I don't care enough to search their minds for the answer. Aksel is too drunk to see how they all laugh at him and the Jannik name. These gardens are nothing but weeds in comparison to their own. The house itself looks like it might collapse at any moment, and no one wants to stand too close to the edge of the cliffs, in case the wind—particularly strong this afternoon—takes one of them into the sea below.

Marieke and the slave girl Agatha hurry from guest to guest with offerings of sugarcane wine. The personal guards are lined up and sweating in the hot sun. Only Løren stands in the shade on the porch. He tries to hide there. Even with the wall between us, I feel this truth. He doesn't hide because he's afraid; he hides because he doesn't want the attention of his brother, or any of the other kongelig. He doesn't feel like pretending to have respect or love for any of the pale-skinned Fjern today.

Patrika Årud doesn't bother to keep her thoughts to herself. "Pathetic," she whispers to Olsen. "Aksel Jannik needs to learn to mourn in privacy."

She sees Løren. She knows he's here, but she keeps her back to him. If there're any rumors of the nights she'd forced the boy to her bed, she doesn't need to inspire more, not when they're in the middle of the storm season, not when they need the king's support. Patrika doesn't lie to herself; she might be a narcissist, but she knows the king doesn't have her name in mind to inherit the crown. Why would he, when he has Lothar Niklasson and the man's nephews, safely hidden away on Niklasson Helle? Lothar Niklasson is the obvious choice. He might be older than all of the other kongelig, but he'll know how to keep control of the islands of Hans Lollik after the rule of Konge Valdemar, will know how to smoothly transition his rule to his successor. Even if the king were not to choose Lothar Niklasson, other names would come to mind first before Patrika and her husband: Erik Nørup, or even Jytte Solberg, though she's an unwed woman. There's no reason Konge Valdemar would choose the Årud.

Patrika needs to do what she can to change his mind, she knows, and quickly. She needs to prove her family's worth, the strength of their coin and guard. She's been looking for opportunities, but it seems that Hans Lollik Helle has become nothing more than a circus this year, with me joining the table and the death of that girl Beata Larsen. And now this party, where the slave son of Engel Jannik stands on the porch. She doesn't want to know if he's as aware of her presence as she is of his.

Her husband knows, of course. Olsen has known of every man and boy Patrika has brought to her bed that wasn't him. He has even brought slaves to Patrika some nights, as gifts to his wife, though he's never had any interest in joining them or even watching, as some men might. He'd been the one who first brought Engel Jannik's slave to her. The boy was still growing, no more than thirteen. He hadn't known what Olsen Årud had requested him for, only that he had to obey. Olsen had his own personal guard bring the boy from the slave's quarters. Løren had been afraid. It was clear he thought he would be whipped, or even killed, and Olsen couldn't blame him. Olsen had his own particular interests, and just as he didn't interfere with his wife's pleasures, she didn't interfere with his, as long as he didn't choose slaves who were worth more to them alive. The boy clearly thought that Engel Jannik had given Olsen permission to kill him, the way he trembled so, fists balled, ready to fight for his life.

He was confused when he was brought to Patrika's chambers, it was easy to see on his face; he was confused when the door shut behind Olsen, leaving the boy and Patrika alone. His screams of pain had echoed all through the night as she worked her kraft on him. Olsen sees and recognizes Løren as well. Olsen is surprised the boy's still alive. He thought Løren would've gotten himself killed long ago, with that look of defiance always in his eyes.

Aksel shouts and stumbles, dropping his glass of sugarcane wine so that it shatters. A slave girl hurries forward to pick up the shards. Aksel yells at her to hurry up—then, deciding she moves too slowly, drunkenly pushes her out of the way to snatch up the glass himself. A shard cuts his finger, and red drops onto his shirt, his pants.

Some of the guests look away, embarrassed for him, but Olsen laughs with his wife. Aksel Jannik behaves like a commoner, as did his father; both were born on these islands. Only the Elskerinde Freja Jannik had any grace. Olsen has known nothing but riches all his life. Nothing but jewels and gold. These islands are only a small piece of the Fjern empire of Koninkrijk, a sliver of paradise that he's happy to own—but there's so much more to take in this world. Olsen comes here for the storm seasons, but he mostly travels to the other nations under the Fjern empire, conducting his business and buying new lands while his wife stays on Årud Helle for the rest of the year. Patrika and Olsen Årud do not love each other. That's easy to see. Theirs is a business, a partnership. Patrika Årud wants to rule these islands as queen. The power is too magnetizing, and over such beautiful lands, too—the most beautiful in all the world, all the other nations agree.

Aksel raises a fresh glass of sugarcane wine. "I'd like to make a toast," he announces. The guests and their polite conversation pause, unease trickling through them. "Beata Larsen," Aksel tells us, "was the most beautiful woman to have ever graced these islands."

Erik shouts his agreement, but the others glance away in discomfort, or look to me to see how I'll react. I have a flinch of pity for Aksel. He tells everyone that he loved Beata Larsen. "I don't care who knows now. I was married, yes, married to this snake"—he gestures at me, pausing to look at me as he sips his wine—"but I loved Beata Larsen more than anyone else, and now she's gone."

He takes a long swallow, and the guests raise their glasses politely to Beata's memory. But Aksel isn't finished. He turns his toast to Erik Nørup now, thanking the man for being such a good friend.

"You've always supported me," Aksel says, "even when all the other kongelig were elitist snobs who looked down on me and my family."

Erik's eyes slide uncomfortably to Patrika and Olsen Årud. The two watch without expression, hiding the ripples of anger at the insult, amusement now gone. Erik nods to Aksel, raising his own glass. "Here, here." He takes a sip.

Erik Nørup has always hated coming to Hans Lollik Helle, and all that he ever looks forward to are these parties with their sugarcane wine. He feels sorry for Aksel, but Erik is the only guest who doesn't laugh at his friend. They'd been friends once, anyway, long ago; children, racing through the groves of Hans Lollik Helle, putting spiders in Alida's hair and laughing as she screamed, chasing the brown boy who had Aksel's eyes. Erik had heard the rumors, of course—everyone had—and Erik had been particularly good at hiding under tables to listen to the adults' affairs. He and Aksel chased the boy through the groves, threatening to hang Løren Jannik by his neck. Erik had thought it had all been in jest, nothing but a game, but one day Aksel had actually brought rope and told Erik how they were to catch Løren before he could run back to the slaves' quarters. Erik had wanted to tell Aksel no, he wouldn't help the boy kill his brother, but he'd been too afraid. Aksel had a fury in him that Erik had never witnessed in anyone else—besides, perhaps, Aksel's father, Engel Jannik.

They were both twelve years old, the slave boy only ten; it was easy to catch him, easier than Erik thought it would be. They slipped the rope around Løren's neck, and he screamed and cried and fought, biting and scratching—Erik still had a pale, thin scar on his collarbone, even all these years later—but Aksel was determined. He threw the rope over a branch, pulling, and Løren was lifted into the air, feet kicking, hands to the rope around his neck as he choked, his face swelling—until the branch snapped, and he fell to the ground with a gasp.

Aksel could have tried again: The boy's fight had left him, and he was gasping for air and crying. Erik was relieved when Aksel, instead, decided to run. Aksel and Erik had done many cruel things on this island as boys, Erik could admit; but somehow, this was what had split their friendship apart. Erik couldn't quite look at Aksel again after the two nearly took Løren Jannik's life. If he continued to play with Aksel, it was because his father, Johans Nørup, now dead, told him to.

But it took the death of Beata Larsen for Erik to become allies with Aksel Jannik once again. He couldn't help but feel sorry for the man, and though Erik did enjoy sugarcane wine, I notice that he's been drinking from the same glass all afternoon, though he laughs just as loudly as Aksel does when he stumbles.

Aksel points at the slaves lined up and demands that they sing a song. "You're always singing," he tells them, "making your loud music in the fields. Sing for us now. We need music, and I want to dance."

The slaves hesitate. One starts a shaky tune, and the others know it, so they join in. It's a slow song, one that makes my heart ache. I'd heard Tante singing it long ago. A song about a woman who, on her deathbed, isn't sure she'll live long enough to see her daughter, who must cross the sea. Aksel either doesn't listen to the words or he's too drunk to care; he claps his hands and twists around to his imagined beat, grin split across his face, as though the song is festive and full of joy. He pauses. He's spotted Løren, standing in the shade of the porch.

Aksel claps his hands once again, then points at his brother. "You aren't singing," he says.

Løren doesn't respond, not right away. The kongelig are watching, however, even Patrika and Olsen Årud, and he knows he's expected to respond to his master. "I don't know this song," he tells Aksel.

"Don't all you slaves know the same songs?" Aksel asks.

Løren doesn't reply this time. This angers Aksel, it's easy for everyone to see. Aksel takes another glass of sugarcane wine from the slave girl, then makes his way up the steps and to the porch, into the shade. He speaks only to Løren, but his voice carries on the wind.

"Maybe you should learn it," he tells Løren. The slaves are still singing in the garden, under the hot sun. "See? There are the words, and the tune. You can learn it, can't you?"

Løren tells Aksel, "I don't want to."

Aksel slaps Løren's cheek, and Løren's fist flies back, knocking Aksel in the mouth.

The slaves stop singing. There's an intake of breath from everyone, islanders and kongelig alike. Aksel has been hit so hard that he stumbles backward, into the railing, another glass of sugarcane wine falling to the ground, though this one doesn't break. It rolls, down the stairs and into the grass. Aksel straightens now, shock filling his being. The rage in Løren settles, and I can see it plainly on his face: the realization of what he's done.

Aksel doesn't speak. For a long while, he doesn't move. When he finally does, it isn't to throw himself at Løren, to beat the boy into submission, as I thought he would. He leaves—walking down the dirt path, toward the groves. The kongelig share my confusion, but it's clear to all that the party is now over. Glasses are handed back to Marieke and Agatha, and they give me tightened smiles as they curtsy and bow with their gratitude, Erik now sober. Patrika compliments me on a lovely party with a smile.

When the guests and their slaves are gone, I turn to the porch, but Løren has disappeared. Marieke hurries to me. "We have to find him," she says. "We won't have a lot of time."

I'm not sure what she means, and in her impatience, she pushes an image at me, her thoughts: Marieke has seen this before. A slave dares to rise their hand against their master, and the master returns with a group of men, ready to hang that slave from the nearest tree. She believes Aksel is looking for those men now. Some kongelig, perhaps, but likely other guards from the slaves' quarters. Marieke wants me to find Løren now—to hide him and save him.

We hurry into the house, through the halls, calling Løren's name. He isn't in the kitchens, or even the library. I realize where he might be, and leave the house again, taking the path that cuts into the groves, trees leaving patterns of shadow and light on the ground, flickering sunshine into my eyes, until I reach the shore. He stands on the rocks again, a figure so still he may be nothing but a shadow, and whereas before I wondered if he might be waiting for a wave to come and take him into the sea, now I'm sure he's trying to find the courage to jump.

I take off my sandals, clutching them in my hand, and race across the rocky grains, ignoring the sting of stone cutting into the bottoms of my feet as I call his name. There's no block between us. He doesn't care to keep me from his thoughts now. He knows I'm there, but he doesn't look at or acknowledge me. I stand behind him, willing him to turn.

"I'll make your brother see my way," I tell him. "I won't let him touch you."

But Løren knows Aksel far better than I do. Aksel has wanted his brother dead for years, and he's attempted to kill Løren multiple times. Racing through the groves, telling all of Løren's power. Aksel had been so sure that his father would have the slave boy hung from his neck when Engel found that Løren had kraft in his veins, and it was to be so, at first; Løren had been locked in a room, and Engel had decided to hang his son the following morning. It was the law of Hans Lollik, the law of the kongelig, and there were to be no exceptions. The noose was set up, the slaves gathered to watch. Aksel was happy to not have a boy his father would compare him to, yelling at Aksel, hitting him across the face, telling him that his brother, subhuman, was faster and smarter and stronger than he.

But even as Løren was brought from his room, hands tied, Aksel could see his father's waning determination. His jaw clenched and unclenched, and his voice wavered as he began to speak of the law of the kongelig. The boy didn't fight or struggle—he must've realized that there was no chance he would win this fight, and so there was no point. He stood on the chair obediently as his father came to him and placed the noose around his neck. But here, Aksel saw with a dropping heart, Engel hesitated. He wouldn't look away from the boy's face, and Løren wouldn't look away either. He held his father's stare with courage, anger, and hatred burning, as though Løren meant to let Engel Jannik know that his own spirit would haunt his father until the end of time. Engel took the noose from around the boy's neck and ordered him released. He might be a slave, but he was still a descendant of the kongelig, and so Engel announced that Løren would live. Even all these years later, Løren's eyes looked too much like his own.

Engel Jannik was no longer here to hesitate. Fever, a storm-season illness, had taken the man years before. A pitiful way for Engel Jannik to go. Løren could see that Aksel didn't mourn his father. Løren, in a sick way, had. It was because of Engel Jannik that Løren had lived. Engel had been the only barrier between Løren and Aksel, even after the man had nearly beaten Løren to death for so many years. Aksel refused to look at the truth within himself: He couldn't help but feel a connection to this man with his brown skin and dark hair and eyes, knowing that he and this islander shared the same blood and flesh. Aksel wanted the boy dead, but every time he tried to kill Løren himself, he would hesitate, just as his own father would.

Løren and I both know that, right now, Aksel won't hesitate. He has too much sugarcane wine in his stomach and rage flowing through his veins. Løren will be dead by nightfall, he is sure of it, and if Løren is going to die, he wants to die on his own terms: making one last bid for his freedom, even if it means he will drown.

I ask him to come down from the rocks. "I won't let Aksel kill you."

"There were witnesses. If he doesn't have me executed, they'll consider him weak. He would never allow anyone to consider him weak."

"Come back with me," I tell Løren. "I won't let anyone come near you. I promise you that."

Løren hesitates—but if there's a chance he might live, he'll take it. We hurry back to the house, the other slaves continuing their work but unable to keep from watching us race past. I walk Løren to the library, where he's been sleeping these last weeks in his corner with his blanket and pillow. Løren watches me as I close the door behind him. I can see how his eyes might've looked when he was young—how there might've been a mixture of rage and fear and hope. Though the rest of his face is blank, and I can't feel any emotion because of the wall he holds between us, I can see in his eyes that he feels like a child again, and that he hates that he has to depend on me now.

I go outside to wait for Aksel on the rocky path. The wind grows stronger in the setting sun, whipping my dress around my legs and my thick hair into my face so that it brushes against my cheeks. I can see Aksel coming up the path from afar, a line of men trailing behind him. As they get closer, I count ten. They're mostly kongelig, Erik included. A few are guards, one of them Malthe.

Aksel doesn't bother to speak. Malthe steps forward, his expression grim.

"My lady," he tells me, "Herre Aksel Jannik has requested the presence of the slave named Løren."

"Aksel can't have him," I tell Malthe.

Malthe hesitates, looking to Aksel, who only continues to watch me. Malthe turns back to me again. "My apologies, my lady," he says. "I know that Løren is your personal guard, but he attacked Herre Aksel Jannik. This can't be overlooked."

"Aksel attacked Løren first," I say. There's an uncomfortable shifting of feet. "Is that not so?"

Aksel speaks, though he still doesn't look at me. "Løren is a slave," he says, "my family's slave, and so it's impossible for me to *attack* him. Does the butcher attack the goat when he cuts the animal's neck?"

"Løren is mine," I say. "He's been mine since the day you sent him to kill me."

The kongelig who are gathered had heard the rumors, of course, the same as everyone else: how much Aksel and I despised each other, how Aksel had tried to have me killed so that he could be free of our marriage and escape with Beata Larsen; how, though Lothar Niklasson had declared me innocent, most on the island still believe I found my revenge by strangling the girl and leaving her body to the sea. They believe that I'm a black snake, think that I'd somehow found a way to deceive the kongelig. The hatred Aksel and I have kept for each other, and his attempt to take my life, was a secret I'd so desperately wanted to hide in the face of the king, with the chance that Jannik might be named regent; but now that it's obvious to me that he's a puppet king, it's not a fact worth hiding.

Faced with the truth, Aksel turns red with rage, still unable to look at me.

"Do you deny it?" I ask Aksel.

"I don't," he says.

"Løren reacted in self-defense," I tell all gathered.

"A slave has no right to defend himself against his master," one of the kongelig, a Solberg cousin, tells me. He's disgusted that he even has to address me, an islander. "The boy should be dead."

Aksel is a coward. He's too afraid to fight me on this. He knows of my kraft and knows I'd best him before all gathered. He knows I would delight in the chance to humiliate him and force him to his knees to kiss my feet if he attempts to attack me here and now. I would prove to all of them that my power is stronger than theirs—not in spite of the darkness of my skin but because of it, because of my ancestors and the fury filling my bones.

My husband finally looks at me. He clenches his jaw, then walks, boots crunching the rocky dirt, and stops so close beside me that I can smell the sugarcane wine on his breath. "He can't go completely unpunished for what he's done," he says.

A negotiation. I shake my head. "I won't let you touch him."

"The guests of my party saw him hit me. What will it do to the Jannik name, for him to hit his master and no harm come to him? I won't kill him," he says, and here his voice is lit with rage, "but I want to see him punished."

I'd promised Løren that no harm would come to him, but I can see that this is the compromise that Aksel expects, the compromise that will allow Løren to keep his life without this spectacle of a standoff between me and Aksel. I agree to Aksel's terms with a stiff nod. This is the best way to end this quarrel, and the safest. I tell Malthe where Løren is hiding. Aksel snaps his fingers impatiently at Marieke, and all the slaves who work the Jannik house are gathered from the kitchens and the groves, as is custom. Marieke stands with her hands folded one atop the other, her yellowing eyes empty. She doesn't look at me because she doesn't want me to feel her judgment, and so I give her the privacy she deserves, but even then the disgust radiates from her skin. Was *there really no other way, Sigourney? Is watching my fellow islanders whipped how I spend my time on the island of Hans Lollik*

Helle now, instead of finding a way to make the kongelig pay for what they've done? Marieke wants to know, but she doesn't see how I'm twisted in this game the kongelig play.

Løren is dragged out from the library. Malthe binds his hands, though the boy doesn't fight back, doesn't struggle. He's a fighter, yes, but Løren has never fought back when he's known it was a fight he wouldn't win. There's no point in wasting the energy. He won't look at me as he's forced into the center of all who stand to watch. Aksel is handed a whip.

I leave. I know that, as the Elskerinde Jannik, it's my duty to stay and see that this punishment be carried out, but I can't watch. Already I feel a sickness churning in me, and I can't trust myself not to enter Aksel and force him to stop, to turn the whip on himself and the other Fjern. Even from inside, in the shadowed hall and up the stairs, in my chambers with the doors closed, I can hear the crack of the whip. It's a long time before Løren lets himself scream.

CHAPTER SEVENTEEN

I don't visit Løren, because the first time I tried to, he let me feel the fullness of his hatred. I'd felt the hatred waver in his questions, his wondering of whether I do, after all, care for my people—whether I could ever find redemption in helping the islanders find freedom from the Fjern—but now, he lets me see what he thinks of me: this woman who has fooled herself for her own comfort, who has tried to pull others into her lies so that she can use them for her own gain, this islander who has betrayed her people out of what she pretends is love. There's no one in this world who is worse than I am, he wants me to know. Though I tell myself I saved him, this is just another lie to make me feel like I'm the heroine in my own fairy tale. I didn't save him: I allowed my husband to whip him.

Marieke says that Løren remains in the library and that she goes to him every morning, and afternoon and night to reapply salves of aloe to his back and legs. Løren already has a webbing of pale, raised scars covering his skin. This doesn't surprise Marieke. She's seen boys like Løren before: reckless, fearless, believing they don't care if they die but knowing they really do want to live, just like anyone else. She'd once known a boy like this, on Rose Helle, before my father married my mother. The boy had belonged to my father, when Koen Rose was just about my age. Marieke was told that this boy was her brother, though she didn't see many similarities between them. Marieke preferred to hide the anger and hatred within her, to keep patience for the day she might finally find an opportunity for revenge. This boy, who might've been her brother, wasn't patient. He'd whispered to the other slaves in the night. They'd collected their machetes and knives and buried the blades in the sand by the bay. They had planned to kill Koen Rose.

It had been Marieke who told her master the truth. She told her master, knowing that if she didn't, Koen Rose would have killed not only her brother and his friends but more of his slaves as well. It was common practice to kill islanders who hadn't been a part of the rebellion, both in punishment and to create fear so that there would never be another uprising again. Marieke didn't want innocents to die. She didn't want to risk that she would be one of those innocents killed. And so she told Koen Rose of her brother's plans.

He and his friends were gathered to be killed, as Marieke expected. Her brother spat at her feet as he passed by. This didn't surprise her, either. What did surprise her was when Koen Rose, before the boys' execution, decided he would extend his punishment to five innocents anyway. Two girls and three boys, all as young as Marieke, were selected and brought forward, screaming and crying and pleading with their master for their lives, promising they had nothing to do with the rebellion. And her brother watched Marieke, accusingly—all of these deaths were because of her, it seemed he wanted her to know.

Marieke tells me that Løren asked her why she cares for me.

"And what did you say?"

"The truth," she tells me. "It's not like I have much choice."

Marieke isn't happy with me, either, I can tell, but I want to ask what she would rather I have done. Should I have let Aksel hang Løren from his neck? Should I have let Løren jump into the sea? He's in pain now, but his wounds will heal and join the thick netting of scars across his skin.

"You came here to destroy the kongelig," Marieke tells me. "You came here to take the throne back from the Fjern, to find your revenge and free your people. What have you done since you've arrived here on Hans Lollik Helle? You've done nothing but kill an old man on behalf of the king and have one slave boy nearly whipped to death."

"You don't understand the way the kongelig work," I tell her, but I can feel shame radiating from me. "If I didn't have Løren whipped, I would've lost the respect of the Fjern, and he would've been killed anyway."

"The kongelig will never have any respect for you, no matter what you do."

"Herregård Constanjin is false, nothing more than an illusion. I've been looking into the minds of the kongelig, to see who might be controlling the puppet king, who might be killing the other kongelig. I know that it's either Alida Nørup or the Årud. I only need to find a way to question them."

"Why question them when you can simply kill them?"

"You always tell me to have patience, Marieke," I say. "I can't simply murder Alida Nørup and Patrika and Olsen Årud in their sleep."

"And why not?" she asks me. Her eyes burn. "You should have patience, yes—but not to the point that you miss your opportunity. The storm season won't last much longer."

The house isn't a welcome place for me. It never was, but especially now, the slaves who walk the halls watch me with loathing and disgust. I've never allowed any of my slaves to be beaten or whipped. Though I hadn't given the slaves their promised freedom, this, at least, was what held me apart from the Fjern. I shouldn't let myself be run out of my own home, but I do. I wander the groves, picking mango and guava, trying to think on what my next steps should be. I'm no closer to knowing who among the kongelig control the king—who has killed Beata Larsen and Ane Solberg and Jens Nørup.

I find an alcove in the sea: a little patch of sand surrounded by rocks, and a calm swirling tide that allows for a miniature world of life to flourish. Baby crabs are nestled in the rocks, along with sea urchins and starfish. I eat my fruit and stare out at the blue of the ocean, remembering the days I would spend with Ellinor. We'd pretend that we were the queens of Hans Lollik Helle, even as children. We'd tell each other that if only we had the crown of these islands, the Fjern and the islanders alike would learn to love us as much as our mother taught us to love ourselves.

I can feel the presence long before she arrives at the shore, so I'm not surprised when I see Alida Nørup, though Alida is surprised to see me. I remember Marieke's suggestion to simply kill the woman. She catches a glimpse of me and begins to slow her walk, hesitating, unsure if she should join me; then, determined, she speeds her steps until she's by my side. She wears white, loose-fitted pants and a white shirt, as her brother might; unlike her brother's blond hair and blue eyes, her eyes and hair are dark. This had been a source of pain for her, once; the Fjern have always admired blond hair and blue eyes, so as a child, Alida could feel the love and attention her brother received for looking the way he did, while she received none. Her mother had been disappointed. She felt it would be difficult to find a suitable match for Alida, and it didn't help that the girl had little interest in dresses and dolls. She always wanted to read, or ride horseback, and gods above, the girl was wild: attempting to race after her brother to play with his friends, running through the mud. It took years before Alida finally seemed to compromise: She stopped acting like a little boy, chasing after her brother, but she wouldn't wear the pretty little dresses and stand silently and demurely at the garden parties, either. Instead, she locked herself away in the library, poring over her books, unwilling to meet with any men who called upon her. Erik would send his thoughts to her: Just do what their mother wanted. It wouldn't hurt anyone, would it, to act like the other girls of these islands? This perhaps was the first crack between the two.

I see in Alida that she noticed me a while ago, walking through the groves, but she's still surprised that I managed to find this hidden section of the shore. Her cousin Jens Nørup had been found dead, but she doesn't seem to be in grief over the man; they'd never been close, and there's even disdain—Jens had always been the type to claw at whatever power he could. Alida isn't like this. The games of the kongelig disgust her.

"You've found my favorite place on Hans Lollik Helle," Alida tells me. She doesn't hesitate to sit on the sand beside me; she helps herself to one of the mangoes I'd picked, biting into the yellow skin, juice leaking down her arm and staining her shirt. Alida is odd. Everyone on Hans Lollik Helle, on Nørup Helle, throughout all of the islands, knows this.

She doesn't seem to mind. She only smiles at me while she sucks on the mango seed. "My brother likes you," she tells me, "very much."

Alida and Erik's kraft connect them. They know each other's thoughts, their feelings. I can see that when they were younger, the two could even hop into each other's bodies, but in the same way that my power had once been impossible to control, their own power has evolved as well, and that part of their kraft died long ago now.

"He feels sorry for you," Alida tells me. "He's too kind-hearted, my brother. He sees anyone who's been outcasted and thinks he loves them."

I don't want Erik's pity, or the belief that he's kindhearted, when I've seen the way he chased Løren through the groves by Aksel's side. "And what do you think of me?" I ask Alida.

She has a smile for me. "I think you're interesting. The most interesting thing to happen to Hans Lollik Helle in a long time, in fact."

I ask if she isn't as upset as the other kongelig are—Jytte Solberg, Patrika and Olsen Årud—but I can already feel the truth brimming in her. There are some whose minds are more tiring to read than others, and there are some who are so open, and want me to know their thoughts so desperately, that each thought comes to me whether I'm looking for it or not. I might be wrong, but I now don't believe that Alida is behind the false king, or the killings of the kongelig. If not her and her brother, then the last two I have to suspect are Patrika and Olsen Årud.

"Why should I be upset?" Alida says. "I can't stand this island and its politics. I fear that Konge Valdemar will choose my brother only because he looks the way the Fjern hope a regent would look, and then all of the islands' responsibilities would fall to me. Gods above, it's my worst nightmare. But you already knew this."

She thinks I'm interesting, yes, but most interesting of all is my kraft. It's the strongest she's seen in some time, and Alida has long since wondered if power can be taken. Whether kraft fills the veins, and if blood were to be spilled and poured and sipped like a fine wine, would the drinker then take the power of the other? Ancient stories fill the Fjern empire: regents of Koninkrijk would slaughter their enemies and drain their bodies. They would drink their blood in their attempts to take the powers of others, and though some claimed success, these were more the legends one might tell a child as they fell asleep at night. Alida has seen from her own experiments firsthand that drinking the blood of another isn't enough to take their kraft. She believes that their kraft must fill your veins wholly, replacing your own; but then, Alida wonders, what if there was a way to take all of the blood of one person and replace it with the blood of another?

Dark thoughts for a woman of her standing, but as I sink into her further, I can see that although Alida may be curious about my kraft, she has no interest in killing me. Alida believes the hatred the kongelig hold for me is something that belongs to the older generations. She has seen much of the world, even if most of the Fjern would expect her to stay home and wait to be married. She's seen the wealth, the culture, the civilizations that people with skin like mine have built, and she knows that a person with dark skin is her equal; in many cases, her better. The lies the kongelig tell themselves in these islands—that's what she can't stand, more than anything else. They've taken what they consider a paradise and set it up as a child might in their own kingdom: the feeling that they are somehow better, stronger, more important than others. And why? Why do her people conquer others? Alida's always wanted to know, ever since she was a child.

This is what Alida tells herself, anyway—but still, she was raised in these islands. She tells herself I'm her equal, but there's still a flicker, in the back of her heart, that says otherwise. The surprise that I would sit beside her, speaking as I do, without using Alida's proper title of Elskerinde Nørup; the confusion over why I'm not in the groves, where I belong, and why I picked the mangoes to eat them myself, when they belong to the Fjern.

She knows she holds these feelings and detests them. So she pushes them as far away as she can, pretending that they don't exist. Instead she looks at me with a smile, as she's supposed to look at any equal. "You've had a difficult time on this island," she tells me. "I'm surprised that you're still here."

"Why would that surprise you?"

"The kongelig have tried to kill you," she says, "and they'll undoubtedly try to do it again. You know that you won't be chosen for regent. The king announced this for all to hear. And yet you're still here on Hans Lollik Helle. Why?" she asks me.

Alida envies my kraft. She wishes she could ask any question and have it automatically answered. If there were a way to simply switch the blood of two bodies, without killing the other, she'd certainly try. She's already made her attempts, draining the blood from one mouse and attempting to filter this blood into another. She tried to do this in over one hundred ways—slowly, so that neither mouse would lose too much blood; quickly, before the heart had a chance to stop—but neither mouse would ever survive the experiment. It was difficult to know whether the mice died because they were mice or if by a fault of her own. She wanted to attempt her experiment on humans. On one particular night, one filled with shame, she did wonder if she could simply try to switch the blood of two islanders. The islanders wouldn't be missed, and if they were slaves of the Nørup, then those slaves were technically the property of her family anyway, and hers to do with as she pleased. It would ultimately be to help the islanders, she told herself. The exchange of blood could be a way to save the poor islanders of Hans Lollik who have kraft in their veins, when it's no fault of theirs. The kongelig could simply take their blood and put it into the bodies of young Fjern who were not given the divine gift. This would be a kindness, she tells herself, and the two islanders who might die in her experiment would have sacrificed their lives for a worthy cause. This is what Alida tells herself.

"I have to remain on Hans Lollik Helle. It's my duty to stay here as Elskerinde Jannik."

"If I were you," she says, "and I had a husband who hated me and tried to kill me, I would've left him long ago, and I would've traveled the world twice over by now. There's so much more to see than just these islands. I feel trapped here every time I come."

This is easy for anyone to see, whether they have my kraft or not. Alida Nørup detests these islands and Hans Lollik Helle. Girls aren't supposed to ask as many questions as she does; girls aren't supposed to want to read and learn the sciences or attend universities in faraway empires. Yet she asked her questions and learned the sciences and went to her university, where she was one of the top students in her field, researching the properties of various plants and herbs and taking note of their medicinal uses and their effects on kraft. After all of this, Alida could have stayed away from Hans Lollik Helle. She could have taught at one of the many universities, or continued her research of the sciences and of kraft. So many things Alida Nørup could have done—and yet she returned, and why? Her brother, her brother, always her brother. Erik Nørup has always been a child, always needed her help, and as much as Erik annoys her, Alida finds that she can't abandon him.

"It's your brother who's expected to be here more than any-one else," I tell her. "Why don't you simply leave?"

She laughs at me. "Erik? He can't spend a day here without me. He always whines whenever I threaten to leave him here. He's a baby, you know, a child. I hate my brother sometimes. And he knows it. He can feel it, the same way I can feel how sad he is to know that I can't stand him. That's what's most tragic of all," she tells me. "Even knowing I hate him sometimes, hate his ways of drinking and dancing and gallivanting all across the islands, he can't return any anger. He wants to. He's tried. But he's just too innocent, my brother."

I want to tell her about what he used to do in the groves, hunting Løren with his friend Aksel; want to tell Alida that her brother came with the other kongelig earlier today, to hang Løren by his neck. What's funniest is that I don't believe Alida means to lie to herself. This Erik she describes is the only version she's ever seen.

"Elskerinde Jannik," Alida says, "I want to hear about your life. You're fascinating to me, you know."

I hesitate. I don't know what information Alida might one day use against me. But I can also feel that she has no plans to take what she learns and race to the nearest kongelig, to plot against me as some might. She really is just curious, and bored. There's never anything to do on Hans Lollik Helle except watch the other kongelig whisper their gossip and play their games and murder one another as they sleep, and even that becomes tiresome after coming to this island once a year for the past ten years of her life.

And so I tell her. At this point, I don't see that I have any other choice. I have no allies among the kongelig, and the longer I sit here next to Elskerinde Nørup, the more I begin to wonder if I could use her friendship—if there could be a way to ask for Alida's help against the other kongelig. I describe the deaths of my mother and sisters and brother at the hands of the Jannik guards, explain how I escaped Rose Helle with Marieke and traveled the northern empires, and how I decided to return and use my kraft to convince Elskerinde Freja Jannik to let me marry her son. I even decide to tell Alida a story, of when I'd traveled the north with Marieke, and together we hoped to make it to Koninkrijk, for I'd never been to the empire that had taken these islands and oppressed my people. I wanted to see for myself the fields, the groves of elder trees and the mountains with white tips in the distance; I wanted to look at the people who shared the same blood of the ones who'd killed my family, to see if the evil was one they all shared, and if it was an evil that'd been passed on to me.

We crossed the border on horseback, and there was nothing momentous about the occasion, nothing special. We were only surrounded by craggy paths and fields of grass that stretched on like the sea. I'd heard of the cold ice that fell from the sky in Koninkrijk, but had never seen it, and so I was most intrigued by the frost that seemed to cover the leaves of some of the trees, the ice like glass that cracked beneath my feet.

Marieke rode me through the groves and to a stone inn, helped me from the horse and took the animal to the stables. She held my hand as we walked inside, fireplace roaring. There weren't many people: the innkeeper and two other guests who sat in the far corner. It'd already been quiet, but it seemed the silence became physical when we walked inside. We dusted our jackets of ice and sat. I'd only had my kraft for a few months, and I still had difficulty controlling it. Sometimes thoughts and emotions came to me unbidden; other times I would purposefully try to enter minds, but find it impossible.

I tried to know the thoughts of the two men in the corner, the woman who walked to us hesitantly. The woman gave us a careful smile. She looked at us as though she'd never seen people with skin our color before. It was possible she had not.

She asked us if we were planning to stay at the inn, and if so, for how long; Marieke gave her an answer, I can't remember what she'd said. But before Marieke could finish speaking, one of the two men in the corner stood. He said he wouldn't be sharing his quarters with people like us—beasts, creatures, monsters—this is what he called us, and all because of something like the color of our skin. I shouldn't have been surprised, because these were the same people who had come to my islands, who killed and tortured and enslaved my people, but I couldn't help but be shocked and hurt. It's always shocking when someone claims you aren't as human as they.

I don't think Marieke was as shocked. She'd been hesitant when I first requested we come here. I'd wanted to understand the people who had conquered us, but Marieke had told me that sometimes there's nothing to understand.

The man went on, demanding we leave. The other laughed, saying that perhaps they could make coin off of us: take us captive, sell us to any of the Fjern territories that kept their slaves with skin as dark as ours. Marieke trembled. She understood how easily these two men could take us and sell us. These were people who didn't believe we deserved our freedom. The woman, the innkeeper, had given us a smile when she approached, but now she only watched.

Marieke took my hand, and we left. She put me onto the back of the horse, ignoring my complaints—I was used to my life of privilege, and I had exclaimed that the men could attempt to hurt us, but they wouldn't get away with it, we could simply write to my cousin and he would right any wrongs—and she got onto the horse behind me. She raced through the groves, no matter that we were both hungry and tired. She didn't stop until she found a cave, not unlike the one she'd found me in years before. It was wet and cold, but she wouldn't let us light a fire that night. I found out why as I lay awake. There was rustling, footsteps and voices. One man asked another if he was sure he'd seen us come this way, and a third said that yes, he was sure. Marieke held me close, and neither of us moved or breathed until the footsteps became fainter, the crunching of boots ending, the torchlight they held fading.

We got back onto our horse in the morning and didn't stop riding until we reached one of the free nations.

I speak until my voice is hoarse, and the sun begins to fall, the trade-winds breeze blowing off the sea and prickling my skin. I speak more openly to Alida than I have to any of the kongelig before, almost as openly as I would when telling Marieke all of my worries and fears. I begin to wonder if Alida has somehow concealed her true kraft: the ability to make me feel comfortable with her, to tell her all of my secrets. It's a relief, I realize, though not one I would willingly admit—a relief to feel like, for one moment, I might have an ally on this island.

"Did you mean to take the title of regent for the Rose name?" Alida asks, her curiosity genuine, and I tell her that I did mean to, even though this admits that I'd also planned to kill Aksel, because it makes no difference whether Alida knows or not: I won't be able to receive the title now anyway. She has a spark of judgment at this. In her mind, no matter who the person is or what they have done, taking a Fjern's life will always be a sin before the gods. Alida, though she practices her sciences and studies her kraft, believes in the gods as much as any of the Fjern of Hans Lollik. There can be no other explanation for the start of life, for the power that runs through the veins of the blessed.

"Who do you think will receive the regent's title?" Alida asks me.

I don't know why she asks; it's clear to everyone that Lothar Niklasson will be chosen. I say this, and she nods, but I can feel hesitation bubbling within her. The king, she thinks, has been strange. She means no disrespect to me, of course she doesn't, but for the man to invite me onto the island was startling. And when she was young, Lothar Niklasson had always been the king's most trusted adviser; the two would be seen taking their strolls around the island together, and the king always did as Lothar suggested, without hesitation; but now, this storm season, he openly questions Lothar and shows his frustration with the man.

Alida has wondered if the king is ill, or, perhaps in his old age, has gone a little mad. She thinks he might be more unpredictable than anyone would expect. We sit in silence for some time. Alida buries the mango seed and its skin beneath the sand. There aren't many whom I trust with the truth about the king. Only Marieke and Løren know that I can't sense a soul within the man, that Herregård Constantjin itself is a lie. Maybe it's the feeling of desperation that makes me want to tell Alida Nørup now.

I ask her what she knows of Konge Valdemar's kraft, and because Alida has made it her life's mission to know all that she can about the kraft of those who surround her, she tells me without hesitation: Konge Valdemar's kraft is over the dead. Since he was a boy of ten years, it became clear that the king could speak with the deceased. Their spirits would come to him, and they would tell him how they had died. They would ask him to send a message to a loved one, or to curse someone they had hated. The Fjern do not believe in the spirits as we islanders do, and many, including Valdemar himself, felt the voices of the dead were inspired by madness. But the spirits wouldn't leave the king alone, and so he sought help from the divine gods, though Alida can't say if the gods really did give him peace.

Konge Valdemar has a power to communicate with the dead, and whenever I look at him, I see nothing more than a corpse dangling by an invisible thread. I'd thought on the possibility that the king himself was dead, but decided that Konge Valdemar had to be ruled by a kongelig—but perhaps I was wrong. This could well be the king himself, already dead for a storm season. A ghost haunting his own royal island.

There're shouts. Alida frowns, looking up the path. We both stand, dusting the sand from our legs and clothes, and walk up the dirt path and into the groves. The groves are empty. They're usually filled with slaves, overseen by a Fjern on his horse, but now there's no one. As we walk, the smell of smoke becomes stronger, and my eyes and nose begin to sting. Slaves begin to run past us when we reach the clearing. We hurry with them, quickening our steps until we've reached one of the manors. The house is on fire. Flames burn and blacken the walls, ash and smoke flying into the sky. The fire has already spread to the nearest trees. The fire is like a breathing thing, growing when the wind blows, heightening to the tops of the groves. Sparks spit onto the grass near our feet. Slaves run around us, carrying pails of ocean water, but the water turns to steam the moment it hits the flame. They shout to one another, and their tactics change: Some begin to dig around the manor, while others start a fire of their own, killing the brush before the fire has a chance to spread farther.

Alida and I stand and watch in shock. Alida has spent more storm seasons on this island than I, but she's never seen a fire erupt like this, engulfing an entire manor. This is the Årud manor, she knows. She'd once been forced to come here with her brother when they were children, to politely stand and smile in their uncomfortable clothes while the adults socialized around them. She wonders about the Herre and Elskerinde Årud. The roof collapses with a crash and explosion of fire and smoke. Even the slaves who'd been desperately working to prevent the fire's spread stop now, all of us standing and staring at the fallen manor. Anyone who might've been trapped inside the manor is surely dead now.

"There's nothing we can do," Alida tells me, shouting over roar of the flame. "Best to go to the safety of our homes."

We part ways as more slaves and guards arrive. Alida hurries down the path, and I run in the opposite direction, unable to stop looking over my shoulder at the crumbling mansion and the smoke darkening the sky.

Marieke is already waiting for me on the porch when I arrive at the Jannik house. She'd been worried for me, she couldn't help it, even with the anger she holds for me now. We sit on the balcony outside of my chambers and watch the fire in the far distance. The fire's spread is stopped, thankfully, but the house burns until it's nothing but blackened embers, the smoke filling the sky into the night and even as dawn breaks. Marieke's thoughts are empty as she sits beside me, unblinking as she stares at the fire in the distance. She doesn't feel surprise, or even fear, but I do. Even knowing the kongelig—knowing that they're willing to kill for the chance at winning the regent's title—I'd always thought their murder would at least be quiet, poison or a knife in the dark.

"These are the people whose respect you so desperately craved," Marieke tells me.

"Only to heighten my chance of inheriting the throne." I pause. "I may have an ally. Alida Nørup. She can't be trusted fully, none of them can—but if I pull her over to my side, to my way of thinking, maybe there's a chance..."

"A chance of what?" Marieke asks.

"Using her to help me attack the kongelig."

As we sit and watch, the sun lightening the sky, a slave comes to us with news, sent by Malthe to deliver the message. At least nine were killed in the fire, the bodies charred, but it's impossible to know who the victims are. Marieke has gotten no sleep for the night, but she doesn't complain. She gets to her feet to ready for the day. There was a fire, yes, and lives were lost, but there's still a meal to prepare for both me and my husband, halls to sweep, weeds to pull.

I try to sleep, though I only lie in my bed, tossing and turning in the heat. I finally close my eyes, the darkness of a shadowed hall calling me—there's a figure at the end of the hall, but I can't see their shape, can't make out their face. Heat sears my skin, and when my eyes open, my bed is on fire, sheets eaten by flame. The fire burns through me, but when I wake up again, sitting up with a gasp, the fire is gone. I hide my face in my hands and try to breathe. The nightmares have been getting worse. It's difficult to breathe on this island—difficult not to feel that I'm falling into madness.

Marieke's too busy to comfort me from my nightmare, to

reassure me that our house on the hill won't be set on fire, and besides that, I'm too old now for her to wrap me in her arms and kiss my cheek as she did when I was a child. There were days when Marieke, I knew, pretended I was her daughter. She tried not to; she knew this was offensive to the memory of her little girl, but there were some nights when I woke crying that she couldn't help but see her own child crying from a nightmare, afraid that the Fjern had come onto Rose Helle to take her away from her mother. The little girl had heard stories of other children being stolen away from their homes, and this was the nightmare that had plagued her. Marieke believes in the spirits that fill these islands. She believes in the ancestors who watch and protect us. But she wonders why, then, the spirit of her child hasn't come to her. She wonders if she will ever be able to see her daughter again.

Marieke wouldn't want to comfort me now, and I shouldn't want her comfort, either. I'm a grown woman. The days of Marieke's reassuring whispers have passed. I go to the sitting room, staring from the window, curtains parted and allowing in the breeze that smells of ash. I think on Alida Nørup—the plans that begin to build in my mind.

"Elskerinde Jannik," a slave girl says, standing by the glass doors. "I have a message for you."

She passes me the note, sealed with the sunburst insignia of Hans Lollik Helle. Patrika Årud survived the fire—she'd been on a boat, watching the passing of the whales—but Olsen Årud and eight slaves are dead. There will be a funeral ceremony for Herre Årud in the coming day.

I mutter an automatic prayer, as is customary at receiving such news. I don't feel sorry for the man. He was wicked, heartless, and didn't treat me with the respect I deserve. But I don't feel gladness at his death, either. I can't summon happiness at knowing the man is dead, when I can only think about the fire and who might've had a hand in setting it. The person who killed Ane Solberg, Jens Nørup, Olsen Årud, who killed Beata Larsen, and who attempted to kill me is to blame. I don't believe they'll stop in their plans until every kongelig on Hans Lollik Helle is dead.

I look up from the message, and I'm surprised to see the slave girl Agatha still there, standing and watching me. "Is there anything else?" I ask her.

She seems shy, but I can tell there's a question on the edge of her tongue. I could enter her mind, force the question from her lips, but I hesitate. Hatred for me lives and breathes in the minds of the other islanders, and I don't want to feel her hatred now.

"Is it true that you have kraft?" she asks me. Her question seems innocent enough, but I don't know why she asks it. Everyone knows I have kraft.

"Yes," I tell her.

"I didn't think any islander could have kraft and be allowed to live," she says. "You must truly be blessed by the spirits."

I frown. The girl must know the risk, to openly praise the spirits. I could order her hung by her neck. But I have no reason to, and we're alone in this room. "I don't think that I am."

"No?" She gives me a hesitant smile. "I think that all of the spirits watch us and care for us. They love their people." Her smile almost seems mocking, but this could be my own fear of how the spirits see me. "You can know another's thoughts and feelings," she says. "This is what I heard. Won't you use your kraft on me, Elskerinde Rose?"

I don't want to do this. I don't want to know what she thinks of me, what she and the other slaves whisper about me once I've turned my back to them. I already know how they hate me. I already know how I'll never be accepted by my own people. There's no greater loneliness in the world than this. My enemies, yes—I understand that the Fjern and the kongelig will never accept me. But it's natural for me to want to be accepted and loved by my people, who understand the pain of having lost our history and our land. It's understandable not to want to see the disappointment and betrayal in the minds of those who expect me to be like my mother—to fight not only for myself but for their freedom as well.

"Please," she tells me. "I want to know what it's like to feel someone as blessed as you use their ability on me."

"It doesn't feel any different from how you are now," I tell her, but she insists, in the same way that a child might insist that one play a game. She doesn't seem afraid that I'm one of the kongelig and that I might be annoyed. She watches me as she waits, so I take a breath and close my eyes, sinking into her mind.

She hides something from me. This I feel immediately, but I can see at its roots her hatred for me, which isn't surprising. Even as she smiles at me, she hates me, this woman who has betrayed her people and wears the white of the kongelig. But though she hates, Agatha so badly wants my attention. She wants me to believe that she's worthy. She's seen what happens to unworthy slaves—to those the masters have found no use for, the ones who become broken and discarded, not even worth enough to be sold on the docks of Niklasson Helle. Agatha came not from one of the kongelig families but from a Fjern plantation owner on Årud Helle. Agatha has seen cruelty. She's witnessed cruelty like no one else I've known.

As a little girl, she huddled with the other children in a room, afraid that the master would come for them—and come he did, every night, choosing a new girl so that Agatha and the others would have to hear her screams from the main house. Agatha was sometimes the girl he chose, and she prayed to the spirits for forgiveness whenever she wasn't chosen and felt relief. Sometimes the children didn't come back at all. When Agatha became too old for the master to bring her to his bed, she began to work the fields from dawn until well into the night. She begged the spirits to not let her faint. The last girl who had fainted was whipped until she was dead, right where she'd fallen. Agatha prayed she wouldn't accidentally cut herself; the last girl who had cut herself got an infection that wouldn't heal. She lost her hand, and the master didn't find her life worthy anymore, and so had her drowned, rocks tied to her feet as she was thrown from a ship. Agatha knows what happens when a slave is no longer considered worthy. She wants me to see that she can be useful to me, more useful than any of the other slaves of this house.

I leave her mind. It's always exhausting, this ability of mine— tiring to become another person, to feel their emotions more than I feel my own, and it's always painful to see the hatred of my people directed toward me. But there's something about Agatha's mind that's more exhausting than all the rest. I don't want to know these burdens, these horrors. I don't want to know them.

"You're dismissed," I tell the slave girl. She nods her understanding, curtsies, and leaves.

CHAPTER EIGHTEEN

Olsen Årud's funeral ceremony has a boat empty of any body. I can see in the minds of the kongelig what they'd witnessed: the bodies charred beyond recognition, blackened bones and mouths twisted open, eye sockets empty. Olsen Årud had been found in the ruins near a window. He'd tried to escape, but the window must have been barred. His golden rings and glittering jewels, some partly melted and fused to his bone, were the only pieces that could identify his body. The slaves had seen the house crumbling to embers as the fire raged. The heat was too intense, the fire spreading purposefully and quickly. This fire wasn't an accident. Everyone on the island knows.

We kongelig stand on the sand, as we had for Beata Larsen, but the wind is stronger today. It's difficult to hear the words of prayer. I can feel the stares of distrust, hear the thoughts of those around me: They think I'm to blame. They said as much, before the funeral even began. As I walked down the sand, approaching the kongelig who stood in respect of Herre Årud, Jytte Solberg immediately asked me where I'd been and what I'd been doing when the fire had been set. Luckily for me, Alida answered that we'd been sitting on the bay together. Even so, most of the kongelig aren't convinced. They remember my guilt in using my kraft on Elskerinde Jannik. They believe I could've just as easily used my kraft on Alida. And Jytte Solberg won't look away from me. She thinks to herself that it's possible I could've sent a slave to do my work and waited with Alida on the bay, using the girl for an alibi—for all her intelligence, Jytte believes that Alida Nørup is far too naive.

Patrika is distraught. She stands closest to the water, her shoulders shaking with emotion she tries to hide. This isn't a lie. She truly is devastated by the death of her husband. The emotion that scours through her surprises me. I thought she'd hated him; she'd laughed at him, thought him a fool. But I can see now that though she didn't love Olsen Årud, he was her partner. They'd plotted and planned together many a night, strategizing how they would help the Årud name claim the title of regent. The two had helped one another achieve their goals. Patrika knows that she's supposed to be dead as well. She'd left to go whale watching unexpectedly, out of boredom; if she'd stayed, she'd have been a charred corpse on the ground beside her husband. She feels guilty she survived, while Olsen is now dead. She should've invited him to come watch the passing of the whales with her, but she'd fought with him just the night before, argued over the value of this island and whether the title of regent would be worth their lives.

There's one thing that Patrika knows for certain: This fire was set, and she'll have the person who set it. She'll torture whoever killed her husband, slowly, for many months, until the murderer has bitten off their own tongue, choking on blood, in an attempt to escape her. She considers the many ways she might torture her husband's killer; her kraft won't be enough. She wants to see the inside of the murderer's skin, bone peeking through flesh. Patrika Årud may be a more vengeful woman than I am.

"A second member of the kongelig, dead in as many weeks," Jytte whispers, her eyes fastened to me, "and a newcomer who is welcomed by none but the king."

*   *   *

Konge Valdemar calls for another meeting with the kongelig in a handwritten request brought in by a trembling slave girl. I haven't seen Aksel in days, and don't know where he's hiding on the island, or if he's even on the island at all. It's possible that he got on a boat and left for Jannik Helle, or any of the other islands of Hans Lollik; possible that he left these seas altogether for the northern empires, cities, and nations he's always wanted to witness, even if it means he won't see them with his beloved. I hope that he's left, not only for me but for himself as well. I thought that I needed Aksel Jannik, once, but it's become clear that he's only in my way the longer he stays on this island. I know that I won't be handed the title of regent by the puppet king, but if I can discover which of the kongelig is behind the murders, and who is behind the control of the regent, there's still a chance I can expose them—kill them if necessary—and take control of these islands. Aksel is only a dangerous distraction.

I leave for the main house without him, Løren behind me. He's able to walk now, though he walks with a limp. The pain that flares in him with each step is so strong that he's unable to keep the block between us as he normally does. I tell myself it's out of respect that I don't abuse his pain to read his thoughts and answer more questions I have of him, always unending questions and curiosity for the man—but I'm only telling myself a lie. I'm too afraid to see what he really thinks of me right now. I'm too afraid to see the hatred he feels for me. I don't know what I can do to convince Løren that I don't deserve his hatred. I'm not sure there's anything I can do, except to free him and all the slaves of the Rose, Jannik, and Lund names.

We come to the main house, and I don't know if he thinks about the night we'd come here together—the rot of the walls, the weeds that filled the gardens, which look so perfectly manicured now, shining under the sunlight. The window I'd shattered to climb inside has been fixed, or has been brought into the lie that's the perfection of this manor, I don't know which. This only makes my heart tighten in my chest. Løren goes to stand beside the other slaves lined up outside of the wall, and I enter through the grand doorway alone.

I shiver, walking down the halls. The wallpaper had been torn and stained, bloated with water; the floors, scuffed and cracked and covered with dirt and abandoned pots and pans. Now the wallpaper is intact, floral patterns shining with glittering gold, paneled wood floors gleaming. The staircase, which I've never seen anyone walk up or down, I now realize, remains as grand and unbroken as it did before, marble glistening under the golden chandeliers. A lie, all of it.

I come to the meeting room with its walls and chairs and table of mahogany. My vision flickers and wavers as I sit at the table. I can feel the rot beneath my skirts, smell the must and mold, though the room looks as beautiful as it had the first time I walked through its doors. I look for the cracks in the lie, but the more I strain to find even a hint of mold on the walls, the more my vision tunnels and blackens. I clench my hands together in my lap.

Today Lothar Niklasson is also already in the room, along with all the other kongelig. It's clear they'd just been discussing me. Lothar tilts his head as he examines me. Alida and Erik watch me with a mixture of curiosity and guilt, before looking at the surface at the table instead. Jytte Solberg stares. A small smile twitches on her face. She thinks to herself how I might look when I'm finally brought to justice, rope strung around my neck. Patrika looks forward at the opposite wall without expression, without blinking. She trembles across the table from me. She forces herself not to use her kraft on me, though she so desperately wants to.

I can see that she doesn't believe it was me. She knows I sat on the bay with Alida Nørup; she knows I would have to be a fool to kill another of the kongelig right now, when so many accuse me of the death of Beata Larsen, and that though my skin is dark, I'm clearly not a fool if I've managed to make my way onto this royal island. Patrika Årud knows I didn't kill her husband; but still, she wants to see someone scream. She wants to watch me beg for mercy, to end my life just to let the torture stop. If enough of the kongelig believe it was me—if they all hate me so, all want to see me dead—then perhaps this is something she could do without repercussion. She considers this strongly.

No one speaks. There's nothing to say. There's only a beat of silence before the doors open and the false king enters. We all stand, and he takes his seat, waving at us impatiently to be seated as well. I can't look away from the man. I think on his kraft over the dead. Is it possible that he truly is nothing more than a ghost welcoming us into his haunting? I can't imagine what a spirit would want with the world of the living. And if he isn't a ghost, but a result of kraft? How well this lie must be upheld; the power of whoever holds the king in their grasp, and presents this lie of beauty around us, awes me and shocks me and terrifies me all at once.

The regent asks me for my husband.

"I don't know where he is, my king."

Konge Valdemar raises a brow. "You don't know where your husband is?"

At one point in time, Patrika and Olsen Årud would have exchanged smiles. Jytte Solberg, perhaps, would've looked satisfied that the Jannik name continues to be no more than a joke before the king. Beata might've stared at her hands, too afraid to look my way at the mention of my husband. Today there's only hard silence. Patrika has barely registered that the king has spoken. She shouldn't have come, she now realizes. She's close to standing with a scream, close to throwing herself at me, close to demanding that Konge Valdemar allow her to use her kraft on me.

The regent doesn't seem to realize the depths of Patrika Årud's struggles. "Is it not suspicious," he asks, "that you don't know where your husband is, and there's just been a fatal fire?"

It might be foolish of me, but I hadn't considered the possibility. Aksel has been in mourning, and doesn't have any reason to burn the Årud manor to the ground, unless he'd drunkenly mistaken the manor for the Jannik house, hoping to take my life. The others around the table, however, have thought about the possibility. Lothar's colorless eyes flicker to my own. He wouldn't know the motive, but Aksel Jannik has been crazed since the death of Beata Larsen. Perhaps he wouldn't need a motive to want to see this island burn. Lothar has never liked Aksel Jannik, his father, or even the former Elskerinde. He, along with Patrika and Olsen Årud, had been in the room when the Herre and Elskerinde Jannik invited the other kongelig to their home. Arranged around the sitting room carefully, as though posing for a portrait, Herre Engel Jannik began to describe their plans. The king was ill, frail of mind; he didn't understand his implications in inviting an islander onto Hans Lollik Helle for the storm season. And while the Rose family had been nothing but an inconvenience for generations now, partnering with the Lund and taking a hold on the business of sugarcane in these lands, the inconvenience had now officially become dangerous. Each of the kongelig could agree that Mirjam Rose must be killed.

Lothar remembered the discomfort of Freja Jannik as her husband began to detail the plan: the annual ball that the woman threw in her late husband's honor. The children, who would be in attendance, and who must also die. Even the Fjern guests who attended the ball must be killed, if they wanted to ensure no survivor went to the king with the truth. The Fjern guests weren't islanders, and so this would be considered a sin by the gods above—all of the kongelig in the room knew this—but still, Engel acted as though anyone who would attend an islander's ball was deserving of their death.

Lothar had felt sick. It didn't matter to him that my family was made of islanders. He'd never met the Rose family and had never seen me before as a child, but he knew that I'd been only six at the time, my sisters ten and thirteen, my brother barely a man at fourteen years old. It didn't sit well with him, this plot to slaughter innocent children. But Lothar couldn't afford to put himself in a dangerous position, either. If he were the only one who spoke out against the Jannik plan, then the kongelig might very well put a target on his back next. It was easier—safer—to go along with the group's decision than to argue on behalf of my family's lives.

Though Lothar could understand the murder of my mother, there was little reason to kill my sisters and brother and attempt to kill me; we were far too young to be invited onto Hans Lollik Helle for the storm season, and even if we had been offered a chance to replace our mother, the king obviously wasn't as interested in us as he was in Mirjam Rose. Lothar had fully expected that he'd be the next regent, and as he also agreed that a family of islanders had no business holding a monopoly of one of the most lucrative businesses of Hans Lollik, he would simply find a way to tax our family until our coin ran dry and we were forced to leave for the north. A simple, logical solution.

The Jannik family wasn't logical. Aksel was becoming more like his father with every passing day: drunk, shouting and stumbling incoherently; if Beata had lived, and the two had been wed, Lothar was certain Aksel would have eventually turned his fist to the poor girl. It was reasonable to assume that Aksel Jannik, in his pain and fury, would drunkenly stumble through the groves and decide to set fire to the first house of the kongelig he saw. He might've even have planned to set fire to every single house, including his own, before he understood the depth of his mistake and ran away like the coward he was.

Alida's thoughts on the possibility of Aksel's guilt are similar; she, too, has never respected the Jannik. Even Erik worries that his friend might be to blame for the death of Olsen Årud. It's only Patrika, barely aware of the suggestion in the conversation that takes place, and Jytte, who is convinced of my guilt, who don't place blame on Aksel in their thoughts.

It doesn't matter. Konge Valdemar waves a hand at Lothar, who nods and stands. He begins his questioning of each of us. What do we know of the fire? Were we the ones who set it, or did we send someone to set the fire in our stead?

Erik was drunk, asleep—in bed with a slave girl; Alida, with me. Patrika was whale watching, just as she'd said. Jytte had been answering letters from Solberg Helle pertaining to her estate. The only person whose answers we don't have is Aksel. I glance at Lothar. It isn't lost on me that we don't have his answers to his own questions, either.

Lothar speaks, taking his seat beside the king once again. "Assuming Aksel Jannik's innocence, there's another suspect we must consider," he tells the king. "The Ludjivik wouldn't have let the death of their patriarch go unanswered. Gustav Ludjivik's cousins could easily be behind these deaths."

I don't see how the Ludjivik cousins could've spread their grasp onto the royal island so easily and quickly, but it's not my place to question. The king seems to consider this. He nods, and in his silence, my vision flickers; I see the truth behind the screen of kraft. The king isn't there, and behind him is the rotting wallpaper, the black mold spread across the empty chair that waits at the helm of the table. The lie returns, and the room is glistening in its mahogany and velvet and gold once again, the king with his soured pale skin and empty eyes. He smiles at me. For only a second, so quickly I can't be sure any of the kongelig have even seen. He smiles, as though whoever has created this vision wants me to know that they're aware of what I've realized, about the king and the house and this island itself.

"If it is indeed the Ludjivik," Patrika says, suddenly invested in the conversation, "then I'd like to find my revenge myself." She hadn't been paying attention, had wished she hadn't come to this meeting room, but now she hears a chance, finally, to release the pain and anger building beneath her skin.

The king asks her, "And how will you do this?"

"I'll take my guards, and the guards of anyone else who is willing to offer them, and I'll go to Ludjivik Helle and burn the island to the ground. There will be no survivors. The Ludjivik cousins knew this would be the response, and so they have no care for their people."

"That isn't fair to the innocents," Alida tells Patrika—a surprise, to all around the table. Alida usually doesn't speak. She tends to daydream, counting down the seconds to her freedom from the meeting room, but I can see that she's shaken by the fire and Olsen Årud's death. Beata Larsen's passing was a tragedy, but now this is no coincidence. She sees the situation as I do: There has always been death on Hans Lollik Helle, yes, but now someone in this room means to be rid of each of the other kongelig, until they themselves are finally guaranteed the throne. Alida won't look at Patrika, but I sense a suspicion in her: She knows that Patrika Årud didn't love Olsen. Couldn't it have easily been the woman, sacrificing her husband's life in order to receive the crown she so desperately wants for herself? She could've killed him to take the guilt and blame away from herself by pretending to be in mourning, while she then continues to kill each of us without suspicion. The only question is how she—how anyone in this room—might've managed to trick Lothar Niklasson.

Unless he himself is lying, Alida thinks—declaring that everyone in this room speaks their truths.

Patrika doesn't look away from the king. "The Ludjivik signed away their lives the moment they killed my husband."

"You have no proof that it was them," Jytte says. "You only look for somewhere to place your anger. The answer might be closer than we think," she tells Patrika, her eyes meeting mine.

"I've proven my innocence."

"You've lied and tricked and schemed your way onto this island."

"She's proven her innocence," the false king says, and Jytte falls silent in her seat. The king regards Lothar. "How do you know that it was the Ludjivik?"

"I can't think of who else it might be."

Konge Valdemar agrees to Patrika's wishes. She's to attack Ludjivik Helle and take the island for herself, to place under Årud rule. I swallow down my own arguments, trying not to think on the children who had raced after my carriage, the villagers washing their clothes and picking weeds from their gardens with their distrustful eyes. It's impossible to justify the murder of innocents, the deaths of children. They'll all be dead in a few days' time because of this one woman's need for revenge.

CHAPTER NINETEEN

Løren walks me back to the Jannik house as the sun begins to set. Once I've walked through the front doors, he turns, heading for the slaves' entrance to the kitchens so that he can go down the hall and to the library, where he still sleeps to this day; he can't stand the slaves' quarters on this island, there're too many memories that haunt him at night and make it impossible for him to sleep, and no one has yet told him that he can't make the library his own personal chamber, so that's where he stays. I tell him to wait, so he waits. I ask him to join me in the sitting room. He doesn't move. He doesn't want to. He can't be around me for much longer without letting the hatred inside of him seep into the air, into his words and expressions, and he's supposed to have learned his lesson on how, exactly, he should treat his Jannik masters.

But he also can't tell me no. He follows me inside, down the hall and through the sitting room doors. The nights have been cold enough to want a fire, to fight against the breeze that forces itself through the cracks in the house. The fireplace here hasn't been lit, and Marieke has gone to bed. Agatha busies herself with lighting the fire.

"Is there anything else you require, Elskerinde Jannik?" she asks.

I dismiss her, and as the fire crackles, Løren stands where he

usually would, against the wall and at attention. I ask him to sit.
He doesn't want to, but his leg where the whip cut in pains him.
He sits on the sofa opposite me, on the seat Aksel had taken just
a few weeks before.

"How're your wounds?" I ask Løren. "Are you healing well?"

He doesn't believe I actually care to know, but he still answers.
"I'm healing slowly."

"It seems you should be used to such beatings. You have a lot
of scars."

He isn't sure what the point of me mentioning this is; he sits
in silence.

"I want to be your ally, Løren," I tell him, "but you don't help
me if you do such things—hitting Aksel, that could've been a
fatal mistake. You're lucky I was able to convince him and the
other kongelig to spare your life."

"Is that what you think you did?"

He doesn't say any more. I sit and wait, but it's clear that he
won't speak. The minutes pass, and finally I break under the
pressure of the quiet and his hateful eyes.

"I tried to help you."

"Yes," he says, "that's what you continue to tell yourself."

"You can feel it for yourself," I tell him—an invitation to use
his kraft on me, to take my ability and read my own thoughts,
my own feelings, but he refuses. He feels unsettled whenever
he enters my mind. I'm used to knowing the lives of the people around me, to slipping in and out of the minds and souls of
others, becoming an entirely different person from one moment
to the next; but Løren has never known anything but his own
life. To suddenly become me—to see the world through my
eyes, and to feel, for even a moment, the freedom I feel—takes
a toll on him. It's like having one of the many dreams he had
as a child, dreams of his freedom, of walking from a boat and

onto an island filled with escaped slaves of Hans Lollik—only to wake, still in the slaves' quarters, still as trapped as he has been since the moment he was pulled from his mother's stomach.

He'd had a friend, once; yes, hard to believe, but he did. No one had ever wanted anything to do with Løren: He was Engel Jannik's son and had the blood of the Fjern in him. The other slaves believed Løren thought he was better than they, and he can admit now that he did think this, not because of the Fjern blood in his veins but because he wondered why they wouldn't fight for their freedom. They seemed content to wake day after day and do their masters' bidding, without considering for a moment that they might take the machetes they used to work the fields and cut their masters' stomachs open instead. He wondered why they didn't run. He ran, time and again, and received the beatings and whippings, knowing all the while that he would still try again, even if it meant that he failed, even if it meant that he would lose his life. He couldn't imagine living as the other slaves of the Jannik household did: as though their freedom wasn't worth fighting for. As though their freedom wasn't worth dying for.

They hated him for it, yes, and he told himself he hated them as well. But there was one boy. He was soft, touched in the head, as the other slaves liked to say, dropped as a baby and not worth much coin. He might've been drowned as an infant by Engel Jannik, if Engel had taken enough notice of him. The boy was eight years older than Løren, but acted as though he were five. He wanted to play games with Løren all of the time, even when he was nineteen years old, a man who should've been working the fields. They'd play hide and seek in the groves; if they were caught, they'd be whipped, but Løren's friend didn't seem to care. One day Løren saw an unused cave, well hidden by the mangroves. It was stocked with supplies. A forgotten hiding spot for smugglers, most likely. Løren knew that he could survive in the cave for an entire week, and once the search party gave up looking for him on this island, and even the nearest islands—once they all assumed he'd drowned trying to escape—he'd leave in the dead of night.

He told his friend his plan, and even offered to let the boy join him; and though he seemed uncertain, the boy said yes. It was on the night that they were meant to escape together that Løren got to the cave first. He waited, afraid that his friend had gotten lost or had changed his mind or become too scared to look for the cave without Løren there to guide him. Løren soon heard the hurried footsteps of his friend, but he'd brought someone with him: Engel Jannik and a set of guards. The boy pointed to Løren with a smile, hoping for Engel's approval. Løren had received the majority of his scars that night. It was bad enough, yes, that he so often plotted to escape on his own, but the idea that he might consider taking any of Engel's other slaves with him was too dangerous. Engel had actually meant to kill his son; when Løren was still breathing at the end of it all, Engel had ordered the guards to hang the boy by his wrists and let him starve. A night later, and he was still breathing. Three days later, and he was still alive. The other slaves grew afraid of him and wouldn't come near the tree from which he hung. They whispered that he'd been cursed—that a vengeful spirit had entered him, and that this was why Løren wouldn't die.

Engel didn't believe in the superstition of the savages, but he couldn't help but feel dread, fear, seeing his flesh and blood hanging by his wrists, head lolling and eyes half-open. He had Løren cut down and fed and washed, his wounds covered in salve. Still, Engel Jannik was angry that Løren had managed to survive his punishment, and so he had Løren's friend brought forth and hung from a tree, before all of the plantation. The slave hadn't been worth very much coin anyway.

"Do you believe the spirits mean to keep you alive?" I ask him.

I can feel the answer in him, but before he says a word, the doors
to the sitting room open, and Aksel stands before us, machete in
his hand. I barely have a moment to open my mouth before he
runs at Løren, barely have a chance to scream before he tries to cut
his brother's neck. Løren grabs his brother's wrist, straining against
him as the blade aims for his chest. The blade is knocked from
Aksel's hand, and the two lunge for it as it slides across the floor.
I try to force myself into Aksel, to control him, and I can feel no
thoughts in him, only a hollowness—he runs at Løren again, and
Løren stabs the machete deep into his brother's gut.

Aksel gasps. Blood seeps from his stomach and onto the floors.
He looks up at Løren with surprise, but his eyes are empty now.
Red spills from his open mouth. He drops to the ground.

I stand where I am, trapped in my shock—but Løren is quick
to move. He begins to pull his brother's arms. He wants my
help, needs my help, it's easy to see. My hand, trembling, reaches
for the handle of the machete still sticking from Aksel's stomach,
but Løren snaps at me not to touch it.

"He'll bleed out," he tells me. "Pick up his feet."

I pick up Aksel's feet. His body is heavy. He was spineless, a
coward, but he'd been even larger than Engel Jannik. His eyes
are stuck open, wide with shock. I pray to the spirits and the
divine gods above that no slave will see us now, and my prayers
are answered. We carry him through the hall, back out into the
gardens. I want to be rid of the body as quickly as possible, and
start for the cliffs, but Løren again shakes his head. We carry
Aksel, both of us sweating and heaving, down the dirt path until
we reach the rocky sand. Here Løren pulls the machete out, and
he was right: Blood spurts, but dies down quickly. Løren throws
the blade into the sea, and he and I wade out into the water with
Aksel as far as we can, up to our shoulders, my dress floating
around me, coral scratching the bottoms of my feet. We let him

drift. The tide will carry him out to the ocean, where hopefully his body will be torn apart by the sharks. I can only pray that the water won't bring him back to shore.

The two of us stand where we are for some time, as though the roots from my nightmares have wound their way around our feet. I can't speak, can barely breathe. The shock of it all begins to take over my body now. The memory of him suddenly appearing, as though out of thin air, rushing at Løren in such a way, he meant to kill his brother, completely unprovoked—he might've tried to kill me next, might've succeeded...

We walk back up onto the sand, breathless. Løren won't meet my eye.

"He tried to kill you," I tell him. "He came out of nowhere, and he tried to kill you. There's nothing else you could've done."

"If anyone learns the truth, I'll be hung," he tells me. There's no excuse for a slave to kill their master. I don't bother to argue with him on this; he speaks the truth.

I can attempt to speak on Løren's behalf, as I've done before, but Løren didn't simply hit Aksel across the face this time. The kongelig won't leave this slave's punishment to me. They will come and they'll force their way into this house and they'll drag Løren to the groves to hang him from his neck. I do have my kraft, but I've never been able to control more than one person at a time. It's a fight that I will lose.

We walk back along the path to the Jannik house. I expect him to follow me inside, to go to the library, but he doesn't step through the threshold. He lets me see that he needs to walk, to think. He wouldn't be able to sleep anyway. The shock vibrates through Løren as well, though he keeps his face impassive. His muscles are taut beneath his skin. He'd acted in self-defense. He wouldn't have allowed his brother to take his life. He couldn't help that he'd fought back, but now he knows he'll die anyway.

★   ★   ★

Marieke can plainly see that something is wrong the next day, but I'm afraid to tell even her the truth. I know what she would say to me: that I'm not so weak as to imprison myself—that I can't be afraid to face the kongelig. The killer is getting closer to seeing their own goals won, and if they learn of Aksel's murder, they'll be glad to see me executed next. But the more the kongelig kills as they control the king, the more that kongelig helps me as well. There're fewer people in the room now, and if I'm to believe Patrika's grief, and if I'm still to trust that Jytte Solberg would not act against me so aggressively, then the killer can only be either Lothar Niklasson or the Nørup twins. I still want to trust that Erik and Alida Nørup have no desire for the crown—and so I feel my focus on Lothar Niklasson growing.

My plans have had to constantly shift and evolve since I came to this island, but new plans begin to build in my mind now. I can't trust any of the kongelig, this is certain, but there are ways I can use them. Patrika Årud and the Nørup twins might be particularly helpful.

I stay in my bed, peering out over my balcony for a sign of Løren's return, but I don't see him. I sleep, fleetingly, falling in and out of dreams where one moment, I open my eyes and Freja Jannik sits beside me, dirt and leaves tangled in her hair, and the next, I'm walking through the maze of the Rose manor, listening to my mother's screams.

I hear a voice, low and laughing. I fall into sleep again, and when I wake, the voice is louder. It strikes me that the voice sounds like Aksel's, but I think only that this is another trick of my mind. But the laughter doesn't end. I stand from my bed, wandering the hall and walking down the stairs. I find him in the sitting room. Erik is there with him. The two have been drinking. Aksel's pain darkens the air. Even with a grin cracked across his face, I can see that with every pulse he mourns Beata. He's alive, without a machete's wound in his stomach. Both men notice me and stop laughing. They look at me with confused frowns. I'm still in my sleeping clothes, and I'm staring at Aksel as though a fever has taken me and driven me into madness.

Erik asks, "Are you well, Elskerinde Jannik?"

I'm not well. That much I do know. Perhaps another storm-season sickness has taken me without my realizing it and I've been sick for weeks now; perhaps I never recovered from the first, and my entire time spent here on Hans Lollik Helle has only been a hallucination, a dream. I might've convinced myself that the king is only a puppet, pulled by invisible strings; might've convinced myself that one of the kongelig holds a kraft so powerful that they control reality itself. Nothing feels real now, nothing certain.

I don't answer them. I turn, walking quickly through the halls. When I enter the library, Løren is sitting in his corner, a book open in his lap.

He snaps the book shut. A slave shouldn't know how to read, and I've caught him now for a second time. But when he sees the look on my face, his fear of punishment leaves him.

Løren doesn't care for me, not in the slightest, but even he can't resist asking me what's wrong, and if something has happened.

"Your brother is alive," I tell him.

He stares at me, expressionless.

"He's in the sitting room right now, speaking with Erik Nørup."

"Is everything all right?" Løren asks me.

I'm shaking now, trembling. "You killed him," I tell Løren. "Last night. You stuck a machete into his gut."

Løren shakes his head, looking at me with confusion and the slightest touch of pity. He never thought he'd feel such a thing for me, but I look as mad as I feel, I can see it in his eyes: My hair tangled, in my sleeping gown, dark circles beneath my eyes, and telling him stories I'm so certain are real. Last night had been real, I know that it was, but the look on Løren's face tells me otherwise. He would love to have killed his brother, there's no doubt about that, but he didn't. He walked me back to the Jannik house last night after my meeting with the kongelig, and he left me at the front door as he went around to the back, to the slaves' entrance of the kitchens, and came to the library. He's been here since last night, hoping that I wouldn't call on him, hoping that he could hide away for the rest of the day. He hasn't seen me since then. He most certainly didn't kill his brother. All of this he thinks to himself—but for the glimmer of a moment, I don't believe him. I wonder if it's possible that he's found a way to lie to me. If he's only playing a game with me, just as the kongelig do.

Løren tells me he'll call for Marieke, and walks past the library's doorway, leaving me behind. I make my way to the shelves, to the book he left on the floor. It's on the history of these islands, as told by a Fjernman. I know this book. Claus had read it in the libraries of the manor of Rose Helle. He'd told me the history of these islands, a history passed down from one mouth to the next, stories belonging to our ancestors and our people; but it wasn't a history we were supposed to remember, nor one we were supposed to keep. The history as told by the Fjern could be the only truth. Their divine right to take these lands from the savages, to hold us captive in our own home. Marieke enters the library to find me crying. I'm afraid that she'll be annoyed with me, but she isn't, not this time. She takes my arm and guides me back to my bed. She feels my face and tells me that I don't have a fever but that I might be at the beginning of another bout of storm-season sickness. She makes me broth and lemongrass tea. I drink it all dutifully, and she smooths down my hair and hums a song to me as she did when

I was a child. I close my eyes, and she pulls my sheets up around me and leaves my chambers, but I can't sleep. I stand from my bed and go to the balcony overlooking the churning of the sea.

"Are you feeling better?"

I turn, and Løren is standing at my threshold. He walks inside and shuts the door behind him. It's just as he pulls a knife that I feel the truth: This isn't Løren. He has no soul, no emotion. He rushes at me, and the blade pierces my stomach. Pain flourishes, fire spreading through my gut and over my skin. My vision flickers. I fall to the floor. I must've screamed, because the door bangs open, and my vision goes black, then white, though I can hear Marieke's voice.

CHAPTER TWENTY

I'm still alive, though I probably shouldn't be. I want to ask Løren if the spirits who've kept him alive all these years have now decided to protect me as well, but I don't see him in the days that follow, and I don't ask him to come to my rooms. I'm too afraid to look at him, when his face had been the last thing I saw before I was stabbed. I know that Løren's thoughts would insist on his innocence, but I know also that nothing is a coincidence on Hans Lollik Helle.

Marieke stays by my bedside, though at first I'd screamed at her to leave, uncertain whether she was real or another one of the ghosts haunting Hans Lollik Helle. She sits at my side, holding my hand, eyes closed as she whispers her prayers to the spirits to heal me. It shouldn't have happened this way. Marieke knows that I'm in her mind, but she doesn't argue with me when I sink into her memories. She'd been in the kitchens, readying another pot of lemongrass tea for me, when she heard the scream and the crash that'd followed. She raced down the hall and up the stairs, only to find me on the ground with a knife in my gut. The blood on my hands suggested I'd stabbed myself, though where I'd gotten the knife I couldn't say. I didn't recognize the knife. It hadn't come from the kitchens. Marieke decided it had belonged to a vengeful spirit, enraged that I hadn't killed the kongelig and freed my people. She'd taken the knife from my room and thrown the blade into the sea.

I couldn't speak at all for the first few days, and I could barely open my eyes. I mostly slept, but when I woke for a few moments of each day, Marieke was always by my side. Marieke wasn't sure I would survive, even with the herbs and salves she'd applied and reapplied without stop, praying to the spirits not to take me yet. I know this is the truth, because I'd heard her prayers, even as I ran across the shore with a laughing Ellinor, and while Inga sang her songs, tying ribbons in my hair. I asked them both where our mother was, and they only smiled. I walked the maze until I came upon the sitting room of the Rose manor, and there she sat, fiddling with a needle and thread. She wouldn't look at me as I called for her. Tante's voice whispered in my ear.

When I woke, Marieke was praying beside me, my hand in hers. I gripped her fingers, pain moving through me like a living thing. My voice was harsh and low as I said her name. Marieke's eyes widened. She murmured that her prayers had been answered. Maybe they were. She asked me what happened, but I could only speak a few words. Marieke patted my hand, understanding the effort, and told me that it was all right, to be quiet and to rest. Even as I felt her spirit, her memories, fear built in me. I sensed Marieke's presence, the life that filled her, but she could also draw a hidden blade and plunge it into me. She could just as easily be a product of my mind.

When I wake again, Marieke speaks to me without stopping, filling the silence with her soothing voice. She tells me of memories we shared, traveling the north. She'd never seen anything like it, the cobblestone streets and towering buildings and people, so many people. She'd longed for the islands, longed for her home by the cliffs of Rose Helle, missed her little girl and the child's father as well. She'd hidden her sadness from me, over the years, and her rage. She'd put all of her energy into raising me as if I'd been her own. But there'd been days, yes, when she'd considered leaving me—taking the money she carried for me and finding her freedom. She never considered it for very long, thinking of what my mother's spirit might do to her if she ever had.

She tells herself she grew to love me. This, along with needing to see her little girl's killers dead, is why she stays beside me.

I don't leave my bed for days. I sleep, listening to Marieke's voice and Tante's whispers. Freja Jannik takes my hand, and Ellinor's laughter sounds like my mother's screams. Fire licks at my bed, the curtains, my hair and skin, and when I try to shout for help, it's gone. A storm lashes at the windows, blowing rain and wind all around me, sky illuminated with purple lightning, but when I cry in Marieke's arms, it's over.

I sit up in my bed with a gasp, yellow sunlight filling the room and blinding me. Pain bursts, and I stand to my feet, pulling up the ends of my dress. My wound has been stitched, black thread woven through my skin. My head feels foggy, as though I've been asleep for weeks.

When I leave my room, the halls are shadowed, windows shuttered and closed, curtains pulled. The heat and dust swirls with every step. It's hard to breathe. Water and mold swell in the wallpaper. The sitting room furniture is pushed to the side, dirt spread across the floor. I go to the kitchens, and a slave stirs a pot of stew. I ask for Marieke, and the girl tells me she's in the gardens.

Marieke bends over a basket filled with weeds, sweating in the heat. She stands, eyes wide, when she sees me.

"You shouldn't be on your feet, Sigourney," she says.

I see the state of the garden: the uprooted trees and dead brush. There'd been a second storm while I slept.

She walks with me, back into the shade of the house and to my room, my balcony so that we can enjoy the breeze.

"The house is all right, for the most part," Marieke tells me, "and the manor on Lund Helle is still standing."

"What about the kongelig?" I ask her. "Konge Valdemar?"

"No one else has been killed, if that's what you mean to ask." The murderer hasn't been found yet, either. I think of the nightmares—wandering a maze in my dreams only for Beata Larsen to die; Løren, knife in his hand, when the only hand that had held the knife was mine. I've thought the other kongelig have been behind the deaths, the killings, and Konge Valdemar himself—but it could all be me. This could all be my paranoia, my imagination. This is what I think, for the briefest of moments—but no. Nothing is a coincidence on Hans Lollik Helle. This is the kongelig, the same who want me dead, playing their games with my head.

Marieke hesitates to tell me something, but I don't read her thoughts. I want to respect her privacy, especially since I owe her my life. "Aksel refuses his duties as Herre Jannik. He's allowed the house to fall into ruin. He won't give us the tools to fix it. And there's something else," Marieke tells me. "His brother, Løren, has run away."

Løren had waited until the height of the storm. The slave girl Agatha had seen him leaving, walking through the lashing wind and rain, knowing no one would dare to follow him. He went to the shore. No one has seen him since. It's possible he jumped into the waves, or took a boat he'd dragged there, but the end result must still be the same: Løren wouldn't have survived the sea.

"His body still hasn't washed ashore," Marieke tells me.

Løren shouldn't have survived the sea, but he's always been under the protection of the spirits. It's possible he finally found his freedom, escaped Hans Lollik Helle and is on his way to the north. He could find happiness there. Simple work that would allow him to earn coin, a house he could call his own. Løren wouldn't need much to be happy, I can tell; he would leave his memories of Hans Lollik behind, like a distant dream that would only return to him in his nightmares while he slept.

I ask Marieke to pass a message to Malthe: Have the guards search the shores and groves of the nearest islands, and especially Larsen Helle.

The kongelig sit around the mahogany table of the meeting room. While I was healing, Patrika had attacked Ludjivik Helle, just as she promised she would. She left Hans Lollik Helle on a ship that met with ships of Niklasson and Solberg Helle. There were over five hundred guards at her command with the guards of the combined houses, and she didn't plan for mercy. The killings were easy. The guards marched from the bay, walking into villages, killing the Fjern who attempted to fight, finding the children who hid beneath their beds. They marched to the failing plantations and estates, rounding up each of the masters. They were all executed, tied to stakes and burned before their slaves. Only the slaves were kept alive: They were taken onto the Niklasson ships, to be sold for a profit; the coin would be split evenly among the Årud, Niklasson, and Solberg treasuries. Patrika Årud is certain that no one survived the massacre of Ludjivik Helle.

They'd considered the attack a success at first—but while they focused on Ludjivik Helle, the cousins of Gustav Ludjivik had already moved on. Patrika had taken all of her guardsmen from Årud Helle, and so it was an easy attack. Most of the plantations on Årud Helle were burned, many of the masters and their slaves killed, and the Ludjivik cousin at the helm of the battle, Hannes Skov, took the manor of the island, Herregård Mord, for himself. The manor is like a fortress, I've heard. He's comfortable there.

Patrika is quiet at the meeting as she listens to the updates on Hannes Skov. She's embarrassed that she was tricked so easily, and while she won't admit it, she's still in mourning over the loss of Olsen. She's not as adamant on finding her revenge, nor as determined to win the crown as she had been. Now she silently questions why she is still on Hans Lollik Helle; thinks to herself on the many times Olsen had wondered why she wanted this throne. She can't remember her answers now, what she'd told him, but I can see them in her memories: how she'd wanted the power of a crown over the most beautiful lands in all the world.

Lothar describes the most recent attacks. Smaller rebellions have started on Nørup and Solberg Helle, though each has been stamped out. It seems Hannes Skov means to attack each island of Hans Lollik, taking control in the kongelig's stead, until he finally reaches the royal island itself. Lothar tells us we'll have to attack Årud Helle, of course; we have no choice if we want to regain control of the situation, which is rapidly disintegrating before our very eyes.

The false king is silent today. If the kongelig who controls him has any thoughts, they keep those opinions a mystery, having Konge Valdemar add nothing to the discussion as the guards of the families are chosen to battle for Årud Helle. No one asks for the Jannik or Lund families to join the fight; all know that the guardsmen are untrained in comparison to the armies that Jytte Solberg and Lothar Niklasson have built for themselves.

I could leave the meeting without having to worry about the oncoming battles at all—but I also know where the real fight lies. I hadn't planned it, but the opportunity presents itself.

"Valdemar Helle is closest to Solberg Helle," I say.

Jytte looks annoyed at the interruption in their plans. She asks why this matters. "The island has been abandoned since Konge Valdemar moved onto Hans Lollik Helle at the beginning of his reign." She's impatient. Everyone knows this.

"That could suggest the perfect position for the Ludjivik to hide as they plan their next attack. If I'm wrong, your campaign won't have suffered at all," I say. "But if I'm right, it's worth me taking some Jannik guardsmen to scout the island and ensure there are no spies. Perhaps even rebuild fortifications for ourselves, so that when they attempt to fall back, we'll be ready to attack."

I can see plainly that Lothar agrees—there's no harm in sending me to Valdemar Helle—but Jytte doesn't trust my intentions. She wonders what secret plans I might have in wanting to be on Valdemar Helle, away from the other kongelig and away from potential witnesses. She doesn't know, but if she can, she'll find out. The king doesn't speak his opinion. As I peer at the king through my eyelashes, I believe I can see my vision of him flicker. I wonder if the kongelig who controls him is growing weaker from the amount of energy it must take to uphold this lie, and for so long, too.

The meeting is adjourned, the plans set. I stand to leave along with the rest of the kongelig, but the king stays seated. "Elskerinde Jannik," he says, "a word."

The kongelig are surprised. I can see it in their glances, in the flare of thought around the room. Lothar Niklasson wonders what the king could have to say to me. He and Konge Valdemar have always discussed their tactics and plans. The king would never have spoken to any of the other kongelig without Lothar first knowing he would. Cristoff Valdemar has changed, yes, that much is certain; changed from the friendship the two had once shared, generations before under the rule of a different king an entire era ago. They had planned and schemed, Cristoff and Lothar, two young boys who envisioned a future where all of

Hans Lollik would belong to them. Their friendship was close; their alliance was natural. They don't have to work to convince anyone that they belong to this world and that the world belongs to them. They aren't like Jytte Solberg: emotionless so that no one will question her ability to rule. They are nothing like me, certainly. What could two pale-skinned Fjern boys have in common with a dark-skinned islander like myself? They'd been taught my people are savages—that we have an inability to think for ourselves, to feel as other humans do. Both boys had been taught that they own the world, and that I'm a part of the world they own.

Lothar is confused. He and Cristoff had been handed the power they were owed, and Lothar was ready to be passed the title of regent, as they'd agreed so many years ago. The Nik-lasson family would continue in the vision the two boys had for these islands: the profit in crops, in sugarcane and tobacco, would reach a height previously unseen. These islands could become so strong in coin, so abundant in crop, that the Kon-inkrijk Empire would come to rely on Hans Lollik. Though Lothar hadn't shared his thoughts with Cristoff, Lothar was cer-tain that his own successors could even declare independence from the Koninkrijk Empire, that the Niklasson name could become regent of its own nation of islands, the wealthiest in all the world. There were still steps to follow, plans to be made, but they were both so close to reaching their goals, the islands under Cristoff's rule with Lothar's guidance—and as the king had promised so long ago, Lothar and his nephews were to be in line to take the crown.

But now, Lothar's trust in the king wavers. He worries that Valdemar's promises won't be met. Konge Valdemar has been cold to Lothar—and confusing. The first moment of confusion, certainly, had been the invitation to Mirjam Rose to join Hans Lollik Helle for the storm season all those years ago.

Lothar had asked why, and the king had been compelled to answer honestly: "I wonder, sometimes, if the islanders might be better fit to rule themselves."

There'd been no reason for it, no inspiration for him to betray Lothar and the Fjern people; and now, here I am in my mother's place. Lothar is prepared to take the regency for himself, rather than rely on his alliance with Valdemar. He's worked nearly all his life for this moment, and he won't let go easily.

All of the kongelig leave slowly, their questions and curiosity following each out the door, but Lothar hesitates, unmoving.

"Leave, Lothar," the king commands.

Lothar jolts—he's become increasingly used to this anger in the king, this anger that Valdemar shows, but it still sends a shock through him. They'd been the closest of friends as children, the best of allies and partners as they grew. Lothar watched as Cristoff was married to a Niklasson cousin. Lothar watched as they had their child, though the girl had been sickly and didn't live past her first year. The woman fell ill and passed away as well, and Cristoff never bothered to remarry or have another child; he'd already agreed to pass the regency to Lothar at the end of the era. Lothar had sometimes wondered if he should ask Cristoff if he'd ever, at any point in their friendship, considered Lothar the way that Lothar considered him: in the way that both boys were expected to look at the women of these islands. Lothar had felt this, when they were young. It was difficult not to love Cristoff Valdemar. He'd been golden, filled with light and laughter. He exuded the confidence only a person who knows the world belongs to them can exude: There's no need for self-consciousness, or to second-guess your actions, or the words that fall from your mouth, when you know there will be no consequence—when you know that the world will still be yours. Cristoff held this confidence, though it started to shake once he was visited by the voices he called the spirits of the dead. They must've whispered things to him that made him question his standing in this world, for him to turn to the gods for help. Lothar wondered, too, if perhaps these spirits had influenced Cristoff's when he invited Mirjam Rose onto his island.

Lothar had loved him, but he knew that such a love between them could never be. Lothar's love for Cristoff Valdemar had to be kept a secret; he couldn't risk asking his friend if he might've felt the same, couldn't risk the humiliation if Cristoff had declared Lothar's love a sin, as the empire of Koninkrijk had done many eras before.

Lothar leaves the table and makes his way for the door. He glances at me, and he thinks that I must have something to do with this change in the king. It's too much of a coincidence for him, that the storm season I, an islander, am wrongfully brought onto Hans Lollik Helle is the same storm season that Konge Valdemar has begun to push Lothar away. Herre Niklasson wonders if I'm behind everything: the murders, and perhaps even the Ludjivik uprising. Though Lothar had questioned me himself, he doesn't trust me; he never has, but especially now, he wonders if I plot to destroy Hans Lollik Helle.

The door closes behind him, and I'm left alone with Konge Valdemar.

I stay seated. The lay of the room—the shining mahogany and velvet and gilded gold, the chandelier above us—remains, and I think this is more chilling than if the false vision had finally dropped, revealing what I know is the truth.

The king doesn't smile at me. His mouth, I realize, has started to sag, his eyes have yellowed, his pale skin turning blue. He looks the way his corpse should look, just as it's beginning to rot.

"Are you surprised that I've asked you to sit with me, Elskerinde Jannik?"

I'm not sure what he expects me to say. "Yes, my king, I suppose so."

"Why is that?"

He watches me emptily, without any presence or life, and I know the risk I take now—but I know, too, that whoever controls the king must also suspect me of my truth. "I'm surprised because I know that you're not real, my king."

He smiles, slowly, waiting for me to continue, and so I do.

"You have no presence, no life. I look at you and I see a corpse." The longer I watch him, the more he seems to rot before my eyes, skin drooping around his cheeks. "Why don't I feel life from you?" I ask him. "Why don't I feel any presence?"

The king thinks it's funny that I've dared to ask outright. His smile widens, his eyes bright. He tells me that I'm brave. He doesn't answer my question. Instead he asks one of his own. "Why are you going to Valdemar Helle?"

I'm startled by the quick change in topic. "It's as I said before," I tell him. "It'll be useful to our campaign against the Ludjivik if I'm stationed there."

"You're not a very good liar, for someone who depends so much on lies."

I don't answer, and so he continues.

"You stayed here on Hans Lollik Helle, even knowing I wouldn't pass along the regency to you, even knowing the other kongelig want you dead. I was giving you a chance to escape this island, but you didn't take it. Why didn't you, Elskerinde Jannik?"

"Do you want me to leave?" I ask him. "Leave, before I figure out your truth?"

"I was showing you a mercy," he says. "That mercy won't be extended much longer. Leave," he tells me. "Leave Hans Lollik Helle and return to your home. Better yet, leave the islands of Hans Lollik altogether. You'll be giving up your potential power, your coin—but you'll have your life."

I can't pull my eyes away from him. "Who controls you?" I ask him. "Who among the kongelig?"

He laughs at this, his voice rasping, as someone might on their deathbed. He only stops when I say that I'll tell the kongelig. "And what will you do then?" I ask him. "If the kongelig know the truth, and Lothar can see that I'm not lying?"

"Go ahead," he tells me. "Let the kongelig know the truth."

The words hang in the air. "Do you mean to kill until we're all either dead or we've left the island and given up our claim to the throne?"

He stands to leave, his chair scraping behind him. "Let it be known that I did give you a chance."

Konge Valdemar vanishes before the words are even fully from his mouth. The room turns to rot, the wallpaper peeling, dark without the light of the chandelier that hangs from the ceiling, buried in unlit candle wax. I stand, expecting to see an assassin ready to cut my throat in the shadows, but no one comes. I leave the room, run into the hall, once again fallen beneath the lie, dirt smearing the floor—and I hear the echoes of footsteps. I follow them, running, but the footsteps are quicker, farther and farther away down the darkened and rotting halls, until I can't hear them any longer.

CHAPTER TWENTY-ONE

There are eighty guardsmen under the Jannik and Lund names combined, not nearly as many as the Solberg's three hundred, but enough for a small scouting expedition. Malthe takes command of the men as our ships arrive at the bay of Valdemar Helle. There's no wind. The sea is still, unmoving. The guards have to row the boats, and though I expected to arrive before dawn, by the time we reach the sand, the sun is already high above us in the sky, sweat running down my back. The men make camp on the seashore, ready for their orders. At least if there're enemies hidden in the brush, they'll have to make themselves known before they attempt to strike. The island is small, and made mostly of volcanic rock. The Valdemar family had been poor and relied mostly on the trade of fishermen. As a boy, Cristoff Valdemar had wanted more. He'd believed he deserved more.

Malthe is silent and steady as he follows me away from the clatter of the making of camp. I walk along the shore, the sand ashy and mixed with sharp black stones. I've grown to appreciate Malthe's calming presence. His mind is meditative in its silence. He doesn't pass judgment and he doesn't expect anything of me, except for my command, which he will follow, as is his duty. Malthe's mind is so carefully curated that when I sink into his thoughts, I can only access a few memories that I can sense he wants me to see.

It's the mind of someone who has something to hide. I think that Malthe would want to hide the hatred he has for me, and the disgust. He's by my side every day—has sworn his loyalty to me. His hatred isn't something he would want me to know.

Malthe had never known his mother or father. He'd been sold, like most of the boys in the guard, from the moment he'd barely been able to walk on his own two legs. Sold and trained and beaten and whipped with every mistake he made. He wasn't afraid of the beatings. He didn't follow the gods of the Fjern. He believed in his ancestors, the spirits, and he knew that he had been blessed. They wouldn't allow him to be killed, not so easily; they would help him find his peace and happiness. Malthe knew that the spirits would even grant him his freedom, without him even needing to escape.

He fell in love with a sweet island girl. Many boys did, though as guardsmen, they were forbidden from marriage. This girl belonged to Skov Helle, while he'd belonged to Hans Lollik Helle, but she would come once a week to pick up a delivery of fresh rose mallow and lemongrass for Elskerinde Skov's tea. At first it was the smallest of smiles between them; then conversations that lasted minutes before Malthe could hear his trainer shouting for him. Finally, a kiss. He told her he had fallen in love with her, and she said she had fallen for him, too. Every time they saw each other, even for only the smallest of glances and fast whispers, they built their life together. The plans they had made: Malthe would work in the guard until he found enough coin on the bodies of dead men to buy both his and her freedom. She would tell him of the house she would make for him, the children they would have.

And one day she was gone. Malthe looked forward to seeing her again the next week, as he'd grown accustomed to—even his commander had begun to allow the two a few extra moments whenever she visited, he'd grown so used to seeing this island girl with her sweet smile—but she never came. Malthe waited week after week, but the girl never returned to Lund Helle again.

Malthe still didn't know if she lived or if she'd died; if someone had learned their secret, and wouldn't let her return; if Elskerinde Skov had simply grown tired of rose-mallow and lemongrass tea.

That was all Malthe needed to realize, finally, that his life wasn't his own. He'd known before, knew that he was owned by a Fjern-man, knew that he would have to die for this man if his master ever commanded it. But now the life he imagined for himself—having a small house on the edge of the plantation, coming home to the sweet island girl who smelled of lemongrass, having a child of his own—everything he'd imagined, he now lost.

I want to ask Malthe why he doesn't ask about the girl. Gossip flows so easily through these islands, and surely there's someone who would know of a slave who once made deliveries to Lund Helle, but I realize that he's thought of this too, of course he has—he simply doesn't want to know. It's easier for him that way. He's already mourned what he lost. If he were to find the girl again, what would he expect of her, and himself, when he can no longer ignore the fact that they don't own their lives, their free-dom? It's better not knowing where she is, if she still lives.

He's silent as we walk the path, which is more rock than dirt. That anything grows on this island is a miracle, but the trees prove themselves to be worthy of this feat: thick and gnarled, roots creeping up from the ground. The brush is made of thorns, snagging my dress and my hair and my skin. We walk in the heat, mosquitoes swarming around me, though I don't see any water where they could have laid their eggs. Sweat trickles down my back, and I'm sore and scratched, the sun reaching its highest point in the sky. I'm about to turn to Malthe, to give up on find-ing the manor of Valdemar Helle, when I see it.

The manor is a small thing, burned black from fires long ago, its back crumbled to the ground. It stands in a clearing of trees, though a garden takes over the house's entrance. I walk closer and see that the sugar apple trees still bear their fruit, swollen and falling and rotting on the ground. The windows of the house are open or shattered. It's easy to see inside, to see that there's no furniture or paintings that hang on the wall. Cristoff Valdemar was born and grew and lived in this manor, up until the very day he was passed the crown from the former regent; Cristoff had been the rightful heir, even though he was only a distant cousin. The king's sons had been killed in battle, in an uprising of the Ludjivik. It might've been a coincidence that the Ludjivik suddenly received the coin and resources to begin their uprising just at the end of the regent's era. It might still be a coincidence that Lothar Niklasson is so eager to destroy the Ludjivik name, now that their resources have dwindled.

I examine the house, the crumbled stone. The structure itself is unsafe, but still I walk into the open entryway, all signs of a door itself already gone. Wood-paneled floors sink into the dirt, from which weeds and wildflowers bloom. Remnants of a fireplace hold brush, growing from the earth. It's difficult to tell what might've once been the sitting room, the dining room, the kitchen. I'd hoped there'd be a clue—some piece I could add to the growing puzzle of Hans Lollik Helle, something that would illuminate the answer to all my questions. But there's nothing here except a broken manor, a ghost of itself, and some overripe fruit that hangs from the trees.

Malthe waits while I walk around to the back of the house. I see two large stones, out of place—walk to them, and read their engravings. The graves of Dagny and Karine Valdemar: Cristoff's wife and daughter. It's strange that they've been buried here and not out at sea. Burying bodies in the soil is a tradition of the Koninkrijk Empire, who have no access to the ocean to bury their people. It's possible that the king decided to bury them in the dirt as a devoted Fjern would. Dagny and Karine Valdemar have both been dead years now, taken by the storm-season sickness. There's another stone beside the grave of Dagny Valdemar, smaller and unmarked. This strikes me as odd, so I call for Malthe. He sees the work that needs to be done and leaves me where

I stand. I wait, listening to the birdcalls, the rustling of leaves. I begin to regret being left here alone. It feels as though a pair of eyes watch me—as though there's a presence nearby, waiting for the moment it can strike. There's a crunching of stone, but it's only Malthe returning. He carries a shovel he'd brought from camp. He begins his work without complaint.

I stand and watch him dig. His hands become bloody, his legs and feet crusted with dirt, and still he digs, until the sun begins to set and the sky becomes purple, the wings of fruit bats fluttering across my vision in shadow. He digs, until finally he stops, and I can feel the shock in him, the disgust. I walk to the edge of the grave. I'm not as surprised as I should be.

"Keep digging," I tell Malthe.

I stand unmoving at the edge of the grave and watch as the pale hand that appears from the dirt becomes connected to an arm, a head with patches of its hair still connected to the skull. The body of Konge Cristoff Valdemar, empty eye sockets decayed, mouth eaten away to show his teeth, skin purple and blue. The gash in his neck is so deep that his head was nearly severed.

"What will you do?" Malthe asks me.

The Ludjivik are not on Valdemar Helle. Guards had scouted the island from one bay to the next, and no spies or Ludjivik soldiers were found, so we move deeper into the groves; ships are hidden behind the island, ready to swerve around and attack once the Ludjivik appear. I wait on a ship that remains motionless in the stagnant water, wind lifeless—rare, especially when we're so near the end of the storm season. It almost feels as though the spirits have forced their way into the world of the living; the air, heavy with the ghosts of my ancestors, is so unmoving that there isn't even a breeze. This isn't helpful for the attack. Though the guards have been trained for land and sea and are used to rowing when necessary, we will be fighting against the tide, making the Ludjivik ships swifter than ours.

The battle begins, and in the distance I can see the movement of ships as the Solberg and Niklasson armies attack. Even so far away, I can see the streams of smoke that rise and hear the screams. We wait—wait so long the sun begins to fall, and bodies of the battle begin to float by; sharks rise, breaking the surface of the water with an explosion of fins before the bodies are ripped apart, pulled down beneath the surface in a tide of red.

Ours proves to be a useful position for the first of the ships that attempt to flee the Solberg army. The Lund guards that waited on the island come from hiding, arrows lit with fire flying. The ships attempt a wider berth, but the Jannik ships block their escape. The Solberg is close enough behind. The fight is brought before me, and I can see the Solberg guards board the Ludjivik ships; see the men cut, screaming, falling into the water and to the sharks below. These men are all dark-skinned, all islanders, all slaves who have no choice but to fight and die for the Fjern who own them. Refusing would mean execution; it's better to fight now, with the chance that they might live. And so the Fjern pit my people against one another and watch comfortably from their seats while islanders die around them.

The battle isn't long. The Ludjivik guards are untrained and unmotivated; they fight knowing that they'll die. Hannes Skov is captured, but he continues to struggle, even in his chains, and so Jytte executes him herself, slicing off the man's head and placing it into a bag to bring back to the false king Valdemar, to share with him what she hopes will be rewarded with succession to the throne.

I think of the offer the king had given me: to escape with my life and never return to Hans Lollik Helle. It'd be easy to do, to simply get onto one of my ships and order Malthe to take me to the northern empires, Marieke beside me. As she would say, she has nowhere else to go. The Fjern, certainly, wouldn't miss me. They would rejoice. And for a moment, I do consider that I could simply escape. It would be easy to have the life of peace I'd once

daydreamed about with Friedrich at my side, easy to live out the
rest of my days without having to worry if I would die. Whoever
rules the king knows that I'm close to learning their secrets; they
offered me the chance to escape, and I didn't take it, and so I'm
sure that they'll attempt to kill me. They may well succeed.

Marieke waits for me as I approach the Jannik house. One side
of her face is swollen, her eye bruised shut and her lip cut. She
twists her hands together, watching with unease as I come to
her. Before I can ask what's happened, she sends her thoughts
to me. I sweep past her and into the sitting room, where Aksel
waits, sprawled across one of the sofas. There's no guavaberry
rum in sight, but I can still smell the alcohol rising from his
clothes, his hair, the pores of his skin.

Aksel had been waiting for me to leave, Marieke thinks; as
soon as my ships departed for Valdemar Helle, he returned to
his house. He asked for Marieke. He sat where he does now as
he made his commands: a grand dinner of roasted goat, though
he knew the kitchens didn't have the supplies. Sugarcane wine,
even knowing the Jannik house held no such fineries. Every
time Marieke had to apologetically tell him that his commands
couldn't be met, he slapped her. He demanded entertainment:
slave girls to dance before him, music to be sung. This, Marieke
shakenly helped in—two girls from the kitchens, embarrassed
and trying not to cry. The slaves who had gathered to sing were
not even finished with their song when Aksel grabbed the girl
Agatha and tried to drag her from the room, pulling at her dress.
She screamed. Marieke stepped forward quickly. She pleaded
with Aksel. He hit her, but she wouldn't stop, speaking in a low
and rational tone—the girl is too young, and she isn't a slave of
Jannik Helle but of Hans Lollik Helle, what will he do if she
bears a child? She followed them all the way to the bedroom,
and wouldn't stop asking her questions even when he slammed

the door in her face. He grew so tired that he had barely taken off his shoes before he swung the door open again and kneed Marieke in the gut—but, spirits remain, he had left the room with the crying girl inside.

This was only hours before. I stand before him now.

"I haven't seen you in some time," I tell Aksel, but he ignores me, eyes closed and hand resting on his head, as though this world is too difficult for him to bear. "Have you been with Erik Nørup?"

"You don't have the authority to question me," he murmurs, thinking to me that he's not his brother, not one of my little pets of whom I can demand answers and make commands.

"You're needed at the king's meetings," I tell him. "You're needed as head of the Jannik house. If you won't do either of those things—if you won't fulfill your duties as Herre Jannik—then you might as well leave Hans Lollik Helle."

"So that you can take full control of the Jannik household?" he asks me, laughing with his eyes still closed.

"You don't even want to be here, Aksel," I say. I try to control the fury in me. Marieke's memory of Aksel's hand knocking into her cheek, her nose, her lip—I want to wrap my hands around his neck as I had his mother's, wrap them and hold them there until he draws his last breath; but I know I can't. The kongelig would take the opportunity to have me hanged. "Leave Hans Lollik Helle."

"An islander, a slave, taking control of the family name. My father would drown himself before he saw the day."

Yes, Engel Jannik wouldn't have been able to stomach the sight of me, standing in his house, in my dress of white, making my commands as though I'm a part of the kongelig and deserve respect. But Aksel is wrong; Engel wouldn't have killed himself. He would've cut me open with a machete instead. The man had always been violent, hateful, beating anyone who happened to be near. Aksel had often been a victim of being near Engel Jannik. His father was drunk almost every day, angry at the debts he'd caused

his family. Engel asked, once, why the boy was a failure in everything he attempted, and Aksel dared to respond that he was, after
all, Engel Jannik's son. The fist came before Aksel could register it,
and the fist wouldn't stop coming until Freja Jannik came screaming, begging her husband to stop, that he would kill the boy. Aksel
was sure that this is what Engel had wanted. Aksel wasn't the only
person he beat. He'd beaten Freja Jannik many nights, so many
nights that Aksel would fall asleep listening to her scream.

He didn't mourn his father when the man died. Freja Jannik,
though she organized the man's ceremony, his body lit on fire
upon his boat and sent to the sea, didn't cry for him either. Aksel
didn't ask how Engel Jannik could have died of the storm-season
sickness, when the man had never been sick before in his entire
life, as far as Aksel could remember. He didn't ask his mother
why, when he reached for a particular glass of lemongrass tea,
she told him not to drink it—that the tea wasn't for him, but for
his father. Freja Jannik made the man a cup of lemongrass tea
every morning for three months as Engel Jannik became frailer,
until finally he succumbed to his illness.

Aksel had worked so hard to not become his father. His father
had hit and hurt Freja Jannik, and Aksel would never have hurt
Beata in such a way. He would only have shown her and their
children kindness and love. He would've praised Beata Larsen
as though she was one of the Fjern gods. He would've brought
her flowers and sugarcane wine, refusing to leave her side, not
even for the politics of Hans Lollik Helle. Aksel had been ready
to prove that he was nothing like Engel Jannik. And for all of
his patience and understanding, Aksel is now alone in this place,
trapped here with me.

"I won't leave Hans Lollik Helle," Aksel tells me. "I want to
be here when you die. I want to watch."

"And how do you know you won't be killed before me?"

"I don't," he says. "It's a chance I'm willing to take."

CHAPTER TWENTY-TWO

Another storm comes, but this one is quick, winds rattling the windows and tree branches for just a morning, sun shining through the blackened clouds before it moves on. The end of the storm season is near, in just two weeks' time, and the false king will be announcing his choice among the kongelig soon, assuming that the remaining kongelig are still alive. I'm no closer to knowing the truth about Konge Valdemar—who controls him, who has tried to kill me, and who has already killed Beata Larsen and Olsen Årud, Herre Jens Nørup, and Dame Ane Solberg. The other kongelig assume that there's no longer any threat. They believe Gustav Ludjivik sent in his assassins and that Hannes Skov had meant to finish killing the rest of us—that the murders are a thing of the past. At the kongelig meetings with their updates, and at the garden parties with their laughter and wine, their focus remains on who will be chosen to succeed Konge Valdemar and win the regent's rule.

A messenger brings a request: Konge Valdemar has asked for my company as he watches the passing of the whales. It'll likely be the last passing of the season, and it's generally considered a great honor to be invited by the king. The message reads that this watching of the whales will be in celebration of the defeat of the Ludjivik.

Not all of the kongelig have been invited. Aksel had been invited to attend alongside me, but he's disappeared once again. There isn't any way I can control him, and now that there isn't any way that I can win the crown, this isn't my concern, either. There are larger games at play than Aksel's comings and goings. Lothar Niklasson and Jytte Solberg, for their victory over the Ludjivik, are in attendance as well. I'm surprised to see that Erik Nørup is also here. He didn't have much to do with the quelling of the uprising, and everyone knows that he's useless compared to his sister, who isn't even on this boat. Still, it's not my place to question. Everyone lines up on the sand by the mangroves, hands folded politely above our laps, no one looking at one another or speaking. We're dressed in our finery—our lace and silks and cotton trousers.

A boat arrives to bring us to the ship, one by one. It's only as I'm on the boat, waves swelling beneath me, that I feel a spark of fear. It would be easy for any of the kongelig not invited to this venture to have most of us killed, blaming our deaths on an accident: The ship we're on could knock into an unseen coral reef and sink, drowning everyone aboard. A fire could be set, forcing us all overboard and sending us to the sharks. But when I arrive on the ship itself—smaller than the warships, barely any larger than a fisherman's boat—none of the other kongelig appear worried. Jytte Solberg stands at the railing, peering not at the sea but at the rest of us, her eyes landing on me, her hate swelling with the tide. Lothar Niklasson speaks to her softly as he holds a glass of sugarcane wine, speaking of memories he's had of Jytte's parents, now passed. But even Lothar barely listens to the words that politely stream from his mouth. He wonders only why the king isn't here.

Erik comes to me. He's already had a glass of sugarcane wine and has begun another. His face turns red in the heat, and he has a wide smile. He's embarrassed; he can feel that his sister has already told me that he admires me—not romantically, of course not, he would never have any romantic love for someone with skin as dark as mine, for he's been taught that there's nothing beautiful in my skin and he's been too foolish to realize that he's wrong, too ignorant to carefully look at the depth of the darkness that covers me, the hues of purple and blue, as deep as night; but he is curious. He's considered me entertainment from the very start of the storm season, someone who is much more interesting to watch and listen to than the older kongelig around him. He has no respect for me. He only finds me amusing.

"I've heard that Aksel isn't well," he tells me. "Is it true that he left for Jannik Helle?"

"I wouldn't know," I say, without care of the implication, that I don't know the whereabouts of my own husband. Any other number of the kongelig might have been offended, but Erik only smiles.

"Do you see me in the same way that you see the other kongelig?" Erik asks me, lowering his voice. I can feel here that he wants me to use my kraft on him. He wants me to know his thoughts, feel his emotions, even take control of his body. It's curiosity, for Erik, always curiosity; his sister has always been curious too. She has always wanted to learn as much as she could, reading her texts and studying her sciences, doing her experiments on herbs and blood; but for Erik, his curiosity appeared in other ways. His was a curiosity for life. Curiosity for others: for their bodies, for their lives. He longed to know the stories of the people around him. Longed to know their motivations, their desires. Erik is like his sister: He envies my kraft as well. But Erik isn't like Alida in one way. She tries to convince herself that she doesn't mind that I have such a kraft with power over her and all the other kongelig. Erik does mind. He finds it unfair, that he should have a kraft that only allows him to know his sister's thoughts, when I should have a kraft that allows me to know all the people of the world, anyone of my liking. I don't deserve such a kraft. Erik has been taught that my skin makes me less intelligent than the Fjern, so he thinks such an ability is wasted on me.

Gods, what he could do with this kraft of mine: learn the secrets of all those around him, learn of their desires so that he can fulfill them. Erik doesn't believe in forcing the loyalty of others. He believes in inspiring such a love in followers that they would die for him. I realize that I've been too quick to dismiss Erik Nørup, believing his love of drink and hatred for the kongelig meetings meant that he had no ambition. Erik is ambitious, yes; he simply knows that he doesn't have to work as hard as everyone else for the power he holds. Even if he doesn't become regent, the Nørup family will remain strong among the kongelig. He, like Lothar Niklasson and Cristoff Valdemar before him, recognizes that he owns this world. It was handed to him since the moment he was conceived.

"I do think you're similar to the other kongelig, yes," I tell him. There's a slip of disappointment from him. He wants to be seen as different from the rest.

"I'm sorry for the ways you've been treated on Hans Lollik Helle, Elskerinde Jannik," Erik tells me. Surprising, because I can feel from him that this is genuine. "You're a kongelig, even if you're an islander; you deserve a certain level of respect, yet none show it. I think you're brave," he says.

I don't answer him. Even though I can feel the sincerity in his words, I can't help but think that Erik is only mocking me. I don't like to admit it, but it can be easy to trick my kraft. Easy for anyone to show me their disingenuous thoughts and feelings. He takes another glass of sugarcane wine, offered by a passing slave.

The kongelig wonder about the whereabouts of the king, and the longer we stand, the more I begin to worry, until my worry turns to fear. An assassin might be lying in wait, ready to kill us all. The kongelig who has murdered Beata and Olsen might even be here now, ready to slaughter us with a smile.

There's a disturbance in the water, and I see them—only a little ways away, close enough that I could jump into the water and swim to the whales and touch them. They turn gracefully in the water, tails breaking the surface and smacking the waves. There are three of them, one a calf. Their skin is covered with barnacles and algae, and as they come closer, the smell of salt becomes stronger. They turn so slowly, so gracefully, that it's clear they don't mean any harm. They won't attack, but they're so large that my heart begins to pump with fear. It would be easy for them to kill us—to crush us beneath their weight. They don't eat humans, I know this, and yet they could swallow us whole. This is the first time I've seen whales with my own eyes, but the other kongelig have each seen the passing of the whales since the time they were children.

The king never comes. An assassin doesn't attack, and a fire isn't lit. The whales pass us by, and we each return to the boat, to be taken ashore once more.

Patrika Årud accepts my request to visit for lemongrass tea. She grows paler with each passing day, and her hair seems thinner, the makeup she always pasted on now melting in the heat, showing the pockmarked skin she hides beneath. I have no love for Patrika Årud, and I never will, but I can acknowledge the pain she feels, the hollowness that's begun to fill her. I've lost loved ones before, so I understand the questions she begins to ask herself: whether there's any point in her staying here on Hans Lollik Helle, or even on any of these islands. How she can possibly continue to live her life when nothing is the same as it had been before.

Since the fire that burned her manor to the ground, she's

moved into one of the empty houses, hidden even deeper in the groves. Slaves work around us, fixing the gardens and sweeping the dirt out of the sitting room and whipping the dust out of the curtains and rugs while we sit in the shade on her patio. She's lost all of her belongings on Hans Lollik Helle in the fire and has had to borrow dresses from others of the kongelig while one of her slaves fetches her things from Årud Helle.

Her hatred, through everything, remains. She can't even look at me. She believes I've come to laugh at her. She sweats in her dress of white, heavy with lace, and clutches the steaming tea-cup, smelling the lemongrass. Lemongrass had always been her favorite scent. Its rich sweetness reminds her of the few months she would spend on Årud Helle each year. She'd lived in the north with her mother, a woman who had wealth but wouldn't say how she'd come to so much coin, when she'd been born in the gutters like everyone else around her. The other little girls would laugh at Patrika. They would say she was the daughter of a whore and that she would grow up to be a whore as well.

Once every year, on Patrika's birthday, a man with hair as red as her own would come to say hello. He would give her a gift of unimaginable wealth: a necklace of gold, a ring with a ruby in its center. He would ask her how she was and whether she was keeping up with her studies, and she would always say that she was well and that she was doing her best. And then the man would disappear, forgotten until the next year.

It was when Patrika turned eleven years of age that her mother learned that this man was dead. He was married, but the woman had never given him any children, so Patrika inherited an island in the center of paradise. It had been unimaginable: The child of a woman who worked the brothels, scrounging for scraps, was suddenly a princess. Her mother would bring Patrika to Årud Helle so that the child could look upon all the riches that were now hers, but her mother didn't love the islands. She claimed that she didn't want Patrika to forget where she'd come from, but even as a child, Patrika could see the truth plainly: The woman was simple, afraid to live a life different from the only one she had ever known. The islands and their savages scared her, as did the bloodthirsty Fjern, who would take any opportunity they could to seize more wealth and power. She and Patrika lived in the north, struggling for coin, knowing all the while that Patrika owned an entire island, a manor, and all its riches. Patrika's mother allowed Årud Helle to crumble with no Elskerinde. It became an island for bandits, an island where slaves attempting to escape would hide in the groves before moving on.

Patrika came of age the same year her mother passed. She had nothing in the north, so she traveled the seas. She arrived at Årud Helle, a desolate and abandoned island, one for smugglers and pirates and heathens, and there she felt her ambition grow. She had been deliberate in her decision to marry Olsen Damgaard of Koninkrijk; had been deliberate in keeping her surname of Årud, to match the island she now owned, though it was unheard of for a woman to keep her own last name in marriage.

"I hope you're not using your kraft on me, Elskerinde Rose," she tells me. It's deliberate of her now, too, to call me by my mother's name.

"I was," I admit. "It can be difficult to keep my boundaries sometimes. Another's thoughts become my own, and I forget myself."

"Is it so difficult?" she asks. "Thankfully for you, I can keep my abilities to myself."

A threat, maybe—at least, it's what Patrika hopes it will be, but even she doesn't feel the force behind her words. She wants to know why I'm here, why I've asked to sip lemongrass tea on her porch. I hesitate to tell her my reasons. I know it's desperation that has sent me here. Someone who knows the pain I feel might better understand the possibility of a truth like the one

I've come to tell her. The hopelessness in her, the ambition that died along with her husband, might make her more willing to hear what I have to say, whereas anyone else on the island might only think I've come to fill their mind with lies. Patrika isn't an ally I would ever have love for, but I don't need an ally whom I love. I need an ally who might listen.

"The king is dead," I tell her.

Patrika drinks some of her tea. I'd always thought it was universally agreed that it was too hot to drink tea on these islands, but Patrika doesn't seem to mind the heat, even as she sweats. She swallows, and holds the teacup in her lap.

I continue. "I went to Valdemar Helle to help in the defeat of the Ludjivik, yes, but I also wanted an opportunity to search for clues. The king has been strange," I tell her, and with this she can agree. All on the island have witnessed the ways Konge Valdemar has changed, seemingly with no logic behind his sudden transformation. Patrika had attributed it all to Valdemar's old age. She believes the man has lost his mind.

"My kraft allows me to feel the emotions in others, to control them if I wish. Konge Valdemar has no being to control, no feelings or life to command."

She narrows her eyes. She doesn't believe me. I didn't think she would, not so easily.

"I saw the man's grave on Valdemar Helle," I tell her. "His body had a neck wound. He'd been killed."

"And you believe he was killed by one of the kongelig on this island?" she asks me.

"Yes," I tell her. "I know that it wasn't you. You wouldn't have killed the king, just to then murder your husband. With Herre Årud's death—" and I feel a sting of pain here, a shock on my hand that makes me drop my tea. The teacup breaks, large pieces of porcelain falling apart and smaller splinters flying. It'd been purposeful, Patrika's kraft.

"Don't speak of my husband," she tells me.

I swallow, rubbing my hand, and nod. "I don't believe that it was you. I don't know who else of the kongelig I can trust with the truth."

Alida, though she shows me her smiles, could just as easily have been behind the king's death as her brother; the two could plot together, her brother distracting all with his drunken charm, both pretending they have no interest in the crown so that eyes won't fall on them. Jytte Solberg's ambition is clear; she fights for the king's approval, but it's possible that this is an act to pretend her innocence while she kills all of the kongelig to secure her throne. Lothar Niklasson I trust least of all. The man's kraft over truth and his position as the king's closest adviser make him the most likely to hold the king's strings, a puppet who speaks and does as he commands. Each of the kongelig, knowing my kraft, could work to hide their thoughts and emotions.

I never imagined I would find myself coming to Patrika Årud with the truth, with the hopes that she might agree to make herself my ally and use her resources to uncover the kongelig who means to kill us all. She's surprised as well. She doesn't believe me—she thinks this is a trick I mean to play on her, a cruel and elaborate game to laugh at her mourning. She thinks on the slave I keep, that boy who she believes is my pet. She worries he has told me of the nights Olsen would bring Løren to Patrika— lock the boy in the room so she could use him as she wished.

"Where's your proof?" she asks me.

"Still on Valdemar Helle," I answer. "I had my slave cover the body again, in case the murderer returns and sees that we know the truth."

"And if the king is dead," she says, "who is it that we see in the council meetings and garden parties?"

I don't have the answer for her, because I don't know. It could be his ghost. His ghost, controlled by a kongelig; his ghost, returned to the world of the living to find his vengeance.

"Even if this is the truth you tell," Patrika says, "why would I help you?"

I can feel in her the disinterest she has in these islands. This mystery of the king feels like a faraway dream to her now. She stays here on this island because it's her duty, but she has already decided to return to the north and relinquish her position among the kongelig. It's the right choice for her now, allowing her to move on from the death of her husband, but disappointment crawls through me. It occurs to her, briefly, that I might be seeing her thoughts, her emotions, but she simply doesn't care—her husband is dead, her grasp on the throne lost, and nothing matters to her, not right now.

Patrika tells me she had respect for my mother. I think that she means to say this to hurt me, and she does, this mention of my mother; but she means what she says as well. "I hated her," she acknowledges, "this woman with her black skin, just as black as yours, thinking that she was our equal and looking each of us in the eye with her defiance. I was disgusted to be in her presence," Patrika tells me. "But still, I had respect for her. I have respect for such a woman who finds herself in situations as she did—surrounded by people she knew held no love for her, wanted to see her fail, wanted to see her dead—and still holds pride for herself." Patrika thinks of her own childhood: the girls, surrounding her, pulling at her hair and her dress, telling her that she was the daughter of a whore. "It becomes easy to think, after all, that they might be right."

Marieke scrubs my back and plaits my hair. I know she wants me to leave Hans Lollik Helle. This switch in her is surprising to me, but Aksel's attack has shaken her. Though the swelling on her face has gone down, the cut on her lip scabbed over, she's still unsettled from the beating she received. She wants her revenge against the kongelig, yes, revenge for the deaths of her daughter and the girl's father, revenge even for my mother and sisters and brother, revenge for all our people who have been massacred and tortured and enslaved; but she doesn't believe there's any vengeance to be had on this island. Not for her, not for me, not for our people—not now, not for this storm season. She thinks this is a battle that we've lost, and Marieke has always been patient. She thinks another battle will come again. There will be another chance. Maybe in one year, maybe in ten years, maybe long after we're both dead and in the ground—but there will be another chance for us to find our revenge.

"It's important to know when to surrender," she whispers to me. "Surrender, and keep your life while you still have it."

But if I were to leave Hans Lollik Helle, I would be consumed by this anger inside of me. Consumed, knowing that justice still hasn't been served. Knowing that I failed to take the throne from the Fjern as I'd promised my mother I would.

When I sleep, I'm in the halls of the king's manor. The wallpaper rots and boils in fire as I run, roots of the maze wrapping around my ankles. I tell myself that this is a dream, that it's just another nightmare of Hans Lollik Helle, but even as I tell myself this, I don't wake. I fall, and dirt buries me. I can't breathe—I choke on the dirt that fills my nose, my mouth, my throat and lungs. It's dark, and I can't see, but I can feel the body I'm trapped in the dirt with—can feel the squirming of its maggots, the blood leaking from its neck.

I open my eyes, sweating in the yellow sun that fills my room. The king, his neck leaking blood, stands before me. By the time I've sat up, he's already gone, curtains shifting in the breeze. I can't stay inside this house. I can hear Aksel yelling at the slave girl, can hear the chatter rising from the kitchens. I slip out of bed and wander down the hall, shadowed in the afternoon breeze, and down the stairs. I slip, almost fall—and see that I've stepped in blood. It pools from the floorboards, leaks from the walls. I close my eyes and take a breath, waiting to wake, but I don't—the blood rises like the sea around me, rising to my knees. I run from the house. The slaves have all disappeared, the sound of the wind following me, and I can feel that something or someone chases me, though I can't see who or what—I race into the groves, and bodies hang from the branches, ropes tied around their necks, eyes bulging and mouths trapped open in silent screams—

I gasp, sitting up. I'm still in the groves, but I'm on the grass, yellow sunlight shining through the trees, which are empty of bodies. I stand slowly, my limbs sore as though I really had run from my chambers, through the halls, and down the dirt path. Memory comes back to me now: leaving my room for a walk, deciding to sit and enjoy the afternoon sun. I had thought about my brother, Claus; my sisters, Ellinor and Inga. I had thought about my mother. I wondered what each would do if they found themselves in the position I do now. Whether they would decide to stay on this island and fight to outlive all the rest of the kongelig. I know that Ellinor would stay, but only because she would want the approval of the kongelig. I loved my sister, but her memory reminds me of our father: eager to kiss the feet of the Fjern, who kicked him in the mouth. Inga wouldn't have stayed. This island would be too bloody for her, and like Beata Larsen, she would have attempted to leave at the first chance she had. Only Claus, perhaps, would've stayed on this island; but he was always sick, frail. He wouldn't have lived long, even if he'd survived our family's massacre. Claus always knew this, I think, knew that he would die young. Perhaps this is why he was always forthright with the truth. There was no time for lies. My mother, I already know, would have stayed—stayed on the island, just as I do now. Is this why I was the only one out of my sisters and brother to live?

I hear the shouts long before I reach the Jannik house. I hurry my pace until I see the house standing on the cliff. There's a fight: Malthe and three other slaves are trying to subdue someone, a man, Løren, who tries to break free. Malthe holds Løren's arms behind his back, but Løren nearly pulls himself away. It's only when I stop before them that he surrenders. He allows himself to be pushed down to his knees.

Malthe is out of breath. "He was found," he tells me, gasping for air, "on the shores of Larsen Helle, my lady, just as you said he would be."

Løren is thinner now, his muscles and bones straining against his skin. He'd been burned by the sun on his cheeks and shoulders. His hair is tangled, longer now. He smells of the sea, like salt and hot sand. But his eyes. His eyes are the same. The burning hatred, the fury for me and everyone around him. There's also a softness—regret, perhaps, maybe a feeling of betrayal. He never should have let me know his plans of escaping Hans Lollik Helle.

Aksel emerges from the house. He stands on the porch, leaning against the railing, watching with his arms crossed. He has no smile on his face, but I can feel that he mocks me. This is the boy I've made such an effort to protect, and this is how Løren has repaid me: challenging my authority over him, my ownership as his mistress. Aksel wants me to know that this is how Løren has always been, and always will be. He wants me to know that if I give Løren enough freedom, one night he will strangle me in my sleep. Aksel wants me to put Løren to death. He won't say it, won't demand it, because this time it's clear to all that he's right—has been right all along about Løren. There isn't any way

I can let the boy attempt to escape without showing all of my slaves his punishment.

"Why would you do this?" I ask Løren.

He doesn't respond. He's still on his knees, squinting at me in the sunlight.

"Why did you run?" I ask him. "I treat you well, don't I?" My voice lowers, though all gathered can still hear me. "I let you come and go as you please. I let you speak to me as though you are my equal, when we both know that you're not. And yet you work to embarrass me, to undermine me, to challenge me."

And even now, he challenges me—watching me as he does, refusing to look away, his wall carefully in place. He dares me to have him killed. He believes I'm too much of a coward, I can see it from the look on his face; he doesn't believe, not for a moment, that I will prove to him that I am a true kongelig. Not when I have so badly wanted his approval, his friendship, his love—not when I have made him a symbol of the people who will never accept me.

I tell Malthe to prepare for Løren's execution. He will die by hanging tomorrow night, before all of the slaves and kongelig of Hans Lollik Helle.

CHAPTER TWENTY-THREE

Konge Valdemar requests the presence of the kongelig, and so we all return to the meeting room as the sky turns purple and as the moths and gnats and fruit bats take flight. The manor Herregård Constanjin is in shadow, the windows black. It's easier to see the cracks in the walls, the tears in the wallpaper. The council room's mahogany gleams, but the light feels grayer.

I sit at the table with Patrika Årud, who won't meet anyone's eye, and Alida and Erik Nørup, who're silent as well, both of them tense as they exchange their questions and thoughts, a conversation between the two that no one else can share. They argue about their responsibilities to this island and to all of Hans Lollik. Erik wants to leave, despite the ambition I can feel in him. With Beata and Olsen's deaths, it's become clear that someone among the kongelig is willing to kill for the title of regent, and Erik is far from willing to die for such a thing. Alida agrees, yes, but she also knows that their titles as heads of the Nørup family require them to stay. Erik wonders to his sister if I might be using my kraft to spy on their thoughts, and the two glance at me as one as I turn my gaze to the surface of the table.

Lothar Niklasson is here as well, sitting to the side of the empty chair that awaits the king, who hasn't yet come. Jytte isn't here, either. This is strange. Jytte is usually the first to arrive, eager to please the king and earn her place above Lothar. It's a lofty goal for a woman like her to hope to rise to power over the king's trusted adviser, but it's been her goal nonetheless. Lothar meets my eye, and he knows that I, too, am wondering where Jytte is, where the king is, and whether a Solberg assassin waits to kill us all. The king is meant to choose the next regent in just one week's time. Jytte's ambitions could make her act irrationally—try to have us all killed, try to convince the king that she had nothing to do with our deaths so that she can be chosen.

My tension eases into relief as I sense the familiar presence of anger that always accompanies Jytte, but my relief turns to confusion, then alarm as the doors of the council room slam open and Jytte strides inside. Alida stands and hurries to Jytte's side without hesitation. Erik gapes. Patrika rises from her seat as well, turning toward the door to see if a threat follows, but none does.

Lothar is calm. "What happened?" he asks.

Jytte's hands are cut, red flowing where she'd caught a blade, held and kept it from cutting her neck. Alida rips the bottoms of her white dress and wraps the fabric around Jytte's palms, saying that they need to be washed with hot water and salt.

"It was in the groves," she tells us. "Olsen Årud called to me. He stood to the side of the dirt path."

Patrika's attention snaps to the woman. "You play a cruel joke."

"I don't," Jytte says, her eyes steeled. "Olsen Årud called to me. I was afraid, confused—someone came behind me. They tried to cut my neck, but I grabbed the blade before they could. I pushed away from them and turned around."

I know what she's going to say before she does, her eyes fixed on me. She tells them that it was me. It had been me holding the machete, Jytte's blood on my hands.

"It must have been a trick," Alida says. "Elskerinde Jannik has been here this entire time."

"A trick, yes," Jytte agrees, "played by Elskerinde Jannik. She has a control on us. You all refuse to see it. She plays her mind games, and you're all too foolish to see the truth."

"It wasn't me," I say.

"It was you, in that very dress, holding your blade."

"If I wanted you dead, Elskerinde Solberg, I wouldn't be foolish enough to try and kill you myself."

This wasn't the right thing to say. Jytte is trembling in her anger. She might have attempted to strangle me if the pain in her hands weren't so strong, growing by the second alongside her rage.

Lothar puts an end to the argument before either of us can speak again. "I don't see how it could've been Elskerinde Jannik," he tells Jytte. "She's been here, in this meeting room, as Alida had noted. But someone clearly has made an attempt on your life. I propose we retire to the safety of our homes. I'll have a message sent to the king about what's taken place."

I can see in Lothar that he's starting to suspect that the king was never going to appear in the meeting room tonight, in the same way that the king didn't appear for the watching of the whales; Herre Niklasson's worry for our lives, and especially his own, grows. We leave, Jytte storming from the room first. The others have their unspoken questions as we trail down the halls. Questions on assassins and the possibility of ghosts.

Aksel waits for me in my chambers, standing on my balcony overlooking the churning of the black sea. I hesitate, unsure whether it's really him, or if he's just another trick. He doesn't have a smile for me—Aksel will never have a smile for me, I'm sure of this—but he doesn't look at me with burning hatred, either. He doesn't watch me, wanting me to know how badly he wants to see me hanging from a tree, rope cutting into my neck. He isn't staggering, rum filling his veins. He almost looks as he did months before, glaring at me from the halls of his dead mother's house. He'd still been in control then. He'd made his choice to marry me and was resolved to live with that decision. He wasn't yet filled with regret and loathing, both for me and for himself. Now he's returned to a similar peace. He still mourns Beata Larsen—he will never stop mourning his beloved—but he has at least come to a place where he realizes that the past won't change, no matter how much rum and wine he drinks, no matter how hard he hits. And so Aksel is ready to move on. There's also an odd feeling in him, one I never expected to find: He's grateful to me. Grateful, that I've commanded the death of his brother, when he never had the courage to do so himself.

"People have always liked to pretend his innocence," Aksel says. "They pity him, act like he's some sort of martyr. Even my father had an odd love for Løren."

A love that he never shared for Aksel, it seemed. Aksel had never been good enough for his father. The man would give Aksel a challenge and delight in the boy's failures: memorize the history of the islands of Han Lollik, or beat Løren in a skirmish; climb a coconut tree as though he were a slave and bring his father back a seed; or, for once in his short life, manage not to embarrass his father at one of the kongelig's garden parties. Aksel had tried so hard to appease his father and bring the man pride, but it seemed all he ever managed to do was bring shame to the Jannik name.

There was a morning when Engel Jannik wanted to test his son's swimming. Aksel didn't know why; there was never any real need for him to go into the sea, and his father knew the boy had a fear of the ocean. He demanded that Aksel swim out as far as he could—added, in a spark of inspiration, that Aksel was to swim out as far as he could in a contest against the slave boy Løren. If Løren managed to swim farther than Aksel, Aksel knew his father would beat him, as he always did whenever Løren managed to best him.

The two swam. Barely half of a minute passed before Aksel was already exhausted, his limbs heavy, but Løren swam like he was made of the sea. The waves became rougher, the tide's pull became stronger, and Løren only swam alongside Aksel the way a fish might move through the water. Aksel was out of breath, a stitch in his side, salt burning his eyes. He kicked, but hadn't been able to feel the seafloor for some time, and only saw darkness beneath him, when he was so used to seeing the sand and coral. He stopped, gasping, wave after wave knocking him down. Løren stopped as well. He watched Aksel. He watched the boy, drowning, and he did nothing. He watched as though waiting for Aksel to die.

Aksel turned around. He wasn't sure he would make it. He had such a fear that he would die that he still has nightmares of drowning sometimes. But finally he did make it, stumbling onto the sand. Løren came in behind him, standing tall and breathing steady. Aksel well remembers the beating he received that day, because although Engel usually waited until they were inside of the house, today he beat his son right there on the beach for everyone to see. Aksel didn't want to bring the Jannik any more shame, and so tried to take the beating in silence, but this somehow enraged his father even more. He'd beat the boy unconscious. Aksel was confined to bed for three days before he could stand on his own two feet. And all the while, Løren had stood by, watching.

"Your father couldn't have loved Løren," I tell Aksel now. "It's impossible to both be a master and love your slave."

Aksel shrugs. He doesn't care enough one way or the other

to argue. He's decided to leave Hans Lollik Helle—that's all he wanted to tell me, out of courtesy to our marriage, no matter that it's a sham. I hadn't considered a life of marriage with Aksel, living together on Jannik Helle. I'd always assumed that either I would die here on the royal island or I would kill him myself. Aksel is ready to move on from Hans Lollik Helle and the memories that haunt him. Beata's ghost follows him wherever he goes. He sees her in the gardens, hiding behind the flowers. He sees her in the groves, smiling in the shade. He sees her body on the shore, yellow hair tangled in seaweed. He knows that her ghost will follow him to Jannik Helle and that he will likely drink himself to death—even he's aware of this. He also knows that his death means I will inherit Jannik Helle and his manor, but he doesn't care. His only request is that he never see me again.

"Don't come to Jannik Helle with me," he says. "Please— spare me having to see you again, as a mercy."

I can agree to this, so Aksel turns his back on me to leave my chambers. He hopes to leave tomorrow, as soon as possible.

"Don't you want to watch your brother's execution?" I ask.

But Aksel has no need to see Løren die. The very thought scares him, though he wouldn't easily admit to such a thing. Aksel only wants to know, finally, that Løren has died, as he should have so many times.

The house is busier than it's ever been once morning comes. Slaves pack Aksel's belongings, taking them to the mangroves and its bay so that each item can be rowed to a ship. Other slaves prepare for Løren's execution. A proper hanging tree must be found, and it isn't an easy thing, testing branches for their strength to ensure they'll be able to hold the weight of a man. Still other slaves rush back and forth, cleaning and cooking as they do each day.

Marieke scrubs my back, my shoulders, and combs my hair.

She wants to know if I really mean to kill the boy. She doesn't believe that I do. She knows that I'm angry, and when I'm angry, I tend to be impulsive. I don't think as I should, my own emotion filling my veins and my chest and my head. It doesn't help that when I'd made my decision, I was surrounded by so many others who expected to see Løren dead. There was no way for me to know whose thoughts and feelings I'd had—those around me, or my own. This is what Marieke says.

"Should he not be punished for trying to escape?" I ask Marieke, but she only thinks again that I don't really mean to have the boy killed. Something like this would be impossible of me. This is what she believes. Marieke might not know me as well as we both thought she did. She doesn't know how badly I'd wanted Løren's acceptance, how much I want the love of my people. I'm executing Løren, I know, to punish both him and the people who hold no love for me.

The other slaves of the household are less certain of their faith in me. I can see it in their eyes. Their hatred of me scalds my skin, twisting through my stomach, threatening to cut open my chest. I leave for the groves, twigs breaking under my feet, speckled shade leaving patterns on the ground. A hanging tree has been chosen, a noose looped over its branch, a chair placed beneath.

Alida answers the door herself when I knock. She wasn't expecting me, wasn't expecting any guests, as the Nørup twins very rarely receive visitors. All know that Erik leaves the house they share whenever fun is to be had, and Alida knows, too, that all the other kongelig of the island consider her too odd, too unambitious, to make a proper ally out of her. They don't visit her, and they don't pass along invitations to her, either, requests to visit for tea. She prefers to remain in her home or in her secret alcove by the bay, though she's abandoned the alcove now that she's found me sitting in her favorite spot on the island. The alcove suddenly doesn't feel quite as special anymore.

She welcomes me into her home, ushering me to the sitting room, gesturing at an awaiting slave to bring us rose-mallow tea. The sitting room is all white and lace, blue floral designs to match the lily of the Nørup crest covering the wallpaper and the chaise chairs.

"I hope you don't mind rose-mallow tea rather than lemongrass," she tells me. "Rose mallow is far healthier for digestion. Not something the fine people of Hans Lollik Helle often want to discuss, but an important topic nonetheless."

We sit together, the windows open, sunlight shining, breeze calming. Despite herself, Alida is excited to have a visitor. She'd been poring over her books all morning, as she tends to do every day on Hans Lollik Helle, but even that becomes a bit tiresome after a while. She misses Nørup Helle, misses the room where she keeps her different herb mixtures and experiments. She misses her ability to simply leave the island whenever she pleases, taking a ship to the northern empires. She wishes she could simply leave the islands for Koninkrijk. Alida feels no connection to these islands; she never has, not even as a child. It's only a sense of duty that keeps her here, watching over her brother.

We speak on the coolness of the morning breeze, how it'll certainly become hotter by the end of the day, how we hope we'll be spared another storm before the end of the season. Her slave brings the tea, and we blow on the steam. Alida is too polite to speak on the topic, but she knows that my slave boy, Løren, ran away and was recaptured; she knows, too, that I'll have him executed this evening. She's surprised. She'd thought I'd be a little more merciful with my slaves, seeing as we have the same color of skin, the same texture of hair, the same ancestors of these islands.

After we've exhausted all polite conversation, Alida asks, "What brings you here, Elskerinde Jannik?" She knows it isn't just a pleasant visit. This doesn't disappoint her. She doesn't wish to be a part of the culture of the Fjern on this island, with their meaningless garden parties and teas. She's excited by the prospect that I may have come with news, or a question perhaps—something that would be far more interesting than the time she usually spends sitting alone in this manor.

I hesitate. I don't know yet if I trust Alida Nørup. I have no proof, besides her seemingly innocent thoughts, that she isn't the one behind the murders of Hans Lollik Helle. There's no way to know with certainty that she isn't somehow linked to the murder of the king. And yet I'm running out of options—and time. The Fjern who means to see us all dead won't wait until the end of the storm season before taking another kongelig's life. I can't guarantee that kongelig won't be me.

And so I tell her. I tell her of my suspicions, I tell her of Valdemar Helle, I tell her of the king.

"There's a kongelig who means to be rid of us all." I ignore the prickling in the back of my throat, to tell Alida that there's another possibility as well: that the king is only a ghost of himself. That this island has been claimed by the spirits and that we'll all become victims of their vengeance. The thought feels too ridiculous to mention to Alida. She'd find the spirits of the islanders laughable.

I continue. "The kongelig will see us all dead, until finally the false king declares them to be the rightful heir to these islands. It's purposeful. The kongelig will not spark any wars if they're declared by the king to be the next regent, and if they aren't found guilty of all the murders of this island."

Alida sits in silence and watches me as she might watch one of her experiments: calculating, brow pinched in concentration. She's always been matter-of-fact, and a grand story such as mine must be taken into careful consideration. "Does anyone else know what you've told me?"

"Patrika Årud."

Alida hides her surprise well. She doesn't understand why I

would approach Patrika Årud with such concerns. She believes that, even with the murder of Olsen Årud, Patrika is a hateful woman, and that she'd remain a prime suspect. The woman could've easily killed her husband, Alida thinks, to take suspicion away. Alida believes I'm foolish to have confided in Patrika Årud with such information. Still, she says nothing on the topic.

"What do you propose?" she asks me.

"A questioning," I tell her. "An interrogation of Jytte Solberg and Lothar Niklasson."

Alida watches me plainly. "And you?"

Her suspicion of me and Aksel Jannik isn't emotional. It must be considered rationally. What a grand ploy this would be: Aksel and I could honestly have a hatred for each other, but a hatred that in itself could become a tool. A murder of even Aksel's beloved, for the purpose of inventing his emotional pain and clearing him from the desire for the throne. Aksel, even, could be behind the murders. And how easy would it have been for me to force my false king to declare my accession to the throne? It'd be just as easy to have Konge Valdemar publicly change his mind, once all other kongelig are dead.

"What else is there to say?" I ask her. "You'll have to choose whether you can trust me or not."

She isn't sure if she can. There aren't enough facts presented for her to make the most logical choice possible. Yet if I'm innocent, and also correct in my assumptions, and it's either Jytte Solberg or Lothar Niklasson who is behind all these deaths, all this bloodshed, then she'd also be wasting time attempting to gather knowledge. The end of the storm season is near. She also knows the danger in this. She's been worried—not afraid. Alida hasn't been afraid that she'd be killed, hasn't been filled with anxiety at the thought. Nightmares haven't been pursuing her as they do me. She thinks to herself that the kongelig must see how little she and her brother desire the throne. She believes that whoever is behind these murders would let her live. Nonetheless, she's concerned—nervous, that perhaps she hasn't been taking this matter seriously enough.

"We need to form an alliance against Elskerinde Solberg and Herre Niklasson if we're to succeed. We can't let them leave the island and have access to their islands' resources or their guards."

"You'd like to take them prisoner?" she asks.

"Yes."

This is certainly one way Alida would find herself killed, she thinks. Jytte would cut her neck herself if Alida attempted to capture her. Elskerinde Solberg is terrifying to Alida, which is surprising, because she doesn't fear much. She tends to answer her fear with logic. Even as a child, if she found no evidence for the monster beneath her bed, then she wasn't scared. If she sees no proof that there're spirits on this island, ready to kill us all, then she has nothing to fear. But with Elskerinde Jytte Solberg, there's little room for rationality. The woman tends to act how she wishes, in the most unpredictable ways.

"We can have our guards called onto the island," I tell her, "and hidden in the mangroves. The night of the kongelig meeting, we can have the guards storm the room and take Jytte and Lothar."

"And what of Jytte's kraft?" This, Alida also fears. It isn't the possibility of death or pain that she thinks about in this proposed battle. She's more concerned about the irrational fear Jytte can cause in others with just a glance.

"There'd be too many of us. She can't use her kraft on everyone in the room at once. There's only one concern." I clench my hands together, imagining the battle that would inevitably take place—the guards that line the outside of Herregård Constantjin, who'd be required to fight the guards who attempt to take Jytte and Lothar. Løren, who will be dead and not a part of this fight. "Our heads of guards would be outnumbered by the guards of Hans Lollik Helle. We can't bring an entire force onto the island. They'd notice. But we need at least ten more to overpower them. Hopefully the sheer number would force them to surrender."

Alida wonders whose guards I propose we include in our number—hopes that it isn't Patrika Årud that I think of, but I can't think of who else we could ask. Her island is the closest, and she's the only other of the kongelig families who remain.

"Patrika could betray us, Elskerinde Jannik," Alida tells me. "She could easily turn her guards on our own, have them unite with the guards of Hans Lollik Helle." This isn't a risk that Alida is willing to take.

"We need to be in a position to overpower them."

Alida hesitates. She wonders if this is a conversation that should involve her brother, but she knows he's too much of a fool to seriously involve himself in such politics. She'd once been ashamed to have such thoughts on her brother, especially once he knew how she felt about him. But now it's expected, this feeling inside her. Gods above, how she can't stand her brother.

We reach an agreement: Alida will attempt to convince Patrika Årud, where I failed, and at the next kongelig meeting, we'll have our combined guards storm the room. Jytte Solberg and Lothar Niklasson will be arrested, and we'll call the king what he is: a fraud, a by-product of kraft. The real king is dead. We'll have his body exhumed as proof. The interrogation will begin, and the murderer executed for their crimes. Alida thinks, briefly, on how this might mean the deaths of two of my own rivals—how the path to the throne might be made all the clearer for me—but she doesn't think on this for too long, because it was never a throne that she herself wanted. What does it matter to her if I'm given the title of regent over these islands? She pretends not to notice the prickling under her skin, the slight sneer of disgust that mars her smile at the thought of an islander ruling all of Hans Lollik.

The sun has reached its height, and our cups of tea have cooled enough to sip. Marieke, I think, might have gone to visit Løren where he's been locked in the library. She might've offered him prayers and words of comfort. Spirits remain, she'll have reminded him. He won't be gone, not truly—not from this world, not from our memories.

The sun begins to fall, and so it's almost time for the slave Løren to die. The slaves of the Jannik house are gathered in the groves. The trees darken in the lessening light, shadows against the sky, leaves shifting in the breeze. The slaves stand in a silent circle surrounding me and the hanging tree. I think on how easy it would be for them to decide that they won't execute one of their own. Malthe could put the noose around my neck instead, and all the slaves gathered would watch me swing. Marieke stands beside me. She doesn't speak. She's beginning to believe, finally, that I truly mean to kill Løren. Marieke doesn't hide her feelings toward me. She wants me to know them. There's disappointment, disgust, and for the first time, Marieke allows me to feel the full brunt of her hatred. I've always felt this hatred in Marieke, hidden beneath the love she tells herself she feels for me. I was eager to believe her when she told me she didn't hate me. There have never been more comforting words. But I can now see the truth. Just as Marieke hated my mother, she can't help but hate the kongelig, and there is no mistake now: I am a part of the kongelig.

Løren is brought, hands bound. He doesn't bother to look at me. He instead looks into the eyes of each of the islanders he passes. Some murmur words of comfort. Others whisper their prayers to the spirits. Løren doesn't hold the wall between us. He never believed for a moment that I wouldn't kill him, as Marieke had so hoped. He knows that I'm a member of the kongelig—knows that I'm no better than the Fjern. He's grateful. It'd been a great risk, but he's lived as long as he needed to on Hans Lollik Helle. Now his death will serve the islanders well. They'll know, finally, the truth about me: that I'm not one of them, and that I never will be.

I want him to know that I can't be to blame. I tell him this silently, sending the thought to his head. I can't be to blame for his recklessness. Attempting to escape, attacking my guard. What other choice do I have now but to execute him? I remind him that he should've been killed months ago for attempting to take my life and for killing Friedrich. I can't be to blame for this. But he knows the truth: that I hope to punish him, and my people, for not loving me as I claim to love them.

Malthe guides Løren to the chair. He whispers into Løren's ear: a prayer to the ancestors—I don't know which, since I was never taught the prayers as I should have been as a child. I'd seen my mother praying to the spirits many times. She'd walk onto the shoreline before the sun would rise, barefoot and in the salted sea. She'd close her eyes, and her mouth would move in its whispers. She must've known I followed her, must've known I was watching from the trees, but she never reprimanded me. She'd simply walk back to the manor and pretend I had never seen her on the beach. I was too afraid to ask her why she'd pray to the spirits but never allow her children to do the same.

Løren steps onto the chair, which wobbles beneath his weight for only a moment. Malthe puts the noose around his neck. It's a thick rope, strands woven like interlocked fingers wrapping around his throat. I want to look away, as I always have for the executions I've ordered, but this is a death I know I must witness. As angry and betrayed as I am by Løren's choices, his is still a life I respect, and so I must not look away when it ends.

I step forward and speak the words I must as Elskerinde. "The law of the kongelig is clear," I say. My voice wavers under the weight of the hatred of the islanders around me. "You're property of the Jannik household, and yet you attempted to escape as though you own your life."

He's silent. He doesn't look at me still. He stares at the islanders and at the air above and beside me, as though he can see spirits that I can't see. I open my mouth to continue my speech, but Malthe wants to spare the boy the mercy of having to hear my speech as he waits to die. There's nothing worse than waiting. He kicks the chair out from beneath Løren, and he falls.

Løren's neck doesn't break. His neck and face swell, body jerking. Marieke gasps beside me. A long moment passes as we wait, his legs kicking, the air hushing through the leaves of the trees. The branch snaps. Løren falls to the ground with a heavy thud. His hands, still bound, grasp at the rope around his neck to loosen it, and he breathes in a strangled breath. His neck is bruised, bleeding from scratches where the rope dug into his skin. No one moves. Malthe looks only at me, fear building in him—fear that I will order Malthe to behead Løren.

I can't think of what to say. What is there to say, when Løren still lives? He coughs on the ground, gasping for air. He looks up at me, the first he's looked at me since we came to these groves, and the gaze of defiance and hatred sears through me. Even so close to death, he won't be subdued. I feel as Aksel must have felt once, I think—anger coursing through me, disappointment but also relief.

"The spirits really won't let you die, will they?" I ask. "Why won't they let you die?"

He doesn't speak, but his thoughts are clear, even with the pain that wraps around his neck. The spirits need him alive still. They aren't done with him yet.

CHAPTER TWENTY-FOUR

It feels as though the only thing left is to free Løren. He's too defiant, even toward death, and if I keep him on this island, I think that he'll kill me as soon as any of the kongelig. But still I can't bring myself to say the words. To admit defeat between us. And so I let him be. Let him be as I let my people be—I'm undeserving of their love, I know this, and there's never been anything I can do to force them to accept me. I pretend that Løren's dead, even as he roams the house's halls as though he's become one of the many spirits on this island.

I distract myself with other matters, which I tell myself are more pressing. Alida and I prepare for our attacks on Jytte Solberg and Lothar Niklasson. She tells me that she's approached Patrika Årud, but that the woman declined to join in our mission. She doesn't care for these politics, and if the battle doesn't go as we hope, she doesn't want to be imprisoned and beheaded beside us. The one favor the woman will do for us now is to not warn the others of our plans. She'll allow us to attack, watching from the sidelines. Patrika's refusal gives Alida pause, I can tell; she wrings her hands together as she stands in my sitting room, pacing from one end to the next, her thoughts a flurry of confusion. The kongelig meeting is this very night, and our guards are waiting on the shores behind the mangrove trees.

"And if we fail?" Alida asks me.

"We won't fail."

"You wanted Elskerinde Årud's guards to join us for a reason," she says. "You believe there's a possibility we'll fail."

There's a strong possibility this won't go as we hope, of course, but I don't wish to tell Alida and add to her anxiety. I need her as much as I need the guards who will take Jytte and Lothar prisoner. If she crumbles beneath the pressure, and calls off her guards—or worse yet, betrays me when we arrive at the meeting room—Jytte and Lothar will have me executed without hesitation.

"This will work," I tell her. "Remember the consequences if we don't find the murderer now: We'll be killed by the end of the storm season."

She hesitates. Isn't it better, then, to simply leave while we still have our lives?

"It's duty that keeps you here," I remind her. "Duty to the Nørup name—to your brother."

Alida doesn't appreciate that I've seen into her thoughts, that I know her feelings—but she also knows I'm right. This overwhelming sense of Alida's duty has always been what's made her different from her brother. Her parents, while they still lived, had allowed Erik all the freedoms they wouldn't allow their daughter. She held a bitterness. While Erik was able to live a life of freedom, Alida's parents had tried to force her into a marriage. If they'd still been alive—if their ship had returned from Koninkrijk as expected and hadn't sunk to the bottom of the ocean floor—Alida would've been married into another of the kongelig families. She wouldn't have gone to university. It took her parents' deaths for her to find her freedom, but even so, she can't be free from their memories, nor from her responsibility: to take care of the family name, and to protect her brother, too. At least if our guards do lose the battle, only she will be arrested.

Lothar will be able to question her and see plainly that her brother had nothing to do with this plot. As it is now, neither one of them will survive the murderer among the kongelig. This is a chance she must be willing to take.

Alida leaves me in my sitting room to return to her own manor. I remain seated as the sun begins to set and the night breeze becomes cooler. There's a creaking footstep, but I feel no one's presence pass me by.

Malthe waits outside for me in the gardens. I'd requested that he send for the guards of Lund Helle. They wait in the mangroves, alongside the Nørup guards. Malthe knows that he's helping me commit a crime against the kongelig, which is punishable by death—for me and for all of the guards under my command, Malthe included—but he also can't disobey a direct order from his Elskerinde, especially when I claim that it's for the good of Hans Lollik Helle. We walk the path together in quiet, Malthe's mind still in its silence. I can only feel from him how easy it would be to run his knife along my neck and be done with it.

The guards hidden in the mangroves come forth from the water and join us on the shore. The sky becomes a dark green. We move toward the manor, Alida and her head guard joining us at the center of the path, her ten guards following as well. The guards that line Herregård Constantjin see us coming. The head guard steps forward and opens his mouth to speak, but I sink myself into his blood, and he silences himself, pushed back and out of the way. We pass through the doors, down the halls, and into the meeting room.

The room becomes cramped with so many bodies filling the space around the mahogany table. Patrika, Jytte, and Lothar are already in attendance. Patrika doesn't bother to pretend that she's surprised. She watches as Jytte immediately stands to her feet.

"What is this?" Elskerinde Solberg demands. She begins

to call for the guards. Lothar watches in confusion, but he's alert. He assesses the situation quickly and sees Alida standing beside me.

"Elskerinde Nørup," he says, keeping his seat, "I'm surprised."

Alida is unsure what to say. She's surprised, too—surprised that she has actually followed me on this plot of mine.

"Where is the king?" I ask.

"Do you mean to take Konge Valdemar's life?" Jytte asks.

"There's no life to take," I say. "The king is already dead."

Jytte nearly laughs in her confusion, her disbelief, but Lothar remains still, frown deepening. "What do you mean?" he asks.

"Konge Valdemar hasn't been at the kongelig meeting in over a week. He wasn't at the passing of the whales, nor was he with us for the battle against the Ludjivik. Where is he?"

"The king doesn't need to come to such trivial—"

"The king is dead," I say again, my voice echoing against the walls, even filled with so many bodies, the guards and the Fjern. "I've seen his corpse. The king that we've seen in the past months has been nothing but a figment of imagination."

Silence and confusion meet me. The guards glance at one another, and Malthe waits for the order to take Jytte and Lothar. Before I can speak—before another thought can pass through me—emotion shudders through the air. Alida's hand trembles, then goes to her neck, her eyes widening. I feel the shock that jolts through her, the stopping of her heart. It stops for a full second before it begins to pump again. She screams. She screams so loudly her voice pierces my skin. The anguish that passes from her and into my chest is a physical pain. I clutch at my neck as well, tears spilling from me, and Alida's scream lowers to an agonizing sob.

All in the room are alarmed. Questions, thoughts, emotions bombard me, and my vision begins to blacken. I force myself through the bodies of the guards that crowd the room and out into the hallway, leaning against the walls until I stagger out the front doors and into the heated night. I make it to the gardens, where I heave into the grass. There're shouts behind me—they've made the discovery, I can feel the shock and disgust that fills the courtyard.

It was cruel, I think—even crueler than simply killing Erik Nørup and leaving his body to be found: His head, abandoned on the ground beside the fountain, leaves a stream of red, his eyes closed and his lips parted, as though he'd been beheaded in his sleep. Alida screams from within the manor's walls, again and again. She can feel the absence of her twin. She's always been able to feel her brother, as though his spirit was her own. They'd been born with this connection, this kraft that runs through their veins. Most come into their power when they're around ten years of age, but Alida and Erik had always known of their ability. It'd been even stronger when they were younger, and both could feel in themselves and each other what a shame it was that their kraft had become weaker as they grew older. They weren't as close as when they were children. This alone was a tragedy, but at least Alida could sometimes feel how Erik wondered to himself how he might be able to become closer to his sister one day, and Alida knew Erik could also feel this desire in her. The twins didn't want to hate each other. After the deaths of their parents, they were all the other had.

Alida had never considered that she might find herself alone in this world. It was an illogical thought, to be sure, but she'd always felt her brother would be a part of her. No matter how distant they became, the possibility of finding their way to each other again had always remained.

I try to block the emotion that explodes from her and all the guards, Jytte who runs out into the courtyard and covers her mouth, Lothar who follows and shakes his head, unsurprised but still angry on behalf of Erik Nørup. Malthe runs down the path and into the groves that surround Herregård Constantjin looking for a sign of anyone who might be hiding behind a tree, watching the devastation that's unfolded, but no one is there.

News has already spread by the time I reach the cliffs. Slaves whisper to one another of this third murder of the kongelig. Aksel has already left. His things are cleared from the front of the house, where chests had been stacked. The house is quieter now that the slaves who'd been bustling about for his departure have finished their work. It seems that even the usual chatter and laughter has been covered by silence. The sun sets red, and when I close my eyes, all I can see is Erik Nørup's parted mouth, the serenity of his brow. He hadn't died fighting. I hope that when my murderer comes for me, they aren't so cowardly as to take me with my eyes shut.

CHAPTER TWENTY-FIVE

The days pass on Hans Lollik Helle, and I don't leave the Jannik house. I sit in the quiet, enjoying the coolness of the breeze that passes through the open windows. I listen to the crashing of the waves below from my balcony, my eyes closed, my eyelashes fluttering against my cheeks. I should leave the royal island. I can feel the thought in Marieke each time she comes into my room with newly folded sheets. I should leave while I have my life. But still I don't. There's a stubbornness in me. My mother had always called me a stubborn child: I wouldn't take a bath when I was ordered to; wouldn't eat my food, screaming that I wasn't hungry; wouldn't put on the pretty little dresses of lace. She'd called me stubborn—with love sometimes, anger others—but I think she mostly said this with pride, perhaps knowing this was a trait she'd passed on to me. I would be too stubborn to let myself be ignored; too stubborn to allow the Fjern to take my voice, my power, my life. The stubbornness I inherited from my mother pulses in my blood. I have a desire not only to live, to force others to hear my voice, but also a need to see myself succeed—to prove my worth to myself and all the Fjern and my own people. A need to see the kongelig burn.

Neither Jytte Solberg nor Lothar Niklasson have sent their guards after me. I thought that they would, but perhaps it's out of respect for Erik Nørup's death that they hesitate—or maybe they're only waiting for the right time to strike. I received a letter from a messenger, Konge Valdemar's signature scrawled along the paper. The false king is to choose the regent who will replace him in one week's time. It seems impossible, this fact. All of my life has led to this moment. I'd planned for years. Once I decided that I wouldn't let myself die, I knew that I had to return to the islands of Hans Lollik Helle; so I learned. Learned of the kongelig and their descendants. I looked for the weaknesses of each family, plotted how I'd convince Elskerinde Freja Jannik, finally, of my worth. I returned to the island of Lund Helle, and I killed my uncle. Poisoned his tea every morning, slowly, so that no one would suspect me when he became sick. I didn't have to do much to convince the man to name me Elskerinde of Lund Helle on his deathbed; he had no one else to name. I met with Elskerinde Jannik for two years, taking her memories and inserting my own thoughts. And finally I'm here. It goes beyond ambition: Getting onto Hans Lollik Helle and surviving this island long enough so that the king might choose me as regent was my reason for living. Even as a child, when I thought on how Tante had whispered to me that my mother would've wanted me to live, I'd wanted to die. I'd wished that my mother hadn't sent me back to my bed that night. That I'd stayed in the gardens, dancing to the music with Ellinor, laughing beneath the stars.

The kongelig are called to the meeting room by the false king. A final meeting, before he's to declare the new regent. I sit at the table with Patrika Årud, Lothar Niklasson, Jytte Solberg. There're no guards in sight, no desire of Jytte or Lothar to find their revenge against me. I can feel their questions, their suspicions. It's true that the king hasn't been seen for some time, and they remember my accusations—but at the forefront of everyone's mind is the memory of Erik Nørup's head.

Patrika's face is pale, her lips blue, her eyes red. She hasn't put on her cracking makeup as she normally would, and I can see the lines of her face, around her eyes and mouth. Lothar is lost in his own thoughts, his mouth set, gray-and-white-speckled hair uncombed and tangled. Jytte doesn't look away from me. Her pale-blue eyes capture my every movement.

We are only four, out of the nine kongelig who'd originally started the storm season on Hans Lollik Helle. I'm not surprised that Alida didn't come. I'd be surprised if she didn't leave Hans Lollik Helle immediately that morning. I can't help the pinch of fear that Alida might not have any plans to leave Hans Lollik Helle alive. Her brother had been a part of her soul. They hadn't been as close in recent years, and she'd regretted this; now she mourns his loss so violently that I fear she'll take her own life, just to be reunited with him.

Not much time passes before the door swings open again. Konge Valdemar—his ghost, his corpse, the puppet of the false king—enters. The eyes of each of the kongelig flit to meet my own, and they think: Here is their proof against me and my accusations. The king is alive and well. He stands before us all. None of them notice that he brings with him the strong scent of wet, overturned dirt. We barely manage to stand in respect before he takes a heavy seat, waving at us to sit down again.

"Alida Nørup has withdrawn as a kongelig of Hans Lollik Helle," the false king tells us.

There's no measure to Jytte Solberg's ambition. She sits straighter in her seat, the desire for the regent's power emanating from her. She'd been told, since she'd been a child, that she'd been made to rule. Her father had been older than the other girls' fathers on these islands; he had white hair, a face lined by age, a fragile back. The girl's mother had been dead since her birth. Jytte had never truly belonged with the other little girls of Hans Lollik. She stayed on Solberg Helle, content in her isolation. She studied war. She studied politics. She studied how she might one day become regent, earning the honor for the Solberg name. The Solberg line had once been kings of Koninkrijk; hundreds of eras ago, a rebellion forced the family into exile, but royalty remained in their veins. Jytte Solberg doesn't care about these islands of Hans Lollik. She sees only a plan that will take many generations: She'll take Hans Lollik Helle, allowing her future descendants to come one step closer to growing their power and taking back the crown of Koninkrijk.

The king speaks. "It won't be an easy decision," he tells us. "Each of you has the true qualities of regent, and yet I must choose."

"My king," Patrika Årud says, "if I may."

My eyes glance to both Jytte Solberg and Lothar Niklasson, watching their expressions as Elskerinde Årud speaks.

"I, too, would like to withdraw from your consideration as regent," Patrika says.

Her voice doesn't tremble or shake. There's no emotion in her tone, or beneath her skin. She's embraced numbness. If she doesn't embrace numbness, she can't escape the questions that eventually haunt us all: whether there's any point to life, when we will inevitably be found by death in the end.

Patrika hadn't really been in the running, not more than the others; but still, I can feel the relief from Jytte, the increased focus in Lothar. I myself am not eligible, after the king's decision and announcement weeks before, so now the choice is between the two of them.

"Lothar, you've been my trusted ally for many years now," the Konge Valdemar says. "It'd only be natural if I chose you."

"It would be an honor, my king."

"But of course," Valdemar continues, "Jytte Solberg would also be a strong candidate. Fresh eyes, which is so needed in these islands."

"Thank you, my king."

Careful words, gazes fixed on the surface of the table. The

king asks for updates on our respective islands, our crop and coin. I relay that the latest storms had done more damage to the Lund Helle plantations than before. There'll have to be rebuilding, replanting, and perhaps a higher taxation of the Fjern who live on my island. Jytte speaks of her plans to expand her army, after the success of the battle against the Ludjivik.

While she speaks, Lothar thinks that it's strange the king hasn't acknowledged the murder of Erik Nørup. Erik had been up for strong consideration, after all; the Fjern would've wanted a king like him, regardless of whether the boy had the intelligence or the talent for ruling. Lothar thinks on the murders of Beata Larsen and Olsen Årud, the attempted assassination of Jytte Solberg. He meets my eyes. He hasn't wanted to admit it, not when the suggestion implies a weakening in his kraft, but he wonders if I've figured out a way to deceive him, just as the others have suggested.

"My king," Lothar says, "there was an incident. Before the discovery of Erik Nørup's death, Elskerindes Jannik and Nørup had brought their guards onto Hans Lollik Helle. They stormed Herregård Constantjin."

Konge Valdemar makes no expression, speaks no words. His reaction is calm and still.

"I believe that either Jytte Solberg or Lothar Niklasson are to blame for the murders of the kongelig," I say. I don't speak to the king. I know that he's false. I look between the two, seated at the table.

"It could just as easily be you, Elskerinde Jannik," Jytte says.

The king speaks. "What do you propose?"

"Punishment," Lothar answers. "Execution. Exile. Anything to get her off of Hans Lollik Helle."

"One of you is the murderer," I say, "and the other a fool. If you aren't to blame for these killings, then trust me now. All that I say is true."

"The king sits before us in perfect health," Lothar says. "What answer do you have for this?"

I can't honestly say. It becomes easy to think that I've fallen into madness when the king, who should be dead, sits before me—an illusion, a spirit, I'm not sure which. Lothar says again that I should answer for my crimes. Kongelig aren't supposed to bring their guards onto the island. It's an affront, and besides that, I used my guards to threaten both him and Jytte.

The king leans back in his seat, studying Lothar. "I could have Elskerinde Jannik punished," he says, "but I'd rather this fall to the next regent. Whoever inherits Hans Lollik Helle will have the task of deciding Sigourney Jannik's future. Is this agreeable?"

Lothar and Jytte have no choice but to agree with the king's command, and so they nod dutifully. I can feel in them easily what each would decide: Jytte would have me killed immediately, of course, there is no question in that; but Lothar has never had much stomach for blood, and he's never seen me as a true threat, even now. He only wants me gone, and it would be easy enough to send me into exile—force me to leave these islands, never to return again. I would have to find a new home elsewhere, perhaps in the north. I wonder if I would finally find my peace.

The Jannik house on the cliffs is stark white against the setting sun and the darkening sky. The breeze lifts into a wind, threatening to grow stronger into a storm for what would be the last of the season. The house is silent as I approach, but I don't think anything of it until I open the door. It creaks, and I pause. There're no footsteps, no laughter, no chatter or shouted orders. I step inside. A slave girl sits on the couch by my fireplace, her throat cut open. Red spills down her front and to the floor, and her eyes are wide, staring. I swallow a scream and step into the shadows. My breath becomes uneven, ragged. I force myself to close my eyes and breathe in, slowly. This could be another trick, another dream or vision.

I don't feel a presence with murder on its mind, don't feel anyone alive. No life, when this house is usually filled with bustle, chatter, laughter, Marieke shouting her orders. My heart pumps harder, faster, as I walk down the hall. Another slave, the stable boy, has been cut across his chest. He lies on his back, staring at the ceiling, blood spreading across the floorboards. The women who worked in the kitchen are spread across the ground, stomachs open, eyes stuck open in death. When I walk through the door to the gardens, it's all I can do to stop myself from heaving. There're dozens dead here, sprawled on their backs and sides as though they had been running for their lives. The killer mocks me. They know that the last time I saw so many dead like this, taken to the gardens to bleed, was the last time I'd seen my family.

And when I climb my stairs, I can already feel the fear building at what I know I will see. The floorboards creak beneath my feet, the smell of the dead already rising in the heat. I open the door to my chambers. Marieke lies as though asleep, eyes closed and neck cut. I must've screamed, must've cried, because my throat feels raw, but I hear nothing. I run to her, afraid to touch her—afraid to harm her—but wanting to stop the flow of blood. It's only when I touch her neck that I realize the blood that covers her and the sheets stopped pumping long ago. It pools like a jewel in the hollow of her collarbone, stains her skin, and drenches the sheets of the bed like its own salted sea. I crumple to the ground, the floorboards sticking to my skin with her blood, and I stay there, even after the tears have dried. I can't move. I can barely breathe. I wait there for some time, wait for the horror to end, for my eyes to open once again and find myself in the groves or on the rocky shore, another trick of the kongelig who wants me dead; but the longer I stay, the stronger the scent of blood becomes, and I know that this is no lie.

And so I've lost. Marieke was the only person in this world who had any love for me, the only one who cared for me at all—and now she's gone. I've lost, and I can't stay on Hans Lollik Helle—not anymore. The kongelig can take what they want. They can have these islands. They can have my people. I'm done.

I don't know if Malthe is alive or dead, but I suppose it doesn't matter. I leave my chambers, ready to walk to the barracks and ask for a boat to take me from this island. I want to leave Hans Lollik Helle and all of the islands under its rule—return to the northern empires, live the rest of my life on Bernhand Lund's coin. I'll buy a house in a city, far away from Koninkrijk, with the hope that I'll never lay my eyes on the Fjern again. I'll have a life of solitude. I can't see any reason I would need to attempt to make alliances or friend-ships. I can't imagine wanting to touch or be touched—imagine wanting to speak to another person again. Thoughts and emotions will come to me, and I'll know strangers' lives as thoroughly as I'll know my own, with all their sadness and heartbreak and joy, and I'll try to pretend their life is my own so that I won't have to remember this pain. This is what I want most of all now: to forget everything.

It's only when I step from the porch that I think of him. I hesitate. He I should want to forget, too. I should want to leave him here on this island, leave him here to hang and burn, but I can't. I can never leave that man alone. I turn down the halls, toward the library. I turn the knob, afraid of what I'll find inside, but Løren stands, watching and waiting like it seems he always does. He'd heard the screams, the pleas for mercy, trapped in this library. He'd been prepared to fight, even knowing it was likely he would die. After surviving so much, this wasn't how he wanted to leave this life.

I should free him. I can feel it in all of my being, vibrating beneath my skin. I should free the man who stands in front of me and allow him to escape to the north.

We leave the house, him following behind as he has always

done. I'm ready to burn the house down. Burn the house and all the bodies within it. Marieke deserves a proper burial, I know this, but I can't imagine stepping across that threshold again without breaking apart. I need to keep moving, get onto the boat, and go, or I'll return to that house and set it afire with me still inside.

Løren expects me to ask him what happened, but I don't want to know. I don't care, I tell myself, not even if he knew the name of the kongelig who's to blame. I can't let myself care, because the grief that is building in me will explode and rupture me, and I know I won't leave this island. If I think of the pain, let myself remember Marieke in my bed, I'll walk into the sea and keep walking, as so many of my people have escaped these islands before me. I have to keep moving. I can't allow myself to think on Marieke.

Løren is surprised to see me in mourning. He didn't think I had true feelings for anyone other than myself, and most certainly not a slave. It's interesting to see myself as Løren sees me: the black island woman, skin as dark as night, wearing the white dress of the kongelig. There was so much potential for me to be the heroine I'd always wanted to be. If I'd stood up against the kongelig; if I'd led my people in battle against them, not because I wanted to lead them but because I wanted freedom for them. I could've been a symbol of hope in these islands; a daughter of the beloved Mirjam Rose, rising from the dead to lead her people to freedom. I could've destroyed the Fjern, run them from these islands, and made them the land of my people once more.

And why didn't I? This is something Løren has wanted to know. Is it because it would be so difficult for someone like me? I've hated the Fjern, but I've always wanted to be them; have envied their power, have desired the title of regent. Løren wonders if I've been unable to admit to myself, all along, that what I've wanted above all else is to prove my worth to the pale-skinned Fjern; prove that I belong in their world, and earn a respect I know they'll never give. I've wanted this, and the love of my own people, even while knowing I could never have both. I leave these islands now with neither—nothing, but the hatred Løren believes I'll always hold for myself. He pities me. Løren has always pitied me. Someone like me, with my dark skin and the opportunity I hold, can't afford to make the mistakes that I've made. Someone like me, an islander with no love, can't afford to sin. Sins are for the Fjern, to be forgiven by their divine gods; sins are for the islanders, to be forgiven by the spirits of our ancestors. I have no one to forgive me.

"We're leaving Hans Lollik Helle," I tell him. "You're coming with me."

Løren leaves for the slaves' quarters with orders to have the boat and ship prepared. I can't wait outside the Jannik house knowing what lies within. I walk the path that takes me through the groves, and I can feel the eyes of someone on me, their breath on the back of my neck, but I see no one. I run to the hill that holds Herregård Constantjin and I walk up the slope, rocks cutting the bottoms of my bare feet.

The courtyard looks as it did the night I'd come with Løren: desolated, cracks in the cobblestones. I enter through the main doors, not bothering to hide, and I scream that they've won. My voice echoes through the empty halls, and I can hear a laugh, though I can't see the body it belongs to. The laugh lets me know that, yes, they're happy to know I've surrendered in this game. The laugh echoes, fading. I should leave, I know this—leave and wait for Løren, escape the island for good. But my feet move, my legs running. I chase the laugh, racing through the halls that twist and turn like a maze of rot and mold, until I come to a room I haven't seen before: the throne room.

The room is brightly lit with chandeliers and candles that line the walls, empty of furniture except for the throne that presides at the far end of the hall itself. Something sits on the throne. I walk closer, and closer, over the red velvet carpet—stop when I see what it is, and gag despite myself. The head of the king. Its eyes bulge, tongue lolls, and from the skin that has been eaten away, the chunks of hair missing from the skull: the king's head. The person who placed the head here must know that I went to Valdemar Helle. They must know that I've seen the grave. It could be the king's real head, but I'm used to their tricks now. They could have put this false vision of the king's head here to taunt me, to laugh at me.

There are footsteps. I spin around, and Jytte Solberg stands with her guards. One guard already holds Løren, his hands tied, his face empty of emotion. Jytte's eyes are wide, moving from me and to the throne.

There's shock that echoes as the guards and Jytte realize what it is they see. Jytte steels herself from showing the emotion her body releases through her pores. She's had to be careful, all these years, not to show emotion as anyone else would—this emotion is considered a weakness on these islands, and the men of the kongelig have always gladly searched for any excuse to have her removed as Elskerinde Solberg. She shows an icy expression now as she turns to her guard, pointing to me.

"Arrest her," she says, and so they do. They grab my arms, yanking them behind my back. I could fight. I could enter one of the guards and have him attack his brothers—have him attack Jytte even, and try to kill her in an attempt to escape—but I know that this is a fight that I would lose. I suddenly understand why Løren doesn't bother to fight when he knows he cannot win. There isn't any point spending that energy—energy that could easily be saved for another opportunity to fight again, to fight and win.

One guard kicks the backs of my knees, forcing me to the rough surface, my skin stinging; Løren is forced to his knees beside me.

"It's not real," I tell her, but Jytte isn't listening. She only moves closer to the throne. "It isn't real. None of this is real, Elskerinde Solberg."

She thinks I speak nonsense. She thinks I'm crazed. She truly believes I've been to blame for each murder on this royal island; has believed that I have been the snake planning each of their deaths, and now here's her proof. She's glad to have it now, finally, but she only wishes she could have made the others see sooner. The guards flank us, bringing us from the throne room, halls now restored to their marble and gold. We march through the groves, which had been empty before but are now filled with slaves who finish their work, staring only at the fruit they pick. We're taken to the Solberg house. It's difficult to see the outside of the house in the nighttime, but within, the fireplace roars with life and golden chandeliers light the rooms, with their gilded wallpaper and gleaming wooden floors. The guards take me and Løren across the hall and to a staircase, down into the darkness of a cellar. There are bars here, locked doors. We're told to stand within, and the door clangs shut behind us, key turned.

Løren is unbothered. He's found himself in similar situations many times before. Things always tend to work out for him in the end, so he isn't afraid as he finds a comfortable space on the hard stone floor to sit. And even if he were to be killed—accused of helping me in the beheading of the king, hung before all on Hans Lollik Helle—what would that matter? Fate will have finally found him, after all these years. It's interesting to me that he can feel confident that he'll live, but is also resigned to die.

"Are you really so willing to die?" I ask him.

He doesn't bother to respond, doesn't even bother to hold the wall between us. I can slip into him easily, can feel the calmness in him with the strength of the rising tide. There's a memory, deep within him, one that he'd forgotten himself but, as he feels me witnessing it, remembers with some nostalgia, the smallest of smiles. Løren knows he's protected. He knows the love his ancestors hold for him. He'd been a boy, barely able to walk, and he'd come to the rocky shore. He'd gotten too close to the water, and a wave washed him into the sea, tide pulling him beneath, the dark water swirling around him. He'd nearly drowned, just as I had almost drowned so many years ago, too. But a woman had waited for him under the waves. Løren couldn't remember much else. It's possible he'd lost consciousness, unable to breathe. It's possible he actually did die that day, and the spirits didn't want him, and so sent him back into the world of the living. He was left on the sand for one of the slave girls to find. Løren has always been blessed by the spirits of these islands. So blessed that I can't help but begin to wonder if he's a spirit himself.

"You loved Marieke," Løren tells me. This isn't a question. He doesn't need confirmation. It's only an observation of his, one with slight surprise.

I don't want to discuss Marieke. I want to forget her. The pain that fills me numbs my mind, and it becomes difficult to think, to breathe. I'm not a stranger to death. Death has followed me all my life, and I know this grief well.

"I did love her," I tell him.

"You don't believe the kongelig can love a slave they own."

"Marieke wasn't my slave," I tell him. "I'd granted her freedom."

He's impatient at this. Yes, of course Marieke was my slave, when I wouldn't grant her the coin my family owed her for her years of service, along with the coin owed her dead daughter and the girl's father. How could she be anything but a slave, when she had nowhere to live, no food to eat, no opportunity? She'd had no choice but to stay with me, Løren believes, and this perhaps was the worst sort of slavery: one that's mocking as it declares its freedom, punishing Marieke for making her imagine it's her own choice in staying.

But still, Løren must admit that I did love Marieke, even with the lies I'd told myself. He offers his condolences. They're genuine, in respect for Marieke. He wonders if there might be hope for me after all, but this is something he's wondered before, and something I've proven him wrong in time and again. I'd tried to have him killed, he reminds himself. But he can't help but hold hope for me. Hope that I can be better—that I can change.

"Have you ever mourned anyone?" I ask him.

He tells me yes. He mourned the death of his friend who was hung by Engel Jannik after revealing Løren hiding in the caves.

"Why would you mourn that boy, after he betrayed you?"

"He didn't know any better," Løren tells me, and I can feel that he doesn't mean because the boy was touched in the head. "He didn't know anything else. How can I expect someone to imagine freedom if they've never seen freedom for themselves?"

"You've never seen freedom," I tell him, "yet you imagine it whenever you can."

"I don't know why I'm different," he says, "but I do know that I am. And so it's my responsibility to imagine something others can't see, and to show it to them."

I stand, waiting for Jytte's arrival. I know that she means to have me and Løren killed—I just don't know when. I try to come to terms with my death. I should have died along with my family when I was a child, so perhaps this is only what I had denied the spirits so long ago. They've come to collect on the debt I owe. So many have died because of me; because I lived, because I fought to return to these islands, because I wanted the power the kongelig denied me. It's only right that I be punished now. I don't know if the spirits would welcome me as they must have welcomed my family. I don't know whether my family would have any love for me, or if my mother would be proud of me. This is what I fear more than dying: to be greeted by my mother, and to see the disappointment in her eyes. Disappointment not that I failed to rise among the kongelig, but that I betrayed her and my people. And what of Claus, Inga, Ellinor? I fear that

they'd look at me with the same hatred that all the other islanders around me do. That I'd be exiled from my own family—my
own people—even in death.

I fear this more than I do the act of dying, but I do still want
my life—it's natural, isn't it? To want to stay alive. To want to
keep the body that I have, to not feel the stopping of my heart in
my chest as I have felt in the bodies of so many before me. Løren
falls asleep, and I can see snippets of memories mixed with his
dreams—the rope and its tree, the water that swirls around him,
the islanders who stand in the grove awaiting his return.

It's hours before I hear footsteps approaching. A guard opens
the door to the cell, Jytte Solberg by his side. I can see in Jytte the
chaos that has befallen the island. The king is dead. The kongelig,
upon learning the truth, have started their escape. They have all
packed their things, ready to leave for the ships that will take
them to Koninkrijk. None want to be here on Hans Lollik Helle
when the inevitable battle for power begins. They believe there'll
be an outright war between Jytte and Lothar, and Jytte thinks
that they may be right in this. She hasn't seen or heard from
Lothar, and though she has known Herre Niklasson to be gentle,
she also knows that he wants the power that he feels has been
promised to him; and so if he has to kill her and all of her guards
to sit atop the throne, he will do so. If this is how it must be, then
Jytte will fight Lothar, and she'll kill the old fool herself.

But first there is me. Jytte knows it was a risk imprisoning me
and my slave. She had no proof that I have done anything wrong
on this royal island; can't say with any absolute certainty that I'm
the one who has been behind the murder of the king, beyond
finding me in the throne room as she did. But she knows, too,
that no one will speak for me. No one will care if I, with my
dark skin, am imprisoned and left to rot in these cellars. I have
no friends. I have no allies among the kongelig. Alida Nørup has

already left for Koninkrijk, before she could even properly bury her brother at sea.

Jytte should simply kill me. This is what she'd planned, at first—but now that my allies are gone, and I'm imprisoned, no longer a threat, she considers another option. I could be of use to her. This is what Jytte thinks; she's had hours to consider this carefully, this spark of inspiration she couldn't help but feel over the past weeks. That, though I wouldn't work with her willingly, my kraft and my ability to know the thoughts and emotions of others, to even control their bodies, would be valuable if she can learn to control me. It would take work. The stripping of my kongelig status, of course—that would be as easy as a few spoken words. She'd send her guards to overtake Lund Helle, making it the property of the Solberg name along with the plantations, the crops, and coin. Next would be the stripping of my freedom. She would declare that, since Lund Helle would belong to the Solberg, and I am no longer a protected member of the kongelig, I'm no longer deemed a person of these islands who can control my own future. I would be made a slave. I would have to be broken in first. I've only ever known freedom my entire life and I would need to be reminded of my place. Jytte would keep me in this cellar. She would use her kraft on me. Drive me insane with my own fears and anxieties. Have me screaming for my own death within only one month's time. She would offer me comfort. End the torture as a reward, whenever I did something that she wished. Bring another slave into my cage, perhaps, and order me to kill the islander to prove that I'm willing to do the work she needs me to do. Jytte would make me come to learn that if I do what she asks, my life would be bearable. She would successfully break me. Jytte is certain of this.

"I would rather take my own life," I tell Jytte. She's surprised, frustrated that I can know her thoughts so easily, but impressed as well. I've only solidified her desire to take me and make me a slave of Solberg Helle—to use my kraft as she wishes.

The questioning doesn't take place in the dungeons as I thought it would. Løren and I are brought above to the sitting room, as though we're welcomed guests, though our hands are still tied, Løren told to stand against the wall as one of the slaves. Jytte sits across from me, wearing her pants and shirt, her hair tied up in a bun. Lothar stands over us. I'm surprised by this. Jytte and Lothar both think on how they'll have to battle for their position as regent—that they'll have to attempt to take one another's life for the crown within just a few days' time. But the time for that hasn't come yet, and in the aftermath of the regent's death, they act as allies. Both need answers still.

The grief from Lothar comes in waves. He tries to hide it—tries to pretend that he's nothing more than a kongelig who mourns the death of the king as any loyal adviser would. Lothar knows that the king had changed—knows that he wasn't the man he loved when they were both boys—but he can't help but mourn the boy Cristoff Valdemar had once been. He'd been beautiful, filled with light and hope and ambition. Lothar had always been drawn to Cristoff, a moth drawn to a flickering torch. And now the man is dead. He should be happy, too, for the clear path toward the throne. Lothar tries to remind himself of his goals, of his successors, of his legacy; but it's difficult to feel that such things matter when he's lost someone he loved. I know what Lothar feels. I try to forget Marieke's death. I need to forget now if I'm to keep my mind sharp and have any chance of surviving the kongelig long enough to escape Hans Lollik Helle.

"Elskerinde Jannik," he says, "did you have a hand in the death of the king?"

"I did not," I say, and he knows that I'm not lying—but still, he wonders again if I've found a way around his kraft. Lothar knows that something's wrong, not just about me but about all of the island of Hans Lollik Helle. It can't be a coincidence that the season that I'm invited to the royal island is the same season that so many kongelig have met their ends, and that those who survive have escaped from the island, passing on the chance to become regent. This is all interconnected, he thinks; he just doesn't know how.

I watch both of them with equal suspicion. Many have hidden their thoughts from me before, but as I enter the thoughts of Jytte and Lothar, each time I can find no hint that either one is the true murderer. They both seem sincere in their belief in my guilt, but one of the two must be hiding the truth. Which of the kongelig is to blame—for the murders of the others, for the death of the king? Lothar Niklasson has questioned each of the kongelig, and interviewed me multiple times—but he's never been questioned himself.

"I'm not the guilty one," I tell him, and he's unsurprised that I know his thoughts. "But I can't help but wonder if you are."

He is surprised by my accusation—even smiles, then laughs, exchanging looks with Jytte, whose expressionless face remains still. There's a spark within her. It would be most helpful if she could, in fact, find a way to blame Lothar Niklasson for the death of the king, even if she knows that it was me. This would be a way to be rid of Lothar Niklasson without having to take her guards to battle, risking her own life in the process.

"Me?" he says. "You know my thoughts, feel my emotions. If it was me, you would've known before now."

"People often become rather good at hiding their thoughts and emotions from me, with enough practice," I tell him.

"I have nothing to hide." His heart hammers in his chest at the thought that I might have learned, might have realized, the sort of love he'd held for the king. This is the only secret that Lothar Niklasson has to fear. He's killed before, yes; of course he has killed to become as close to the title of regent as he has now. But he hasn't killed the kongelig of Hans Lollik Helle. He hasn't killed the regent. This he feels—or wants me to feel, forcing a lie into my kraft.

"Who have you killed?" I ask him. "Tell me, and I'll see if your memory includes Erik Nørup. You want me to see that you feel badly for the boy, but you could have killed him yourself. And Olsen Årud? Couldn't you have ordered your guard to burn down the Årud manor? Beata Larsen might have been an easy first choice to kill, to get her out of the way."

"This is ridiculous," Lothar says. "I'm not the one on trial here, Elskerinde Jannik—you are." He turns to Jytte. "See how she turns the truth around? How she makes me defend myself?"

Jytte hesitates. "It is true that we're at a disadvantage," she admits. "Your kraft to force all to tell the truth works on everyone but you. But still, Elskerinde Jannik must also answer for her own crimes."

"I have nothing to answer for," I tell her. "If you're looking for an excuse to punish me and strip me of my title and my legacy, then you won't find one."

She clenches her jaw and raises her chin. Jytte knows I've seen her thoughts, her plans. She would make me a personal slave of hers if she could find a way to control me, and she's sure that she can find a way. She's false in her anger for the death of the king. Jytte Solberg can't hide that she's relieved the king is dead. She's glad, even—happy, that I've cleared a path for her to the throne.

If Jytte is successful in all her plans—in becoming queen of these islands—I'll be trapped on Hans Lollik Helle for the rest of my days, without my freedom, living as the rest of my people do. I should be ashamed that this is a fear of mine, to be treated as my people are treated. To lose the privilege of freedom, and of being a member of the kongelig. I know the pain my people have suffered, and I have done nothing to help them. Because of this—because of me—Marieke is dead.

It doesn't matter if Lothar is to blame for the king or not. It doesn't matter if Jytte ever realizes the truth, or if she succeeds in taking the throne. I don't care for these politics any longer. I've lost, and I'm willing to leave, to escape these islands as long as I have my freedom and my life. "Am I guilty or am I innocent?" I ask him.

Lothar, regardless of his personal feelings for me, doesn't lie. "As far as I can see, you're innocent."

"Then I'm free to leave."

I stand, and Jytte hesitates—but she can't argue with Lothar's judgment, not openly, not unless she means to start this war here and now. Both sides still need to prepare. If she decides to hold me against Lothar's will, the battle will be sparked, and she still needs the guards of Solberg Helle to arrive, to attack and take Lothar captive. Her guards will arrive by tomorrow's end, and Lothar's head will be hers. Jytte doesn't want to let me go, but I'm not worth risking the crown.

A slave comes forward, cutting through the ropes that bind my and Løren's hands. I demand a boat be prepared to take me to a ship. I declare that as I wasn't able to become regent of Hans Lollik Helle due to the king's ruling before his death, I have no more ties to the royal island; and so I'll leave for the north, as so many of the other kongelig have before me. Jytte tries to think of a way she can stop me—keep me imprisoned here, without anyone else's knowledge—but she decides to let me leave. Allow me to find my peace in the north, as she focuses on becoming regent and grasping these islands in her control. And when the time is right, she can find me again. She'll send her scouts to the north to search for me, the dark-skinned islander who speaks with the lilting tone of those from Hans Lollik, who acts like I believe I'm of equal worth to the Fjern. It should be easy to find me again, and with the connections Jytte has, she could have me kidnapped and drag me back to these islands as her slave— there's no one in this world who would care, no one who would miss me. I would kill Jytte Solberg myself before I allowed such a thing to happen.

CHAPTER TWENTY-SIX

I don't take many of my belongings—only enough dresses to last the trip to the north, and Løren, who remains silent. He stands on the deck, watching the passing of the islands, the darkness of the ocean beneath us. I wonder if he plans to jump into the sea just to escape me. Løren has never left Hans Lollik before. He'll see, for the first time, waters that aren't clear with the blue of the sky, nor pregnant islands of green. He thinks to himself that he won't necessarily miss these islands—only that this is all he's ever known. The idea of going to the northern empires, with people he knows nothing of, the cultures and languages... for the first time, I feel unease in him. Fear, even.

He'd been afraid as a child. He was scared most of his days, running and begging for his life, trying to escape his brother and his father, praying to the spirits for their protection. But now his life has purpose. A mission, a plan. This mission gave him more than just a goal. It made him fearless. If he died, then so what? It was only death, and he had achieved so much in this short life of his. He was willing to die for this plan—and for his people.

It had been a slow start, over the years. A network of whispers across the islands, whispers that he hadn't been allowed to hear. He had the blood of a Fjernman, after all, and couldn't be trusted. The other slaves would whisper about taking their machetes and cutting the necks of the masters while they slept, but they would become silent whenever they saw Løren, gazes filled with a hatred I'm familiar with. At first, Løren accepted this hatred. There was nothing he could do. He had the blood of a Fjernman, his skin lighter than the islanders around him, and there wasn't anything he could do to change the hatred in their hearts. But after Løren hid in his cave, and his friend had come to him, pointing—and when his friend was hung by his neck— Løren had grown tired of running, tired of being helpless and at the mercy of his brother and father. If he was going to die, he wanted to know he would die with a purpose.

There was a slave who trained him and the other young guards during the storm season on Hans Lollik Helle. In Løren's memory, Malthe was as quiet as he is now, intimidating in his silence. Løren knew the risk he took. If he was wrong, Malthe could easily have Løren killed, called a traitor to the guard and to his masters, executed before all on the royal island. But he hadn't been wrong. Løren had asked if Malthe knew of the whispers. He'd been fourteen, and the other boys in the quarters where Løren slept had been subdued for many years now, the memory of their friend, accused of holding kraft by Aksel, fresh in their memories. Løren was annoyed that they'd given up so easily, at just the reminder that they risked their lives for freedom.

Malthe told Løren to leave the matter alone; told him that he was just a child, and he'd find himself dead and ruin all of the years' worth of work if he attempted to force his way into their plans. But Løren was relentless. He had kraft, and as far as Løren knew, he was the only slave with kraft who had been allowed to live. Løren also knew his kraft was special, powerful. Not many of the slaves of Hans Lollik Helle had kraft. Only two others did, kraft that they kept hidden, knowing that they'd be killed if the kongelig ever learned of their power. One eventually was: an older man of Jannik Helle who had the power to see others' dreams. And then there was the girl, the child, who the others kept hidden as often as they could, afraid that she might accidentally use her kraft and be killed, no matter that she was only ten years old. Løren whispered to Malthe that he could be of use. They needed someone like him.

He was right about this. Malthe hadn't wanted to admit it, but it was true. So far, everyone involved had been slaves Malthe could trust with his life—islanders who were willing to die for the freedom of their people, and to kill for their people, too. Malthe was willing to kill. He was the head of the Lund guard, and so this meant he often had to complete his duty as my captain. He'd killed many of his own people. He'd executed slaves with kraft. He thought of them often, the innocent islanders who had done nothing to deserve their deaths. Their only error had been in being born with skin as dark as his. He whispered his prayers to them, thanking each for their sacrifice. The girl in the fields of Lund Helle—he thought of her often, as she'd so reminded him of his beloved, who smelled of lemongrass and rose-mallow tea. He had to act as the head of my guard would, or he would cause suspicion and lose his position. He needed to keep my confidence, to best serve in this uprising. He was willing to do anything for his people—was willing to lead a rebellion against the kongelig—but they had no power among them. Those with kraft had been so routinely rooted out and killed that there were no known islanders with the power left. After Løren asked Malthe to allow him to join for the entirety of the storm season all those years ago, he was allowed to hear the whispers—the quick and hurried meetings by the bay, in the groves, within the kitchens under the loud clang of pots and pans and shouted orders.

This plan of theirs would take years of careful thought and action. The slaves on the royal island could have attempted the smaller uprisings, as so many did across the islands of Hans Lollik. But Malthe was insistent that they wait for the right opportunity. If they didn't, then just like all the rest before, their uprising would be quickly quelled, all of them killed—especially on an island that held all of the kongelig and all of their power. There was no point in attempting to band together as one to kill the kongelig and their descendants in one attack. The kongelig would simply use their kraft to subdue the islanders, and Malthe was realistic as well. He knew that there'd inevitably be slaves who would refuse to join in the fight, and who would even fight on the side of their masters. So is the extent of those who had no imagination for their own freedom. It'd be a battle they would easily lose, and there would be little hope for the islanders to find their freedom again.

The group agreed that they had to be patient. They had to wait for the right opportunity. Make their connections across all of the islands; learn which slaves to bring into the fold. They'd known of Marieke, even so far away in the northern empires, speaking to the network of islanders in the streets of the cities we crossed. At an inn, there had been a keeper with his lilting tone who held letters for Marieke, sometimes for years, knowing she would return to him again. The regal islanders in the street, who knew their freedom and did not question their worth—they, too, had messages for Marieke, and wished her luck in finding freedom for her people. Marieke had always reminded all the slaves of Hans Lollik Helle to have patience. Even if it meant continuing the plans into the next generation; even if it meant none of them would be able to witness freedom themselves, she reminded them to wait.

She'd told them of me. After the Jannik guards had slaughtered my family, Marieke saw the potential in the role I could play. I was the bridge that the slaves of Hans Lollik Helle needed. The kongelig who was an islander. The woman who could spark the revolution. My growing powers of thoughts, my ability to control, and the skin of my people: I was the key they needed.

Marieke couldn't help but feel love for me at times—she would sometimes pretend that I was her daughter, brought back to life by the spirits—but still, she knew who I was. She never forgot that I'm a daughter of the Rose, and that I feel love for myself and for my family name first. She didn't believe me when I told her of my plans to take the title of regency for myself so that I could free my people. She could see the hunger in my eyes—this desire for power of mine, to become queen of these islands. She wrote to Malthe and the others of Hans Lollik Helle: I wouldn't be an ally in their plans. I couldn't be trusted. I was a true member of the kongelig.

Marieke knew I was nothing like my mother; and even if my mother had still been alive, Marieke and the other slaves would not have trusted her for their freedom, either, just as they did not trust me now. I wouldn't be raised a martyr, a leader in their revolution. Instead, I would be used as the perfect target of the Fjern of Hans Lollik Helle. The islanders would work slowly, carefully, so that no blame could be placed on the slaves, and so that no one would see the revolution until it had already passed, and each of the kongelig were dead. I would work as a distraction. With every death of a kongelig, the Fjern would place the blame of the murders on me, focus on their plots to have me killed, without seeing the truth before them, the truth that was so plain. They wouldn't think to question the slaves, who remained so docile and obedient.

Marieke helped me with my own plans to arrive to Hans Lollik Helle—my return to Lund Helle, my betrothal to Aksel Jannik. She was always there, guiding me and pushing me to return, always so wary of me knowing her thoughts and her motives. She called my kraft evil and taught me to respect her mind—but still she was always so careful to hide any thought of the uprising whenever I was near. What strength this must've taken her, to keep the secret of her betrayal from me for so many years. She primed me, readied me for my role in the game, but still she worried that once I arrived on Hans Lollik Helle, I'd be able to learn the truth quickly—she'd had practice, but what of the others of the uprising?

It'd be too easy for me to pass by any of the slaves and know even a snippet of their thought. As easily as that, the uprising would be over. Marieke traveled the northern cities when she learned of Løren, the boy who held the kraft to end the power of those around him. She had been patient, and finally her patience was rewarded: Løren was the missing piece that was so needed. Løren would be kept close to me, to use his kraft to hide the truth of the rebellion, to block my ability from the slaves who worked around me. If I ever attempted to enter their minds, to know their thoughts or motives or feelings, I would only be met with the same mask I was so familiar with when I attempted to read Løren's thoughts and he didn't want me to see into him. I didn't notice; I was dismissive of the slaves, didn't consider that their minds might be worth reading. I only felt their hatred following me, avoided their thoughts out of fear, so focused was I on the kongelig and who among them might be the murderer of Hans Lollik Helle.

Aksel had been drunk in his mother's sitting room, eyes closed, whispering of his love for Beata Larsen; and Løren had whispered to him that it would be nice if someone could simply be sent to kill me. Aksel had agreed. He gathered the guards he felt he could stand to lose, and when his brother volunteered to join the guards to ensure my death, Aksel had agreed. He didn't think his brother would survive such a battle, but he hoped that Løren would kill me before his own neck was cut.

Yes, Løren could have killed me that day, easily; he had been trained to kill from such a young age with a sword and a machete. But he had no plans to take my life. He needed to only cut me, to make it seem like he'd wanted me dead as he'd been hired to do, so that I wouldn't question his true motives. The slaves

of Hans Lollik Helle had agreed: They needed to take the risk
that I might have Løren executed without a second thought.
Malthe had whispered his prayers as they approached the grove.
So much depended on my choice, and whether I would keep
Løren alive. They couldn't force Løren upon me on Hans Lollik
Helle. I would be as dismissive of him as all the other slaves, and
would avoid him just as much as all the rest. I would never have
realized the kraft he held. The islanders knew that if I learned of
his power, this kraft would draw me to him. I'd always needed
to control those around me, after all—and if I couldn't control
Løren as I could others, I would inevitably do what I could to
oppress him. Malthe and Marieke needed to take the risk and
hope that Løren would be spared; hope that his kraft, and the
wall between us, would make me curious enough to keep him
alive, and to keep him near. This worked better than they could
have hoped, of course; not only did I allow Løren to live but I
made the man my personal guard. He was able to follow me and
block the thoughts of any slave I approached.

The king was killed by the slaves of Hans Lollik Helle. They
killed him as he sat on his throne. It had been an attempted
beheading, though the machete wasn't sharp enough. His body
was carried to Valdemar Helle—the islanders didn't want to drop
his body into the water, in case it washed ashore again, and it was
only out of spite that they didn't burn Cristoff Valdemar. Denying
him his entry to his Fjern gods was only the start of the uprising.

An invitation was sent to me to join the kongelig on Hans
Lollik Helle for the storm season. Once I arrived on the royal
island, so many years after their planning had begun, the uprising would spark. All of the kongelig on Hans Lollik Helle
would be killed one by one. The killings would be careful, cal-
culated. Each murder would create confusion, distrust among
the kongelig, interrupting their rituals as uncertainty spread—
uniting them against me in their distrust as they had a target

to focus on, a target that was not the slaves, waiting for their freedom—until they were all dead.

The slaves wouldn't attempt to murder all of us at once. What if they attempted to put us all into a room and burn that room down? The kongelig were powerful, each with their own kraft; we could have fought back, could have survived, and then? The slaves would be realized in their plan, the uprising stopped with their beheadings. Patience, Marieke had reminded them—have patience and move slowly to remain unseen, unsuspected. The plan had worked. None of the kongelig considered that this could be the work of the slaves around us. We each thought that the murderer was of the Ludjivik family, or another of the kongelig, eager to be rid of the rest of their competition. The uprising, so far, has been a success.

They used me against the kongelig as they organized the rebellions of the other islands through their network of whispers. Løren had escaped—run away in the middle of a storm—just so that he could get to Larsen Helle and relay the first of the messages, which spread from one island to the next. Each of the rebels on the islands of Hans Lollik agreed that the uprising will be this very night. The royal island, in chaos without its regent and without any one of the Herres and Elskerindes left alive to make their orders, will lose its grip on all the islands of Hans Lollik—and as one, the conquered will rise. They will take back these islands. They will kill every Fjern and kongelig. They will have their freedom.

Løren can feel that I know the truth. He hasn't bothered to block this from me. He wants me to know his mind now, to know the truth, now he knows that the attacks on the royal island have already begun. Jytte Solberg has proved difficult to kill, but if all has gone as planned, she will already be dead. Three of her guards are a part of this uprising; they will overpower her and cut her throat before any of the other slaves can stop them. Lothar Niklasson will be the last remaining kongelig. He will be kept alive as the most valuable hostage, something Marieke had suggested might prove useful based on her observations of the Fjern in the northern nations. The Fjern tend to barter and bargain, and if the islanders have someone the Fjern might consider valuable, there could come a point in time when they might be able to use Lothar Niklasson to cement their freedom.

And Løren will kill me. He lets me knows this now. Løren had always been meant to kill me. This had been the greatest source of conflict among the slaves of Hans Lollik Helle. They knew that I was a true kongelig, and that I had no use to them after the uprising; they knew that my kraft was too powerful, and that I would have to die. But Marieke, time and again, couldn't stop herself from asking the others if I could be spared. Perhaps there was hope for me, that I could change—that she could teach me to be like my people, to respect the spirits and to treat the islanders as equals rather than to dismiss them as slaves. Malthe has not wanted to consider this. I'm too dangerous. I could easily take over any one of the slaves and force them to kill themselves or someone else. Malthe didn't want to take such a risk. And Løren—he hasn't known what to think. He'd wanted to believe that there was a hope for me. In a way, I have been enslaved as well, he thinks—enslaved to my own mind, relying on the power the kongelig have granted me. He can't help but want to show me a world I haven't had the imagination to see for myself: a world where islanders walk with freedom and power in their veins. And yet he also knows the truth, plain before him: I have whipped him. I have beaten him. I have tried to force him into my bed, and I have tried to have him killed as well. And so I will have to die.

This is the only reason he's allowed me to sail away, to let me have these final moments of peace before he ends my life. He'll kill me once we come close enough to Valdemar Helle. After I'm dead, he'll return to Hans Lollik Helle, where the others wait for him now.

"Are you afraid?" he asks me, still looking to the sea. I can feel my kraft reflected in him, so he knows the answer to this. He only wants to hear me say the words.

"Yes," I tell him. "I'm afraid."

"I've never understood fearing death," he says. "I was scared, yes, when I was younger. I wasn't ready to die. But now? What is there to fear?" he asks me. "Once you're dead, you feel nothing."

"I'm afraid to die before I've experienced my reason for life."

"You've fulfilled your reason."

"A pawn in your uprising?" I ask. "I'd hope I had more purpose than that."

Løren shrugs. He doesn't know if I have any other purpose than this; it isn't his place to say. I ask him how he plans to kill me, and he assures me that he'll kill me quickly, with mercy, even if he isn't sure I deserve such a thing. But when I ask if he can kill me on Hans Lollik Helle instead, he hesitates.

"Why would you want to die there?" he asks.

I tell him it's a promise I'd made to myself; if I'm going to die, then I'll at least have died trying to become the next regent. If I'm going to die, it will be on the royal island. We haven't sailed for long, only a few hours; Løren doesn't see the harm in agreeing to this. He tells the other slaves, all of whom follow his orders, all of whom know of the uprising that's to come, all of whom rejoice in my death, and we turn back for Hans Lollik Helle.

Hans Lollik Helle is on fire. I can see this in the distance, the bright spots burning as the fires had once burned Rose Helle so many years ago. The sun is setting now, smoke billowing into the darkening sky. The fire of Hans Lollik Helle acts as a signal to the nearest islands: They, too, start to burn, first the fields and then the groves, the plantations in the far distance alight.

The ship anchors, and the same man who had rowed me onto Hans Lollik Helle at the start of the season is here to row me

once more. This man, too, has been a part of the uprising, sharing his whispered messages to the slaves who come and go from
the royal island. The answer to all of my questions had been
so obvious, and yet I'd focused on the kongelig, believing only
they to be capable of having the power to take these islands. And
hadn't Løren himself told me, not so long ago? His pity for me,
that even those closest to me plan for my death.

Løren is patient as we make our way into the mangroves, the
branches snagging at my dress and hair. The fear in me churns,
and though I've accepted my death, I feel sick as well, my hands
slick, my vision blurred. I'm not ready to die.

"Where should I do it?" he asks me. "The Jannik house?"

I ask for him to kill me inside of Herregård Constantjin,
where I'd so hoped to be named regent, and so he takes me
there. Løren is more merciful than even he gives himself credit
for. He doesn't rejoice in my death, doesn't celebrate having to
kill me, even when he thinks of how I have treated him these
past months, even when he thinks of his whippings and that I
had ordered his execution. This isn't revenge for him. This is
simply what must be done, a step toward the freedom of our
people. I should be willing to die. I should be a willing sacrifice.

We walk up the dirt path that runs alongside the shore. We
can't take the usual path because the groves are burning, the
slaves who had worked there for the storm season now disappeared. I can hear screams in the distance. The relatives of
the heads of the kongelig families, I can feel in Løren. They had
decided there would be no survivors. The elderly, and even the
children that had been kept in the manors—each will be killed.

I think of Marieke, the slaves who were massacred in the Jannik house, and I know now what a trick this must have been.
The slaves of Hans Lollik Helle had been playing a game with
me as much as with the other kongelig. They wanted to keep me
confused, wanted me to be distracted by the murders that sur-

rounded me. There's the last slave in Løren's thoughts, of course, the girl who had been a child, hidden away from the kongelig and told not to use her kraft unless she wanted to be hung by her neck. She is nearly grown now, and her kraft is stronger than anyone has ever before seen in these islands—stronger than even my own. She has delighted in the games she's played with me, to the point where she'd become carried away, attempting to take my life before I was supposed to die, nearly walking me over the cliffs of Hans Lollik Helle. That had been a reckless and dangerous choice, one that she'd been berated for many times.

Herregård Constantjin is the only house that doesn't burn. Its facade is gone now; it crumbles in the night, torches unlit, smell of decay finding its way to me. The king has been dead for only one storm season now, but the slaves of Hans Lollik Helle stopped caring for the house many storm seasons ago, allowing the castle to fall into disarray around the king while the kraft of a perfect manor surrounded him. I'd thought for so long that the person behind the false king and the lies of this royal island must be one of the other kongelig. It was arrogant of me to assume that there couldn't be another islander who held kraft as well.

"I don't think she'd want to see you now," Løren tells me. He has seen why I wanted to come to Herregård Constantjin. I could see in his memories that this is where he and the others would meet. "She told me not to force her to see you killed." Another reason, I realize, he'd allowed me to sail away from the island.

"Please," I tell him. "I only want to see her for myself. I won't attempt to fight."

"She told me not to force her to see you die," Løren says again. Løren knows that this is where they all are, waiting for his return following his final mission as my guard. We're already so close to the meeting room now anyway, and since he's done me this mercy and granted me this final wish, I might as well be brought before them.

The council room is dark, save for a few flickering torches. It is as the meeting room has always looked, without the kraft that created a perfect image. Malthe sits at the head, where the king would normally sit. Beside him is Marieke, alive; I'd seen the truth of this, too, in Løren. I saw how Marieke had decided she couldn't stand to be at my side any longer, not when she knew she would have to soon betray me and allow Løren to end my life; and so her death, and the deaths of the slaves of the Jannik house, was created as a mercy to her. Marieke's eyes widen when we walk through the doors. The slave girl, Agatha, sits beside her.

Løren takes his place on Malthe's other side, though he doesn't sit. He stands above the chair, and there's some shame in him, this I can feel. He knows he should have killed me, shouldn't have listened to my wishes and brought me back to this island and to this room. Løren is too merciful, despite himself. The three look at him with a range of emotions. Anger, for bringing me here as though I'm a guest, when Løren knows that I should be dead. Amusement, for the boy has always done exactly as he pleased, truly. Sadness. I can feel this come from Marieke, even as I also feel the surprise in her that I'm still alive. Seeing Marieke here—this is the deepest cut of all. I had loved her, I had mourned her, and I thought that she had loved me, even as she hated that I was a kongelig.

Sinking into her, feeling even only the briefest of emotions, I see that she has grieved, thinking me already dead. This has been painful for Marieke. She grew to love me over the years, and so knowing that she would have to guide me to Hans Lollik Helle and ultimately to my death has been difficult, and nearly impossible. She's betrayed her own proposal more than once: come to the others with the suggestion that perhaps I don't have to die after all. The kongelig, and the ways of the Fjern, are all that I've ever known. I could be taught, she said.

She asked Malthe to show me mercy, but Malthe could not.

Marieke has had no choice but to agree. She has mourned me a thousand times. The others see a kongelig, traitor to her own people, and Marieke knows that this isn't a lie; but she has also seen me as a child grieving the loss of her family, a girl with determination and strength. She has seen me crying, she has seen my smile. She knows me as a mother would, and what sort of mother would leave her child to die? This is what I want to ask her, but no words leave my tongue.

Agatha watches me. She knows she's tricked me. She knows I'm most surprised to see her. I'd been so dismissive of the girl. I'd thought her silly, not worth my thoughts as she tried so hard to impress me. Even now she wants me to be impressed by her—her power, her kraft. The girl isn't any more than seventeen. Even at the young age of nine, she knew of the path she must take. She was so powerful that the slaves of Hans Lollik Helle protected her and showed her how to hide her skills. They had all depended on her for this final game they must play. She practiced over the years. Practiced conjuring the images she'd created in her mind. A flower for the Elskerinde, beautiful and blooming, actually rotting; a dress of lace, clean and pure, actually stained and torn.

After the slaves killed the king, Agatha replaced his image for the storm season, carefully always in the background, standing against walls alongside other slaves, but just enough to fade. She maintained the image of the castle, even as it began to decay. This storm season has been most exhausting of all, as she aided in the deaths of each kongelig, one by one. Beata Larsen's death was easiest. She simply made the girl dream that her parents were still alive on Larsen Helle, that they held her hands as they walked with her through the fields of their plantation. Beata Larsen was instead walked to the bay. Malthe waited there. He wrapped his hands around her neck and strangled her, and then left her body to the sea.

Olsen Årud was next. The fire that took his house had been real, yes; his body burned. The slaves who had been killed in the manor were only a piece of Agatha's imagination. Nine bodies found total—she'd thought this was a nice touch, a symbol of each of the kongelig who would die. She'd had little to do with the death of Erik Nørup. This was again Malthe's doing; Erik had been given herbs to put him into a deep sleep and then brought to the courtyard of Herregård Constantjin. Each of the slaves lining the manor's walls had been brought into the fold, and they watched. Malthe had been swift with the machete.

Agatha was eager to kill me. She was disappointed when she was scolded for nearly walking me off the cliffs, angry when she was told to wait. She didn't want to wait. She's waited years to release the fury building in her; waited, silently, as the Fjern raped her and killed our people. I can't blame her for the rage— the desire, the need, to take her revenge and to show her power. She'd tried to trick the others. Tried to make me stab myself and make it seem it had been my own doing, my own willingness to die, but both Malthe and Marieke had seen through this lie, and she was scolded again, told that she risked the freedom of all the people of these islands.

Agatha had been angry, too, when she failed in the killing of Jytte Solberg. Agatha had been the one who held the knife, a perfect image of me—but she had been too weak against Jytte, and so had to run when the woman fought back. But she was given her chance once again. Jytte was brought to the throne room, hands bound, and Agatha asked if she could be the one to kill Elskerinde Solberg, and so she was given the knife to cut the woman's neck. Now she watches me; she has enjoyed these last few months of killings. She hopes she will have the chance to take my life next.

Malthe wants to know why Løren has brought me here. "She's supposed to be dead."

Here, Løren shows a piece of truth he hadn't wanted me to

see. He knows I should die. It's what I deserve. But the pity in Løren has also grown. He wants others to believe he is merciless; has needed all of them to think this so he could be a part of this uprising. If he had shown himself to be soft all of those years ago, he would never have been brought into the fold. With the blood of the Fjern, Malthe might have believed Løren would warn his brother and his father, and so he worked to cut that softness from his heart. Why would he want to show mercy to the kongelig? These are the people who have ruined these islands, taken our people's freedom, tortured us—and I am one of them. It was easy to force himself to think that he's without mercy. He hates me—hates all of the kongelig, as he should. But Løren has also always wondered if a person should have a chance for redemption.

Løren admits it: He hesitates to kill me, though he knows that's what he must do. "Perhaps she could still be of some use."

"We decided she would die," Agatha says, frustration leaking into her voice, her eyes still on me. She finds Løren weak to even consider such a thing. She's struggled to force herself to smile at me all these long months, to pretend to be the overeager slave and hide her true thoughts, but now, finally, she can look at me as she's truly wanted—with all of her hatred, with all of her glee that she'll get to watch me, traitor to her people, die as I should. Agatha hates me. Yes, all of the slaves of these islands do, but Agatha hates me like none have before. Agatha's kraft is the only one I've met that is stronger than my own. She's powerful. She's more powerful than all of the other kongelig. Her kraft has grown so strong that, even across islands, she can envision a lie and have it appear as a new reality. Agatha knows her strength. She's known that she's more powerful than all of the Fjern who surround her, making their orders, beating her and forcing her into their bed. She has been a slave of Hans Lollik Helle all her life; the royal island that might have been hers, had she not been born with skin as dark as mine.

And she saw me—the woman who managed to avoid chains and scars, who was allowed onto the royal island as a kongelig. Agatha hated me for betraying my own people, yes, but she hated me all the more because she wanted my freedom. She wanted the opportunity to sit at this table as I did, among the Fjern, and prove herself—her worth, her power, her strength. Even knowing that this was all a lie, she wanted to be a part of it, and this is what she hated more than anything else. She looks at me and she sees herself—what she might have become if she had been born a daughter of the Rose.

Marieke doesn't speak. She can't even look at me. She holds her hands together tightly, breathless. She loved me—still does love me, she can't help that. But she also knows the cost of freedom, not just for herself but for all of the islanders. If my death means the freedom of her people, then Marieke will sacrifice me.

"You can let me live," I tell them. I should be above begging for mercy, begging for my life, but I can't stop the words. Agatha's smile widens. "I don't have to die for this uprising to be a success."

"You never planned to free your people," Malthe says, his voice low. Even now his mind is steady and quiet. I wonder how many years of practice it must have taken him to prepare to work as captain of my guard, knowing of my kraft. "You would have taken the title of regent and you would have allowed all of us to remain enslaved."

"This isn't true," I say, but Løren can feel the guilt in me. Had Konge Valdemar offered me the crown and had I kept the power over all of Hans Lollik, I can't know for sure what I would've done. Freeing my people would've meant losing control of these islands, and isn't that what I'd been working for? It's the reason I studied the kongelig and the Fjern, why I prepared for nothing else for nearly half of my life: to inherit these islands in the name of the Rose, to honor my mother's legacy, to fulfill my family's revenge. It's easy, I think, for anyone to say what they would've done if put in a situation other than their own, easy to look away from the suffering of others and avoid the truth, to pretend that they're not the villain of their own story.

Agatha stands from her seat. It is, I realize, the seat I'd taken for so long in each council meeting. Agatha had attended quite a few of these meetings, standing against the wall with her sugar-cane wine, refilling glasses whenever asked. She knew I hadn't even noticed her, had barely recognized her as one of the slaves who so often helped Marieke in the Jannik house.

"Let me kill her," she says, her eyes on mine.

Malthe hesitates. "Løren would be better suited. His kraft would protect him if Elskerinde Jannik attempts to fight back." He realizes he has called me by my former title. I'm not an Elskerinde anymore. Hans Lollik Helle is now under the island-ers' rule, and the kongelig are no longer. But this is an old habit that will take time to break.

Marieke stops herself from speaking. Maybe I could be locked away, kept alive as a hostage as they keep Lothar; but she already knows that the Fjern would have no desire for me. I wouldn't be useful kept alive.

Agatha's kraft builds in her veins. "I can protect myself. I'm the most powerful person in this room, am I not?"

Malthe is concerned. The child has been growing fond of her power. She's already disobeyed his orders several times, and Mal-the is certain that she'll continue to disobey him. If he doesn't learn to control her soon, Agatha could become another problem he hadn't anticipated, and he doesn't relish the thought of having to kill the child. Still, he knows it doesn't matter who takes my life. Løren was supposed to—he was in the best position to do so—but instead he has brought me here, and Malthe is impatient with Løren's hesitancy. If the girl will kill me, then so be it. He waves his hand, and Agatha's smile widens.

"Elskerinde Jannik," she tells me, "you should start to run."

CHAPTER TWENTY-SEVEN

There'd been a fire on Rose Helle when I was young. I'd stood in the gardens alone, watching the fire spread across the groves. The flames looked as though they were coming to take me to the gods. I had heard them calling my name frantically—my mother, Ellinor, Inga, Claus, and the slaves of the manor, searching for me as the fire raged, terrified that I had walked toward the flames. I still don't know why I didn't answer them. I waited where I stood—waited for them to find me or the fire to take me, whichever came first.

My mother found me first. She slapped me and demanded if I hadn't heard her calling my name. She didn't wait for a response before sweeping me up into her arms, into the manor, ignoring my cries from the sting on my cheek.

No one is here to save me now, to take me into their arms, as I run into the fire that sweeps across the groves. The flames have heated the dry, cracked ground, stones like embers blistering the bottoms of my feet. Sweat slicks my skin in the heat. The air is so full of smoke that my eyes and throat burn, and I cough as I run, stumbling over the brush that hasn't yet been taken by the flames. Bodies greet me. Bodies of the Fjern and islanders, necks and guts cut open. It's impossible to know what's real and what's another of Agatha's games.

I slow down, breathless, fire sparking in the brush beside me and crackling through the trees. I cough as ash flies into my throat. I hear the laughter, and I know I have to keep going—but I can't run forever. Agatha will catch me and take pleasure in killing me herself. I could run toward the sea, but I know that I would never survive the ocean's waves, and I don't want to die with water filling my throat, my lungs, pressure building in my chest as I gasp for breath—

I burst out of the groves, looking over my shoulder, and though I see no one, it's the fear that Agatha could be only a few paces behind me that makes me run faster. I race toward the Jannik house on the cliff. I'm surprised that the house still stands. I run up the porch, into the hall—the bodies that had been spread across the ground are now gone, never there to begin with—and I hurry to the kitchen, where I find a knife. I spin around, expecting to see Agatha, but instead there's nothing but the spark of flame, building—overtaking the wood and spreading toward me.

I back out of the kitchen and down the hall, up the stairs to my chambers, the fire growing around me, boiling the wallpaper and cracking the wood. I make it to the balcony, wind whipping my hair. Agatha laughs, though I can't see her. A sting of pain burns my arm—blood drips, and there's another cut across my stomach, my shoulder, my chest. Red stains my skin and dress as the fire rages. The laughter grows louder and stops only when I stab my knife into the air before me, pushing into flesh.

Agatha hadn't seen the knife. She appears before me now, looking down at her stomach where the knife sticks from her gut. She looks back to me, fury and pain in her eyes. She throws herself at me. The railing is at my back as she claws at me, the knife's handle digging into my ribs. I fall over the railing, Agatha on top of me.

Air is knocked from me. Pain flourishes across my back.

There's a wetness on my head, my vision darkening and lightening all at once. Agatha is on the ground beside me, on her stomach, eyes wide and unmoving. I scramble to my feet, palm to my head—it comes back red, and the cuts across my skin aren't shallow. I'm losing blood. I can't return to any of the houses, can't hide in the groves—if any islander sees me, they'll kill me where I stand. I have to go to the beach. The hidden alcove where Alida had once found me. I'll hide there and wait until I can attempt to run again.

I barely take another step before there's a scream. Agatha stands, wavers, then runs at me, knife pulled from her stomach and in her hand. I fall back to the ground, kick at her—try to crawl away, but she pulls at my feet. I manage to kick her in the stomach, where blood still pours—she doubles over in pain as I run, through the gardens, looking over my shoulder.

She catches me, pulling at my arms. Agatha won't let me go—even if it means she'll die, she won't let me leave this island alive. The edge of the cliff is only a few feet away, crumbling into the ocean below, waves crashing into the rocks. I wrap my arms around her middle, and I jump.

We fall through the air. I miss the rocks. Cold water hits me like a shock, salt rushing down my throat. I open my eyes, try to see, but the water is black as night. The only light is from the fires of the Jannik house above and from its gardens. I try to swim toward the light, but something tugs at my foot. I kick, but the harder I kick, the stronger the pull. My chest burns, and I feel as though my lungs may burst. Darkness covers me.

CHAPTER TWENTY-EIGHT

My mother sits in the center of the maze. She'd been reading a book. Slaves had never been allowed to read, and so she was happy for the chance to learn once she was freed. I came to her, and she rewarded me with a smile. I sat on her lap. The book she read was meant for a child—a fairy tale, one of my favorites, though Ellinor didn't like it as much. The fairy tale told the story of a girl who had grown up alone in a tower, with no one to love but her own reflection in a mirror. She couldn't stand the sight of her reflection for some time, and she waited for a knight to save her, to rescue her from this tower and take her away into a foreign land. But a knight never came, and so she slowly learned to love the reflection. Loved it enough to pick the mirror up and hold it close to her chest. She died in her sleep this way, with no one to love her but herself. My mother said she'd so wished she could have read as a slave. Then, she told me, she would've known what it was like to be free.

I stand before my mother now, a woman. I ask my mother if she can forgive me. She doesn't have an answer for me. She only turns the page of her fairy tale, and she continues to read.

Sunlight floods my eyelids, sending a pain through my scalp and down my neck. The pain is a living thing, wrapping itself around my skin and into my chest, shifting with every breath.

I crack my eyes open, staring through my lashes. I'm in a room. There is no window; the stone wall is half-crumbled, vines crawling toward me. The blue of the sky is above me. I'm in a bed, thin mattress as hard as dirt ground, sheets so ragged they begin to tear.

Løren is also here. He'd woken me by saying my name and waited for me to open my eyes and look at him as I do now. He looks older, lines around his mouth and on his heavy brow, but not so much time has passed—only two weeks.

Marieke had argued with the others to let her nurse me. She'd wiped me clean, tipped broth into my mouth until I would swallow. She'd stitched my wounds: the cut in my stomach, which had ripped open again, the gashes on my legs and arms where Agatha had cut me. I shouldn't have survived. The fall, the ocean waves, the blood—I should have died, but I'm still alive. Marieke told Malthe and Løren that this was for a reason. The spirits wanted me here, even if they wouldn't reveal the reason yet. She argues that now, with Agatha's death, they need someone like me—need my kraft if they're to continue their fight against the kongelig. It can't be a coincidence that I survived the fall from the cliffs, while Agatha's body was found on the rocks.

"Malthe wants to kill you," Løren lets me know. "He's waiting for Marieke to turn her back."

I can't speak; Løren knows this, and he's glad. He's always hated the sound of my voice. I speak as though I think I'm better than he, more important than my own people. He leans back in the chair he'd dragged to this room: a tower, broken and forgotten after a passing storm, in one of the wings of Herregård Constantjin.

"Agatha is dead," Løren says.

There's no emotion in me, no anger, remorse, or even glad-ness. Agatha had been a child. She'd wanted to fight for her free-dom. I can't blame her for this. Still, I also can't fault myself for wanting to live, and if Agatha were still alive, I would not be.

"Marieke believes it's for a reason. She thinks that Agatha died and you lived for some greater purpose. She thinks you can be redeemed."

Air catches in my throat, and I cough, unable to breathe. Løren watches me as I choke. He waits for the coughing to end. I can feel him hope that I will die now. It would end this con-stant debate between Marieke and Malthe, a debate where he has been trapped in the middle for some time.

"She thinks you're meant to replace Agatha," he says. "To join our revolution."

I manage to force out a question, hoarsely. "And what do you think?"

Løren has a knife in his lap. Malthe has asked him to kill me many times now, and today he came to my room, unsure him-self what he should do. I wasn't meant to survive. I'm a kongelig, enemy of my people.

He picks up the knife by its handle and stands. I close my eyes again. I can only hope he'll be quick, merciful. I've fought for my life for so long now, and I'm tired. This isn't a fight I'll win. There isn't any point in trying.

Løren rests the knife on the bed beside my hand. He doesn't say anything else as he leaves the room, clicking the door shut behind him. The knife's meaning is clear: Join the islanders, and fight for the freedom of my people, or accept my death here and now. It seems a question that's haunted me for all of my years, since the night my family was ushered into the gardens. I know that it's a question that'll follow me until my last breath.

The story continues in...
King of the Rising
Book 2 of the Island of Blood and
Storm series
Keep reading for a sneak peek!

ACKNOWLEDGMENTS

I've been fortunate to have the love and guidance of so many. My agent, Beth Phelan, who is always patient and understanding of my lofty goals, offering steady advice as well as a treasured friendship. I've also had the support of the entire Gallt & Zacker team, who have welcomed me into their family.

Thank you to my editor, Sarah Guan, who saw the potential in *Queen of the Conquered* and gave me the courage to explore Sigourney's complexities. Thank you to Paola Crespo and Laura Fitzgerald, my Caribbean people! Thank you to Ellen Wright, Alex Lencicki, Andy Ball, Lisa Marie Pompilio, Lauren Panepinto, Derrick Kennelty-Cohen, and everyone who has touched *Queen of the Conquered* at Hachette Book Group and helped put Sigourney's story into the world.

Thank you to Nikki Garcia, the first reader of a very terrible draft, as well as fellow authors who have shown early support by shouting about their excitement online: Justina Ireland, Tasha Suri, Kate Elliott, Aliette de Bodard, K. S. Villoso, Tochi Onyebuchi, Mark Oshiro, and Evan Winter.

When I begin to question myself and my ability, I can feel my family's love pushing me to continue. Mom, Dad, Auntie

Jacqui, Curtis, and Memorie—thank you all for believing in me.

Finally, thank you to the readers for supporting me and other authors like me, so that we can put the stories that we need to see into the world.

extras

meet the author

Photo Credit: Beth Phelan

KACEN CALLENDER was born two days after a hurricane and was first brought home to a house without its roof. After spending their first eighteen years on St. Thomas of the US Virgin Islands, Kacen studied Japanese, fine arts, and creative writing at Sarah Lawrence College and received their MFA from the New School. Kacen is an award-winning author of books for children and teens. *Queen of the Conquered* is their first novel for adults.

interview

When did you first start writing?

I've always loved to write. When I was a teenager, I wrote and shared fanfiction online. Fanfiction offered a lot of people in my generation the space to tell the stories that we wanted seen but weren't available in mainstream media, and that was also the first time I was able to share my stories and get feedback from complete strangers. I started working on original novels towards the end of high school and in my first year of college, about ten years ago now. This was around the time I'd first come up with the initial idea of *Queen of the Conquered*.

Who are some of your most significant authorial influences?

It's difficult to pinpoint only a few authors. Every book that I write tends to be in conversation with another book. *Queen of the Conquered* is in conversation with Marlon James's *The Book of Night Women*, for example. I also wrote *Queen of the Conquered* in response to the overwhelming number of fantasies with white main characters in worlds that use slavery and different forms of oppression, though this is something that people of color have primarily experienced. So many of these books would have stories of slavery as entertainment, with white heroes who need to fight back against the oppressive kingdoms, without acknowledging the pain and struggle of black and brown bodies—throughout history and now, currently, as people of color are still being oppressed by these same systems. Black and brown characters also very rarely survive, or even exist, in the white imagination. Seeing the deaths of these black and brown bodies, both in real life and in white stories, over and over again creates a physical pain in my chest—and witnessing this was definitely a primary influence in writing *Queen of the Conquered.*

How did you come up with the idea for Queen of the Conquered?

The first spark of inspiration was the realization that black slave owners once existed alongside white slave owners. It was enraging and intriguing, the idea of someone who could know the pain of their own people, but then cause that same pain when given the chance to gain power by oppressing others. I then began to wonder what I would have done if I had been black in a time of slavery. What would I have done if having slaves meant receiving some of the same power and privileges and comforts that white people experienced?

I know what I hope my answer would be. I know that I hope I would have been the hero in this situation and done what we all know would have been the right thing to do. I also think that it's a habit of a lot of people, myself included, to say how they would have done differently, how they would have acted courageously, if faced with the same questions and dilemmas humans faced in the past. We would have fought against slavery, fought against the Jim Crow laws, fought against Japanese internment. We would have been braver than our ancestors and would have done what was right. We say and think this without considering the fact that we're all in a time and place where slavery and concentration camps and genocide exist right now. We live our lives of comfort, watching TV and eating out at our favorite restaurants and reading books at leisure without thinking of the people who are suffering to give us the things we currently enjoy. It's easier to think of atrocities like slavery as a thing of the past, or as something that can only exist in a fantasy novel—as something separate from ourselves, something we can't do anything about. I personally feel a helplessness in my privilege and know that I'm a hypocrite, as we all are, for being a part of this system—for thinking we would have done better than our ancestors, when we aren't doing better right now. I wanted to face that uncomfortable truth by creating a character like Sigourney Rose.

This is also a vulnerable story for me, because it takes a lot from my experiences as a black person who often felt in between worlds, and who has often had the privilege to find myself in spaces I've been able to afford, like college and graduate school and a publishing job in New York City—but to then also feel implicit bias and discrimination, because being in these privileged spaces often meant I was one of the only, or the only, black person in the room. The initial idea of a hypocritical, privileged black person who owns slaves began to evolve into a story about the interaction of privilege and oppression, and who is allowed to have literal power.

What research, if any, did you do in preparation for writing this book?

I didn't do any research for *Queen of the Conquered*, except for names and words from the Danish language. The setting of the islands of Hans Lollik is inspired by the United States Virgin Islands, where I was born and raised, and which had once been a territory of Denmark, before being sold to the United States. I chose this setting because the US Virgin Islands is a space that I know well, and is, like Sigourney, in between worlds: a group of islands that is considered "too American" (or in other words, too privileged) by many other island nations to be considered a part of the Caribbean, and a group of islands that simultaneously experiences the oppression of the United States by being a literal territory—owned, like a slave—with its people not having the same rights as other citizens of the United States.

How did you develop the fascinating and unique magic system of this fictional world?

The magic system of kraft (translated as "power" in Danish) was a metaphor not just for supernatural power, but for literal power as well, and who is allowed and not allowed to have this power. Anyone is able to have kraft, regardless of race or identity, and the system is based in mental abilities only (mind reading, body control, seeing the future, seeing others' dreams, etc.) because mental abilities and talents are evenly distributed in real life also. Though islanders could have this power, and their own abilities could be even stronger than the abilities of the kongelig and Fjern, the islanders with kraft are routinely rooted out and executed, for the kongelig declared that only they are allowed to have this power. It's a metaphor for not only systematically hoarding power through oppression, but for how many with abilities and talents are often overlooked and ignored because of their identities.

A major theme of Queen of the Conquered *is complicity: to what degree is participating in and benefitting from a system that oppresses your peers justifiable if it is believed to be the only way to thrive? Is it morally acceptable to perpetuate oppression in the course of overthrowing it? What compelled you to write about this topic?*

As I mentioned before in discussing what inspired *Queen of the Conquered*, I think that, chances are, anyone reading this is currently benefitting from a system that oppresses our peers, and that we're all perpetuating that oppression by not doing anything to stop the atrocities that are happening—not only around the world, but many times right in our backyards.

I also faced this question a lot in specific situations when I found I was the only black person in a room of privilege, telling myself that I wanted to work to create change that I think is important, by writing more books that featured diverse characters, helping to diversify publishing, and more. I do think that this work is also important, but as Løren would question Sigourney, when is the point that you stop perpetuating that system and you tear and burn that system down instead? I was compelled to write about this topic because I wanted to face the uncomfortable truth of my own privilege and what that means in the face of oppression.

Viewpoint characters are usually written to be sympathetic to the reader. Sigourney, however, is not an especially likeable protagonist. How did you reconcile these ideas?

I've spoken a bit about my inspiration behind Sigourney's character as a person of privilege. Knowing that she would be an unlikeable character who would make selfish choices, working in a system that oppresses her own people, doing things—such as having Løren whipped—that would be unforgivable, I knew that it would be equally important to attempt to make her sympathetic so that the audience can have a reason to continue reading Sigourney's story.

Unlikeable but sympathetic characters have always intrigued me, and I take their creation as a challenge. I knew from the beginning that I'd have to make Sigourney as sympathetic as possible, and to give her a motivation that could seem understandable, besides selfishness and greed, that would make her oppress her own people and want the throne of Hans Lollik Helle. To make her suffer great loss at the hands of the kongelig, and to make her believe that she means to oppress her own people so that she can ultimately free them, seemed like the only possible answer to make her actions understandable, even if they are wrong, and make them actions that we would personally think we would never commit ourselves.

Do you have a favorite scene in this book? Which part was the most difficult to write?

My favorite scene was the reveal of the twist at the end, which I won't write too much about in case there's anyone who decided to flip to the back—but to me, the reveal, and Sigourney's realization that she has been wrong in multiple ways (both in who the killer is, and also in her actions as an oppressor), was satisfying to write.

The most difficult scenes were anything involving the pain of the islanders. I didn't want to gloss over the atrocities of slavery. I wanted to portray Caribbean slavery for what it was: horrific. I also didn't want to write about the horrors of slavery for the sake of shock value or entertainment. I wanted to be careful to navigate that line with respect.

Queen of the Conquered *is the first volume in the Islands of Blood and Storm series. What's in store for us in the next book?*

King of the Rising will be from Løren's perspective, starting one month after the final events of *Queen of the Conquered*. I can't say much without spoiling both books, but the first book's question of whether Sigourney can be redeemed will be answered, and another question will be asked: Can Løren try to save everyone in the inevitable revolution, or are sacrifices necessary when burning the system down?

Lastly, we have to ask: if you could have any form of kraft, what power would you choose?

This is a surprisingly difficult question. I think I would want the power to read and write entire novels within seconds. I'd get a lot more work done, a lot more quickly.

if you enjoyed
QUEEN OF THE CONQUERED

look out for

KING OF THE RISING

Islands of Blood and Storm:
Book Two

by

Kacen Callender

It seems that Løren just will not die.

After the revolutionary events that rocked the island of Hans Lollik Helle, Løren doesn't know how many more times he can cheat death. He leads the fight against the Fjern in a bid to free the islands from colonial control forever, but his people's oppressors are relentless in their attacks on the rebels. Løren and the islanders are running out of food, weapons, and options.

As the leader of the rebellion, Løren is faced with difficult choices, including whether to release the captive traitor, Sigourney Rose, to her own people. When Sigourney proposes a daring scheme to infiltrate the islands still under Fjern control, he defies warnings from his fellow rebels and seizes the chance to change the course of the revolution for good—even if it might mean the escape and betrayal of their most dangerous prisoner.

But there's a spy among the rebels on Hans Lollik Helle, and as the Fjern tighten their grip on the islands, inching closer to reclaiming the royal island with every battle, Løren doesn't know who to trust....

They chased me through the groves. My heart pumped, fear slowing the blood in my legs, air caught in my throat. Sharp stones cut the undersides of my feet. Branches and brush and thorns ripped into my legs and arms and cheeks. Wet dirt sank beneath me, the root of a mangrove tree twisting around my ankle. I fell to the ground hard, rocks digging under the skin of the palms of my hands. I could hear their laughter. I knew that if they caught me, I would die. I'd made the mistake of reminding the boy that we shared blood. This wasn't something he liked acknowledged. He didn't like what I'd implied. That he and I weren't so different, even if he called himself master and me slave.

Their footsteps crunched and paused. I hunched in the thorns of brush, air wheezing from my lungs. I could sense the power that that filled my father's son. His kraft let him see the abilities of others. He could see the ability in me. He could sense me as I sensed him. He felt me hiding. He walked closer.

"I see him."

I didn't wait for my brother to grab me, to pick me up and tie his rope around my neck. I leapt to my feet. I ran in the only direction I could, through the thorns and weeds and the tangled roots of the mangrove trees. I burst out of the green and into the sloshing water that pulsed onto the rocky shore. I dove into the seawater, salt burning my eyes and the cuts across my skin, heavy on my tongue. I swam as if I meant to swim to the northern empires and to freedom.

I stopped because my arms and legs were too heavy and weak. I turned to see my brother and his friend standing on the shore, their hair and clothes and skin pale in the white moonlight. They waited, and then they left, bored with the game they'd played. I should have felt relief, but I knew this wouldn't be the last time they would chase me through the groves of Hans Lollik Helle. It was impossible to feel relief when I knew I would forever have this body and forever have this skin.

The thought crossed my mind. It's a thought that often does. The question of whether there's a point to living this life. I'm going to die, whether it's by the hands of my brother or by the whip of my father or by the years that always manage to catch up with us, regardless of the color of our skin. Does it matter if I die in a few days or a few years or now, saltwater filling my lungs? The result will be the same. The result, if I were to allow myself to sink beneath the waves, would be a death that would bring mercy. No more racing through the brush of this island, hiding from my brother. No more beatings and whippings, layers of scars growing on my back like the rings of bark covering the trees, marking how many years I have lived and what I have survived. And there would be no more nights when I was called from the corner of the wooden floor I slept on, marched through the groves to the pain that waited. Letting myself sink into the sea would bring me peace. It would bring me freedom.

The thought had crossed my mind so many times, but so had the urge to live. My desire for death and life was a contradiction. Both desires battled inside of me. In the end, life always won. Not because I loved life so much, despite the pain. So many wanted me dead. My brother, my father, and even other islanders waited for me to die. I wanted to live out of spite.

I began to swim back for shore, but I didn't notice that the waves of the ocean had already begun to suck me farther away from the island. The tide moved against me as I kicked. Waves became higher, knocking me beneath the surface. Seawater forced its way down my nose and into my mouth, filling my lungs. I choked with every gasp. Blackness covered my vision. I'd decided to live, but fate disagreed.

When I opened my eyes again, I sat on the sand of a shore. It was powdered white without any sign of sea shells or footprints or life. The ocean was as still as glass. The sky was red with fire. Islands grew from the sea. Waves rippled as the hills formed, spreading toward the black clouds. My mother was there with me. She stood in the shallows. I could only see her back and the thick scars that wove over her skin, but I knew that it was her. This was often how she came to me, in my nightmares and in my dreams. She would tell me stories. Stories forgotten. Stories buried. My mother told me to listen.

"You'll want to save them all," she said, "but you can't help the ones who think they're already saved."

I woke coughing, vomiting saltwater that burned my throat. Hot sand stuck to my face and my wet skin and clothes. The sky was blue again, the white sunlight scalding through my skin. Waves pushed and foamed around my legs. No one was on the shore with me. I couldn't see anyone who might've saved me.

It wasn't a surprise that I hadn't died.

It seemed the spirits weren't done with me yet.

if you enjoyed
QUEEN OF THE CONQUERED

look out for

THE COURT OF BROKEN KNIVES

Empires of Dust: Book One

by

Anna Smith Spark

It is the richest empire the world has ever known, and it is also doomed. Governed by an impostrous emperor, decadence has blinded its inhabitants to their vulnerability. The Yellow Empire is on the verge of invasion—and only one man can see it.

Haunted by prophetic dreams, Orhan has hired a company of soldiers to cross the desert to reach the capital city. Once they enter the palace, they have one mission: kill the emperor, then all those who remain. Only from the ashes can a new empire be built.

The company is a group of good, ordinary soldiers for whom this is a mission like any other. But the strange boy Marith who walks among them is no ordinary soldier. Though he is young, ambitious, and impossibly charming, something dark hides in Marith's past—and in his blood.

Chapter One

Knives.

Knives everywhere. Coming down like rain.

Down to close work like that, men wrestling in the mud, jabbing at each other, too tired to care any more. Just die and get it over with. Half of them fighting with their guts hanging out of their stomachs, stinking of shit, oozing pink and red and white. Half-dead men lying in the filth. Screaming. A whole lot of things screaming.

Impossible to tell who's who any more. Mud and blood and shadows and that's it. Kill them! Kill them all! Keep killing until we're all dead. The knife jabs and twists and the man he's fighting falls sideways, all the breath going out of him with a sigh of relief. Another there behind. Gods, his arms ache. His head aches. Blood in his eyes. He twists the knife again and thrusts with a broken-off sword and that man too dies. Fire explodes somewhere over to the left. White as maggots. Silent as maggots. Then shrieks as men burn.

He swings the stub of the sword and catches a man on the leg, not hard but hard enough so the man stumbles and he's on him quick with the knife. A good lot of blood and the man's down and dead, still flapping about like a fish but you can see in his eyes that he's finished, his legs just haven't quite caught up yet.

The sun is setting, casting long shadows. Oh beautiful evening! Stars rising in a sky the color of rotting wounds. The Dragon's Mouth. The White Lady. The Dog. A good star, the Dog. Brings plagues and fevers and inflames desire. Its rising marks the coming of summer. So maybe no more campaigning in the sodding rain. Wet leather stinks. Mud stinks. Shit stinks, when the latrine trench overflows.

Another burst of white fire. He hates the way it's silent. Unnatural. Unnerving. Screams again. Screams so bad your ears ring for days. The sky weeps and howls and it's difficult to know what's screaming. You, or the enemy, or the other things.

Men are fighting in great clotted knots like milk curds. He sprints a little to where two men are struggling together. Leaps at one from behind, pulls him down, skewers him. Hard crack of bone, soft lovely yield of fat and innards. Suety. The other yells hoarsely and swings a punch at him. Lost his knife, even. Bare knuckles. He ducks and kicks out hard, overbalances and almost falls. The man kicks back, tries to get him in a wrestling grip. Up close together, two pairs of teeth gritted at each other. A hand smashes his face, gets his nose, digs in. He bites at it. Dirty. Calloused. Iron taste of blood bright in his mouth. But the hand won't let up, crushing his face into his skull. He swallows and almost chokes on the blood pouring from the wound he's made. Blood and snot and shreds of cracked dry human skin. Manages to get his knife in and stabs hard into the back of the man's thigh. Not enough to kill, but the hand jerks out from his face. Lashes out and gets his opponent in the soft part of the throat, pulls his knife out and gazes around the battlefield at the figures hacking at each other while the earth rots beneath them. All eternity, they've been fighting. All the edges blunted. Sword edges and knife edges and the edges in the mind. Keep killing. Keep killing. Keep killing till we're all dead.

And then he's dead. A blade gets him in the side, in the weak point under the shoulder where his armor has to give to let the joint move. Far in, twisting. Aiming down. Killing wound. He hears his body rip. Oh gods. Oh gods and demons. Oh gods and demons and fuck. He swings round, strikes at the man who's stabbed him. The figure facing him is a wraith, scarlet with blood, head open oozing out brain stuff. You're dying, he thinks. You're dying and you've killed me. Not fair.

Shadows twist round them. We're all dying, he thinks, one way or another. Just some of us quicker than others. You fight and you die. And always another twenty men queuing up behind you.

Why we march and why we die,
And what life means . . . it's all a lie.
Death! Death! Death!

Understands that better than he's ever understood anything, even his own name.

But suddenly, for a moment, he's not sure he wants to die.

The battlefield falls silent. He blinks and sees light.

A figure in silver armor. White, shining, blazing with light like the sun. A red cloak billowing in the wind. Moves through the ranks of the dead and the dying and the light beats onto them, pure and clean.

"Amrath! Amrath!" Voices whispering like the wind blowing across salt marsh. Voices calling like birds. Here, walking among us, bright as summer dew.

"Amrath! Amrath!" The shadows fall away as the figure passes. Everything is light.

"Amrath! Amrath!" The men cheer with one voice. No longer one side or the other, just men gazing and cheering as the figure passes. He cheers until his throat aches. Feels restored, seeing it. No longer tired and wounded and dying. Healed. Strong.

"Amrath! Amrath!"

The figure halts. Gazes around. Searching. Finds. A dark-clad man leaps forward, swaying into the light. Poised across from the shining figure, yearning toward it. Draws a sword burning with blue flame.

"Amrath! Amrath!" Harsh voice like crows, challenging. "Amrath!"

He watches joyfully. So beautiful! Watches and nothing in the world matters, except to behold the radiance of his god.

The bright figure draws a sword that shines like all the stars and the moon and the sun. A single dark ruby in its hilt. The dark figure rushes onwards, screeching something. Meets the bright figure with a clash. White light and blue fire. Blue fire and white light. His eyes hurt almost as he watches. But he cannot bear to look away. The two struggle together. Like a candle flame flickering. Like the dawn sun on the sea. The silver sword comes up, throws the dark figure back. Blue fire blazes, engulfing everything, the shining silver armor running with flame. Crash of metal, sparks like a blacksmith's anvil. The shining figure takes a step back defensively, parries, strikes out. The other blocks it. Roars. Howls. Laughs. The mage blade swings again, slicing, trailing blue fire. Blue arcs in the evening gloom. Shapes and words, written on the air. Death words. Pain words. Words of hope and fear and despair. The shining figure parries again, the silver sword rippling beneath the impact of the other's blade. So brilliant with light that rainbows dance on the ground around it. Like a woman's hair throwing out drops of water, tossing back her head in summer rain. Like snow falling. Like colored stars. The two fighters shifting, stepping in each other's footprints. Stepping in each other's shadows. Circling like birds.

The silver sword flashes out and up and downwards and the other falls back, bleeding from the throat. Great spreading gush of red. The blue flame dies.

He cheers and his heart is almost aching, it's so full of joy.

The shining figure turns. Looks at the men watching. Looks at him. Screams. Things shriek back that make the world tremble. The silver sword rises and falls. Five men. Ten. Twenty. A pile of corpses. He stares mesmerized at the dying. The beauty of it. The most beautiful thing in the world. Killing and killing and such perfect joy. His heart overflowing. His heart singing. This, oh indeed, oh, for this, all men are born. He screams in answer, dying, throws himself against his god's enemies with knife and sword and nails and teeth.

Why we march and why we die,
And what life means... it's all a lie.
Death! Death! Death!

Chapter Two

"The Yellow Empire...I can kind of see that. Yeah. Makes sense."

Dun and yellow desert, scattered with crumbling yellow-gray rocks and scrubby yellow-brown thorns. Bruise-yellow sky, low yellow clouds. Even the men's skin and clothes turning yellow, stained with sweat and sand. So bloody hot Tobias's vision seemed yellow. Dry and dusty and yellow as bile and old bones. The Yellow Empire. The famous golden road. The famous golden light.

"If I spent the rest of my life knee-deep in black mud, I think I'd die happy, right about now," said Gulius, and spat into the yellow sand.

Rate sniggered. "And you can really see how they made all that money, too. Valuable thing, dust. Though I'm still kind of clinging to it being a refreshing change from cow manure."

"Yeah, I've been thinking about that myself, too. If this is the heart of the richest empire the world has ever known, I'm one of Rate's dad's cows."

"An empire built on sand... Poetic, like."

"'Cause there's so much bloody money in poetry."

"They're not my dad's cows. They're my cousin's cows. My dad just looks after them."

"Magic, I reckon," said Alxine. "Strange arcane powers. They wave their hands and the dust turns into gold."

"Met a bloke in Alborn once, could do that. Turned iron pennies into gold marks."

Rate's eyes widened. "Yeah?"

"Oh, yeah. Couldn't shop at the same place two days running, mind, and had to change his name a lot..."

They reached a small stream bed, stopped to drink, refill their water-skins. Warm and dirty with a distinct aroma of goat shit. After five hours of dry marching, the feel of it against the skin almost as sweet as the taste of it in the mouth.

Running water, some small rocks to sit on, two big rocks providing a bit of shade. What more could a man want in life? Tobias went to consult with Skie.

"We'll stop here a while, lads. Have some lunch. Rest up a bit. Sit out the worst of the heat." If it got any hotter, their swords would start to melt. The men cheered. Cook pots were filled and scrub gathered; Gulius set to preparing a soupy porridge. New boy Marith was sent off to dig the hole for the latrine.

Tobias himself sat down and stretched out his legs. Closed his eyes. Cool dark shadows and the smell of water. Bliss.

"So how much further do you think we've got till we get there?" Emit asked.

Punch someone, if they asked him that one more time. Tobias opened his eyes again with a sigh. "I have no idea. Ask Skie. Couple of days? A week?"

Rate grinned at Emit. "Don't tell me you're getting bored of sand?"

"I'll die of boredom, if I don't see something soon that isn't sand and your face."

"I saw a goat a couple of hours back. What more do you want? And it was definitely a female goat, before you answer that."

They had been marching now for almost a month. Forty men, lightly armed and with little armor. No horses, no archers, no mage or whatnot. No doctor, though Tobias considered himself something of a dab hand at field surgery and dosing the clap. Just forty men in the desert, walking west into the setting sun. Nearly there now. Gods only knew what they would find. The richest empire the world had ever known. Yellow sand.

"Not bad, this," Alxine said as he scraped the last of his porridge. "The lumps of mud make it taste quite different from the stuff we had at breakfast."

"I'm not entirely sure it's mud..."

"I'm not entirely sure I care."

They bore the highly imaginative title The Free Company of the Sword. An old name, if not a famous one. Well enough known in certain select political circles. Tobias had suggested several times they change it.

"The sand gives it an interesting texture, too. The way it crunches between your teeth."

"You said that yesterday."

"And I'll probably say it again tomorrow. And the day after that. I'll be an old man and still be picking bloody desert out of my gums."

"And other places."

"That, my friend, is not something I ever want to have to think about."

Everything reduced to incidentals by the hot yellow earth and the hot yellow air. Water. Food. Water. Rest. Water. Shade. Tobias sat back against a rock listening to his men droning on just as they had yesterday and the day before that and the day before that. Almost rhythmic, like. Musical. A nice predictable pattern to it. Backward and forwards, backward and forwards, backward and forwards. The same thinking. The same words. Warp and weft of a man's life.

Rate was on form today. "When we get there, the first thing I'm going to do is eat a plate of really good steak. Marbled with fat, the bones all cracked to let the marrow out, maybe some hot bread and a few mushrooms to go with it, mop up the juice."

Emit snorted. "The richest empire the world has ever known, and you're dreaming about steak?"

"Death or a good dinner, that's my motto."

"Oh, I'm not disputing that. I'm just saying as there should be better things to eat when we get there than steak."

"Better than steak? Nothing's better than steak."

"As the whore said to the holy man."

"I'd have thought you'd be sick of steak, Rate, lad."

"You'd have thought wrong, then. You know how it feels, looking after the bloody things day in, day out, never getting to actually sodding eat them?"

"As the holy man said to the whore."

Tiredness was setting in now. Boredom. Fear. They marched and grumbled and it was hot and at night it was cold, and they were desperate to get there, and the thought of getting there was terrifying, and they were fed up to buggery with yellow dust and yellow heat and yellow air. Good lads, really, though, Tobias thought. Good lads. Annoying the hell out of him and about two bad nights short of beating the crap out of each other, but basically good lads. He should be kind of proud.

"The Yellow Empire."

"The Golden Empire."

"The Sunny Empire."

"Sunny's nice and cheerful. Golden's a hope. And Yellow'd be good when we get there. In their soldiers, anyway. Nice and cowardly, yeah?"

Gulius banged the ladle. "More porridge, anyone? Get it while it's not yet fully congealed."

"I swear I sneezed something recently that looked like that last spoonful."

"A steak...Quick cooked, fat still spitting, charred on the bone...Mushrooms...Gravy...A cup of Immish gold..."

"I'll have another bowl if it's going begging."

"Past begging, man, this porridge. This porridge is lying unconscious in the gutter waiting to be kicked hard in the head."

A crow flew down near them cawing. Alxine tried to catch it. Failed. It flew up again and crapped on one of the kit bags.

"Bugger. Good eating on one of them."

"Scrawny-looking fucker though. Even for a crow."

"Cooked up with a few herbs, you wouldn't be complaining. Delicacy, in Allene, slow-roasted crow's guts. Better than steak."

"That was my sodding bag!"

"Lucky, in Allene, a crow crapping on you."

"Quiet!" Tobias scrambled to his feet. "Something moved over to the right."

"Probably a goat," said Rate. "If we're really lucky, it'll be that female goa—"

The dragon was on them before they'd even had a chance to draw their swords.

Big as a cart horse. Deep fetid marsh rot snot shit filth green. Traced out in scar tissue like embroidered cloth. Wings black and white and silver, heavy and vicious as blades. The stink of it came choking. Fire and ash. Hot metal. Fear. Joy. Pain. There are dragons in the desert, said the old maps of old empire, and they had laughed and said no, no, not that close to great cities, if there ever were dragons there they are gone like the memory of a dream. Its teeth closed ripping on Gulius's arm, huge, jagged; its eyes were like knives as it twisted away with the arm hanging bloody in its mouth. It spat blood and slime and roared out flame again, reared up beating its wings. Men fell back screaming, armor scorched and molten, melted into burned melted flesh. The smell of roasting meat surrounded them. Better than steak.

Gulius was lying somehow still alive, staring at the hole where his right arm had been. The dragon's front legs came down smash onto his body. Plume of blood. Gulius disappeared. Little smudge of red on the green. A grating shriek as its claws scrabbled over hot stones. Screaming. Screaming. Beating wings. The stream rose up boiling. Two men were in the stream trying to douse burning flesh and the boiling water was in their faces and they were screaming too. Everything hot and boiling and burning, dry wind and dry earth and dry fire and dry hot scales, the whole great lizard body scorching like a furnace, roaring hot burning killing demon death thing.

We're going to die, thought Tobias. We're all going to fucking die.

Found himself next to pretty new boy Marith, who was staring at it mesmerized with a face as white as pus. Yeah, well, okay, I'll give it to you, bit of a thing to come back to when you've been off digging a hole for your superiors to shit in. Looked pretty startled even for him. Though wouldn't look either pretty or startled in about ten heartbeats, after the dragon flame grilled and decapitated him.

If he'd at least try to raise his sword a bit.

Or even just duck.

"Oh gods and demons and piss." Tobias, veteran of ten years' standing with very little left that could unsettle him, pulled up his sword and plunged it two-handed into the dragon's right eye.

The dragon roared like a city dying. Threw itself sideways. The sword still wedged in its eye. Tobias half fell, half leaped away from it, dragging Marith with him.

"Sword!" he screamed. "Draw your bloody sword!"

The dragon's front claws were bucking and rearing inches from his face. It turned in a circle, clawing at itself, tail and wings lashing out. Spouted flame madly, shrieking, arching its back. Almost burned its own body, stupid fucking thing. Two men went up like candles, bodies alight; a third was struck by the tail and went down with a crack of bone. Tobias rolled and pulled himself upright, dancing back away. His helmet was askew, he could see little except directly in front of him. Big writhing mass of green dragon legs. He went into a crouch again, trying to brace himself against the impact of green scales. Not really much point trying to brace himself against the flames.

A man came in low, driving his sword into the dragon's side, ripping down, glancing off the scales but then meeting the softer underbelly as the thing twisted up. Drove it in and along, tearing flesh. Black blood spurted out, followed by shimmering white and red unraveling entrails. Pretty as a fountain. Men howled, clawed at their own faces as the blood hit. And now it had two swords sticking out of it, as well as its own intestines, and it was redoubling its shrieking, twisting, bucking in circles, bleeding, while men leaped and fell out of its way.

"Pull back!" Tobias screamed at them. "Get back, give it space. Get back!" His voice was lost in the maelstrom of noise. It must be dying, he thought desperately. It might be a bloody dragon, but half its guts are hanging out and it's got a sword sunk a foot into its head. A burst of flame exploded in his direction. He dived back onto his face. Found himself next to new boy Marith again.

"Distract it!" Marith shouted in his ear.

Um...?

Marith scrambled to his feet and leaped.

Suddenly, absurdly, the boy was balanced on the thing's back. Clung on frantically. Almost falling. Looked so bloody stupidly bloody small. Then pulled out his sword and stabbed downwards. Blood bursting up. Marith shouted. Twisted backward. Fell off. The dragon screamed louder than ever. Loud as the end of the world. Its body arched, a gout of flame spouted. Collapsed with a shriek. Its tail twitched and coiled for a few long moments. Last rattling tremors, almost kind of pitiful and obscene. Groaning sighing weeping noise. Finally it lay dead.

A dead dragon is a very large thing. Tobias stared at it for a long time. Felt regret, almost. It was beautiful in its way. Wild. Utterly bloody wild. No wisdom in those eyes. Wild freedom and the delight in killing. An immovable force, like a mountain or a storm cloud. A death thing. A beautiful death, though. Imagine saying that to Gulius's family: he was killed fighting a dragon. He was killed fighting a dragon. A dragon killed him. A dragon. Like saying he died fighting a god. They were gods, in some places. Or kin to gods, anyway. He reached out to touch the dark green scales. Soft. Still warm. His hand jerked back as if burned. What did you expect? he thought. It was alive. A living creature. Course it's bloody soft and warm. It's bloody flesh and blood.

Should be stone. Or fire. Or shadow. It wasn't right, somehow, that it was alive and now it was dead. That it felt no different now to dead cattle, or dead men, or dead dogs. It should feel...different. Like the pain of it should be different. He ached the same way he did after a battle with men. The same way he did the last time he'd got in a fight in an inn. Not right. He touched it again, to be sure. Crumble to dust, it should, maybe. Burn up in a blaze of scented flame.

If it's flesh and blood, he thought then, it's going to fucking stink as it starts to rot.

There was a noise behind him. Tobias spun round in a panic. Another dragon. A demon. Eltheia the beautiful, naked on a white horse.

New boy Marith. Staring at the dragon like a man stares at his own death. A chill of cold went through Tobias for a moment. A scream and a shriek in his ears or his mind. The boy's beautiful eyes gazed unblinking. A shadow there, like it was darker suddenly. Like the sun flickered in the sky. Like the dragon might twitch and move and live. Then the boy sighed wearily, sat down in the dust rubbing at his face. Tobias saw that the back of his left hand was horribly burned.

"Pretty good, that," Tobias said at length.

"You told me to draw my sword."

"I did."

There was a long pause.

"You killed it," said Tobias.

"It was dying anyway."

"You killed a bloody dragon, lad."

A bitter laugh. "It wasn't a very large dragon."

"And you'd know, would you?"

No answer.

"You killed it, boy. You bloody well killed a bloody dragon. Notoriously invulnerable beast nobody really believed still existed right up until it ate their tent-mate. You should be pleased, at least. Instead, you're sitting here looking like death while Rate and the other lads try to get things sorted out around here." Wanted to shake the boy. Moping misery. "At least let me have a look at your hand."

This finally seemed to get Marith's attention. He stared down at his burns. "This? It doesn't really hurt."

"Doesn't hurt? Half your hand's been burned off. How can it not hurt? It's the blood, I think. Burns things. It's completely destroyed my sword. Damn good sword it was, too. Had a real ruby in the hilt and all. Bloke I got it off must have thought it was good too, seeing as I had to kill him for it." Rambled on, trying to relieve his racing mind. At the back of his racing mind this little voice basically just shouting "fuck fuck fuck fuck."

"The blood is acid," Marith said absently. "And boiling hot. Once it's dead it cools, becomes less corrosive." He turned suddenly to Tobias, as if just realizing something. "You stabbed it first. To rescue me. I did nothing, I just stood there."

Absurd how young the boy seemed. Fragile. Weak. Hair like red-black velvet. Eyes like pale gray silk. Skin like new milk and a face like a high-class whore. Could probably pass for Eltheia the beautiful, actually, in the right light. From the neck up at any rate.

Couldn't cook. Couldn't start a fire. Couldn't boil a sodding pot of tea. Could just about use a sword a bit, once someone had found him one, though his hand tended to shake on the blade. Cried a lot at night in his tent. Emit had ten in iron on him one day breaking down crying he wanted his mum. Eltheia the beautiful might have made the better sellsword, actually, in the right light.

"You just stood there. Yeah. So did most of them." And, oh gods, oh yeah, it's the squad commander pep talk coming unstoppably out. Let rip, Tobias me old mucker, like finally getting out a fart: "Don't worry about it. Learn from your mistakes and grow stronger and all that. Then when we next get jumped by a fire-breathing man-eating dragon, you'll be right as rain and ready for it and know exactly what to do."

Marith shook himself. Rubbed his eyes. "I could really, really do with a drink."

Tobias got to his feet. Sighed. Boy didn't even need to ask things directly for you to somehow just do them. A trick in the tone of voice. Those puppy-dog sad eyes. "You're not really supposed to order your squad commander around, boy. And we haven't got any booze left, if that's what you mean. There's water for tea, as long as it's drawn well up river of...that. Seeing as you're a hero and all, I'll go and get you some." He started off toward the camp. "Want something to eat while I'm at it?"

An attempt at drinks and dinner. Get the camp sorted so someone with a particularly iron stomach could get a bit of sleep in that wasn't mostly full of dreams of blood and entrails and your tent-mate's face running off like fat off a kebab. The final butcher's bill on file: Jonar, the man who had hacked the thing's stomach open, had disappeared completely, his body totally eaten away; four others were dead including Gulius; one was dying from bathing in fire and hot steam. Skie finished this last off cleanly by taking off his crispy melted black and pink head. Another four were badly wounded: Tobias suspected two at least would be lucky to survive the night. One, a young man called Newlin who was a member of his squadron, had a burn on his right leg that left him barely able to stand. Tobias had already decided it would be a kindness to knife him at the earliest opportunity. One of the other lads was bound to make a botch of it otherwise.

They'd only lost three men in the last year, and they had largely been the victims of unfortunate accidents. (How could they have known that pretty farmer's daughter had had a pruning hook hidden under her cloak? She hadn't even put up much resistance until that point.) Losing ten was a disaster, leaving them dangerously approaching being under-manned.

Piss poor luck, really, all in all, sitting down for lunch in front of a convenient bit of rock and it happening to have a dragon hiding behind it. Even if it wasn't a very large one.

They were still pitching the tents when Skie's servant Toman appeared. Reported that Skie wanted to see Marith Dragon Killer for a chat.

"Hero's welcome," said Tobias with a grin. Though you never could tell with Skie. Could just be going to bollock the boy for not killing it sooner.

Marith got up slowly. Something like fear in his eyes. Or pain, maybe.

Tobias shivered again. Funny mood, the boy was in.

Follow us:

f **/orbitbooksUS**

🐦 **/orbitbooks**

▶ **/orbitbooks**

Join our mailing list
to receive alerts on our
latest releases and deals.

orbitbooks.net

Enter our monthly
giveaway for the chance
to win some epic prizes.

orbitloot.com